Against the Tide

A Hudson Novel

J. Foley

Copyright © 2013 J. Foley
All rights reserved.

ISBN #: 978-1-300-34933-4

This book is a work of fiction. All characters in this novel are fictitious. Any resemblance to actual events, locals, or persons, living or dead, is entirely coincidental.

To Anne.
Your love gives me strength.

**Other things may change us,
but we start and end with family.**

- Anthony Brandt

Prologue

THERE IS NO LAND.

She is floating on her back in a calm, open ocean.

Her limbs tense and release, instinctively matching the rise and fall of the waves. She is linked to the tide, adrift on a vast expanse of blue.

He calls to her. "Zoe."

The sun dips below the horizon. The Earth tilts, forever tumbling into its own shadow, and the sea turns choppy and rough. Salt water burns its way up her nostrils and down her throat. She panics, fighting to keep her head above the surface as waves surge and press her under. She thrashes, breaching violently, gasping for air.

"Zoe."

Currents take hold of her, pulling her down again. White noise fills her ears like static over a radio.

She is weightless, water crushing her chest. She cannot breathe. Everything is dark. Words penetrate the depth, searching for her, echoing in her head until the ocean expels her, heaving her against hard, wet sand. She scrapes at the ground, sinking into the shifting surface. Another wave crashes, forcing her farther up the beach. Choking and sputtering, she draws herself to her knees.

"I need you to be brave."

His voice makes her heart ache.

She scans the beach, wanting nothing more than to see him; his easy smile, the weathered lines that fan out from his bright green eyes. She can remember the way he smelled, and the rough timbre of his voice, but his face eludes her.

She hasn't seen her father in years.

Scrambling through sand, she makes her way up the beachhead, waterlogged clothes weighing down every step. Empty shore and an endless ocean of white-tipped waves stretch out before her, growing faint in the gathering darkness.

Her heartbeat pounds in her head, a steady drumming under her skull that morphs, resonating deeper, becoming a dissonant sound, metallic and hollow.

She turns away from the water and towards the dunes. Tall grasses cling desperately to the sand, slender tendrils whipping in the wind.

A man so much like her father waits in the shadow of a burned out house atop the hill. He is alone in the scorched threshold.

"Be brave."

Her head throbs. Pain blurs her vision.

"Hudson!"

A different voice.

Her eyes snap open. The beach is gone, replaced by the riveted metal above her berth. The pounding and yelling, however, is all too real.

She checks the clock: it's way too early for this. She hasn't even missed her shift, and the Trident isn't due to dock for another four hours. She strips off the sweat-soaked sheet and throws her legs over the edge of her bunk. The recycled air feels cool against her skin.

"Open your damn door. I ain't got all day."

Zoe scrubs her face hard and combs her fingers through her hair, pulling it back into a quick ponytail. She searches for a pair of pants in the discarded piles of clothing that litter the floor of her room.

"What?" she yells.

"You got a call."

She pulls on a pair of jeans, buttoning them as she crosses the short distance from her bunk to the door. Her room may be little more than a glorified broom closet, but it's all hers. One of the few perks to being the only woman on a boat full of men.

It would have been great to open the door to any one of those men. Any one other than Erik Bryce. But there he is, leaning against the jamb, a smarmy expression plastered on his tanned face. His eyes begin their descent down her frame, and she becomes keenly aware of the way her tank top is clinging to her body.

She frowns. "Spit it out."

Bryce lets out a low whistle and presses himself further into her room. "Aren't you going to invite me in?"

"Wasn't planning on it."

He cocks an eyebrow. "You can't tell me you've never thought about you and me—"

She turns to snatch a hooded sweatshirt off the floor, tugging it over her head. At least this guy is consistent in his assholedom. "I don't know how many times I have to tell you this, Erik, but you're not my type."

He grins. It is an expression devoid of humor and kindness. She can see his tongue flicking behind his teeth. "I could be your type."

Somehow she doubts it. "Who's on the phone?"

"Do I look like your secretary?" Bryce presses off the jamb. "Call's patched to the conference room. You wanna know who it is, go get it. And try answering when you're paged so I don't have to waste my time coming all the way down here for nothing."

He struts off, heading deeper into the massive ship, and Zoe flips him off behind his back, thankful the conference room is one deck up and in the opposite direction.

She takes the stairs two at a time until she reaches the upper deck. As she winds her way through the halls and towards the conference room, her brain races—trying to remember who has this number and why they would need to call her.

She pads silently past the open hatch to Captain Foster's office and slips into the conference room, closing the massive door behind her.

A red light blinks on the phone base.

She snatches up the receiver, pinning it between her shoulder and ear. The line is full of static.

"Hudson here. Who is thi—"

"Zoe?" The woman's voice coming through the handset sounds panicked and out of breath. "Is that you?"

It's been so long since they've spoken, it takes her a moment to recognize the voice.

"Mom?"

- 1 -

This can't be about her. She didn't do anything wrong. This has to be about her mother. Something must have happen in Baghdad. Nicole tenses, breaking into a cold sweat.

The secretary who escorted her from class holds the door open. Nicole squeezes past and into the cramped waiting room.

"He's finishing up another meeting, Ms. Hudson. Please have a seat." The woman gestures towards the overstuffed couch arranged against the far wall. One is already occupied by a lanky blonde, sprawled casually on the plush cushions, head lolling against the dark tufted leather. It's amazing how one person can manage to take up so much space. Nicole plops into the unoccupied chair, pushing herself as far into the corner as possible. She drops her bag at her feet and begins to fidget with the fabric of her jeans as she watches the door to the dean's office.

"Well, this is convenient." The woman on the couch stretches, grinning at Nicole. "Saves me pestering them for your class schedule."

Nicole is instantly annoyed that the woman is wearing sunglasses indoors. "Can I help you?"

"You pick that up from Mom, huh?" The woman gestures at Nicole's hands as they nervously work the denim.

"Mom?" Nicole shakes her head, confusion shifting to anger. "What the hell do you know about my mother?"

The woman's grin fades. She removes her sunglasses with tanned hands. How long has it been? Almost twelve years—lots of time for lots of changes—but her sister's eyes are still the same.

"Zoe?" Nicole swallows hard. "What are you doing here?"

Her sister scoots in closer, smirking. "What are *you* doing here? Didn't think you were the type to get called to the principal's office." She clicks her tongue. "What'd you do?"

"I didn't do anything." Nicole blushes, and wishes very much so that she wouldn't. "And he's a dean, Zoe, not a principal. This is a university, not grade school."

"But you are in trouble?"

"No. I'm not." Nicole crosses her arms. "Just because he called me to his office doesn't mean—"

"Yeah, it does." Her sister's laugh is sharp. "You're in trouble."

"I am just—"

Zoe shushes her. Something in her expression shifts, becoming tense. Her smirk fades as her attention refocuses, moving past Nicole and towards the sharp sounds of arguing emanating from the dean's office. Nicole watches large shadows move behind the closed blinds. She strains to make out the words being said, and half imagines she can hear her own name. Her pulse quickens.

Zoe's warm hand taking hold of her shoulder makes her jump. "We need to leave."

"But he wants to talk to me." Nicole shrugs out if Zoe's grip. "They pulled me out of class—"

"Get up."

"But I—" She stammers as Zoe grips her arms and hauls her to her feet.

"Up. Now."

She barely has time to snatch the strap to her bag before Zoe is forcing her towards the hall door.

"Ms. Hudson?" The secretary looks up from her computer, confused. "Ms. Hudson, where are you going?"

"Don't talk to her," Zoe whispers. "Keep moving."

As they pass into the hall, Zoe's guidance becomes distinctly more like pushing. The hallways begin to fill with students making their way to class. Zoe snakes them through the crowd and towards the massive double doors leading to the quad. Nicole glances back, watching the office door as she jostles into milling student bodies.

"Don't look back," Zoe barks. Her grip on Nicole's arm tightens uncomfortably as they exit into the late afternoon sunlight. Zoe slips her sunglasses back on. "You got a car?"

"Of course I have a car," Nicole scoffs. She jerks free, and rubs at the sore spot on her arm. She can already feel the bruise forming. "What does it matter?"

Zoe begins to stalk across the cobblestone courtyard. She's different than Nicole remembered, but time will do that. Every piece of her clothing is rumpled and creased like she has been sleeping in them for days. Her skin the color of honey, a tan so deep Nicole wonders if anyone has ever warned her about skin cancer. She adjusts the strap of her bag. "Why are you here?"

Zoe ignores her. "Where're you parked?"

Nicole holds her ground. "What's going on, Zoe? You can't just show up out of the blue without a reason. Who was talking to the dean? Is something wrong with Mom? Is she okay?"

Zoe spins on her heel, taking hold of Nicole's shoulders and shaking her. "Tell me. Where. You're. Parked."

"Not until you answer my questions."

This stubborn streak is clearly genetic. They glare at each other, arms crossed, neither willing to break.

There is the loud pop as doors slam open. Two men burst out of the main building: one in a crisp suit, the other a shaved head brute with a frightening expression. They scan the quad. Nicole locks eyes with the big man and instantly wishes she hadn't. His mouth twists into a vicious smile, and the men begin to shove their way through the crowd of students.

Something is very wrong here. Nicole can feel it in her gut. She can also tell because her sister has grabbed hold of her wrist again and is unceremoniously wrenching her forward.

"Nik, now." Zoe hollers over her shoulder. "Where is it?"

She sputters, "It—It's over by my dorm. On the other side of campus."

It doesn't take long for Nicole to become painfully aware how out of shape she is. Running has never been her strong suit—not that the flip-flops and a bag loaded with text books make things any easier.

Zoe drags her down the steps and around a corner. They bolt through a wide portico, dodging students and faculty. Her lungs begin to burn, heart pounding so hard it feels barely contained inside her chest. The haphazard route they are carving through the campus seems to be equal parts an attempt to shake the men tailing them and Zoe not knowing where she is going. Expletives are barked in deep, angry voices.

Nicole does not need to look back. Whoever these guys are, a chase isn't going to deter them.

"Faster!"

Nicole grimaces. "I can't!"

"You've got to." Zoe jerks at Nicole's arm. She slips around a pair of coeds, pardoning herself as she passes and leaving Nicole to gracelessly slam into one of the girls. The impact sends her sprawling to the pavement, sliding on her knees and scuffing up her palms. The contents of her bag scatter across the concrete walkway. Her hands throb as she presses herself up. Nicole scrambles to recover her possessions, arms flailing wildly trying to gather every book and every paper.

Zoe scoops her up under the arms, dragging her to her feet. "Just leave it! Come on."

"I have to get—" Then she sees him. The big man, the one with the shaved head and the stern expression, hurtling towards her with impressive speed. Her scattered possessions lose their importance. Nicole pushes herself to her feet and runs, runs like her life depends on it, which she's pretty certain it does. She quickly matches Zoe's pace.

They make a sharp turn and pass a shallow alcove. Zoe snags Nicole's arm, twisting her around until she slams into the wall. Her sister pins her in the corner, forearm pressed against her chest.

Through ragged breaths, Nicole manages to hiss, "What are you do—?"

Zoe cups her mouth, silencing her.

His heavy footsteps are unmistakable. There'd better be a plan, she thinks, because hiding in plain sight won't actually work.

Nicole watches Zoe prepare herself, muscles coiling tight like a spring. As the big man passes their hiding place, Zoe's leg lashes out, the top of her foot striking him square in the face.

The impact is accompanied by a sickening crack.

Blood is everywhere. Nicole has never seen anything like it. The man stumbles back, gripping his nose and cursing loudly.

She cannot imagine still being upright after being kicked in the face like that, but somehow he is. He growls, throwing a wild punch that Zoe dodges. The blood from his broken nose spatters the pale concrete. Zoe slips under his arm, bringing her knee up into his groin.

The noise drains away. She watches her sister fight, throwing punch after punch, and feels herself growing numb. Her body refuses to respond. Zoe turns towards her. She looks so angry. Her face is so red. Her mouth is moving, but the muffled words lag far behind the movement of her lips.

All at once, sound rushes back.

"Nicole! I said run! Get to the car! Now!"

She shoves herself off the wall and sprints past the fight, flip-flops slapping down the broad steps leading to the dorm parking lot. Part of her wants to look back and make sure Zoe is okay, but that part is much less significant than the part that wants to get somewhere safe as fast as humanly possible.

She digs a trembling hand into her pants pocket, searching for her keys. They're not there. Where are they? Nicole pats her other pockets as she runs. Nothing.

Think, Hudson. Where did you put your keys?

They were in your bag.

The bag that spilled all over the ground after you leveled a pair of coeds.

Nicole reaches a trembling hand under the flap of her satchel, groping for anything cool and metallic.

A man's voice rings out. "Ms. Hudson! Stop!"

The second man. The one in the suit. She forgot about the man in the suit.

She digs deeper into her bag, weaving in and out of the parked cars as the man hops a guard rail and sprints towards her. Her fingers finally curl around the jagged ends of her keys. Oh thank God.

"Nicole Hudson! Stop!"

She fumbles with the key ring, thumbing the buttons until the headlights blink and the locks disengage. She slams into the driver's side door, hands frantically tugging at the door handle. He is closing the gap and still yelling, but Nicole has no intention of following the directions of a man who has chased her all the way across campus. She flings the door wide, throwing her bag across the interior and allowing herself to tumble into the driver's seat. Nicole slams the door shut. Seconds later, the man slaps the window. She can hear him pulling at the handle.

His voice is muffled through the glass, but she can hear him well enough. "Unlock this door, Ms. Hudson."

Her hand shakes as she twists the key in the ignition, holding it too long. The engine squeals. She lets go and grips the steering wheel, poised to act but uncertain what she's supposed to do. The man digs into his jacket, briefly revealing the shoulder holster strapped to his body.

He has a gun. This man has a gun. Nicole clamps her eyes shut, expecting to hear a bang, not the sound of a badge slapping against the glass. Out of her periphery she sees "FBI" in bold blue letters.

"Please get out of the car, Ms. Hudson." He leans in close to the window, and she finally has a chance to get a good look at his face. Somehow, he doesn't look dangerous. The man tucks his badge back into his coat pocket and speaks more softly. "I can help you, but you have to trust—"

His head jerks back, then strikes the roof of her car with a nauseating smack. Nicole cringes as his limp body slides down her door. Zoe crosses the front of the car, wiping her own blood from the corner of her mouth. She raps on the passenger size window with raw knuckles, body resting against the glass. "Open up, Nik."

Nicole forces herself to breathe deeply, trying to slow her heart and pull her stomach out of her throat. She pops the locks and Zoe slips into the passenger seat, shoving Nicole's bag to the floorboard.

"Drive."

Nicole stares blankly out the windshield, unable to process the last fifteen minutes.

"Now, Nicole!"

Nothing makes sense, the only thing she knows is that everything seemed to go to hell the moment Zoe showed up. Nicole glares at her sister as she slams the car into drive and pulls out of the parking lot.

She can feel her heartbeat in her fingers as she grips the steering wheel. After a few minutes driving, her throat unclenches enough for the question to come out. "Who were those guys?"

Zoe stares out the passenger window, slouching into the seat while anxiously watching the side mirror.

"He had a badge." Nicole swallows hard and continues. "An FBI badge. He said he'd help me. Help me what? What the hell is going on? What did you do?"

Zoe looks away, popping every knuckle. The hollow sound is mildly nauseating. "Next exit."

Nicole hits her blinker, merging on to the offramp. "We should go to the police."

"No."

"Maybe they can—"

Zoe glares at Nicole. "Help? Yeah. Not likely, kid."

"What do you have against the police? Are you in some sort of trouble?"

Zoe begins to fidget.

"Are you?" Nicole presses.

"Look kid, I just left two men unconscious at your school. We turn around and go to the cops, it won't end how you want it to." Zoe sinks deeper into her seat, biting her thumbnail. Nicole swears she can hear her sister thinking. "Our best bet is to get as far away from here as possible."

"But we can explain what happened. We should try to talk to someone—"

"I said no." Zoe's attention shifts back to the window. "No stopping. No cops. And no more questions. Head for the airport."

Nicole is not used to being shut down. She clenches the steering wheel, wringing her hands on its pebbled leather surface.

ZOE WAITS AT THE COUNTER, listening to sounds of jostling luggage mingle with the droning airport PA and the murmuring of travelers. All the movement creates a soothing wall of noise. She feels comfortable at airports, centered, somehow more at peace. The anonymity of being lost in the crowd has always appealed to her, and there is a certain inertia to travel that just makes sense to her. It's all a mass of bodies constantly moving, oblivious to the world passing around them, focused on getting where they need to go.

When they arrived, she told the kid to stay put and keep a low profile. Nicole responded by glowering and dropping herself into one of the uncomfortable chairs across from the ticket counter. She curled into a ball and buried her head in her arms, dark hair spilling over pale skin.

She seems more angry than scared, which is kind of a blessing, Zoe thinks. She can handle people being pissed at her, but having to comfort her estranged kid sister isn't something she wants to deal with right now. As soon as her transaction at the counter is complete, Zoe heads back to Nicole, slapping her freckled shoulder with the wallet she lifted from the kid's school bag. "Here."

Nicole raises her head. Her feet slip to the stiff multicolored carpet that covers the terminal, absently seeking her flip-flops. "Why did you have my wallet?"

Zoe takes a seat next to her, and tosses the leather billfold into her lap. "I needed a credit card."

"Credit card—" Nicole snatches her wallet up and thumbs through it, checking that everything is in its place. "Use your own credit card. Jesus, what is wrong with you?"

She would have preferred not to use a card at all. The things are too easy to trace. But she didn't bring enough cash, and she wasn't left with many options. She had to take the risk.

Nicole tucks her wallet back into her bag, looking vaguely nauseous. "What did you buy?"

Zoe hands her the tickets.

"Brazil?" Nicole balks. "Oh my God, how much did these cost? What— What are you—"

Zoe shrugs. Brazil is the safest place she could think of. The only place on this side of the globe where she has a friend she can trust. And yeah, the tickets weren't cheap, but last minute international tickets are always expensive, and she had to make sure whatever flight they ended up on wasn't going to be canceled or rescheduled. That privileged information cost her half of her spare cash.

"This card is for school! Mom is going to kill me." Nicole continues her tirade, but not loud enough to draw any attention. At least the kid has tact. "No, wait. She's going to kill you."

Pissing off their mother wouldn't be anything new. Zoe shrugs and sinks deeper into her seat, picking at the hem of her jacket.

"I'm calling her." Nicole tugs her bag onto her lap and digs inside its depth, searching for her cell phone.

"Nik—"

"Don't 'Nik' me. I'm calling Mom right now and I'm going to tell her what happened and what you did and—" She stops, sighing heavy and glaring at Zoe. "Where did you put my cell phone?"

"What? I didn't touch your phone."

"You stole my wallet," Nicole holds her hand out, waiting. "Give me back my phone."

Zoe leans in close to her sister. Her eyes narrow. Her words are slow and deliberate, and she makes no attempt to hide how annoyed she is feeling. "I don't have your phone."

They glare at each other until Nicole accepts that Zoe isn't bullshitting her. Defeated, the kid slumps back into her seat and closes her eyes. "I just want to go home. Why won't you take me home?"

Zoe can hear the tremor in her voice. This is not the time or place for a breakdown. "It's not safe. I have to take you—"

Nicole sniffles and slaps Zoe with her ticket. "To South America?"

"Why not?" Zoe stares at her, eyebrow cocked. She digs into her jacket pocket and pulls out the other item she might have taken from

Nicole's bag. "You've already got your documents in order." She tosses the passport at Nicole and the kid catches it out of reflex. "It was in your bag. Why you keep it with you, I have no idea."

Nicole takes in deep, measured breaths and stares down at her pristine passport. She murmurs, "Mom told me to always carry two forms of identification."

"Right. And you always do exactly what Mom says, don't you?" Zoe stands, reaching down for the strap of Nicole's bag, and slinging it over her shoulders. As she stretches her neck, vertebrae adjust, popping loudly. She motions towards the security check point. "Come on. We've got a plane to catch."

ZOE IS ASLEEP, HEAD PRESSED against the seat, chin resting on her shoulder. Nicole's neck hurts just looking at her.

Her goal for the majority of the fifteen hour long flight is to try to ignore her sister, but she's already read the linguistics text book that was left in her bag cover to cover twice, and the inflight magazine is so very poorly written. She has switched to staring at Zoe for entertainment alone.

Being around her is strange. Nicole was six the last time she saw her sister. She vaguely recalls some sort of argument. The yelling was so loud it woke her up. Mom told her to go back to bed, that she wasn't mad at Zoe, that they were just talking.

Even at that age, Nicole could tell she was lying.

Zoe had looked so hurt. So angry. She was just a kid. Only seventeen years old.

Nicole was never able to wrap her head around the concept of running away. It all seemed so selfish and so scary. It changed everything. Mom was different. Broken. And Zoe was just gone.

They didn't talk about her anymore. Mom took down all the photographs. It was like even the memory of her sister wasn't allowed in the house. She was simply erased from their lives.

And now Nicole is on a plane bound for a foreign country, sitting next to a sister she barely knows.

Someone a few rows back lets out a sharp cough. Nicole fidgets in her seat. She can see Zoe's passport, just visible under the limp tips of her fingers. Looking at the document won't explain anything, but it will alleviate her curiosity. She tugs the passport free and begins to flip through its pages.

There are so many stamps from so many different countries. The thing is literally held together with little more than tape and rubber bands.

Near the middle, Nicole comes to a battered photo tucked carefully between the pages, all bent edges and sun bleached emulsion. It is not a digital print, but an honest to God processed image. She unfolds it delicately, not wanting to tear it any further. There's a middle aged woman, their mother. She can only assume the handsome man is Zoe's father, and the grinning little girl he is holding must be some lost version of her sister.

She looks so happy. They all do.

Nicole folds the picture and places it back where she found it, gingerly slipping the document back under her sister's fingers. She winces as Zoe stirs in her sleep. She sinks back into her seat and stares out the window at the clouds as they shift and transform, light fading from the sky, sliding the world into darkness.

Customs goes quickly—not having checked luggage will do that—and before Nicole knows it, they've stepped out of the comfortable atmosphere of the terminal and into the sticky heat of a San Paulo afternoon. The hum and honking of traffic surrounds her. A man pushing a cart filled with baggage hollers at her to move. Nicole side steps the cart, gripping the strap of her bag with both hands like an anchor, scared that if she lets go she might fly away entirely. Smog presses in from all sides. It is a suffocating mix of humidity and exhaust. Lush green planters with vibrant tropical flowers are muted by the sickly grey haze. Zoe hails them a taxi, and trots off to the first that stops.

Listening to her sister struggle to explain their destination to the driver is annoying. It's not like Portuguese is that difficult. Nicole crosses her arms, silently refusing to help. The grizzled old man doesn't seem to want to take them anywhere. But things change once Zoe produces cash. The man gives her sister a pen and a pad of paper on which she scrawls a barely legible address. The driver balks at the location, shaking his head and raising his hands, international sign for "Hell no, crazy lady."

Nicole leans in close to her sister. "Why don't we just rent a car?"

"I don't want to rent a car." When Zoe hands the driver back his pen, she drops a few tattered hundred dollar bills on the notepad's surface. "I want him to drive us."

The broken edges of his fingernails scratch at the bills. He takes the pad and tucks the money into his sweat-soaked shirt pocket.

As he puts the car into drive, Nicole settles back into her seat. She's been cooped up on a plane for fifteen hours. A drive might actually be kind of nice, if she can manage to forget everything else that has happened since she woke up yesterday morning.

Warm sunlight streams through the window, calming her, and eventually the muted sounds of city traffic lull her sleep-deprived body into unconsciousness.

The slamming of a car door snaps her awake. Nicole rubs her eyes, trying to adjust to the disorienting lack of sunlight. How long have they been driving?

Her door opens.

"Come on." No greater explanation. Zoe leans against the car, tapping her fingers against the roof impatiently. Groggy and sticky with sweat, Nicole pulls herself and her bag from the back seat of the cab. The night air is still. There is just the faint sound of water lapping, the chirping of hundreds of bugs, and the low humming of sodium vapor lights that barely illuminate a long, rickety dock. Nicole frowns. Her sister has brought her to a dock. A poorly lit, totally creepy, run-down dock on the Brazilian coast.

The car door closes, and Nicole can't help but jump.

"Relax," Zoe chides.

She shoulders her bag, mumbling to herself. "Not even possible." The dock seems to grow less and less hospitable with each passing moment. "What are we doing here?"

"Visiting a friend." Zoe tucks her hands deep into her pants pockets, heading up the dock and past some large wooden pylons.

She passes a large sign warning against trespassing. Nicole points at the metal notice peppered with small holes.

"So?"

"Does your friend know we're coming?"

Nicole takes Zoe's raised eyebrow and indignant expression as a no. "I don't need to call the guy every time I—"

There is a strange mechanical click. Nicole is still processing the sound when she hears the crack. The deafening noise is followed by a concussion she can feel deep in her chest. Next thing she knows, Zoe is tackling her to rough surface of the dock as wooden splinters shower them both.

It takes her a few moments to add everything together. The sound. The shockwave. Someone is shooting at them. With a gun. She can barely believe it.

Nicole follows Zoe, careful to stay low and in the cover of pylons and smattering of docked sailboats. Another round is chambered, then fired, peppering the bow of the nearest boat.

"Damn it, Jones!" her sister yells. "Stop shooting!"

"Wait a minute." Nicole slaps Zoe hard. "That's you friend?"

Another round is chambered, but instead of the deafening crack, a man's voice rings out. "Hudson?"

"Put the gun down, man. It's just me."

Nicole can just stare at Zoe, shaking her head slowly in disbelief. "The guy who's shooting at us. He's your *friend*?"

"Who you got with you?"

Zoe stands, reaching to help Nicole up, only to be warded off by her flailing hand. "My kid sister."

There is silence, then a high-pitched creaking. Zoe steps out of their cover and into the beam from an aimed searchlight. She squints into the brightness and snaps for Nicole, gesturing for her step out of the shadows. Nicole refuses to move.

"Nik," Zoe hisses. "Come on."

It's going to take a lot more than a searchlight and an informal cease fire to get her to trust this so-called friend. "He tried to kill us!"

The man's voice sounds sheepish. "I'm really sorry about that. I-I thought you guys were someone else."

His apology isn't exactly reassuring. She dusts herself off and steps into the pool of light. She snaps at Zoe under her breath. "You have the shittiest friends."

Nicole bumps her head on the low door jamb as she steps below deck. The sailboat is a modest one, very cramped and very run down, but he clearly lives here. This boat is his home. The whole arrangement is strangely intimate. She can't help but feel voyeuristic as she glances around, taking in the various articles of clothing strewn about, the dirty dishes, the shelves overstuffed with paperback books, their spines split and worn, titles no longer legible. It strikes her as strange that he's a reader.

Zoe seems completely at home, even considering the excessive display of force just moments before. She flops on the small bed, casually propping herself up on her elbows.

"Welcome to Casa de Matthew." Jones smiles at them both, tossing the shotgun onto an upholstered bench. He's a big man, older than Zoe, with a goofy smile and kind eyes hidden beneath shaggy hair and dirty blonde beard. His tattered hawaiian shirt clashes nicely with his camo cut-offs. "Can I get you ladies something to drink?"

"Beer." Of course Zoe would drink beer.

Jones looks expectantly at Nicole. "You want one?"

She is about to reject his offer when Zoe flicks something at him, beaning him in the temple. She points at him playfully. "She's seventeen, Jones."

Jones winces and rubs the point of impact. "Water, then?" He digs into a tiny refrigerator, pulling out two waters and a bottle of beer. He tosses Zoe her drink. "I thought you were in the channel, sucking silver out of the silt on that stupid boat."

"And I thought you quit gambling and pissing off the wrong people?"

He smiles broadly and hands Nicole a bottle of water. "I thought about it."

"I mean, a shotgun salute? How much you owe now?"

Nicole's ears are still ringing from the blast. She grips her forehead, feeling the start of a headache.

"How 'bout we don't talk about it." Jones scratches at his beard and leans against the chipped edge of the counter. "So. What do you ladies need?"

Zoe twists the cap off her bottle and takes a deep pull. "Right now? A place to crash."

Jones gives Zoe a nod. "Not a problem."

She found an old flannel in one of the drawers. It's not much, but it's a lot warmer than her sleeveless top. The oversized shirt dwarfs her. Nicole flops on the bed only to find out that it is not even remotely soft or comfortable, but it's better than the bench-seat in the back of the taxi so she'll take it.

She could almost relax if she wasn't so angry at Zoe. She was told to stay put like a child while grown ups went topside to talk. About what, Nicole obviously isn't allowed to know.

When Zoe enters the cabin and closes the door behind her, Nicole has had plenty of time to work up some indignation. "What the hell is going on?"

"Thought you'd be asleep by now."

"Shut up and answer me."

Zoe flashes her a sarcastic glare. "Wait, which one do you want, Nik?"

"God damn it, Zoe. Why did you bring me here? How do you know this guy? What were you two talking about?"

Her sister sighs, taking off her jacket and slipping out of her shoes. "I brought you here because this place is safe. Jones is a friend. And none of your business." Zoe flops face first onto the mattress. "Go to sleep."

"A friend? Did you not catch the part where he shot at us?"

Her sister shrugs, speech muffled by the pillow. "He apologized. What more do you want?"

"What do I want? I wanted to wait in the office and talk to the dean. I wanted to go to the police. I wanted to call Mom. I didn't want to leave the country and I sure as hell didn't want to come to Brazil and sleep in the bed of a man who almost blew my head off. I apparently trust you for some stupid reason, but the amount of trust that buys my cooperation is pretty much tapped out by this secret squirrel bullshit! I let you drag me this far, but I really, really need some answers!"

By the end, her chest is heaving and her head hurts.

Zoe has rolled over and is staring at her. "Are you finished?"

Nicole takes a deep breath and gives a curt nod.

"First off, your school wasn't safe. I don't know if you noticed, but those men were after you. I'd like a little credit for saving your ass. Second, no cops. And third, Mom was the one who told me to come get you in the first place, so—"

Nicole cuts her off. "You talked to Mom?"

"Yeah."

"When?"

"Does it matter?"

Nicole doesn't mean to be as loud as she is. "When did you talk to her?"

The silence as Zoe tries to remember is unbearable. "A few days ago. She told me she didn't think you were safe. That I had to get to you. I had to ditch work and catch a flight—"

"She called *you*?"

Zoe looks completely bewildered. "Yeah. Why are you getting so bent out of shape over this?"

Nicole doesn't want to cry. Not here. Not in front of Zoe, but she can't quite hold her tears back. She can feel them welling in the corners of her eyes, threatening to spill over. "If she thought something was wrong, if she thought I was in trouble, why wouldn't she just tell me? I—I don't understand." Her mother had left three months before to supervise a multinational restoration project at the Iraqi National Museum. It was the first real project she had accepted in decades. Nicole understood contact with her would be erratic at best, but her mom promised to email as often as possible. The idea that something had gone wrong and her mother's first reaction was to call Zoe was strangely upsetting.

"Look, we're okay. You're safe. This is what mom wants."

Though her sister's tone is earnest, Nicole can't help snapping at her. "What else did she tell you? She must have said what was going on, who those men were. What else do you know that you aren't you telling me?"

Zoe stares at the wall, silent.

Nicole can feel herself shaking. Her loss of control is infuriating. She wipes the tears from her cheeks with the sleeve of Jones's flannel shirt and lays back down, scooting as far away from her sister as possible.

HE MUST HAVE READ HER BRIEF. She had hoped he would have waited, giving her more time to contact her operators and present him with more a complete image of the current situation. No luck.

Her heels click on the concrete, reverberating in the empty hall. She stops, taking a moment to collect herself, straightening her blouse and flattening the line of her skirt. She lets her eyes trace the lines of his door. It is an intricate piece, massive, pulled from some ancient temple —Nepalese, by her estimate—and installed in the compound as an object of function rather than worship.

She takes a breath, and lightly pushes. The ancient door opens smoothly, carved wood swinging inward with mechanical precision.

Sutton's assistant is seated behind the desk, all perfect posture, pristine attire, and immaculate grooming. He glances up from his computer. "Ms. Case."

"Mr. Fletcher."

Fletcher smiles an unsettling smile. "He's expecting you."

She can see him through the smoked glass that separates his office from the waiting room. He is still, staring out the window at the sun rise. His back is to her when she enters, but she does not need to see his face to know his mood.

"I do not appreciate waking up to this, Tricia." He holds up a tablet. Her report is visible on the screen. "Explain yourself."

She clutches the folder in her hand. "My team was unable to acquire the target."

He turns, tanned skin and white hair contrasting sharply to his dark monochromatic clothing. "Are you implying your operators could not handle a seventeen year old child?"

Case inhales sharply. The insult is as much directed at her as her operators. In Sutton's eyes, their failures are her own, valid excuses or not. "There was a complication."

He sets the tablet on the glass desk top and crosses his arms. "A 'complication.'"

"Her sister. Hayden's daughter." She watches his frustration turn to curiosity. "She interfered."

That gives him pause. "Your original assessment claimed they were no longer in contact."

Case meets his gaze. "They weren't."

"It seems you were mistaken." Sutton twist in his chair, deep in thought. "This certainly... alters the scenario. Where are they now?"

It is a question to which she has an answer to. Case sets the folder on his desk, flipping it open to expose grainy CCTV images of two women. "San Paulo. Two tickets were purchased using Nicole Hudson's credit card. Surveillance footage from the airport shows them exiting the terminal and boarding an unregulated taxi. Dempsey and Connor are interviewing the driver as we speak. I am confident we will have their location soon."

He selects an image off the pile—a woman and a girl entering a taxi—and takes a seat behind his desk, rotating his chair away from her.

"Sir." Fletcher stands in the threshold. "Your appointment has arrived."

"Thank you, Joseph."

Sutton clears his throat. "This is a very sensitive assignment I've given you, Tricia. It is very important to me. Do you understand?"

Case moves to collect the surveillance photos, but she does not dare reach for the photo in his hands.

He is focused on the image. More aptly, on Zoe. Sutton places the picture down on his desk. "Find them."

Case closes the folder, tucking it under her arm as she heads for the door. She slips past Fletcher in the threshold.

"And Ms. Case?" His eyes meet hers. "Do not disappoint me."

- 2 -

NICOLE WAKES TO THE SMELL OF BREWING COFFEE. Her body is sprawled out at an angle, bare feet dangling off the edge of the bed. The unfamiliar surroundings and hard mattress beneath her are disorienting enough; Zoe's absence only adds to the mess in her head. She presses herself upright, stretching her arms to work out the tightness in her shoulders.

Coffee is not her thing, but the idea of a dose of pure caffeine is alluring. She pads to the counter and inspects the "I hate Mondays" mug left out next to the battered coffee maker. She snorts as she fills it. Nicole suspects every day with Zoe will feel like a Monday.

There doesn't appear to be a 'be back soon, stay put' note, so Nicole and her Monday mug make their way above deck. This time she is careful to duck, not wanting a repeat of the whack on the head she received the night before. Cool air and bright sunlight assault her. There is a slight sway to the boat that transmits directly though her body, churning her stomach. Abstractly, the idea of being on the open ocean had always seemed so peaceful, even calming. The backflips her gut is doing on the deck of a docked sailboat have pretty much convinced her she has no nautical future.

Jones had mentioned last night that he and Zoe worked on a boat together. It's further proof of how different she and her sister are.

Nicole hears a rhythmic splashing and peers over the rear of the boat. Jones is swimming, his hands cupping the ocean water, propelling himself effortlessly through the blue. The muscles on his back tense and shift, responding to his motion.

She sips her coffee absently as tanned skin shimmers just below the surface of the water. There is a large tattoo on his right shoulder, but no matter how hard she squints, she can't make out the design.

He swims to the edge of the boat and pulls himself out of the ocean, feet slapping on the deck as a puddle of water gathers beneath him.

"Look who's up." He smiles at her, raking broad hands through wet hair. His body glistens in the morning sun, water droplets still clinging to swirls of chest hair. "You sleep okay?"

Nicole realizes she's gawking. Her eyes drop to the deck. All she can do is nod in response to his question, clutching her mug between her hands and pointedly looking anywhere he is not. She can only hope he hasn't noticed she's blushing.

"You found the coffee! Awesome." He grabs a towel from the railing and scrubs himself. "Sorry if it's too strong. Zoe likes diesel fuel."

Nicole takes another sip. He isn't wrong. The brew could double as paint stripper. "Where is she?"

"Zo? She went into town for supplies. Asked me to keep an eye on you, which is easy enough when you sleep all day." Jones scoots past her, toweling off his ragged beard and staring down the narrow dock thoughtfully. He looks concerned.

"Is something wrong?"

"Nah." Jones's sudden grin is reassuring. "She's just kind of a shitty driver, and I loaned her my ride. That's all. Nothing you got to worry about."

Nicole plops onto a bench seat. Zoe didn't even consider waking her up or taking her into town. No, instead she left her with a babysitter. A handsome, scruffy babysitter, which is a plus, but she cannot help but feel insulted.

"Everything okay?" Jones pauses in his scrubbing and lets the towel hang over his head.

When she finally looks up at him, he is smiling at her with an infectious grin. Nicole sips her coffee, trying not to reciprocate. Nothing she is feeling is worth getting in to, and her issues with her sister are definitely not this guy's problem.

Jones cocks his head, towel slipping down and coming to rest on his broad shoulder. He nudges her with a wet, brawny arm. "Want to talk about it?"

She shakes her head and stares blankly at the water.

"You know what? That sister of yours is crap at introductions." He lets a moment pass, then reaches out a hand. "I'm Matthew Jones."

She takes his hand and he gives her a firm but gentle shake. "Nicole. Nicole Hudson."

"Nicole. Okay. I can remember that." Jones takes a seat next to her on the bench. The silence that settles between them is probably only awkward for her. She's never been this casually close to a half-naked man before. It's amazing what you miss out on being a seventeen-year-old senior at an Ivy League school.

Jones is the first to break the silence. "So, you guys are sisters, huh?"

"Half."

"Different…?"

"Fathers."

"Ah." He nods. "Kinda figured. No offense, but you guys barely look related."

It's a pretty obvious observation. They don't. Zoe is all sharp angles, tanned skin, and toned muscle. Her short blonde hair is always pulled back in a sloppy ponytail. They both picked up a strong jaw and a stubborn streak from their mother, but that's where the similarities stop. Nicole is a textbook indoor kid, round where her sister is sharp, soft where she's hard, and pale as opposed to tan. Her freckled skin burns at even the mention of sun, and she has dark, tangled curls that tumble freely past her shoulders and halfway down her back. She has always assumed those traits came from her father, but she can't know for sure. She's never met the man.

Her thoughts begin to stray. Thankfully, Jones keeps their conversation rolling. "So, you're in school, right? What grade?"

"I'm a senior."

"Bet you're excited about college, huh?"

She brushes her hair behind her ear. "I'm a senior at Columbia."

He looks confused. "Is that a good high school? I don't know much—"

"It's a really great university."

"Oh. Oh, that Columbia." He leans back, eyebrow cocked. "So you're like super smart?" There is a level of mischief in his expression Nicole appreciates. "You're definitely only half related to Zoe."

She smiles.

"Well, good for you." Jones bumps her again before rubbing at his chin, flicking water in all directions. "I wasn't that great at school. It was straight out of high school and into the Corp. My dad wasn't too happy about that. Guy's a bit of a hippie. He didn't like me being in the military. I served Force Recon. 'Retired' after I got a few stripes, then picked up a dive gig on the Trident."

"Is that how you two met?"

"Me and your sister?" Jones's eyes twinkle. He leans in close, dropping his voice to a mock whisper. "Man, I could tell you some stories."

Nicole blushes and searches for composure in the dark surface of her coffee. "So you two have been together a long time, then?"

"Together?" He pulls back, his brows knitting with confusion. After a moment his expression relaxes and he lets out a loud laugh. "Whoa, uh, you mean—Oh, no. That's not—" He grinds his thumb against his temple. "You should really be having this conversation with your sister."

Jones must see the frustration on her face because he quickly backpedals. "I swear I'm not trying to be a jackass. I mean, no, Zoe and I —We were never 'together.' Not like that. Just friends."

She gives him a look.

"I promise." He raises his hand. "Scout's honor."

They're interrupted by the rumble of an engine from up the dock. Jones stands, squinting at the rusty truck as Zoe slips out of the driver's side—an easy maneuver since the door is missing entirely. Nicole can only assume from his reaction that the truck is in the exact same condition it was when it left this morning. She can't imagine what he was worried about, unless Zoe is prone to exploding things.

Jones cups his hands to his mouth and hollers at her sister. "What did you get me, sweet cheeks?"

Zoe flips him off and shouts, "Get your ass over here and help me unload, you lazy bastard."

Nicole shakes her head. Her sister certainly has a way with words. "Why do you let her talk to you like that?"

Jones tugs a t-shirt over his head. "Your sister's got a special way about her, Nicole. But under all the attitude, she's a decent lady."

Zoe yells again. "Jones!"

"Duty calls." He gives Nicole an exaggerated salute and makes his way from the deck to the dock.

THE 303 IS LARGER THAN JONES'S BOAT by a good twenty feet. Two sleeping berths and a little more room below deck will make future awkward nights with Nicole a little more bearable. Zoe tries not to think about their argument, opting instead to focus on unpacking canned goods and bottled water into the dusty cupboards.

"So this isn't a vacation. I get that." Jones tosses a duffle on to the bunk. "Mind telling me why you're here?"

Zoe deflects his question with her own. "Where's the kid?"

"Up top. She's fine." He crosses his arms and fixes her with a stare. "Now talk to me."

She does not want to do this right now. "Is that the last of it?"

"Hudson, cut the crap." He sounds so serious. "Does this have something to do with the Trident? Are you in some kind of trouble? What's Foster gotten you in to now?"

Zoe turns and leans against the cupboards. "Why would you automatically assume I'm in trouble?"

"Because you're always in trouble, Zo. You *are* trouble." His shit-eating grin is usually charming, even reassuring, but right now she just wants to knock his teeth out.

His smile fades. Jones sits on the edge of the bunk and waits for a response. When she doesn't oblige, he presses on. "So, you have a little sister. That's new. She's seems nice."

"Nice, and none of your business."

Jones raises his hands. "I'm just saying, she's a sweet kid and she seems really smart."

Zoe steps over boxes of supplies and grabs a beer from a crate, then drops herself onto the built-in bench. "Point being?"

Jones shrugs. "Just not the kind of Hudson I'm used to."

He seems to be expecting some form of physical retaliation for the comment, but Zoe doesn't have it in her. The trip into town was draining. The entire time she couldn't shake the feeling that she was being followed. Everything is so keyed up, and the beer isn't helping. Zoe leans forward and sets her bottle on the floor. She rakes her fingers through her hair, pulling out the band holding it back.

Jones is a good friend. He deserves answers. She's just not sure what to tell him.

"I'll help you, however I can. You know that." Jones sets a hand on her knee. "But if I'm stepping into a shit storm, I'd like to know which way the wind is blowing, you know?"

Zoe takes a deep breath. "My mom called me. She told me Nik wasn't safe."

Jones looks confused. "Wasn't safe? Don't get me wrong, Zo, I'm happy to see you, but how exactly does 'wasn't safe' equal 'South American vacation'?"

Zoe fidgets with the fabric of her jeans. "Please don't take the piss out of me right now."

He stares at her, brows raised. "I'm sorry. I just don't understand."

Brazil wasn't initially part of her plan. She didn't really have a plan. Her mother was not generous with details and Zoe was kind of left to wing it. She snatches her beer off the floor and leans back. Her fingers tug at the label, peeling strips away from the glass. "I got to Nik's school and there were these two guys, real rough looking bastards, and they were asking about her. So I waited in the lobby. Eavesdropped, you know? Tried to get an idea what they wanted. Sounded real shady. They went and talked to some administrator. Nik showed up. Whole thing didn't feel safe. So—" She trails off.

"So—You left the country?"

Zoe shrugs, knees bobbing up and down. "When you say it, it sounds stupid."

Jones chuckles. "Who were they?"

She takes a deep pull of her beer. "Don't know."

He must be able to hear the apprehension in her voice. "You have no idea who they were, but you ran from them any way and skipped the states with a minor?"

"Nik said one of them was armed, and he—" Zoe tenses, preparing herself for his reaction. "He had a badge."

"What kind of badge, Zoe?"

She clears her throat, trying to keep her voice calm. "FBI."

"You ran from Feds?!" he yelps.

Apparently calm is not contagious. Zoe tries to smooth things over. "The guy I tussled with didn't flash any ID."

Jones cuts her off. "Wait. Hold up. 'Tussled?'" He scrubs his face with both hands. "Please tell me you didn't beat up a Fed."

She leans in close to him. "Those guys weren't Feds, Jones."

"But if they were, then you assaulted a federal agent."

Better to be completely honest. She holds up two fingers.

"Two? Jesus, Hudson. I hate to break it to you, now is not the time to start overachieving." He rubs his neck, controlling his breath. "And now you're here?"

She didn't really think about it like that. Not until right now. She has put him in a hell of a position. It wasn't her intent. She didn't have anywhere else to turn. It's not like she has a huge network of friends to go to for help. Zoe scratches at the label of her bottle. "I got scared."

They sit in silence. There really is nothing left to say. All that is left is uncertainty and worry, and neither will do her any good.

"It's gonna be okay." Jones squeezes her shoulder. "The boat is yours as long as you need it. Stay as long as you want."

Zoe nods and watches as Jones scoots past her to inspect their dinner options. She drains the last of her beer and taps the empty bottle against her knee.

SHE HAS TO KEEP MOVING.

Allison slips through a crowded street, tightening her grip on the scarf draped over her head and around her face. Hiding is a futile exercise. She can only imagine how easy it must be to spot a tall Caucasian woman in predominantly Muslim country.

A man in a white polo shirt and dark sunglasses has been in her periphery for the last twenty minutes. He seems to be all too conveniently going her way. Allison tries to keep her gaze forward, focusing on her surroundings and searching for an opportunity. She needs to get out of the open.

The answer is around a corner: a bustling market. So many bodies, stalls, and cluttered alleyways—all distractions that might help shake her tail.

Tail. Even thinking it has her feeling a little crazy, until she sees his reflection in the dark glass of a parked van.

Her pace quickens. She tries to suppress her own heartbeat pounding in her throat. Increase the distance, but don't run. Get some space, then pick an alley, a shop, a restaurant, and hope there is a way out.

Allison tucks into a corner business. Her Arabic is rusty, but 'bathroom' is easy enough to get across. The man behind the counter speaks faster than she can comprehend and points down a dark hallway. Allison takes one last opportunity to check over her shoulder for her pursuer.

Nothing.

She squeezes past the clutter of crates and boxes lining the hall, up a narrow flight of stairs and pushes her way into a claustrophobic bathroom, closing the door firmly behind her and throwing the lock. Her heart is still racing. This might have been a stupid idea.

Allison scans the cramped room. There is a window. It is small and inconveniently located above the toilet. She's tall enough to get to it, slim enough to get through it, but who knows what will be on the other side.

Her breathing slows, returning to normal. Maybe she can just wait. Maybe he didn't see where she went. All she has to do is hide here for a bit, then head back out. There is little dignity in hiding in a bathroom, but today she'll take evasion over dignity.

Her ear is pressed to the door, listening to the din outside. She can hear voices rise from below, then quiet, then rapid footsteps up the stairs. That can't be good.

Evasion over dignity.

Allison presses off the door and steps onto the rim of the toilet, then the tank. She shoves the narrow window open and grips the sill, pulling herself up and half through as the door knob rattles and a fist pounds on the locked door.

"Open this door, Dr. Hudson!" A man's voice. An angry voice. Probably the voice of the man who has been following her, but she is not about to stay to find out.

The drop from the window is short and sets her on an adjacent roof. She can hear the pounding on the door increase, becoming more violent. As she backs away from the window the percussive sound from inside mixes with the hum of the crowd on the street below.

You can't stay here. You have to keep moving.

Allison scrambles to the edge of the building. There is a twisting back alley with multiple exits, at least one leading back to the market. This section appears empty except for a pile of crates and stacks of trash. No people, no witnesses. She sits on the ledge, twisting her body in an attempt to lessen the considerable distance to the ground. Her fingers lose their grip. She slips, falling hard into a pile of uneven wooden crates. The impact hurt like hell, but nothing is broken.

Allison adjusts her scarf and exits the alley, merging back into the crowed street without looking back. She needs to find a place to lay low until she can think of what to do next.

She hopes her girls are doing the same.

ZOE HAS TO HAND IT TO HIM: the guy can cook. It was a simple meal—rice, beans, and some incredibly spicy sausage—but it's the most filling thing she's eaten in days. She is thankful for the hot meal, but almost more thankful for the familiar company.

Jones has been a perfect gentleman, spending the entire evening drinking beers and spinning tales of their shared past to her kid sister. His stories, as usual, are filled with inaccuracy and hyperbole, but she can't bring herself to correct him. It's nice to hear his voice.

Nicole is all too happy to chatter with Jones. Not that Zoe can really blame her. She was only two years older than her sister when she first met the guy, and his easy smile and boyish manner were instantly disarming. He was always looking out for her. After she got the gig on the Trident, he taught her to dive. He even kept the other guys on the boat in line and out of her hair. It was nice, like having a big brother.

If it wasn't for Matthew Jones and Captain Foster, Zoe would still be stuck working a shit dock job in Western Australia, barely scraping by, and completely incapable of continuing to search for her father.

"Isn't that right, Hudson?"

She hasn't been paying any attention to them. "What?"

Jones points his beer bottle at Zoe and closes his free hand in to a fist, motioning an exaggerated upper cut. "She clocked him. Right in the kisser. Guy was like, what? Twice your size?"

Zoe raises her eyebrows. She isn't sure which story he is telling, but if it's about a stupid decision and a fight, it's probably mostly true. She nods, stripping the last of the label from her bottle.

Nicole is swathed in one of Jones's old flannel shirts. Her chin rests on her palms, elbows propped against the narrow table, her freckled cheeks glowing rosy. "Then what happened?"

"The guy was too shocked to hit her back, so Zoe just whaled on him. It was hilarious, until the cops showed up." He stands and gathers up the plates, giving Zoe a solid punch to the arm on his way to the sink. "They dragged her out of that bar kicking and screaming. Captain Foster put up her bail and swore she'd stay on her best behavior. Next week we recovered three thirteen foot bronze cannon and a few hundred pieces of eight from the Indian Ocean. From then on, Zoe getting arrested always seemed to bring the boat luck."

Zoe rolls her eyes. It never had anything to do with luck. More likely, her mouth and stubborn streak stirred up shit often enough it seemed like there was some correlation.

She lets out a labored sigh. "I'm sure Nik doesn't want to hear about—"

"Shhh." Nicole slurs and raises a lazy finger to her lips, shushing her sister. Zoe finally notices the nearly empty bottle in Nicole's other hand.

She's been drinking. *Great.*

Zoe reaches for the bottle. "Hey, Nik, why don't you give me that?"

Nicole cradles the bottle out of reach.

Zoe exhales sharply and finishes her beer. Jones seems oblivious to Nicole's intoxication, likely due to his own. He finishes rinsing the dishes and leans against the cupboard. "We got into some serious shit on that boat. Didn't we, Hudson?"

"Yeah." She's not big on reminiscing, but things were never the same after he left. Everything was so much more complicated. The faces changed, and the crew that used to be a family quickly became strangers. Zoe felt isolated. After ten years, the job was all she knew, all she could see herself doing. Even if the rest of her life was falling apart, diving was her passion. It was all she had.

Nicole's eyelids slip closed, growing heavy from the hot meal and the alcohol. Zoe watches her begin to drift off and takes the opportunity to tug the now empty bottle from her sister's fingertips.

Jones smiles and motions towards to door. They slip outside. The air is salty and still warm, with just the hint of a breeze rustling the rigging of the 303.

Jones leans against the cabin. "How're you doing?"

She rolls her eyes. This is far more responsibility than she is used to. Keeping her own nose clean has been enough of a challenge; now she has Nicole to look after. Three days in and it's already not looking good. "I'm really bad at this."

Jones rubs his neck. "You *are* kind of impressively shitty at being a guardian. I think she's already drunk. How long she been around you —three days? That's got to be some kind of record."

"Thanks." Zoe leans her back against the massive wheel, digging her hands deep into the pockets of her jeans. "She doesn't trust me, Jones. I don't even think she likes me."

"She doesn't know you. That's different." He cocks his head. "You've got to give her time."

"Yeah." Zoe nods. He's right. He usually is.

"Once she knows you, she can learn to really hate your guts just like the rest of us do." His sarcasm earns him a punch to the shoulder.

Jones winces and retaliates by slipping his arm around Zoe's shoulders and pulling her into a bear hug.

She feels stupid, but she hasn't been hugged in a long time, and the physical contact is comforting. His chin rests on the top of her head. Zoe reaches around him, letting herself take comfort in his size and the strength of his arms.

"I don't know what you've gotten yourself into, Hudson." He sighs. "But please try to be careful."

"I'm trying."

Jones pulls back, grinning. "I meant with the boat. Try to be careful with my boat."

Zoe groans and gives him a firm push. "Get out of here."

He disembarks and staggers across the dimly lit dock. After a few deep breaths of warm ocean air, Zoe tucks back into the cabin to check on her inebriated sister. Nicole is completely passed out, slumped at the table, head resting on her arms. Zoe moves behind her and gives her a gentle shake. "Come on, Nik. Let's get you to bed."

The kid groans in disapproval, but Zoe grips under her arms, pulling her upward. Nicole fusses vaguely. "Did Matthew leave?"

"Yup. Come on, up you go."

Nicole rises on unsteady legs and wobbles the few steps to the sleeping berth, sitting with a heavy plop. Her speech is slurred. "He's kinda cute."

Zoe shakes her head. "No. No, he is not." She grabs a pillow and blanket from a drawer under the bunk.

Nicole stabs a finger at Zoe as she tips over onto the mattress. "You *liiiiiike* him."

"No. No, I don't." She hands Nicole the pillow. "How did you get so drunk off one beer?"

Her sister raises four fingers. Four beers. That makes a little more sense.

Zoe opens the blanket and tosses it over Nicole.

"Beer tastes funny." The statement is chased by a loud burp.

Zoe stops and stares at Nicole. "You've never had beer before?" She finds it hard to believe. "You do go to college, right?"

"University." Nicole corrects her, smacking her lips. Her words are slow and sticky, slurring as she begins to drift off to sleep. "I don't drink. Too young."

Zoe carefully pushes Nicole's dark curls out of her face and over her freckled shoulder. 'First hangover' is not really the most impressive milestone to reach with your estranged sibling. Mom won't be pleased. Zoe's hands snake around her neck, rubbing at well established knots.

She sits quietly on the edge of the bunk, watching Nicole as she begins to snore.

Case's office is sterile, all converging clean lines of polished concrete and brushed aluminum. Case watches the waves as they strike the pristine white beachhead just beyond the curtain of lush foliage.

There has been no word from her operators. Not since they acquired the cab driver in Brazil.

All the waiting has given her time to obsess. Her position requires a very delicate balance between knowledge and ignorance. She has to gather enough intel to be effective, but she rarely burdens herself with the sordid particulars of her targets. She prefers, instead, to remain distant. Objective. In control.

But this assignment bothered her from the start. She needs to know more.

There is movement in the reflection of the massive window. The polished metal door to her office opens, and her secretary enters, striding towards her desk and depositing a sleek tablet.

"These are the files you requested, ma'am."

Digging deeper into Victor Sutton's business is ill advised. Case twists the device so that its lines are parallel with the desk. "That will be all."

She waits until she hears the click of the latch, then turns to consider the information at her fingertips, idly swiping through surveillance, documents, phone records, and wire taps. The Corporation has been monitoring the Hudson women for years, but to what end?

A light on her phone receiver blinks.

This had better be worth the wait.

Dempsey is on the line. "Ma'am."

"What took so long?"

"The driver had to be encouraged."

It must be why she's speaking to him and not Connor. "And?"

"We have their location."

Case allows herself the briefest of smiles. "Go get them."

- 3 -

Opening her eyes is a bad idea. Her pupils instantly retaliate, amplifying the pounding in her skull. Nicole pinches her lids shut and groans, limply tugging the heavy wool blanket over her head to block what little light there is in the cabin of the boat.

So this is a hangover.

Note to self: don't ever do this again.

Just the thought of crawling out from under the blanket and searching the cupboards for painkillers makes her body ache. No wonder her roommate was always so useless after a night out. The effects of alcohol are ridiculous. It didn't even taste that good.

Zoe's voice is muffled through the blanket. "You awake?"

Nicole's curiosity trumps her pain. She lowers her cover and squints, trying to focus on Zoe standing next to the berth, water bottle in one hand, big bottle of aspirin in the other.

"You're gonna want these." Zoe shakes the aspirin.

Nicole winces at the sound and sits up slowly, legs slipping off the edge of the bed and dropping to the floor. Her mouth is full of cotton. The theory of water is sound, but her stomach rejects her change of position.

Zoe pokes her with the water bottle until she accepts it, then cracks open the aspirin and shakes out a dose. "Take it. You'll feel better."

Just thinking about putting the chalky pills in her mouth makes her nausea swell.

But there's something else. Something is wrong.

Her stomach is not the only thing pitching and rolling. Gear and supplies hanging from hooks on the ceiling are swaying. She can feel the uneven rise and fall of waves. Comprehension and the desire to vomit overwhelm her simultaneously.

"Nik, I can explain."

She wants to yell at her sister, but more than that, she wants to be able to barf with some dignity. Nicole pushes herself up and scrambles past Zoe towards the narrow steps and out to the deck. Salty air and a spray of mist hit her face, and if the dim light of the cabin hurt her eyes before, it's nothing compared to the explosion of bright noonday sun.

"Nik! Wait."

Nicole stumbles past the wheel and towards the rear of the boat. All her focus is on getting to the edge before she throws up. She grips the railing and as her torso pitches forward her stomach contracts, expelling its contents into the open ocean.

Very dignified.

Her sister takes a seat on the bench next to her and places a warm hand on Nicole's shoulder. "You okay?"

"Don't touch me." She jerks away, shooting Zoe a fierce look through strands of dark hair whipping in the wind.

"Before you get all pissed, let me explain."

Nicole knows the last thing she will get is an actual explanation, and she is not particularly in the mood for excuses. Her hands comb through her hair, tugging it back and out of her face as she spits the remaining bile out of her mouth. Braced against the railing, knees pressed into the cushion of the built-in bench, Nicole gets a look around at the vast stretch of nothing surrounding them.

No land. No dock. Just an endless expanse of forever rolling ocean.

"Where are we?" she mumbles to herself.

"We're on the Atlantic—"

"Shut up!" Nicole's mind races, trying to line up her questions in the right order. "Why would you—When did you—"

Zoe leans back against the railing, squinting into the warm sunlight. "You were asleep. I went ahead and took us out."

All she can do is stare, mouth agape.

"What?"

"Oh my God." Nicole can't tell if she is shaking from anger or having just lost her dinner over the starboard side of a boat. "Why do you keep kidnapping me?"

Zoe cocks her eyebrow. "What are you talking about?"

"It's like you have a disorder or something."

"I didn't kidnap you, Nik." Zoe scoffs. "We're on a boat. What did you think was going to happen?"

Her sister is really fantastic at being infuriating. "You're right! I should have assumed this was a shanghai. That should have been the only obvious conclusion." Nicole jabs at Zoe with her finger. "I cannot believe you. You have mental problems! You're crazy, because a rational person would have *asked* me if I wanted to flee to a foreign country. They wouldn't just take me, without my input. Right? Because I didn't agree to any of this, Zoe. Not Brazil. And not—not this." She gestures around her at the open ocean.

"You're the one who got tanked and passed out. Made it kinda difficult to ask for your opinion." Zoe lets out a heavy sigh. "Jesus, kid, getting wasted? What the hell was that? You're seventeen. What were you thinking?"

Nicole wasn't thinking. She was tired of thinking, and she was tired of unanswered questions. No one offered her the alcohol, but no one noticed her drink it either. It was an opportunity. She took it. She doesn't need Zoe's help regretting it now.

"You drank at my age," Nicole mumbles lamely.

Zoe takes in a deep breath, still staring off at the horizon. "I'm not exactly the best role model."

They both fall quiet, but the world does not. There is the sound of the water crashing against the hull of the boat and the howl of the wind rustling against the sails.

Nicole stares down at her pale feet, toes flexing against the white deck. "Where are we going?"

"Does it matter?" Zoe stands, ducking under the rigging to mind the navigation. She busies herself with the various gauges and instruments. After a few moments she responds, "Cape Town."

Nicole was not expecting an answer. "Cape Town, South Africa?" She raises an eyebrow. "Why?"

"Because it's a good place to get lost for a while." Zoe locks the wheel into position and leans against the cabin.

Nicole wishes her sister's logic made more sense. "Why couldn't we just stay in Brazil with Jones?"

"Those guys who were after you knew where you went to school. I bet they're probably tracking your credit card and they know about the tickets I bought. But they don't know anything about Jones, and no one can track *this* boat."

It's not like Nicole has never watched the Discovery Channel. Of course you can track a boat. Maybe not a homemade raft, but this is a legitimate seafaring vessel. It'll have communications equipment, navigation sensors—all sorts of ways to find their way through the ocean. But Zoe's intonation gives her pause. "'This boat?' What's so special about this boat?"

"I killed the GPS beacon." Zoe ducks into the cabin. "Can't follow what you can't see."

"Why would you do that?" She doesn't mean for the words to come out sounding as panicked as they do. "What if something happens? What if there's a storm? Or something on the boat breaks? Or you doze off and we hit a cargo ship?"

Zoe pokes her head out of the doorway, grinning. "You think I'm that bad of a sailor?"

"I don't know." Nicole can't tell if Zoe is actually offended or just messing with her. It doesn't matter. "Are you?"

Her sister shrugs as she climbs the steps, bottles of water and aspirin in hand. "I'm not total crap at it."

Nicole takes a bottle when offered, unscrewing the cap of the water and drinking deep, washing away the taste of bile. "Zoe, 'not crap' does not equal good."

Zoe plops onto the built-in bench opposite Nicole. "Two decent sailors can cross the Atlantic given good weather and good wind. It takes, like, two weeks. Won't be a problem."

Nicole struggles with the aspirin cap, fumbling it in her hands, confused by her sister's choice of words. "Two sailors?"

"Yeah." Zoe points to herself. "One." Then to Nicole. "Two."

Nicole shakes her head. "Oh no. No. I am not a sailor. I'm a college student. I've read *Master and Commander*, and I don't want to be either. I hate boats. And being on one has already made me violate my strict anti-puking policy. I—"

Zoe stretches her arms out along the railing. "That's too bad. I thought you'd like the challenge, but if you don't think you're smart enough to learn—"

"No one said anything about not being smart. I'm smart enough. I've won two National Merit scholarships and the McKinley Language Grant three years in a row." Nicole smacks her sister on the arm. "And don't think I don't know what you're doing. You're insulting my intelligence in an attempt to motivate me. And you know what? It's going to work." Nicole pointedly stands. "I can sail your little boat, Zoe."

It was meant to be a defiant gesture. A real "take *that*, you jerk." But her stomach and her limbs don't play along. Nicole's gut lurches and her legs don't wobble so much as give out entirely.

Her sister swoops in, preventing a shameful face-plant by catching Nicole in sturdy arms.

It's the last thing Nicole wanted to have happen. She presses back, finding stability of her own and searching for what little is left of her dignity. "Now." She straightens her shirt and pushes her hair out of her face. "Show me what to do."

THE WEEKLY PROGRESS MEETING IS something Case usually attends with a very particular level of disdain. It's sickening to watch every other manager with operatives in the field file into the massive boardroom and jockey for position and favor. The sheer level of ass kissing is appalling, especially since Victor Sutton has never been susceptible to flattery. And, contrary to popular opinion, flattery is not a tactic Case has ever used to curry his favor.

No. She has spent the better part of two decades bleeding and sweating for the man. She made the most of her projects, and brought in revenue from the most unexpected of places. Her successful foray into artifact acquisition eventually caught Victor's eye.

Antiquities trafficking never should have been able to compete with the other facets of the corporation. Private security, arms dealing, information brokering, and inside trading are all worthwhile and lucrative activities. But Case molded her seemingly minor responsibilities into a well oiled machine—all the right contacts, the most loyal operators, and the broadest array of resources. She became Sutton's right hand, the eyes and ears of his eccentric passions.

She earned her place.

But this week brings her no intel and no word from her operators. She has nothing to report. It's a situation that sets her nerves on edge. Every person in the room will be taking note of her lack of contribution, none more keenly than the olive skinned man at the far end of the table. Eli Kostich has been waiting for this moment for years.

When they adjourn, Case excuses herself, heading for the double doors to the main hall. Kostich follows her, slithering past the bodies milling around the table and passing up his opportunity to glad-hand the boss. He heads straight for her.

"Tricia."

She pauses in the hall, gripping her tablet. "Mr. Kostich."

His smile spreads wide. "I couldn't help but notice we didn't cover any of your projects." He presses in, always standing too close.

"No problems, I hope. I know you're kind of new to target acquisition. It's different than digging up relics. Takes a stronger stomach. I'd be happy to loan you some of my boys if you need some extra muscle."

Case rolls her eyes, inhaling deeply in an attempt to swallow the contempt her voice can't hide. "That will not be necessary, Mr. Kostich. I haven't much use for trained apes. Now, if you'll excuse—"

"Don't leave." Kostich steps in front of her, blocking her way. His voice lowers to a hiss. "I'm just offering you a little help. You know. I scratch your back. You scratch mine." He looks her up and down. "I hear you're good at that."

Case shakes her head, unable to hold back her laughter.

"What?" He looks confused.

"I don't want your help."

"Why the fuck not?"

There are so many reasons. Case starts with the most obvious ones. "I don't like you, Eli. You're sloppy. You lack polish and you have zero control over your operatives—"

He cuts her off, stabbing a finger at her chest. "I get results, which is more than you're getting right now."

Her smile is sudden and sharp. "Go to hell." Case strides past him, heels clicking on the concrete. She is halfway down the corridor when he calls after her.

"Why do you always have to be such a bitch, Tricia?"

She turns. "You bring out the best in me, Eli."

It's taken over a week and a half to start to enjoy this forced adventure. Okay, maybe "enjoy" is too strong a word. Acclimate is probably more accurate. She is gleaning the basics of sailing, though it's not even remotely a result of her sister's instruction—Zoe is a terrible teacher. But Nicole observes and absorbs every action. She's a student. It's what she's good at.

They've taken turns monitoring the instruments and the wheel. With how calm the ocean has been, the job is not mentally taxing. The ship's autopilot takes care of pretty much everything, and Zoe is up like a flash if Nicole so much as sneezes. She's pretty sure she's the only one actually sleeping. Zoe seems to be subsisting on caffeine and protein bars. There seems to be an infrequent nap here and there, but no real honest-to-God sleep. Nicole has known students who live like that during finals week, but they were taking tests, not piloting a boat on a transcontinental jaunt. She can't even begin to imagine feeling as tired as her sister looks and still putting in the backbreaking work it takes to run this boat. At least Zoe doesn't get cranky when she's exhausted.

Nicole combs her fingers through her curls, tucking them into a sloppy bun, pulling it out of her face to better see the sky. If there is one thing she has grown to truly love on this journey, it's the sunsets—an eternity of horizon glowing brilliant as the sun slips below the sea, setting behind the boat as they push deeper into shadow. There is nothing quite like it.

Nicole sits on the prow, back pressed against the fiberglass cabin. She's attempting to read a battered copy of Watership Down from the boat's strange library, but it's tricky as the sleeves keep sliding down on the sweatshirt she swiped from Zoe's gear bag. Her sister's attempt to buy clothing for the both of them was charming. Things have either been too small or way too big. She could complain, but there wouldn't be much of a point. At least the sneakers fit and the over-sized hoodie is warmer than the threadbare flannel she swiped from Jones.

Music begins to thump through the ship's tiny speakers. Zoe's evening ritual has commenced. Nicole is thankful musical taste is one of the few things they seem to have in common. The tracks skip around; Zoe is looking for something in particular. When the heavy drum beat and melancholy bass line begin to mingle with the crashing waves, Nicole gets a clear idea what mood her sister is in.

She hears footsteps on the deck. Zoe threads her body under the rigging and settles next to Nicole.

This is definitely not part of the usual ritual.

She nudges Nicole. "Hey."

It takes her a second to realize her sister's shoulder bump means she is expressing interest in communicating. "Hey."

They sit in companionable silence.

Nicole points up to the sky. "I never get to see the stars. Not like this. Too many lights in the city, you know?"

Zoe pulls her hood up and tucks her hands deep into her pockets. She yawns. "Stars are good."

Nicole cannot suppress her smile. Zoe's voice is strangely calming, in its own low, raspy sort of way.

"Want me to take over for a little while? You could get some sleep."

It was worth a shot, but Zoe shakes her head and leans back against the fiberglass.

Nicole sighs. "You have to sleep, Zoe."

"I'm fine."

Nicole doesn't believe her. The dark circles under Zoe's eyes tell a different story, but her sister is stubborn. Arguing won't change that. At least they're talking.

"Anything I need to do?"

Zoe shakes her head. "Just keep an eye on the sail and tack it up if she slacks."

The familiar silence returns, threatening to turn this night into every other night: just the waves, the wind, and the music echoing over the vast ocean.

It's not like Nicole doesn't have questions, beyond the apparently verboten obvious ones. She just doesn't want to mess things up by asking the wrong one. There are thousands spinning around in her head. Twelve years of them, in fact. *Who are you now? What do you like to do for fun? What is it like to be a diver? Is that even a real job? How many countries have you been to? Did you really punch out a guy twice your size in a tropical dive bar?*

Are you happy?

Did you ever miss me?

"What?"

She must be making a face, because Zoe is staring at her.

Now or never. "Can I ask you a question?"

Zoe shrugs. "I guess."

"After you left—" She can feel Zoe wince but continues to her point. "Did you ever think about coming home?"

The answer comes quickly. "No."

"Why?"

Zoe takes in a deep breath, hawkish profile peeking out of her hood, silhouetted in the vibrant moonlight. "That place was never my home, Nik. Not after my dad left. I never—I didn't belong there. Mom made that really clear."

"But we're your family." Her words sound hollow and confused.

"So is he."

Zoe's jaw begins to set in an all-too-familiar I'm-done-talking-now way. Nicole doesn't allow the quiet to stretch between them.

"Do you know where he is?"

Zoe sinks deeper into her sweatshirt, shaking her head. "No."

"All this time, and you don't even—" She trails off.

"I tried. Got as far as Perth before I ran out of money. Mom froze the credit card I stole. Thought I found his house once, but—I was wrong." Zoe's speech is monotone, matter of fact. Nicole wishes she could see her eyes, but they are hidden under the shadow of her hood. "Jones told you the rest. It's really not a big deal."

"Yes it is!" Nicole scoots in close. "Everything changed after you ran away. Mom was different, and I didn't have anyone to talk to."

"Talk to?" Zoe flashes Nicole a confused look. "You were five."

"Twelve years ago, Zoe. I grew up!"

Her sister shakes her head. Nicole doesn't have to see Zoe's face to know she's rolling her eyes.

"So after all that time, with no intention of ever coming home, and not even so much as sending me a stupid birthday card, why would you come after me?"

Zoe opens her mouth, but Nicole cuts her off. "And don't give me that 'Mom told me to' crap. It's not like you have a track record of listening to her."

Whatever Zoe was going to say, she stops, furrowing her brow. Nicole waits, watching her sister's face, hoping for the expression that will reveal what the silence does not.

The wind shifts.

The sail rustles in the breeze, growing slack, sending sloppy rigging slapping into the boom and mast. Hollow echoes drown out the music still coasting out of the ship's tiny speakers.

Zoe sits up, carefully slipping under the sail. She looks back at Nicole. "Give me a hand."

And with that, their conversation is over.

Nicole pushes up her sleeves and follows her sister back to the cockpit.

"Nik! Get up here!"

Nicole rolls her eyes and sets the down the deck of cards. She hollers back at Zoe through the open door. "What?"

There is a thump on the cabin wall. Is she seriously kicking the cabin? Very mature.

Rolling her eyes, Nicole scoots out from behind the table and heads up top. She grips the railing and pads out to the prow to join Zoe. The wind has not let up, but her sister is still perched precariously on the farthest edge of the bow, past the railing, binoculars in hand.

47

There is no way Nicole is going out there.

"What, Zoe?"

Zoe has a cocky grin plastered on her face. She extends the binoculars, beckoning Nicole out to the narrow planks.

Nicole holds the railing tighter. "I'm fine here, thank you. Just tell me."

"You've got to see it, Nik."

Her stomach turns at the idea of leaving the relative safety of the deck to balance out on the ledge with her sister. She'll get close, but she's not going out there. Nicole dips under the tight sail and creeps out to the edge, hands firm on the railing. This had better be worth it.

"Look." Zoe presses the binoculars into her hands.

At first she can't see anything, just blurry waves and sky, then a dark strip comes into focus.

Land.

Zoe slaps Nicole's shoulder as she clambers over the railing back onto the deck. "You are going to love Cape Town. The food. The incomprehensible accents—"

"Hot showers." Nicole smiles stupidly, still staring at the shore. The wind is so loud, whipping past her ears.

Her smile fades. That sound is not wind. She adjusts her focus. Something is headed directly for them. Fast.

The binoculars are snatched from her hands. Zoe must have heard the sound too. "Shit."

She grabs Nicole's shirt and tugs her back towards the cockpit. Nicole stammers, "What? 'Shit', what?"

"Get the sail tight."

"Why?" Her sister doesn't look happy anymore. "Who are they, Zoe? You said you didn't know anybody here."

"I don't."

"Well, who are they and why are you so—"

"They're pirates, Nik!"

"What?"

"Tack the sail. Now!"

Pirates. It doesn't seem real. She's read about bands of heavily armed thieves roving the African coast on CNN, but she always figured they went after bigger fish. Like commercial vessels worth massive ransoms, not thirty foot sailboats filled with canned food and bickering siblings.

Zoe tries maneuvering the sailboat to make a run for it, but the small speedboat is easily gaining on them. Nicole cranks the winch as fast as she can, trying desperately not to let her fear get the best of her.

"Faster, Nik."

Criticism won't stop them from losing ground, and the wind is no match for the speedboat's engine. Nicole glances towards their pursuers—they're gesturing emphatically, guns are raised. One man screams through a megaphone in a language Nicole doesn't recognize. Regardless, she has a pretty good idea what he's saying. When she looks back at the helm, her sister is rummaging through a storage bin under the cockpit benches instead of minding the boat's navigation.

"Zoe?!"

The pirates are closing the distance. Nicole locks the winch down and scrambles for her sister. "What are you doing?"

Zoe presses a red flare gun into Nicole's hands. "Take this. Fire it if…"

"What?!"

"Fire it if shit goes south. Then get your ass down in the cabin and lock it up tight. No matter what happens, do not come out."

Nicole can only imagine what qualifies as 'south' in a situation like this. Things feel pretty damn southerly as it is. "What about you?"

"Just do it, Nicole," she yells.

Zoe makes her way around the far side of the boat as the speedboat slows, bumping its hull into the 303. One of the pirates tosses a grappling hook over the railing, lashing the two boats together with practiced ease.

Nicole's words come out in a whispered jumble. "Shit, shit, shit, shit." She tucks the flare gun into her jeans and hunkers down, shoulder pressed against the wheel housing, trying to hide.

Zoe's voice is loud and calm. "You boys lost?"

The men are yelling, to each other and at Zoe. Nicole can just barely make out her sister's shadow through the thick fabric of the sail. She's going to get herself killed. Nicole scrambles to get a better view. Two men cross over, guns drawn.

Zoe raises her hands slowly. "Looks like you're on the wrong boat, fellas— "

The man with the rifle jabs at her, its long barrel digging into her shoulder, knocking her back.

"This is how you want it, huh?" says Zoe.

What happens next happens fast.

The attack is two simple motions: one of Zoe's hands whips down, striking the barrel and sending the butt of the rifle up into the man's chin, while the other punches him square in the nose. The crack is horrific. Blood sprays out like someone opened a spigot. Paralyzed, Nicole watches as her sister throws punch after punch into the would-be boarding party.

Fingers twist their way into Nicole's hair, taking hold of her ponytail and wrenching her up and on to her feet. The flare gun clatters to the deck, sliding uselessly out of reach. A sinewy forearm stretching across her throat, choking her. She tries to fight back, but no amount of squirming will loosen his grip.

She hears Zoe yell. "Hey! Get your hands off her!"

Nicole struggles, turning just in time to see the butt of a rifle ram Zoe in the gut before she crumples to the deck.

The pirate with the broken nose is screaming, flicking blood all over the white deck of the 303. He has his foot on her sister's chest, pinning her down as his gun toting cohort kicks Zoe repeatedly in the ribs. Nicole feels sick watching it.

The man holding Nicole laughs. His grip begins to loosen around her neck. It may be her only chance. She stomps her heel down on his bare foot with as much force as she can manage. He yowls and Nicole goes limp, dropping to the deck as soon as he releases her.

She kicks out with both feet, striking the lock on the winch holding the sail in place. The boom swings wild, clearing the pirates from the deck of the 303 more effectively than Nicole could ever have hoped. To her horror, Zoe doesn't use her newfound freedom to cut the tether or head for the controls. She leaps over to the speedboat and begins to attack the last remaining pirate, a young man probably not much older than Nicole. Clearly terrified, the boy fumbles with his weapon until Zoe wrenches it away. She shoves the kid back and begins to smash the wooden stock of the rifle into the boat's control panel.

"What are you doing?" Nicole screams.

Zoe points to the tether. "Cut it."

"You cut it!"

"Do it now, Nicole!"

"With what?!"

Zoe doesn't offer any suggestions as she continues to batter the console until showers of sparks and bits of broken glass flail in all directions. Nicole scrambles to the railing and gropes at the coarse rope, tugging until the makeshift hook holding the two vessels together comes free. The 303 begins to slowly drift away. She hurries back to the wheel to change their course, but the wind is too strong. Zoe hurls the rifle into the ocean and makes a jump for the 303. Her feet miss, but her stomach slams hard into the polished railing. Nicole locks the wheel down and runs to her, grabbing hold of her belt and pulling her on to the boat. Her sister pitches forward, crashing to the deck, gasping for air.

Zoe crawls forward, propping herself against the exterior of the cabin. She watches as the pirates swim back to their their speedboat only to find it's dead in the water. A smug smile crosses her lips. "That'll teach 'em."

Nicole kicks at her sister's prone body. "What is wrong with you!"

"Ow! What do you mean what's wrong with me, what's wrong with *you*? I told you to get below deck."

"You are completely insane! You could have gotten yourself killed! They had guns. Why do you do stuff like that?" She's never been so mad, so scared, and so relieved all at the same time. The combination of emotions is exhausting.

Her sister clutches her side but does not answer. As the distance grows between the two boats, Zoe lets out a pained sigh. "That thing with the winch—Where'd you pick that up?"

Nicole shrugs, sinking to the deck. "Physics."

"It was good." Zoe leans her head back, resting it against the hull as she closes her eyes. "Smart. I never would've thought of it."

"Thanks." It's the first compliment her sister has ever given her. A part of Nicole still wants to choke Zoe for the crap she just pulled, but the rest of her is strangely touched.

They sit in silence, catching their breath.

THEY HAVE BEEN WALKING for almost an hour, and Nicole has been nothing but sullenly silent the entire time. At least she is being quiet about it, but Zoe is having a hard time figuring out what her deal is. What happened off the coast was pretty nerve racking, but the kid handled herself well and they both made it out alive. If either of them should be cranky about what happened, it's Zoe. She got the crap kicked out of her. Her ribs ache with every breath, and she can feel her knuckles growing tight as deep bruises settle beneath her skin.

Asking the kid will just open up the can of whatever Nicole is feeling, but the sheer degree of brooding is annoying. "What's wrong with you?"

Nicole squints at her sister grumpily. "You sold the boat."

"Seriously?" Zoe laughs. "That's your problem?"

"I liked the boat. There were books."

"Books?"

"Yeah, you know, things you read. With words and pages." Nicole adjusts the strap of her bag. "Did Matthew know you were going to sell it? I mean, did he give you permission?"

"I'll ask for his forgiveness later. We needed the money for a place to stay."

Nicole mumbles, "We could have just stayed on the boat. For free."

Zoe ignores her, scanning the cramped, bustling street for any sign of danger. They've wandered into a rough part of town, and she needs to stay focused. The men who attacked them in the bay may have friends in the area, and there's no telling if they managed to get back to shore by now.

Nicole lets out a heavy sigh.

"What now?" Zoe asks.

"You keep saying we need to get a place, but we've already passed, like, three hotels. Just pick one and let's get it over with. I want a shower."

"Those weren't hotels, kid."

Nicole stops, pointing indignantly back down the street. "Yes they were. They had signs and everything—"

Zoe laughs to herself as she turns the corner. "Yeah, with rates by the hour."

It takes Nicole a minute to catch on, but when she does, her face turns a satisfying shade of bright red. She quickens her pace.

Their hotel is a four-story Art Deco monster, a once grand building that time forgot. The crumbling facade is punctuated by sections of intricate tile. Airy geometric patterns and architectural details are chipped and broken, their colors fading away in the unforgiving African sun.

Room rates are bound to be cheap, and so long as the doors lock and the water's hot, run down is fine by Zoe. Besides, there's a familiar sort of comfort in its ramshackle decrepitude.

They enter the lobby through rickety double doors that creak with a piercing sound. Particles of dust float through the air, and there is an overwhelming smell of mold and stale cigarette smoke. The lobby is vacant except for an old man sitting behind a counter. He frowns at them, his deep wrinkles falling farther into shadow. As Zoe draws closer, the man taps his cigarette out on an ashtray and watches her with a cautious stare.

"Hey."

The old man glares at her.

Zoe continues, leaning against the sticky wooden counter. "Can we maybe get a room?"

He puffs on his cigarette and begins to speak rapidly, gesturing to the exit.

She can't understand a word he's saying, but he seems to be telling them to leave. Not the best business practice, considering the place looks like a ghost town. All she wants is a hot shower and a few hours of real sleep on an actual bed. Zoe pulls out her passport and unsnaps the brittle rubber bands, thumbing through their cash. "Look, I have money. Okay? We just need a room for a few days— "

Nicole startles Zoe when she slouches against the counter and begins to gibber incoherently. The old man smiles warmly at Nicole, then glares at Zoe. Whatever they're talking about, they understand one another. Zoe feels keenly out of the loop. The old man puffs on his cigarette and holds out his palm.

Nicole nudges Zoe. "Pay him."

"What?"

Her sister snatches the passport and thumbs through the bills, sliding the appropriate amount across the counter in return for a room key.

"What did you say to him?" Zoe stammers as Nicole grabs her sleeve and drags her towards the antiquated elevator. "No, wait, what just happened there?"

"It's not a big deal." Nicole shushes her. "We've got a room. Just drop it."

The metal accordion door slams closed. Zoe can still see the old man at the counter flicking through the stack of cash. "You were talking to him back there. How did you know—"

"It's Afrikaans, Zoe. It's not witchcraft." Nicole stabs at the button for the third floor, and the motor kicks in, drawing them upward.

She's still confused. "How the hell do you know Afrikaans?"

As the elevator grinds to a halt, Nicole modestly lowers her gaze and throws the gate, exiting into the hall and checking the number on the room key. "It's rooted in Dutch."

Zoe follows her out of the elevator. "And you just happen to know Dutch?"

Nicole looks sheepish. "Mom taught me so I could talk to Gran."

The muscles in Zoe's jaw clench, teeth grinding together uncomfortably. "You do that a lot?"

"Talk to Gran?"

Zoe nods curtly.

"Um, yeah. On holidays and birthdays. That sort of thing." Nicole checks the key fob again. "She was kind of a busy lady, you know?"

No, I don't, is what she wants to say. *Old bat never wanted to talk to me.* It's ridiculous, but she can feel the jealousy burning in her gut. Nicole, even at a young age, was always the favorite daughter. It must have been nice for their mother to finally have a kid who fit in with the rest of the family.

School was never Zoe's strong suit. She was better at skipping class, smoking under the bleachers, and clocking football players when they pissed her off. Books and studying never really factored into the equation.

Nicole jiggles the key in the old lock until the tumblers finally give way, swinging open into the cramped, musty room. They dump their bags on the floor and the boards creak with the sudden weight.

"I call shower." Nicole declares, beelining for the darkened bathroom.

Zoe absently kicks the door closed and throws the security chain into its channel.

The room is sparsely furnished with a single bed, a battered dresser, and louvered shutters over narrow windows. It's hot and humid, and every piece of clothing is sticking to her. For everything she's been through, Nicole deserves the first go at a shower. All Zoe can do is hope the kid doesn't use up all the hot water. She flops back on the lumpy mattress and stares up at the cracked plaster ceiling until her eyes drift closed.

There is a knock.

It can't have been more than a few minutes. She doesn't even remember falling asleep. She can still hear the water running behind the closed bathroom door.

Her eyelids feel so heavy.

There is another knock, this one harder than the first. The door to their room jostles with the force.

She sits up, her body slipping off the edge of the bed and moving for the door, every muscle tensed. She pulls it open quickly, without removing the security chain. Wood bucks against metal.

Through the gap she can see the old man from the front desk. He begins to speak rapidly, but even if he weren't, Zoe still wouldn't be able to understand anything he's saying.

"I don't—I'm not good at—Oh, Christ, just hold on. Just one sec. Okay?" The old man seems harmless enough. Zoe closes the door and hollers for her sister. If the man's got something to say, he better say it to the person who can actually talk to him.

Nicole doesn't respond. Zoe fumbles with the chain and opens the door all the way, yelling for her sister. "Nico—"

Zoe stops.

He's holding something that belongs to her: the yellowed photograph from inside her passport. She'd know it anywhere: tell-tale crease down the middle, frayed corners, weathered emulsion. Her father holding her tight, her own youthful smile missing her first tooth, and her mother looking so very much in love with the man clutching their daughter.

It is her only tangible proof that they once were all together, a fleeting memory of a happy family that no longer exists.

"How did you get that? Give it back." Zoe reaches for the photo, but the old man tugs it out of reach, emphatically pointing at her father. Zoe shakes her head. "What? I don't understand—"

He gives her the picture and begins to rummage through his pants pocket. Zoe braces herself, not knowing what to expect.

The desk clerk pulls out a weathered envelope.

He points again at her father's image, then takes her hand, opening her clenched fist. He presses the brittle envelope into Zoe's palm, forcing her fingers closed around it. She stares at him blankly, then turns her gaze to the envelope.

Delicate script on the face reads "Hayden Thomas."

Her father.

When she looks back up, the old man is halfway down the poorly lit hall. Zoe yells after him. "Wait!"

He pulls open the accordion door, stepping inside the elevator and letting it slam behind him. The motor whirs loudly, pulling the carriage out of sight.

Zoe checks the hall. Beams of light cast through filthy windows, puddling on the dirty rug, illuminating a million specks of dust drifting through the thick air. There is no one else.

She backs into the hotel room, locking the door behind her. Zoe folds the photograph and carefully tucks it back into her passport. It must have gotten mixed in with the money to pay for the room. She hadn't noticed. Her stomach twists at the thought. It's the only picture she has of him. If she had lost it—

She pushes the thought from her head and focuses on the envelope. The paper crinkles beneath her touch, dry with age. The postmark is no longer legible, but she can still make out the return address: an apartment in Mombasa, Kenya.

She flips the envelope over, slips her finger under the flap and parts the seal. The paper inside is fine and heavy, the personalized stationary of a man named William Hawthorne. The address and title below his name are hastily scratched out. She holds the letter up to the light, exposing a detailed watermark. A crest. She can just make out the words: Cairo University.

Confused, she squints at the precise, foreign script. Better ask the expert.

"Nik." Zoe barges into the bathroom and is instantly assaulted by steam. "Nicole!"

No response. She doesn't have time for this.

"Come on, kid. Time's up." She trips the lever on the antiquated toilet and waits as the water pressure shifts. Nicole lets out a startled bark from inside the shower as all the cold water evacuates the lines.

"Oh my God!" Nicole cuts the water and pulls at the plastic shower curtain to cover herself. "Get out of here! It's not your turn!"

Zoe hold the letter in front of her sister's face. "Can you read this?"

"What is it?"

"It's a letter, Nik."

Nicole lets out an exasperated sound. "Read it yourself!"

"I can't. It's in squiggle."

"It's not—Jesus, Zoe, 'squiggle?'" She leans towards the paper, squinting through suds at the lettering. "That's Arabic."

"See. You *can* read it." Zoe holds the letter out.

Nicole glowers at her, refusing to take the yellowed paper. "Yeah, I can read it. It says you have boundary issues."

Zoe pulls her arm back, inspecting the script. "No it doesn't."

Nicole's wet hand protrudes from the shower curtain, snapping. "Give me a towel."

"No."

"Seriously?!"

"Tell me what this says and I'll give you what you want."

"You're blackmailing me *with a towel?*" Nicole's face pinches, eyes drawing into narrow, angry slits. "There is something seriously wrong with you." Nicole sighs and pulls the shower curtain tighter around herself, drying her hand against it as best she can before reaching for the letter.

Zoe hands it off and leans back against the legged sink. She inspects the envelope more closely, trying to decipher the smudged and weathered postmark. Her fingertips trace the scratched surface, feeling the depressed channel left by the pen that spelled out her father's name. "What does it say, Nicole?"

"Uh, okay. 'Beware the Southern Cross. The ground is burning. You will find no safety. Keep hidden. They are looking for you.'" Nicole stares at her sister pointedly, wet hair dripping on the tile floor. "Now, give me a damn towel, Zoe. I'm cold."

She tosses her sister a towel and leans against the threshold, thinking hard.

"Where did this come from?" Nicole wraps the towel around her body, tugging the shower curtain aside, her eyes glued to the paper. "Who's William Hawthorne?"

Wherever her father is, he's in trouble. Zoe can feel her chest tighten with the thought.

"Zoe?" Nicole steps over the edge of the claw foot tub, clutching her towel tight as water puddles on the tile floor, dripping from her sopping hair. "Was this addressed to you?"

Zoe snaps, "Give it."

Her sister hands the letter back and takes cautious steps closer. "It said 'Keep away. They are looking for you'? That's creepy. What do you think it means? Does this have something to do with Mom?"

"No." Zoe shakes her head and stalks out of the bathroom, closing the door hard behind her.

The scrap of paper in her hand is the closest she's been to her father in over two decades.

Zoe crosses the cramped room and leans against the window casing, tugging at the louvered shutters. The sun is setting. The crowded street below begins to change, preparing for night.

She tucks the letter into its envelope, nervously tapping it against her thigh as she chews her thumbnail. As night falls, street lights flicker to life, casting warm amber light on the city outside the dirty hotel window.

- 4 -

TWO WEEKS AND STILL NO SIGN of the Hudson women. Nothing from the Atlantic patrols. No leads from South Africa. And still nothing from Baghdad. It's like they simply vanished. The idea is ridiculous and she knows it. Anyone who takes even the most cursory glance at their dossiers would see that Zoe Hudson is not one for stealth, Nicole Hudson is far too sheltered to be of much use in the real world, and Allison Hudson is too identifiable to keep a low profile. Nothing is adding up. Either someone is keeping them hidden, or they have all been exceptionally lucky.

No matter. Luck has a way of running out.

Sutton could not have been pleased with her most recent report. In this particular situation, her lack of intel must look like the sign of a poorly run op, which is not a perception she can afford.

When Case enters the waiting room to Sutton's office, Fletcher is stationed next to the glass door, waiting for her. He opens it, averting his eyes as she passes.

Not a good sign.

Sutton is not alone.

"Sir." She addresses her boss respectfully, then glares at a man who is casually occupying a place he shouldn't. "This is a private meeting, Eli."

Kostich is sitting in the leather chair across from her employer's desk, slouched and smug. His perfectly tailored suit is, as always, slightly rumpled in the most fashionable way possible.

"I invited him." Sutton gestures for her to sit next to Eli. "Please take a seat, Ms. Case."

"I'm fine standing, sir. Thank you."

Her answer is not an acceptable one. "Sit down, Tricia."

Case lowers herself slowly into the seat, making sure to keep her posture as straight as possible, in sharp contrast to Eli's overtly unprofessional presentation. The presence of one of her contemporaries in what she was told would be a private meeting can only be a bad sign.

Sutton begins to pace, hands clasped behind his back. "It has been brought to my attention that you have too much on your plate, Ms. Case."

"Sir, I hardly think—"

He raises a hand to silence her.

Eli leans forward, smile broadening at the sight of her dismissal. "Mr. Sutton, may I?"

The old man gives him a nod.

"Tricia's been under a lot of pressure lately. We've all witnessed her dramatic decline in performance. Now, I realize how important this particular operation is to you, sir, and I sympathize with how hard it must be for Ms. Case to admit she needs help. But the facts are clear. She cannot handle this acquisition alone. Which is why I would like to offer you my expertise."

There is no rational way to respond to Eli's comments. It takes balls to steal her op right out from under her when she is in the room. This has not happened to her in a long time. She feels the weight of her sidearm against her back.

Case sits erect and still, waiting for silence.

"I am certain your skills will be appreciated." Sutton says. "Won't they, Ms. Case?"

She nods stiffly, burning with rage.

Eli turns his gaze and chuckles uncomfortably to himself. "Mr. Sutton, I just wanted to let you know what a pleasure it's been talking to you."

Sutton sits behind his desk, swiveling the leather chair to face the window. "You have a job to do, Mr. Kostich. You are dismissed."

"Yes, sir."

Case rises, her fingers digging into the arm of her chair. She can see Sutton's reflection in the plate glass window as he points at her. "Not you, Ms. Case. You stay."

Eli flashes her a pearly smile. He leans in close as she lowers herself back into her seat. "Be a good girl."

Fletcher enters the office, holding the door open for Eli as he exits. The smoked glass swings silently shut in his wake.

Sutton turns in his chair. "Coffee?" He does not wait for her to answer but gestures to Fletcher, who fills two delicate china cups.

She does her best to control her tone. "What was that?"

"That?" Sutton raises an eyebrow. "That was something I should have done weeks ago. A little friendly competition, something to light a fire inside you."

Fletcher hands them both steaming cups of coffee. Case accepts the mug. "I have things under control."

"'Under control' and 'producing results' are one and the same. You have put me in an uncomfortable position. I do not have the luxury to allow my most senior project manager to under-perform. I had to take action." He sips his coffee. "I'm sure you understand."

"You just stripped me of my op and handed it to a degenerate kiss-ass. Forgive me, sir, but I don't."

"You left me no other option." Sutton's weathered face is unreadable. "Mr. Kostich has more experience with target acquisition as well as deep contacts in the Middle East and will bring Dr. Hudson in within a more acceptable time frame."

Her voice sharpens. "So that's it?"

"This is not a punishment, Tricia. I am allowing you time to focus all your attention on your other objectives."

She cannot stay quiet when challenged. "I can find the doctor, sir."

"You *will* find her daughters. And you will do so swiftly." He sets his coffee down, porcelain clinking on glass. "No more excuses. Is that understood?"

Case nods, placing her cup on the side table. Her fists clench, fingernails digging painfully into her palms. Her composure will not hold much longer.

"You are dismissed."

Fletcher crosses the room, moving gracefully to the door and holding it open for her. Case exits the lobby and enters the hall, finally releasing the breath she has been holding. The corridor is bustling, its early morning activity in sharp contrast to the stillness of Sutton's office.

Case pulls her cellphone from her jacket pocket. Her fingers move out of instinct, unlocking the device and dialing.

"Dempsey?"

He sounds confused. They were not due to report for hours. "Ma'am?"

"Where are you?"

"Cape Town. Connor tracked a lead. Somali pirates who say—"

She cuts him off. "Wrap it up. I want you two back here tonight."

There is silence on the line.
"Ma'am?"
"Was I unclear, Mr. Dempsey?"
"No ma'am."

ZOE IS SLOUCHED ON A BENCH, tapping her boarding pass against her thigh. In under an hour they will both get on some ridiculously small aircraft headed for the largest city in Kenya. Her sister does not seem excited by the concept.

Nicole is sitting on an adjacent bench, looking morose and more than a little exhausted. She lets out a heavy sigh. "I don't understand why we're leaving. You said Cape Town was a good place to lay low."

"We need to keep moving." Zoe props her head back against the seat. At least her sister is talking again. The silent treatment was getting annoying. "It's safer this way."

"That's not what you said before," Nicole snaps. A few passing travelers shoot them suspicious glances. Nicole scoots closer to Zoe, lowering her voice. "We're only leaving because of that letter."

Zoe flicks at the edges of her boarding pass.

Nicole continues, "I understand it seems like a lead on your dad, but—"

"Then what's your problem?" Zoe crosses her arms, curious to see where this is going.

"I think this is a bad idea."

"A bad idea?"

"Yeah. We don't even know who sent that letter. We don't know this Hawthorne guy's relationship to your father. And it barely makes any sense anyway. 'The ground is burning'—who says that sort of stuff?"

Zoe tugs off her sunglasses. "And what do you think we should be doing? What's your bright idea?"

Nicole doesn't have an answer. She slumps back into her seat and stares sightlessly out the window. "All I'm saying is this feels way too convenient. If no one knew we were at that hotel and you've never been there before, why was that letter waiting there for your dad? Doesn't that seem strange to you? It's weird, right?"

Zoe rolls her eyes. It's not like she planned it this way. After all the years of fruitlessly searching, she doesn't want to think about how 'convenient' this help is. She clears her throat. "I'm done talking about this."

"Why are you being so stubborn?" Nicole sounds just like their mother. "Have you ever thought that maybe your dad doesn't want you to find him?"

The words cut deep, and Zoe can't resist the urge to lash back. "I never asked to be your damn babysitter, kid. I'm sorry if you think this detour is inconvenient, but last time I checked, I'm the adult here and I'm the one who gets to make the decisions. So when I say we're going to Mombasa, we're going to Mombasa. End of story. You got a problem with it, tough shit."

Her sister turns red and pulls away, staring beyond Zoe at the planes taxiing down the runway.

THE EARPLUGS DEADEN THE SOUND, but nothing can dampen the full-body concussion of her weapon's discharge. Case feels the crack in her gut every time she pulls the trigger. Round after round exits her pistol and pierces the thick card stock, following the last bullet through the ever expanding hole in the silhouette's head. She has been in this lane for hours, shooting paper effigies until they tear and drop from the target stand.

The range attendant came by an hour ago with boxes of ammunition, a fresh roll of targets, and information. The private jet carrying her operators landed on the mainland.

She has been repeating the cycle of firing and reloading her Makarov. Waiting.

The pressure in the room changes when the door opens. Case removes her ear plugs to hear the echo of footsteps and sound of empty brass shells skittering across the concrete floor. Out of the corner of her eye she sees Dempsey, his dark complexion emphasizing the heavy bags that have settled beneath his eyes.

Case hits the button on the wall of her lane and a motor spins up, whirring loudly, pulling her target towards the counter. "Mr. Dempsey."

"Ma'am." The man is always so polite.

"I'm disappointed." She watches the perforated paper flutter. Harsh fluorescent lights shine through the tight grouping in the center of the target's head. "I was confident I had the right man for the job.

Someone who would temper Connor's unpredictable nature and still produce results. Was I mistaken?"

He remains quiet, aware her question is rhetorical. She can hear him swallow behind her. "In my defense, I've performed my duties to the best of my ability, ma'am. You can't blame me for—"

"I can, in fact, blame you, Mr. Dempsey." The motor comes to an abrupt stop, metal clamp striking the rubber bumper at the end of the line. She rips down the silhouette and unrolls a fresh target, clipping it into place. She punches the red button again, harder this time. The motor switches on, pulling the dark shape down the lane. "This project is overdue. It is unacceptable. All you had to do was pick up a seventeen-year-old girl."

Dempsey sets his jaw. "Her sister interfered."

"I don't want excuses." Case slams the magazine into her pistol, thumbing the slide release and chambering a round. "I want results."

"I apologize, ma'am."

She turns, finger hovering over the trigger, arm extending, the muzzle of her pistol coming to rest on Dempsey's brow. She takes a controlled breath, drawing in as much air as her lungs will hold then releasing it slowly. Her words are crisp. "Give me one reason not to pull this trigger."

He looks calm. She has to respect that. Nothing is worse than a man who grovels. Dempsey speaks in a measured tone. "We had a strong lead in South Africa. We'll go back—"

"No." Her Makarov is still pressed firm to his skin. He is sweating now. Case withdraws her finger, resting it on the trigger guard as her arm drifts to her side. She turns back to her target. "Clear your quarters. Your services are no longer required."

He seems genuinely confused. "You're firing me?"

She holds up her pistol and sights down the range. "Would you prefer I explore other options?"

"No, ma'am." Dempsey nods stiffly then turns for the door. His exit is swift but not hurried.

The heavy metal door closes behind him, reverberant through the indoor range as she squeezes the trigger. The crack of the 9mm ammunition pierces her unprotected ears.

The sound takes her back to simpler times, when she had more control. A time when she relied only on herself, her partner, and her intel. A time long before the promotions and the politics of her job made everything muddy and complicated. Case fires until the slide locks back and the magazine is spent.

She is no longer alone.

"Want me to have him followed?" The man's voice is gravelly, evidence of a lifetime of destructive choices.

Case shakes her head. "No."

"I can kill him."

He is serious, and she is pleased by his offer despite herself. "That won't be necessary, Connor." Case ejects the empty magazine and places the sturdy Russian pistol on the counter.

Connor leans against the wall, kicking brass shells from under his feet. "Bad day?"

She crosses her arms, leaning back against the counter. "Sutton split the op. Gave the mother to Eli."

"Kostich?" Connor scoffs. "Old man bumped you for that piece of shit?"

"Mr. Kostich was able to make a compelling argument regarding my incompetence."

The muscles in his jaw and neck flex in concert with the scowl forming on his face.

Case has to ask. "You had them in Brazil. What happened?" Dempsey had been vague about the details, but the hulking man before her won't mince words when it comes to explaining a failure.

Connor scrubs the crown of his shaved head. "They were gone before we got to the dock. Put the guy who ran the place through it, but we didn't get much."

"What did you get?"

"We know they took one of his boats. Guy was a friend of Hayden's kid. The bitch broke my nose when we tried to grab the kid from her school." When he stares down the lane at her target, Case can see his profile is different, flatter and more crooked than before. She had noticed his discolored eye sockets when he entered, but didn't think much of it. He's never been a delicate man.

"Dempsey seemed to believe the guy when he said he didn't know where they were headed."

"Did you?"

"Believe him?" Connor squints, considering his answer. "I beat the shit out of him and he didn't crack." He shrugs his massive shoulders. "If he knew where they were headed, he would have said something when I started breaking his fingers."

65

Case slams a full magazine into her pistol, thumbing the slide release and slipping the heavy steel frame into the holster at the base of her spine. "Did you leave the Hudson sisters a message?"

Connor's smile is wicked. "Burned the place down. Left him there. If that bitch and the kid head back, they'll hear us loud and clear."

"Good." Case switches off the light in her lane and grabs her jacket, heading for the large metal door. Connor falls into step with her as they exit the firing range.

She missed him. In all the corporation, there is no one she trusts more. When she needs something done, she sends Connor. He has a special way about him, an ability to extract information from even the most resistant sources. Having him out in the field has paid off more times than she can count, but after a day like today, having him at her side steadies her. He moves ahead, his bulky frame pressing against the smoked glass door, opening it wide for her. They trade the air-conditioned comfort of the complex for the sticky humidity of the night.

Connor digs into his pocket, removing a smashed pack of cigarettes. He taps one out and lights it, snapping his silver lighter closed as he draws smoke deep into his lungs. "What now?"

"I'll send a team to investigate the lead you identified in South Africa. See where that goes. If nothing direct comes from it, we wait." She stops at the edge of the path leading down to the personnel quarters, staring intently at the strip of white beach reflecting bright in the moonlight, dark water surging forward then slinking back into itself. "They'll make a mistake. And then we'll have them."

THEIR CAB COMES TO A STOP outside a dilapidated stucco apartment building deep in the heart of Mombasa's urban center. Large patches of plaster seem to be peeling away from the facade in sheets, leaving cracks in their wake as they crumble to the dusty ground below. The surrounding buildings are not in much better shape. The entire neighborhood looks like it's simply waiting to die, longing for a heavy storm to dissolve every structure into nothing more than rubble and memory.

Dusk is settling on the city; the growing darkness litters the street in long, lonesome shadows. The cab driver is speaking to Zoe in broken English. He pulls into a spot on the opposite side of the street, parking and turning off the engine.

Since Zoe is not inclined to share anything with her, Nicole can only assume this must be the address on the envelope. She sighs softly. "Are you sure you want to do this?"

Zoe doesn't respond, checking the address one last time before climbing out of the car and loping across the street. She manages to miss every passing car with a reckless ease. As her sister steps into the shadowed threshold of the apartment, Nicole takes a moment to consider her options: stay in the cab with the driver who is leering at her in the rear-view mirror, or get out of the car and brave an iffy neighborhood with her sister.

Nicole clambers out of the cab. She waits for a gap in traffic and runs as quickly as she can across the busy street. A speeding sedan nearly clips her, and the driver swerves, horn blaring. He leans out his window to yell, but she can barely hear him over the sound of her own heart pounding in her ears. She ducks between a pair of parked vehicles and leans against a crumpled bumper, taking slow, deep breaths until her knees stop shaking.

Off to a good start. Nicole presses off the pickup and joins Zoe in the shaded entry.

Up close, this building has seen better days, and the door is clearly a new addition. The broad expanse of thick glass is crisscrossed with security mesh which is in turn obscured by heavy iron bars bolted to a sturdy wooden frame. Zoe tugs on the massive handle, banging the bolt against the jamb loud enough that Nicole winces. She takes a cautious glance at the street, worried the noise might have drawn some attention from onlookers, but the bustling evening traffic seems to have masked Zoe's effort to rip the door off its hinges.

"I think it's locked, Zoe."

"You think?"

Nicole rolls her eyes and turns her attention to the antiquated call box next to the door. Names are written on brittle, yellowing tape that barely cling to the splotchy metal. She traces the labels carefully until she finds the one they're looking for.

104. W. M. Hawthorne.

She presses the buzzer. There is a faint pop and whir—the mechanical sound of something old working hard to do its job. The tiny speaker above the row of labels crackles softly with static. No response. Half optimistic, half frustrated, she jabs at the button a few more times.

She jumps at the loud click behind her. When she looks over her shoulder, Zoe is pressing the heavy door open.

Nicole stammers, "How—How did you do that?"

Zoe checks the street before tucking into the darkness beyond the threshold. Nicole follows, hip gracelessly bumping the bulky door as she slips through the closing gap. She tugs at Zoe's jacket until her sister comes to halt. Nicole's voice comes out in a panicked whisper. "You're breaking and entering?"

"I didn't break anything." Zoe rolls her eyes and pulls free, surveying the empty foyer, then checking the envelope again before tucking it back into her pocket. "We're just entering."

It's the thready moral logic of a thug. Nicole tries to suppress her mounting disapproval as they head past the narrow staircase and turn down a poorly lit hall. The building seems steeped in a strange odor, an overpowering mixture of dust and antiseptic cleaners. Besides making her sick to her stomach, the smell is making her nervous. The condition of the interior isn't helping: the walls show signs of water damage ineffectively obscured by layer upon layer of mismatched paint. The wooden doors lining the hall are worn and scratched, their surfaces bearing the evidence of careless tenants. Each is marked with brass numbers, shabby and dark with age.

Apartment 104 is the second unit on their left. Zoe's features twitch as she reaches out and raps on the door with bruised knuckles. There's a hesitance in her motion, and for the first time, Nicole can see that she is scared.

She won't want to be comforted. From what Nicole has picked up in their brief time together, it does not seem to be Zoe's way. So she fights the urge to speak and drives her hands deep into her pants pockets, waiting for William Hawthorne to answer his door.

Zoe knocks again, harder, hesitation gone.

The sound echoes through the vacant hallway.

Nicole hears the creak of floorboards groaning nearby. A door down the narrow hall opens slightly, spilling a slender shaft of light onto the soiled runner. A shadowed figure peers at them from the gap.

Nicole tugs on her sister's jacket. "Maybe we should go."

Zoe shakes her head and knocks again.

Nicole's stomach twists. "Maybe he doesn't even live here anymore."

"This is the address on the envelope. His name was on the call box. He lives here. I'm not leaving until I talk to him." Her knuckles strike out a steady rhythm against the wood, echoing through the hallway.

"Zoe, please." Nicole can hears the squeak of hinges further down the hall. All she wants is to be out of this building, but Zoe will not budge. "Maybe he's not home. We should try back—"

"No." She cuts Nicole off, balling her fist and pounding on the dry wooden surface, shaking the door in its jamb. The floor creaks inside the apartment, locks jostle and release. They both take a step back as the door swings inward, revealing an elderly man in a wheelchair. A ragged beard juts out from his chin. His hair is thinning and nearly white, matted to his head by perspiration. Wrinkles fracture his skin, fanning out in all directions. He glares at the both of them suspiciously, his gnarled hand still gripping the edge of the door.

"What?" His voice is low and gruff.

Her sister takes a step forward. "Are you William Hawthorne?"

His eyes flick from Zoe to Nicole, quietly assessing them. After a long pause, he scowls at Zoe and asks, "I don't know who you are. I didn't let you in. You're trespassing, and I want you to leave. Now."

"My name is Zoe Hudson." She holds up the yellowed envelope. "I need to talk to the man who wrote this letter."

His eyes narrow, disappearing into weathered wrinkles. "How did you get that?"

"It doesn't matter how I got it." Aggravation rises to the surface. "Did you write it or not?"

Nicole winces as Zoe's volume raises. She has a feeling getting frustrated and loud is not going to help. The door down the hall closes with a thud. Nicole places her hand on her sister's shoulder. "Zoe. Please."

"Zoe?" The old man says her name under his breath, rolling the syllables around until something clicks into place. His expression shifts, softening. A sad sort of sympathy creeps into his eyes. "You're Hayden's little girl, aren't you?"

Zoe nods stiffly, her chest rising and falling in an erratic pattern.

"I apologize. Please, please come in." He backs up his wheelchair, allowing them space to enter, then closes the door behind them, bolting all the locks tight. He pushes past them, gesturing towards an adjacent room. "Have a seat in the parlor. I'll be right with you."

Nicole peers around the corner.

Parlor?

Not even remotely.

She follows Zoe into the small room and takes a seat on the threadbare couch. The fabric crinkles as her weight settles. A single narrow window faces west and, judging by the sweltering temperature inside the unit, it catches every drop of late afternoon sun. The heat makes the air heavy. It compresses her chest, making it hard to breathe.

Zoe doesn't seem to notice. She's inspecting the photos hanging on the far wall, hands dug deep into her pants pockets.

"Hudson. Your mother's name." Hawthorne pushes himself into the room. His hair is slicked down, parted and combed carefully. The collar of his shirt is speckled with fresh droplets of water that begin to dry swiftly in the stagnant heat. "They never married?"

"No, sir."

"Pity. Those two were a lovely couple. She was good for him. Grounded him."

Nicole can't believe she is the only one caught off guard by this man's apparent familiarity. "You knew Mom?"

"Yes." He nods, gripping the fabric of his pants to manually adjust his limp legs. "I knew Allison when she was not much older than you must be. I had the privilege of being her adviser and later one of her professors while she studied Egyptology at Cairo University. It's been years since I've spoken to her. Decades. But Hayden mentioned her often." He rests his hands in his lap and cocks his head, smiling softly at Nicole. The expression is pleasant, but oddly forced. He turns to Zoe. "How is your mother these days?"

Zoe takes a seat on a wooden chair and changes the subject. "When was the last time you spoke to my father?"

Hawthorne scrubs his beard. "Lord, it was years ago—"

"Was it before or after you sent him this?" She holds up the envelope.

His expression becomes distant. "Before."

Zoe taps the envelope with her thumb. "What were you trying to tell him? Why were you trying to warn him?"

"I don't—" He lets out a nervous laugh and pauses, searching for a response as he undoes his collar button. "It's been so long since I wrote that letter—"

Nicole hasn't been able to get the sweeping Arabic words out of her brain since she read them. "It said, 'Beware the Southern Cross. The ground is burning. You will find no safety. Keep hidden. They are looking for you.'"

Hawthorne swallows hard. His palms rap against the arms of his chair. The loose wooden strut clangs against its metal seat. He looks out the window.

Zoe leans forward. "Who was looking for him?"

His face falls. "It's... complicated."

"I haven't seen my father since I was seven years old." Zoe's voice is getting louder again. "I never knew what happened or why he left us. All I want to do is find him. And if he's in trouble—"

Hawthorne clears his throat. "Your father did what he felt was best. He was trying to protect you and your mother—"

"From who?" Zoe's brow is furrowed, her eyes narrowed to angry slits.

He shakes his head. "Our former employers."

"The University of Cairo?" Nicole asks, confused.

"No, my dear girl." Hawthorne lets out a labored sigh and straightens the fabric of his trousers.

"But you said you were a teacher."

"Without tenure." He grimaces. "I sought a means to augment my meager salary, and found a job assisting Hayden with the identification and appraisal of... ancient artifacts."

"Oh." Nicole sheepishly stares at the cracked floorboards.

Hawthorne continues, his voice unsteady, "It was good money, but highly illegal. Very risky work."

Zoe crosses her arms. "So you're telling me my father was a criminal?"

"For a time, my dear. Yes." Hawthorne nods. "But when he met your mother, everything changed. He told me he wanted to leave the business. To start a family. Finding out Allison was pregnant with you only made his decision easier. I was very proud of him."

Zoe swallows. "Then what changed?"

"He was on assignment when he decided to break free. He never returned the artifact he was investigating."

"Why not?"

"Spite? Maybe he felt they owed him something. Maybe he thought of it as insurance. I don't know. Your father was a strange man at times. Very willful. Very proud." Hawthorne clears his throat. "I tried to help him. Get it out of his hands while he looked for a buyer. I never would have offered if I had known..."

"Known what?" Nicole presses.

"The people we worked for came looking for him. I was less than helpful, I suppose." His gnarled hands fall to his lap and he gives them the weakest smile. "So, they made an example of me. Then, while I was recovering in hospital, they informed the university of my connection to the black market and destroyed my career."

Nicole feels sick to her stomach. She scans the apartment, taking in the remnants of a man's life that have now been crammed in to two tiny rooms on the edge of the world. Hawthorne is forgotten and alone. Everything he owns is covered in a fine layer of dust, all of it waiting to decay.

Hawthorne pushes his wheelchair back and turns in a tight circle. The motion is fluid, if a bit labored. He glides across the room, stopping at the dark wood desk pressed awkwardly against the far wall. With both hands, he works the top left drawer free and sets the cluttered bin on the desktop. Hawthorne reaches into the vacancy, groping for something in the shadowed gap. When he withdraws his hand, he is holding a leather-bound book. Hawthorne rolls towards the couch and hands Zoe the book, taking a deep breath before before speaking. "When I returned home from hospital, this was waiting for me." His smile is brittle. "I think he'd want you to have it."

"What is it?" Zoe asks.

"I don't know." Hawthorne pulls away and heads towards the kitchen. "But I'm sure he can tell you once you find him."

When the old man is out of the room, Nicole leans in closer to get a better look at the aged text. Her sister is lost in thought, fingertips absently tracing the pebbled leather of the binding. "Are you okay?"

Zoe doesn't answer.

Hawthorne comes back into the room, working a precise route past tattered furniture. He pulls close to the edge of the couch and takes hold of Zoe's hand, pressing a tight roll of bills into her palm. He carefully curls her fingers closed around the cash. "I want you to have this."

Her sister stares blankly down at the thick wad of bills resting in her palm. "I can't."

"Your father was a good man, and he always provided for me." He shakes his head and holds her hand closed. "If this money helps you find him, then it has gone to better use."

She tucks the money into her jacket pocket and stands, motioning to Nicole. "We should get going."

"Of course." Hawthorne nods, resting his gnarled hands in his lap. "Good luck."

Her sister walks out of the apartment, but Nicole cannot leave. She gives Hawthorne a sympathetic smile. "Thank you."

He swallows hard, refusing to look her in the eyes. "My apologies I couldn't be of more assistance."

When she exits the apartment, the sky is dark. Flickering street lamps cast dim pools of light, providing pockets of visibility in the overwhelming shadows. Zoe is waiting for her, leaning against the plaster wall of the entry. She is restless, tapping the book against her thigh.

"Well, that was super depressing." Nicole takes a deep breath and digs her hands into her pants pockets. "What now?"

"Airport," Zoe barks, pressing off the wall.

"What?" Nicole grabs hold of her jacket, spinning her sister around."Don't you 'airport' me. How about 'hotel.' How about for once you say something nice like 'Nicole, we're going to check into a nice hotel and you can take a nap.'"

Zoe rolls her eyes. "Why are you always so goddamn tired?"

"Because you are exhausting!" Nicole cannot help but flail. She may be making a scene, but at this point she just does not care. "We have been running for forever and it needs to stop. You can't keep dragging me around with no explanation. We have to open up some kind of dialogue. You have to let me in on this stuff."

"Fine."

Nicole ignores the petulant face Zoe is making. She takes a deep, bracing breath through her nose and continues. "Now, why would we possibly need to go to the airport? Again?"

Zoe checks the traffic and jogs across the street to the waiting cab, hollering back to Nicole over her shoulder. "Because I need to go to the library."

"Excuse me, what?"

THE HOUSE IS DARK. Rain outside is falling in heavy, rhythmic drops, striking the windows with forceful pops and splashes.

Her mother's Connecticut home feels cold. Empty. Unwelcoming. It has always felt that way, ever since she was a girl. But there is something else. Something is wrong. Everything is torn apart. Papers and books are scattered down the narrow hall and wide open windows let in the rain. An ever expanding puddle soaks the documents littering the floor.

Zoe steadies herself against the cool wall.

This place is not her home.

His voice faintly drifts up the stairs. "Zoe."

Her trembling hand traces the worn wooden banister. Broken glass crunches beneath her feet. Framed photographs that had lined the stairwell are no more than debris, shattered on the steps beneath her.

Beyond the stairs, a lone light flickers in the darkness. Every step she takes grinds glass deeper in to the pads of her feet. She can hear the sound but feels nothing.

Zoe grips the newel post for support. The first floor is empty, lit only by the television in the living room, tuned to a dead station. Static crashing like waves, blue-gray glow filling the room like moonlight through deep water.

He is in the middle of the room, staring out the window.

Her steps towards him are tentative. Shattered glass on hardwood gives way to the worn rug of the living room. Every step produces a sopping sound, like walking through a puddle.

Her father whispers, "I need you to be brave."

His clothes are soaked and torn. His shoes are caked with mud. His hands are bruised and raw, each knuckle split and bleeding.

As she reaches out for his hand, his voice fills her ears. It is all around her, everywhere and nowhere all at once.

Disconnected.

Hollow.

"Run, Zoe. Run."

She wakes with a start.

Stale air flows through the vent. She is still buckled into her seat. They are still in the air. It can't be much longer before they land.

Her head is throbbing. Zoe rubs her eyes, the pressure producing brilliant flashes of light behind her lids. She fell asleep, exhaustion finally catching up with her. At her side, Nicole is passed out, seat reclined, head tilted awkwardly against a small pillow. She murmurs softly, twitching in her sleep.

She wonders what Nicole's dreams are like.

Her sister shivers, tucking her body up into a ball. Zoe touches the bare skin on Nicole's forearm. It's cold. She peels her jacket off and lays it over Nicole, careful not to wake her. Not difficult. The kid sleeps like she's in a coma.

The sky out the small porthole is dark, dotted with stars and streaked with clouds. As the cover breaks, she can just make out the distinctive lights of a familiar Parisian skyline.

Zoe sinks into her seat, knees bouncing, her body unwilling to come to rest.

His voice echoes through her head. *Run.*

It can't be much longer until they land.

ALLISON LOOKS TO HER WRIST, instinctively checking the watch that is no longer there, reminding herself she needs the money more. Her hotel room is cheap, but after two weeks, she is running low on cash.

The rational part of her says she should go to the authorities. Tell someone she is being followed. That she fears her family is in danger.

But her gut tells her to trust no one and wait, find out who is following her and what they are after. No one will believe her without concrete proof. Especially when her story sounds as crazy as it does.

Whoever has been following her has to be camping out at airports, waiting for her to make a move. Her passport has probably been flagged. Maybe she's over-thinking this, but her paranoia appears to have paid off so far. When she snuck out today, she didn't notice anyone following her. No cars. No one tracking her through the streets. No watchful eyes behind dark glasses. She exchanged her valuables for cash and headed back to the hotel.

Allison climbs the stairs to her floor. Long legs carry her up multiple steps at a time until she reaches the narrow hall. She digs through her bag for her key, reaching her room as she feels the sharp metal against her fingertips. She gives one last look at the hall before unlocking the door and slipping inside. The suite is dark, as usual, the curtains drawn tight allowing only a sliver of light into the musty hotel room.

Her thoughts drift to her daughters. They haven't tried to contact her at all. And though she told Zoe not to chance calling her, she religiously checks her cell phone every night hoping for a message, only to be disappointed by her daughters' lack of communication. Ironic that now is the time when Zoe decided to start following her directions. Where ever they are, Allison hopes they are safe, somewhere off the map and out of reach.

Allison removes the headscarf, tossing it onto the bed as she heads towards the window, past the open bathroom door. She flips the switch, flooding the hotel room with harsh fluorescent light.

There is a click behind her.

Allison turns slowly.

A dark haired man is blocking the door. His arm is extended, gun drawn. His gives her a menacing grin. "Good evening, Doctor. You're a pretty difficult woman to keep an eye on."

Her brain is racing, eyes darting around the room, searching for a way out or a weapon. Nothing is close enough, and he is blocking the only door. Her best bet is her bag. It's not heavy enough to do much, but it might distract him, get him out of the way long enough to make a run for it. She grips the strap, knuckles turning white.

He flicks the muzzle of his gun at her bag. "Uh-uh. Hand it over."

Allison sets her jaw, muscles flexing in her cheeks. She didn't think it was possible to grip the strap any tighter. He advances, gun trained on her, hand out, insisting. "Give me the purse, Doctor."

Something in his eyes tells her he is more than comfortable using that weapon. She raises her bag slowly, offering it up on the end of a trembling arm. He smiles, interpreting the tremor as fear rather than the rage boiling over inside her.

His chuckle is a short, humorless sound. He tosses the bag out of reach. "Trust me when I say your cooperation is in your best interest. Unless you like the idea of never seeing your daughters again."

Her heart stops, tightening in her chest. He is lying. He has to be lying. She refuses to believe him.

"You haven't heard from them lately, have you?" He presses in close, voice purring in her ear. "There's a reason for that."

Allison shakes her head. "You're lying."

"Don't worry. No one's hurt them. Yet." His tone shifts. She can feel his spit against her cheek as he forces his words through gritted teeth. "But you fuck with me and I will make life very uncomfortable for Zoe and Nicole. That's a promise."

The insinuation is far more effective than any kind of physical intimidation would be. His pistol retracts, but his grips tightens around her arm, fingers digging into her bicep, pinching muscle to bone.

"Be a good girl, Allison." The way he says her name turns her stomach. He pushes her towards the door. "Move."

- 5 -

These morning runs around the island's perimeter are becoming a habit. For the past three weeks, she has been up before sunrise, no matter the weather, pushing herself harder and harder every day until her muscles scream and her mind clears.

Case navigates the secluded beachhead at the northern tip of the compound. Her feet displace the sand beneath her, creating craters that surging waves leap forward to fill. The exercise offers a rare moment of solitude, far from the prying eyes and judgments of her colleagues. A time to be alone with her thoughts and her own steady heartbeat.

She veers away from the ocean, heading towards the lush vegetation at the edge of the beach. Shadows begin to retreat as the sun starts its ascent. The soft soil is replaced by the hard, packed trail leading back to the compound. Case settles into a more conservative rhythm, looking forward to her body's impending exhaustion.

When she rounds the corner, she comes to an abrupt halt.

Fletcher is standing in the middle of the path, arms at ease behind his back, three-piece suit immaculate and completely out of place. "Good morning, ma'am." His dark eyes twinkle under heavy lids.

"Fletcher?" Her breath stutters out, adjusting to her sudden change in motion.

"I apologize for the intrusion. I didn't mean to startle you."

Her hands are on her waist, fingertips digging into her sides, applying pressure to the stitch that has formed in her abdomen. Every muscle turns to lead. She does her best to walk it off, glancing back cautiously at the bizarre young man behind her. "What are you doing out here?"

Fletcher steps closer, posture perfect as always. "I needed to talk to you. Alone."

His tone sets her on edge, but maybe it's just be the endorphins coursing through her system. Her curiosity is tempered by her annoyance. "I'm sure this can wait until I get into the office, Mr. Fletcher."

"I'm sorry, ma'am. It cannot." He checks over his shoulder, eyes searching the path. This is not a heavily occupied trail. Factor in the early hour, and seclusion is a given. He must know that. Fletcher steps even closer. "It's regarding your operation."

He has her attention.

"Your assistant requested complete personal dossiers on the Hudson women."

Case narrows her gaze. "Last time I checked, it wasn't against the rules to research my targets."

"That request was not about research." He raises an eyebrow. "You want to know what is behind Victor Sutton's sudden interest in these women. You want to know why he's been pushing you so hard to acquire them. "You are asking the wrong questions, Ms. Case." His pale skin seems to glow in the sunlight filtering through the foliage.

"What am I supposed to be asking, Mr. Fletcher?" There is a sharp edge to her voice. Case has never appreciated being told she is wrong.

"Victor is a very ill, ma'am. He has been for some time now. I've been able to stabilize him with medications and keep his condition quiet, but he will not live forever." Fletcher stares sightlessly down the lush trail, lost in his own thoughts. "And when the time comes, he has no heir, and someone will have to take his place and lead this organization."

She knows better than to be flattered by his insinuation. For all she knows this is a test, a trap, a simulation conducted by her employer to gauge her loyalty. Fletcher is too close to Sutton to be trusted. There has to be an angle she is not seeing yet. Whatever it is, this interruption has lasted long enough. Case steps past him, advancing down the trail towards her quarters, a hot shower, and the rest of her day. "I have work to do. Excuse me."

He calls after her. "He's after the book again."

She stalls, long legs weary beneath her.

"You know what I'm talking about." Fletcher saunters up to beside her, digging his hands deep into his pockets. "This is not the first time he's sent you after it."

Her brain accesses a long buried memory. A chill runs down her spine.

"I can help you secure your position." He removes a thumb drive from his pocket and extends it to her. His features are soft, almost boyish, but under their gentle surface there is something else, something she can't place.

Her eyes drift to the drive. The black cylinder contains the most precious commodity their business has to offer: information. Fletcher's private stock of unattainable knowledge. A perk of perching so close to the top, and being privy to every facet of the company. He is Sutton's secretary, his errand boy, his private caregiver. A man cognizant of every dirty deed, every twisted deal—the cogs and gears of the entire corporation. If she could find a way to trust him, he would be an invaluable ally.

Case turns towards Fletcher, considering his offer. "What's in it for you?"

Fletcher shrugs. "I would only hope that after all is said and done, there would be a better place for me within this organization."

She stares at the drive, gently grasped between his delicate fingers. This is treason. Sedition. She knows it. But every fiber of her being is screaming to take the drive, dig deeper, and regain the control she has lost.

"Who else have you offered this to?" Fletcher is a smart man. He must have cast a wide net in hopes of finding someone willing to do what she assumes he is suggesting.

"I can understand your trepidation, Ms. Case. You're wise to distrust me." He twists the drive between his fingertips, tumbling it over, letting the polished surface catch the light. "Take it. Look at the information on a secure terminal. Then make your choice."

She snatches the device, clutching it tight. For being held in his hand, the outer shell is oddly cool against her palm.

Fletcher flashes his sickly sweet smile, dimples forming on his broad cheeks. "Ma'am."

Case slips the drive into her jacket pocket, securing the zipper as she nods to Fletcher and walks away, stomach turning, muscles still burning. She can just say no. She can always change her mind. He only asked her to look at the information and consider his offer of help. She doesn't have to accept it.

She has a choice.

His voice rings out clear. "I almost forgot." She glances over her shoulder back in his direction. "He brought the mother in last night. She's in a holding cell on the east wing. I thought you'd want to know."

Every ounce of tension relieved by her run rushes back. She should have expected this. Eli never would have gone to Sutton if he didn't have an ace up his sleeve. Twenty-four hours is ridiculously efficient. Too efficient to be luck.

Case acknowledges the information, and gives Fletcher a another curt nod. Her whole body is vibrating with anger and exhaustion.

At first her pace is slow and controlled, putting on her best show if Fletcher happens to be watching her exit. But as soon as she rounds the corner, she begins to sprint, arms pumping, legs churning, carrying her over the uneven terrain and towards the personnel quarters.

WHILE THEY WAITED FOR THEIR last connecting flight, Nicole's sinuses started to act up and the sneezing began. Passing it off as her usual bout with obnoxious seasonal allergies, she ignored the warning signs and dozed off in the terminal. As a bonus, her nap was an excellent way to ignore her sister. But when she woke, every joint ached, her head felt two feet thick, and her throat was raw.

They touched down in the early afternoon and promptly boarded a cab. She had always wanted to visit Paris, but she hoped for something more along the lines of *on a vacation* than *on the run*. Nicole got what sightseeing she could through the tinted glass of her window. Though her accent was atrocious, Zoe's French was surprisingly passable, and one twenty-minute car ride later they are trading warm afternoon sunlight for the air-conditioned halls of the Paris National Library.

Nicole shifts her bag, moving the strap so it can dig into a fresh part of her shoulder. Walking through the cold corridors of the library is not helping her headache at all. She shivers. The last thing she needs now is to get sick.

Zoe leads her through a pair of tall doors and into a massive chamber. The domed ceiling rises high above them. Circular cut glass windows let in shafts of jewel-colored light that warm a sea of dark wooden tables. Nicole stops in her tracks, disoriented by the sheer quantity of books lining the walls. Columbia's collection is no slouch, but this place puts it to shame. Three stories of shelves, accessible by ornate metal ladders and gridded mezzanines. The space is dotted with columns and murals, as if there wasn't enough going on. "This place is unreal," she whispers. "I've never seen anything like it. It's so beautiful."

"It's just a library, Nik." Zoe takes hold of her elbow and pulls her forward. "Come on."

"But I want to look—"

"We don't have time," she snaps.

Her sister is anything but relaxed. The cool apathy that she has become used to over their extended time together has been replaced by an anxiety so palpable it's starting to affect Nicole. Zoe is still as bossy and irritable as ever, but now her mood is compounded by an indistinct panic.

Nicole scrubs at her nose with her sleeve as they leave the hall and turn down a long corridor. "I still can't believe you actually lived in Paris."

"Why not?"

She shrugs. "It just doesn't fit into my picture of who you are."

Zoe squints at her, annoyed. "What's that supposed to mean?"

"I don't know." There's no way to back out of this now. Nicole searches for an answer that won't sound rude. "I guess I just thought you were a sailor, you know? Someone who drinks a lot, gets into fights in bars, and has stupid tattoos in ill-advised places."

"That's what you think of me?" Her sister sounds genuinely wounded.

Her headache starts drumming behind her eyes. "Come on, Zoe. It was a joke. I didn't mean to hurt your feelings." Nicole sighs. "I mean, I didn't even know I could."

"Yeah, well, I am a person, Nik." Zoe stiffens, popping her knuckles. "Not a damn cartoon character. And for your information, I don't have any tattoos."

"Okay. Jeez. Sorry." Tip-toeing around her sister's feelings is new territory. She'd much rather go back to Zoe ignoring her. A cough rises from deep within her chest.

Zoe looks irritated. "What now?"

Her throat is hoarse. Speaking hurts. "I don't feel so great."

"Jesus Christ, Nicole—"

She feels cranky enough about her own predicament; she doesn't need Zoe making her feel worse. She has a sinking suspicion that jetting around the globe while stressed out isn't doing her immune system any favors. Nicole balls her fists in the baggy ends of her sleeves and grumbles, "I can't help that I'm getting sick."

Her sister ignores her, scanning an engraved directory. Zoe's finger traces down the list of departments until it stops on Education Outreach, C. Royer. She takes a deep breath and points down the wide, sun-bathed hall. "Down here."

"Who are we seeing again?"

"A friend."

Nicole takes a brief moment to be grateful that in a place like this, Zoe's 'friend' might be less likely to say hello with a shotgun. She laughs to herself.

"What's so funny?"

"Nothing," she mumbles, doing her best to keep pace with Zoe as they continue down an ornate staircase and into another expansive hallway. Wide doors line the left wall, their varnished surfaces glowing warm in the natural light streaming through tall mullioned windows.

One of the doors opens. A woman in a tailored pencil skirt and remarkably tall heels steps into the hall. Her dark hair is pulled back in a precise, albeit loose bun, exposing her graceful cheekbones and warm, expressive features. All at once Nicole feels keenly aware that she is a frumpy mess whose pants pockets are full of used tissues.

The woman's gaze drifts their direction, then focuses sharply on Zoe. Her smile fades, replaced by a look of disbelief. "What are you doing here?"

Zoe's voice catches. "I'm here to see you."

The two women seem at a loss for words. Nicole's bag slips off her shoulder and comes to rest abruptly in the crook of her elbow. The pain is nowhere near as uncomfortable as all the silence. She clears her throat and jabs her sister.

Zoe stammers, "Th-this is Nik."

The woman seems to notice her for the first time, moving closer, studying Nicole. Her smile returns, albeit a little more forced. "Caroline. Caroline Royer." She offers her hand. "You're Nicole. You're her sister, aren't you?"

"Unfortunately." Nicole shifts on the balls of her aching feet, shouldering her messenger bag and stretching past Zoe to accept the offered greeting.

"So. What brings you two to Paris?"

It didn't seem possible, but Zoe is radiating more discomfort by the second. "Can we talk somewhere more private?"

"Certainly." Caroline leads them into her office. A reassuring aroma of old books and coffee fills the air. Her space is warm and comfortable. An artfully battered antique sofa faces the clean lines of a modern wooden desk. Trinkets line her shelves, curated and uncluttered.

The door clicks closed behind them and Caroline studies Zoe, her eyebrow cocked. "You've looked better."

Zoe scrubs at her neck. "It's been a rough couple of weeks."

Caroline settles against her desktop, arms crossed. "How much trouble are you in?"

"What the hell kind of question—"

"We don't know." Nicole gladly cuts her sister's indignant tirade short. When Zoe flashes her a pissy glare, she fires one right back. Her swelling sinuses are not having any of this. "Don't look at me like that. We might as well be honest with her if you're going to ask for help."

"Help with what?" Caroline glances from sister to sister. "What's going on?"

"I need you to look into this." Zoe pulls the book Hawthorne gave her out of her jacket pocket. Gingerly, she hands it to Caroline, then retreats, slipping her hands deep into her pants pockets. "It belonged to my dad."

Caroline stares at the object in her hand. Nicole takes a moment to pointedly examine a small model airplane on a shelf. Out of the corner of her eye, Zoe starts to shift with nervous energy.

The words seem to come from deep within Caroline. "After everything that happened between us, how you left, you expect me to just—I just—I never thought I'd see you again." She sets the book on her desk and rubs her temples. "This is all very sudden."

Nicole coughs into her sleeve. "Tell me about it."

"I need your help, Caroline." Zoe's eyes are fixed to a spot on the carpet. "I wouldn't be here if it wasn't important."

Caroline lets out a heavy sigh and begins to flip purposefully through the pages. "Where did you get this?"

"Mombasa," Nicole says as she plops onto the tufted leather sofa.

Caroline pauses in her inspection, confused. "Kenya? What were you doing in Kenya?"

Zoe halts her restless pacing of the office and snaps, "Can you help or not?"

"I don't know what you expect me to do, Zoe." Caroline closes the book. Even Nicole can feel the frustration hidden in her voice. "You can't just drop by my work out of the blue after two years of nothing, hand me a book written in a language I don't even recognize, and expect me to magically know what it is and how it relates to your father. That's not fair to me, and I think you—"

"I had nowhere else to go." Zoe's face begins to turn red. "It's not like I have a lot of people to turn to when shit gets complicated."

"And whose fault is that?"

Nicole shifts in her seat. At least when they were in Brazil, her discomfort ended when Jones put his shotgun down. This is completely different.

"Nice. Real nice." Zoe stiffens and reaches for the book. "You're right, Caroline. I'm an asshole. I shouldn't have bothered you."

"Babe, no. That's not what I—Please, stop." Caroline takes hold of her outstretched hand and searches for her eyes. "When was the last time you slept?"

Nicole is still snagged on the endearment. She stares at this beautiful women, and then at her brash sister. A puzzle piece drops into place.

"I don't really remember." Zoe's shoulders drop, her weakness beginning to show.

"Where are you staying?"

When Zoe doesn't answer, Caroline fishes a key ring out of a carved wooden bowl on her desktop. "Here. Go back to my flat."

"That's not why I—"

"You asked for my help, so let me help you. I'll see what I can find out." She closes Zoe's hand around the keys. "Try to get some rest. We'll talk more when I get home."

Zoe stares at the hand around her clenched fist, and her jaw tenses. "Come on, Nik."

She pushes herself off the couch and follows her rattled sister. Before she steps out of the office, Nicole sniffles and says in her best French, "It was nice to meet you."

Caroline's smile is genuine, if sad. "You too."

BRIGHT LIGHT FILTERS THROUGH the smoked glass of the clearstory windows. The ceiling is high, well over ten feet. The smooth concrete walls surrounding her on all sides seem to lean inward, creating the illusion of collapse. Allison has been over every inch of the ten-by-ten cell. There is one door. Every piece of furniture is bolted to the ground or wall. Except for one chair.

She bashed at the door until the chair bent. After that, she moved on to shouting at the surveillance camera. Neither did her much good, so now she waits for whatever will come next in silence, lying on the narrow bed, staring at the ceiling.

The sound of the lock disengaging startles her. She sits straight up.

The olive-skinned man who apprehended her in Baghdad enters the room. He is the first person she has seen since her sedatives wore off and she woke in this cell.

"Good afternoon, Allison." She watches him cautiously as he inspects the damaged chair. "I see you've been busy."

After taking a seat on the edge of the built-in desk, he drops a tablet onto its surface and selects a program. A red light pulses on the edge of the device, and a time stamp cycles on its screen. He is recording her. "Glad you've enjoyed our hospitality in my absence."

Allison stares past him, uninterested in playing his game.

"Not feeling talkative?" He adjusts his suit jacket. "How about I let you pick the topic. What would you like to discuss, Doctor?"

She swallows the lump in her throat. "I want to see my daughters."

He smiles, exposing a row of perfect white teeth. "That's not an option."

"Why not?"

"They're not available." He gives her a suggestive grin. "But I'm sure we can work something out, if you cooperate."

Allison crosses her arms. "I'm not helping you until I see my girls."

"You are in no position to make demands." His eyes are cold. "Now then, my employer is in search of something, and we have reason to believe you know where it is."

He turns his tablet towards her. There is a photo of a decrepit leather-bound book on the screen. Allison shakes her head. "I've never seen that before in my life."

"Mr. Sutton thought you might say that." He clears his screen, placing the tablet back on the metal desk. "There are lots of way we can do this, Allison. Some are easy. Others are more unpleasant. For you." The pause he takes is uncomfortably long. "And for your daughters."

Allison lurches forward, crossing the room and pressing into his space, fists clenched. "If you hurt them, I swear I'll—"

"You'll do *what*?" The man is not intimidated in the least. He slips off the desk, his height matching her own, his bulk far out-massing her. "Sit back down, Dr. Hudson, and tell me everything you know about Hayden Thomas."

She has not heard that name in years.

"We can start whenever you're ready." He gestures towards the bent chair.

Allison lowers herself onto the cold aluminum seat.

Caroline didn't say anything about a dog.

The hulking mutt greeted them as they entered her flat, loping from his oversized bed by the march of narrow floor-to-ceiling windows to sit on Nicole's foot. No matter how sick her sister may be, the kid seemed all too happy to reciprocate the dog's affection. It's not the animal Zoe objects to; it's the change. But what did she expect? Two years is a long time.

She shows Nicole to one of the flat's generous guest rooms. In no time at all, her sister is in the marble-lined bath, filling the claw foot tub with scalding hot water and settling in for a long soak.

For the first time in weeks, Zoe is alone. She thought it was something she wanted, but being back in Caroline's flat all by herself feels strange. There is absolutely no trace of her ever having lived here. But she remembers vividly the life that they had shared.

Her heart aches.

Zoe heads into the kitchen and pulls open the refrigerator only to be reminded that Caroline Royer isn't much of a cook. The shelves are sparse, littered with condiments, a half-empty tub of yogurt, and a few bottles of white wine.

It's not beer, but it will have to do.

She snatches a bottle and searches for the corkscrew. It is laying out in the open next to the knife block. At least some things never change. The wine glasses are hung under the cabinets, slipped carefully into their slots. They are as graceful as they are delicate. The last thing she needs to do is break anything expensive. Zoe peels the thick foil from the mouth of the wine bottle and takes a deep swig.

When she checks back in on her sister, the kid is huddled down tight under a mound of blankets in the queen-sized bed. Despite the covers, she is still shivering.

"You feel a little better?" Zoe sits on the edge of the bed.

Nicole mumbles an incomprehensible response into the sheets.

"Never mind. I'll let you sleep." Zoe grabs another heavy duvet from the basket at the foot of the bed and tosses it over her sister, tucking the kid in carefully.

Nicole smiles, teeth chattering. "You're worried about me."

"Maybe." Zoe pushes her sister's wet hair out of her face, halfheartedly grinning back at her.

"See, you can be nice."

Zoe heads for the door, its jamb outlined by the late afternoon sun streaming in from the rest of the apartment. "Get some rest, kid."

"Hey, Zoe?" Her voice is muffled by blankets.

Zoe pauses. "What?"

"Caroline seems really great."

She's glad the room is dark, so Nicole can't see the expression on her face. "She is."

"She's really beautiful, too." Her voice is sleepy and drifting towards unconsciousness. "What happened?"

Zoe doesn't even know where to begin. "Go to sleep, Nicole." She closes the door behind her, leaving her sister in the dark.

CASE SITS CURLED UP IN THE leather chair, watching the sunset through the leaves, cigarette dangling between her fingers, sweet smoke curling from its glowing end. The room is cold, sweat on her skin drys quickly in the crisp air. She inhales deeply, smoke filling her lungs and rolling smoothly out her nostrils.

The shower cuts off in the bathroom and Connor exits moments later, body still dripping with water, towel wrapped loose around his waist. If this were her quarters, she would take issue with the puddles now collecting on the hardwood floor. But this is his place, he can drip wherever he wants. She observes him, drinking in his shape and the way the dwindling light accentuates his every muscle. He crosses the room, grabbing a bottle of bourbon and pack of cigarettes off his dresser. Connor offers her the first drink, but Case refuses. She might have accepted a glass, but not the whole damn thing. Connor is crooked that way, simultaneously chivalrous and brutish. Both are qualities she has come to appreciate.

His teeth grip a cigarette from the pack, pulling it free. He leans over Case, water droplets rolling off his body and hitting her bare thighs. She takes in a deep breath, cigarette burning bright in the growing dark, allowing Connor just enough fire to light his own. Once kindled, he pulls the stopper from the bottle and takes a deep drink, dropping himself onto the disheveled bed.

"What are you going to do about Kostich?"

Maybe she does want that bottle. "He bought out my Baghdad operation. Paid off Jacobs and Hussein. They sat on Dr. Hudson for weeks until Eli finalized his takeover. Then they backed up and let him bring her in like a conquering hero."

Connor squints at her, leaning back on the mattress, elbows sinking into the sheets. "How'd you find that out?"

"A little bird told me." He doesn't need to know about Fletcher or his offer. She isn't even positive she'll take him up on it yet. Sutton's assistant still makes her uneasy, and if her colleagues are gunning for her, she needs to surround herself with people she can trust.

"Little shit." Connor drags off his cigarette. "Where's he keeping her?"

"East holding cells." She hasn't been able to get the location out of her head all day, not since Fletcher told her on the trail this morning. If Allison Hudson knows the book's location, a tactful interrogation session could get Sutton his artifact in no time at all. Knowing Eli, he has already screwed that up.

Case has drifted and Connor knows it. He takes a drag, letting the smoke flow out of his mouth as he speaks. "What are you thinking?"

She stubs out her cigarette in the ashtray that's resting on the arm of her chair, fingertips grinding the smoldering remains of tobacco, extinguishing their glow. She rises, moving toward him with effortless grace. He is staring at her, hungry eyes inspecting her figure, drawn to the jagged pale scar running down her left breast. As she draws closer, a knowing leer curls the corners of his lips.

Case strikes him, the back of her hand impacting his face with great force, all her pent up rage releasing itself in one fluid motion. She draws close, gripping Connor's stubbled chin. Her nails dig into his skin. "Did I tell you you could smile?"

"No, ma'am." His tongue flicks out, licking blood from his split lip. His expression grows neutral, but his eyes are still filled with want.

She kisses him hard, forcing his lips aparts, tasting his blood as her tongue searches the inside of his mouth. Connor bites down, teeth gripping her briefly. Her lips pull into a smile as she draws back, his teeth grating over the surface of her tongue. Her hands drift across his broad shoulders and down his chest. As she retreats, Case takes a brief moment to admire the man beneath her before leaving the bedroom to gather her clothes.

IF MAXWELL DURAND CAN'T GIVE her information about the book, no one can. Caroline sits at the end of the bar, nursing a glass of wine while she waits for him.

The bar is packed. Music thumps loud behind her, the low end sending a subtle vibration through her body. The place is swarming with attractive people drenched in sweat, grinding against each other on a darkened dance floor. She's not usually one for clubs, but Max does love the night life.

"Never figured you for a wallflower, Royer." He leans against the bar, smirking.

"Nice of you to show up."

He shrugs, taking a seat next to her and signaling the bartender. "So, tell me. What's this thing only I can help you with?"

Caroline removes the book from her purse, placing it on the bar between them. He flips it open, reaching into his pocket for a slim pair of reading glasses. The bartender sets a drink down, and without looking up, Max scoots it carefully away from the text. "Caroline, this is fascinating. Where on earth did you get it?"

She knows the look of excitement on his face. She has seen it before when she accompanied him to auctions. Whatever this is, it is quite the find. "Is it old?

"Oh, dear heart, this is not simply old." His smile broadens. "It is —Impressively old, and in fine condition."

She scoots closer, looking over his shoulder as he inspects the pages. "Can you tell what language it's written in?"

"Dutch."

He's so matter-of-fact that it takes Caroline a moment to realize he is not joking. French and English are her languages, the by-product of an adolescence split between life in Canada and visits with mother's family in provincial France. She may not be able to speak Dutch, but she is confident she could identify it if she were to see it. "You're joking, right?"

"Not at all." Max traces the words in reverse. "What you have here, lovely, is a sixteenth century sinistral Dutch text."

It takes her a moment to understand his meaning. "Sinistral?"

"You're author was a lefty." Max grins at her. "Or possessed by the devil, though one does not exclude the other."

She rolls her eyes.

"A joke. I apologize. Actually, a fair number of left dominant writers would compose mirrored so they didn't smudge their work before the ink dried." He closes the book, regarding the cover in the dim light of the bar. "I'll take this back to the auction house and get it translated—"

"I appreciate the offer, Max." Caroline pulls the it from his fingers, smiling politely. She shakes her head and tucks the book back into her purse. "But it's not mine to give."

"What kind of librarian are you?" Max sips his drink, eyes roaming up and down her body. "You let me look at the materials, but you never let me check them out."

She takes a deep pull of her wine, remembering all at once why Zoe never liked Max. She fixes him with a look, letting him know he has crossed the line.

Max winces sheepishly. "I'm sorry, Caroline. That should have been an inside thought. Let me make it up to you. I'll buy you another drink."

She shakes her head, setting her glass down on the bar. "I have to be going."

"Suit yourself." He watches her gather her things. "You never did answer me."

"Pardon?" She slips the strap of her purse over her shoulder, fingers pulling her long brown hair free.

"Where did that book come from?"

She considers telling him a lie, but what would that accomplish? "Zoe."

"Zoe Hudson? *Your* Zoe?"

His words sting more than they should. "She hasn't been mine for a long time, Max."

"Well this just became substantially more interesting." He leans back against the counter, drink in hand, ice clinking in the glass. "I'll be over for breakfast. Your place. Early. We can go over your ex-girlfriend's little artifact then."

When she finally arrives home, the door to her flat is unlocked and music is playing softly in the shadowed living room.

Caroline drops her car keys on the console table and sets her purse down. The apartment is dark, illuminated only by the distant lights of the city through the tall windows. She can see Zoe slouched on the couch, staring vacantly at nothing in particular. Caroline can also see wine bottles, at least two of them empty, tipped over on the coffee table.

A vague sense of embarrassment sets in as she takes a seat on the couch next to Zoe. She had said she would be home after work. Technically, midnight is after work, but it must seem like avoidance from Zoe's perspective.

"Hi." She steadies herself by tidying the coffee table. "How's your sister feeling?"

"Sick." Zoe swigs from a bottle, resting it on her chest as her fingers tear at the label. Her speech is slurred, noticeable even with her monosyllabic response. It becomes more noticeable as Zoe continues to talk to her. "You have a good time tonight?"

Caroline sighs. "I'm sorry, I should have called. I didn't mean to make you worry."

"I didn't say I was worried." Zoe leans her head against the back of the couch, eyes moving from the window to the ceiling.

"So—you drank all my wine? For fun?"

A sloppy smile spreads across Zoe's face. "You didn't have anything harder."

Caroline raises an eyebrow, watching her ex drink deep. Enough is enough. "What's going on, Zoe?"

She chuckles bitterly, wobbling forward and setting the half empty bottle down hard on the table. "I don't know, all right? I don't fucking know." She moves to stand, but her equilibrium fails as she rises. Caroline catches her as she teeters forward, arms wrapping around her tight, steadying her. She smells the same as Caroline remembers, sharp and sweet. When Zoe's arms slip around her for support, Caroline's heart skips a beat.

Zoe tightens her embrace, no longer seeking stability. Her breath is ragged and hot against Caroline's ear. "I don't know what I'm doing, or if—if I'm doing the right thing. I want to find him so bad, but Mom told me to keep Nik safe, and I don't know how to do that or why I have to. I haven't heard from her in a month. She sounded so scared, and I don't know how to find her or what she wants me to do now. I'm not good at this shit. I'm not."

Caroline can feel Zoe's chest heave as she starts to sob. She strokes her back gently, whispering in her ear. "It's okay. Everything will be okay. Just calm down, darling. You're going to be all right."

Hot tears hit Caroline's neck and slip down her skin.

Zoe pulls back, her voice hoarse. "What do I do?"

She smiles softly at Zoe, pushing loose stands of blonde hair out of her face, her fingers lingering too long on cheeks streaked with tears.

They are so close. The kiss is like second nature. Easy as breathing. Her fingers snake around the nape of Zoe's neck, finding their way into the base of her ponytail and tugging at the band. She can taste the wine on her lips, heady and sweet.

Desire takes over when common sense should prevail, and Zoe's hands grip at Caroline's blouse, fumbling with buttons as her lips move down the length of her neck.

It feels so good.

And so desperately wrong.

The anger from this afternoon is quiet but still there, twisting in the pit of her stomach. Caroline pulls back, her consciousness raising. "No. No, stop."

As they break apart, Zoe sinks to the couch, head hanging low. The look of shame on her face makes Caroline's heart break.

"I want to help you. I do. But this—" She gestures at the space between them. "This cannot happen. It isn't fair."

"I know."

Caroline winces. She can see how much Zoe is hurting, but that is no justification. "You can't just keep falling in and out of my life like this. I loved you. I wanted a future with you, and you walked away. That was a choice you made."

"I made a mistake." She buries her head in her hands.

There is nothing left to say. Caroline runs her fingers through her hair and leaves the living room as quickly as possible, not wanting Zoe to see her lose control.

***

He can call it whatever he wants.

That was not a conversation. It was an interrogation.

Allison told him everything she knew about Zoe's father, but none of it seemed to be good enough. He kept circling back to the damn book, accusing her of knowing more than she was letting on.

She was relieved when he finally gave up and left her alone in her cell. As night settles in, sleep refuses to find her. All she can do is stare at the surveillance camera mounted high in the corner, red light glowing to reminding her she is under constant scrutiny.

The light goes dark.

That's new.

The door locks snap back. It's a little late for an unsupervised second visit. She sits up on the bunk and looks to the door, nerves buzzing, expecting the worst.

"Good evening, Dr. Hudson."

It's a woman she's never seen before. She is so very tired of these games. "Who are you? What do you want?"

The woman's voice is cold and calm. "Eli is lying to you. He told you he has your daughters in custody."

Allison leans forward, now keenly interested in what the woman has to say.

"He does not."

And with that, the woman knocks on the door and exits after it is opened.

The red light on the camera blinks back on.

- 6 -

SHE WOULD HAVE RATHER FELT nauseous, but the only consequence of the previous night's drinking binge is a vision-blurring, temple-splitting headache. She hates wine hangovers and how they manage to produce the most violent, thumping migraines known to man.

Zoe presses herself off the mattress, unsure when and how she made it into her room. What she does know is that last night did not go well, and she certainly made a needy ass out of herself in front of Caroline.

Way to go, Hudson.

Eyes pinched closed, Zoe rights herself, bare feet dropping to the cool hardwood floor. Her entire body aches. She squints, allowing in only enough light for her focus to sharpen. Her hands look like hell: the area between each knuckle is a sickly shade of yellow green, forgotten bruises from the fight on the boat.

She's a vision. No wonder Caroline assumed she was in trouble.

Zoe crouches at the foot of the bed, digging through her bag for another layer. She tugs a hooded sweatshirt over her head, pulling her arms through the sleeves. The smells of coffee and breakfast hit her at the same time as the voices from beyond her closed door. The distinct sounds of conversation is mixed with Caroline's rich laughter and a man's voice, punctuated by the occasional rattling cough. Nicole must be awake.

Zoe rubs her forehead. Dealing with company is not something she's prepared for, but the promise of caffeine is worth tolerating an interloper. She exits the guest room and heads for the kitchen.

"Look who's finally decided to join us," Max coos from his seat at the counter. "Good morning, Zoe."

No amount of coffee can make seeing that two-faced bastard this early in the morning bearable. She can feel her blood pressure rise.

Caroline is at the stove, busily preparing omelets and doing her best to ignore her. She pours herself a cup of coffee, hoping it is strong. Leaning against the kitchen counter, she occupies herself with glaring at the fancy man seated next to her kid sister.

"How rude of you to hide such a lovely sibling." Max rests his hand on Nicole's. Zoe could clock him for touching her, but Nicole doesn't seem to mind. "She's quite brilliant. Smashing to meet another polyglot. Her Dutch is almost better than mine."

Nicole blushes at Max's backhanded compliment, sniffling and sipping her tea. Zoe guesses it takes years of practice to sniff out a conceited jackass like Maxwell Durand, and Nicole is just too young and sheltered to have the necessary experience.

She speaks into the black surface of her mug. "What is he doing here?"

Max smiles. "Caroline asked me to help you with your little artifact." He gestures towards the open book laying on the counter between himself and her sister.

"It's a journal, Zoe." Nicole's voice sounds better than yesterday, a little clearer, more excited. "From a sailor. And it's mirrored. I don't know why I couldn't figure that out—"

"That's great, Nik." Zoe glares at Caroline. "Can I talk to you? Alone?"

"Problem, Zoe?" Max raises his eyes from the book and flashes her a smug expression.

"I'll deal with you in a minute." She sets her coffee mug on the counter and stalks out of the kitchen and down the long hall.

"Well, that was rude." Caroline follows her. "What is your problem—"

"Him," she barks. "He's my problem."

"Max? What did he do?"

"I asked you for help. *You!*" She tries to keep her voice low, speaking through gritted teeth. "Not him."

"Max knows these things. He identified the age and origin almost automatically. He has the expertise you need "

Zoe cuts her off. "Screw his expertise, Caroline. I don't trust him."

Caroline starts to flush with anger. "I am trying to help you the only way I know how."

The throbbing behind her eyes has amplified. There are so many hurtful things swimming in her brain, but when she opens her lips nothing comes out. She stands there, mouth agape, shaking with anger.

Caroline says nothing. She turns on her heel and heads for her office. After the door slams, Zoe goes back to the kitchen. Her sister and Max are still poring over the book. Zoe crosses the room, reaching across the counter and slamming the leather cover closed. She snatches it up and tosses it across the kitchen.

"Jesus Christ, Zoe." Nicole's voice cracks. "What is wrong with you?"

"Go to your room, Nik."

"Go to my room? What am I, five?" Her sister stares at her, hurt. "He's trying to help us. Why can't he help—"

"Go, Nicole!" She meant to control her volume, but fails miserably.

Nicole slips from her stool. With a wounded expression, she pads silently out of the kitchen.

Zoe fixes Max with a bitter stare. "Get out."

"Ah, my dear girl. I forgot just how charming you can be." He removes his glasses, folding them slowly and slipping them into the breast pocket of his jacket. "Your aptitude for human interaction has always astonished me. Maybe that's what drew Ms. Royer to you in the first place. She has always been so very fond of projects. You know, fast things in need of constant maintenance."

His words sting. Zoe sets the book down on the counter and scowls. "Fuck you."

"You have no idea what you have there, do you?" Max stands, rounding the edge of the counter, fingers tracing the honed marble top. "Sad, lost little Zoe. Not smart enough to figure it all out on her own."

She cannot hold back any longer. The punch is a reflex, something she does without thinking. Her knuckles make contact with the bony flat of his cheek and he stumbles back, shocked.

After he recovers he smiles at her. "Such a brute. Did you treat her like this? Is that why she made you leave?"

"Get out!" she screams.

"No matter." Max touches the tender spot on his cheek and sneers at her as he backs towards the door. "You should have stayed gone, Zoe. It would have been better for everyone."

***

CONNOR SITS ACROSS FROM HER, peeling the skin from an apple with a tactical knife. His blunted fingers rock the blade back and forth, carving out slices. Case sips her coffee, content to watch him eat, enjoying the precision of his cuts through the fruit's flesh.

"Tricia!"

She smiles at the sound of her name being yelled across the crowded corporate dining hall. Eli crosses the floor at a rapid pace, displacing unoccupied chairs and pointing at her, face red with anger.

"Here we go." She whispers softly, directing her attention to her coffee, away from the juggernaut heading towards them.

Connor pauses, knife lodged firmly in the skinned apple. Eli bounds up a series of steps to the table and slams his fist down, leaning in aggressively towards Case. Connor withdraws his blade and clutches the hilt. She raises a hand, wordlessly calling him off.

Eli is loud, drawing stares from curious employees. "What the fuck are you trying to pull?"

Case gestures towards the empty chair at their table. "Will you be joining us for breakfast, Mr. Kostich?"

She can see his eyes shoot around the room, her suggestion confusing him. He pulls out the chair with an exaggerated motion, and drops into the seat like a petulant child. Case can't help but chuckle at his behavior.

"What is so fucking funny, Tricia?" Eli hisses at her, volume now checked.

"Nothing." She sips her coffee, smile still on her lips.

"That little stunt of yours ruined everything. All my progress. Being straight with her tanked my interrogation. You're going to sink your own project." Eli points to his temple. "Are you psychotic?"

She does her best to looked more shocked than humored. "Whatever are you talking about?"

"You talked to her last night. There is a gap in the surveillance, Tricia. I'm not an idiot. The camera was off for over a minute. You talked to her. And now she won't cooperate." He spits as he speaks, fine droplets landing on the table, a few striking her cheek.

Case sets her cup down and gently wipes away the offending moisture, contemplating her fingertips thoughtfully before wiping her hand on her napkin. "But we don't have her daughters, Eli."

He stammers, "We—We would have them if your ape here had done his job!"

Connor glares at Eli, grip tightening on the hilt of his knife. Not the smartest move. He looks at Case, his eyes searching for permission he does not find. Stabbing Kostich in a room full of witnesses would be irrational. There are better ways to deal with this pest.

"I'm still trying to figure out how this is my problem." She leans in close to him, head tilted, eyes narrowed. "You wanted more responsibility. You asked for a bigger op. And you muscled your way into mine. And now you want help? If you are having such a difficult time with Dr. Hudson—" She leans back, returning to her coffee. "I suggest you go cry to daddy."

His reaction is priceless. Eli stands, the force of his movement sending his chair crashing to the tile floor. All eyes are on them as he stalks out of the dining room, shoving a waiter aside on his way out the double doors into the hall.

"Fucking *bitch!*" he shouts.

Connor's lips curl around another slice of apple, muscles in his jaw flexing as he chews.

She traces the backs of her teeth with her tongue, shaking her head. "What a child."

CAROLINE SETS THE GROCERY BAGS down on the counter. She can see Zoe through the double doors off the kitchen, seated out on the balcony, so focused and still, staring out at the city.

She almost steps on the journal. *Why is it lying on the floor?* Caroline leans over to pick it up, and notices something out of place. A business card is protruding from the leather binding. She pulls the it free and inspects it. The heavy stock is embossed with the familiar moniker of a Swiss bank, Julian Baer, and a name, Mr. Fredrick Meier. A series of numbers is written on the back in precise script. She tucks the card into her pocket and finishes unloading the groceries.

Her flat is big, but not so huge that they can spend the next week or so avoiding each other. Involving Max was a mistake, she knows that now, and because nothing says "I'm sorry" quite like the gift of alcohol, she gathers two bottles of beer and heads for the balcony. The doors creak as she exits and Zoe stirs in her seat, a pained look settling on her face as she sees Caroline.

"I'll let you—" Zoe rises to leave.

"Please don't." Caroline offers her one of the cold bottles, droplets of moisture condensing on their surfaces in the evening heat.

Zoe gives her a halfhearted smile as she accepts the offering, sinking back into her chair.

So far, so good.

Caroline sits across from Zoe. She can feel the warmth of the black metal chair radiate through her clothes, the surface freshly baked in the summer sun. The beer is cool and refreshing, its carbonation a welcome sensation in this heat.

She might as well start with the most uncomfortable question. "I heard the things he said to you. Max, I mean. Has he always talked to you like that?"

Zoe responds with a wordless shrug.

"Why didn't you ever tell me?"

"I always knew I wasn't good enough for you." She squints into the setting sun, bottle pressed to her lips, drinking deeply. "Max wasn't the only person in your life who made that clear to me."

She's not wrong. Caroline's father had always been wary of Zoe, never fond of her turbulent past or her slim prospects. He was not a man to keep his opinions to himself, even if it meant hurting the feelings of his only daughter.

"That was for me to decide. Not them." She takes a deep pull and sets the beer down on the table between them. "Can we please start over?"

She gets a sideways glance and her first honest smile. Her heart flutters. Zoe's lips rest on the mouth of her bottle, pausing to speak. "Sure."

That smile could be the death of her. She decides to focus elsewhere. The business card. Caroline digs into her pocket and slides it across the tabletop to Zoe, letting her finger linger on the embossed name. "I found this. It was in your father's book."

Zoe looks confused, but takes the card.

"Julian Baer is a private bank in Zurich. I'm pretty sure that's an account number written on the back."

"How do you know that?"

"My father's done business with them. They're known for being fair and highly confidential."

"Looks like your old man and mine finally have something in common." Zoe's smile doesn't reach her eyes. "Look, I wanted to apologize for last night. I wasn't really at my best and I—"

"About that." Caroline looks at the bottle, the street, anywhere that is not Zoe. "It wasn't all your fault. When we first met, we sort of skipped being friends, you know? We have these very ingrained habits that are difficult to break. It's not an excuse. But—"

"I'm still sorry."

"Don't be." Caroline twists her bottle on the table, leaving streaks of moisture on its surface. "I would really like to be your friend, Zoe, and I want to help you if I can. It would really mean a lot to me if you'd let me try."

Zoe stops her, smile softening her sharp features. "We're okay, Caroline. Really."

"I'm so sorry about Max." She glances down at her hands, thumb tracing the edge of carefully manicured fingernails.

"I don't want to talk about him anymore, okay?"

Change the subject, Caroline. Move past it. "I think you should call him."

"Who?"

She points at the business card next to Zoe. "Fredrick Meier at Julius Baer. His business card was in your book. I think you should call him and see if he can tell you anything about your father."

Zoe sinks into her seat, leaving the card on the table top. "I don't know if that's a good idea."

"You won't know until you try."

Zoe nods. She has begun to absently pick at the label of her beer, thumb rubbing the soft paper until it gives way.

Caroline reaches for topics to fill the awkward silence. "Nicole seems nice. Very bright. How are you two getting along?"

"We're not." Zoe shrugs. "I'm not good at—"

"Being around people?"

Zoe taps the tip of her nose.

Caroline laughs to herself. "She's not people. She's your sister."

"I don't know how to relate to her. The kid's smart. Really smart. Like Mom. I can't—I don't know how to—" Caroline can hear the anxiety in Zoe's voice. "I don't know what to say to her."

"Whatever you two are going through, you're going through it together. You have to try to get to know her and trust her."

Zoe shoots her a lopsided grin. "So says the only child."

"I will remind you I have a very Roman Catholic number of cousins," she chides as Zoe sinks deeper into her seat, and flicks the wadded up beer label on to the terracotta tile of the balcony. "Trusting people doesn't make you weak. You can't do everything on your own. You've have to let people in sometimes."

Caroline waits tentatively for some kind of response, knowing that no matter how honest the advice, it could easily be misconstrued as sticking her nose where it doesn't belong.

Zoe thinks for a moment, then nods. "Where's Nik?"

"She's probably still curled up with Arthur."

Zoe pauses mid pull, beer foaming inside the bottle as it slips out of her mouth. "Who the hell is Arthur?"

"He's my dog, Zoe."

"Oh." Zoe takes another swig of her beer. "Why'd you get a dog anyway? You're never home."

Caroline shrugs, tugging at the hem of her skirt. "I missed having something big and smelly to hold at night."

Zoe laughs, draining the last of her beer. "I smell better than that dog."

Caroline relaxes into her chair and rolls her head towards Zoe. She smiles playfully. "Barely."

WHATEVER HAS BEEN PLAGUING her system seems to be on its way out. Her fever broke some time in the night. Minor aches and congestion still abound, but Nicole is really liking feeling human again.

Zoe also seems to have improved. Instead of yelling at her and telling her what to do, she actually asked Nicole how she was feeling, and if she was up for taking in some sights while they were in the city. When they spoke, she was smiling.

The whole interaction was odd, as far as Nicole was concerned. She had learned to deal with Zoe being obstinate and distant. Nice Zoe is weird Zoe. But the idea of taking a walk seems more relaxing than reading a backwards Dutch journal.

Not that she hasn't made progress, but it's been pretty dull. The structure of the text is so formal. She has never read anything quite like it. She was all too happy to accept her sister's invitation as she is certain she'll go cross-eyed if she keeps looking at the book.

After a shower and a fresh change of clothes, she heads down the long hall towards the living room. It finally sinks in how huge this apartment is. It has to take up the entire fourth floor of the building, and Caroline seems to live here completely on her own. Nicole figures libraries don't pay that well, so what gives?

On her way out she passes a large framed photograph of a handsome man. He has salt and pepper hair and a meticulously kept beard. He is standing on an airfield. A little girl with long brown hair and a blue dress clings to him, kissing his cheek. The off-white mat is signed in numerous languages. The messages Nicole can decipher all seem to be congratulatory.

"That's my father and me." Caroline's presence takes her off guard. "The engineers put that together when I finished my masters."

"Is he a pilot?"

"That's how he started. He got more interested in the manufacturing side of things, and it kind of spiraled out of control from there." Caroline points at the streamlined jet over her father's shoulder. The graphic on the body of the aircraft reads Royer Aviation.

"Wow." Nicole murmurs. Caroline is one of *those* Royers. She cannot believe she missed the connection at first glance. "So you're rich. Like absurd rich. Your dad is basically Howard Hughes, minus all the jars full of urine?"

"That is what he has printed on all his business cards." She gives Nicole a jovial bump to the shoulder. "Have you ever flown?"

Nicole snorts, "What? A plane? No."

"We should go up some time. I bet you'd like it." The more she finds out about Caroline Royer, the more she likes her. How her brash sister ended up nabbing a wealthy, highly cultured academic who flies planes in her spare time is beyond Nicole's understanding.

Caroline gestures towards the living room. "Are you going out with Zoe?"

"Yeah." Nicole nod.

"Tell her to pick up something for dinner, okay?" Caroline calls after her, "And try to enjoy yourself."

They leave the apartment and meander through the city. It's nice not having to play catch up with Zoe. Her sister's pace is downright relaxed, as is her mood. This is a side of Zoe Nicole could get used to. She can't help but wonder what happened yesterday after she fell asleep. "You're in an awfully good mood."

"So?" Zoe digs her hands into her pockets, shrugging.

"You and Caroline work things out?" It's the most obvious conclusion, but the look her sister gives her tells her it's the wrong one.

"That ship sailed a long time ago." Zoe smiles distantly. "We're just friends."

Nicole is not sure she believes her. Caroline had been pretty affectionate towards Zoe this morning, drawing her out and getting her to talk about the time she spent living in Paris. The two women seemed so at ease around each other. Something must've happened, no matter what Zoe claims.

Her sister is a rotten tour guide, but just being out in the sun and around normal people is soothing. They wander down the twisting cobblestone streets and up a few too many hills. Nicole coughs, lungs not ready for this level of exertion. She is about to say something to Zoe when they come to a stop outside a beautiful building. Ornate stonework encases simple double doors and dark, obscured windows. She can see shapes moving inside.

"What's this place?" Nicole stifles another cough.

"Old haunt." Zoe grins, pushing the heavy door open and holding it for Nicole. Rowdy cheers erupt as she steps through the threshold. The smell of sweat hits her hard. Her eyes adjust from the bright sunshine, spots of light slowly disappearing. Punching bags hang from the ceiling. Her sister has taken her to a gym, for some reason. Zoe may have funny ideas about recuperating from illness, but Nicole has no interest in working out.

She has to admit the sight of a dozen muscular men surrounding the elevated boxing ring at the center of the room is pleasantly distracting, but something tells her that is not why her sister brought her here.

Zoe edges closer to the ring, moving through the small crowd. Nicole follows, pardoning herself the entire way. She grabs her sister's arm, whispering, "Why are we here?"

Zoe shushes her and points towards the match about to begin. The men inside the ring advance towards each other, bodies slick with sweat, muscles in their lean legs flexing and tensing with every quick step. Nicole swallows the lump in her throat, unconsciously biting her lip.

Zoe whispers in her ear. "Keep an eye on the chump with the beard."

It's an easy thing to do. His movements are swift and accurate, kicks finding their target even through his young opponent's desperate attempts to block. The kid is outmatched. A sweeping kick topples him to the mat, but he springs back up, tenaciously trying to get the upper hand, attacking harder, body pressed against the bearded man, knees slamming into his abdomen until he receives a crippling strike to his ear that sends him tumbling to the mat.

Nicole whispers back to Zoe. "Who is he?"

But her sister is no longer at her side. Zoe has scaled the ring, ducking under the ropes. "I take winner."

The bearded man looks for the source of the taunt. His eyes settle on her with a little surprise and a good deal of anger. "You got a lot of nerve showing your face here, Hudson."

Nicole watches Zoe saunter to the center of the ring, popping her knuckles rhythmically. "What can I say, Gabe? I missed handing you your ass."

He chuckles, muttering a rapid string of expletives in French. His foot whips out, narrowly missing Zoe, who sidesteps the blow, moving in close to deliver a swift jab. He adjusts his position, blocking her. She bounces back, hips pivoting, the toe of her sneaker snapping up and connecting with his ribcage. He stumbles, wincing.

She called him by name. She must know him, and he sure seems to know Zoe well enough to want to kick her in the face.

Gabe throws a punch that Zoe ducks. The kick that follow his jab is impossibly high, and aimed right at her sister's head. She steps out of the way, but the return motion of his foot connects lower, hooking her shoulder and sending her sprawling to her knees. The crowd noise is a mixture of jeers and clapping. Nicole can't quite tell who they are favoring, but she has to assume it's the bearded home team.

"You haven't been practicing." His body bounces in place, staying in motion, gloved hands slapping together.

Zoe laughs, a wicked smile on her lips. "I don't need any more practice." She rocks back, finding her feet and advancing quickly, tucking under his defense. She swings wildly, punches raining down on his upraised hands. She moves in close, until their bodies are touching. Her knee snaps up, slamming into Gabe's side. When his hands drop to guard his core, Zoe strikes him across the temple. They shove off each other, stumbling back to their respective corners.

Zoe finally makes eye contact with Nicole, shaking her hand in pain. "Ow."

Nicole can't find sympathy for her sister, having just watched her pick the fight with the man she just cold cocked. Nicole cups her hands around her mouth and yells, "You deserved that."

All she wanted was something more relaxing than being sick and looking at the journal. She's had enough violent excitement to last her a lifetime. Boring would have been nice for a change. Nicole rolls her eyes, missing her chance to warn her sister of the movement in their periphery. Gabe grabs Zoe, flinging her backwards, and connecting a practiced, graceful kick with her jaw as she stumbles. The impact sends her crashing to the mat. He advances on her prone body, dropping to her side, hand curling around the fabric of Zoe's shirt, tugging her up, his fist cocked back, ready to strike.

Nicole slaps the surface of the ring, yelling as loud as she can, her voice cracking. "*Stop!*"

Gabe glances at Nicole, smiling softly. "New girlfriend, Zoe? She seems a little young for you." He lets go of her shirt, rocking to his feet and offering her his hand.

"That's my kid sister, you jackass." Zoe slaps his hand away, wiping blood from the corner of her mouth. "Gabriel Beraud, Nicole Hudson. Nik, meet Caroline's jerk cousin."

Knowing the relation, Nicole can see the faint resemblance. They share the same dark, curly hair and clear blue eyes. Gabe slips through the ropes and effortlessly drops to the floor next to Nicole. He takes her hand, gently kissing the top of it and greeting her smoothly in French. She muddles through a response, thanking him and withdrawing her hand.

Gabe turns to Zoe, smirking. "Her accent is better than yours."

Her sister shakes her head, sitting on the edge of the ring and leaning against the ropes. "Yeah, well, that's not exactly difficult, is it."

He grabs a towel off the ropes. "Does *she* know you're here?"

Zoe nods stiffly, stretching her neck. Nicole can hear a vertebrae pop back into place.

"Do you need a place to—Um, what is the term?" He snaps his fingers. "Crash?"

"No. We're good." Zoe answers quickly, slipping under the ropes and dropping between Gabe and Nicole.

He eyes her suspiciously. "Really?"

"We're staying with Caroline." Zoe winces at Nicole for filling in the details. The groan Gabe lets out speaks volumes.

Her sister rubs her jaw. "It's not what you think."

Gabe sighs. "When it comes to the two of you, it is always exactly what I think."

***

FINDING OUT HER SISTER can actually cook is a bit of a shock. Dinners during the two weeks aboard the boat from Brazil to South Africa consisted of canned food and protein bars. Nicole had no idea Zoe knew how to roast anything, let alone an entire chicken. She must have picked it up from Jones, because she definitely didn't get it from Mom.

After successfully consuming her weight in meat and fresh vegetables, Nicole leaves her sister to the dishes and retires to Caroline's office to take another look at the book and hang out with Arthur before collapsing into bed. As soon as she takes a seat, the big guy hunkers down at Nicole's side, sighing heavily as he lays his head across his burly set of paws. She scratches him with her toes, and opens the book to where she left off.

Caroline peeks through the door, eyes settling on her dog curled up on Nicole's feet. Arthur raises his big head, thick tail thumping the floor. "He's not bothering you, is he?"

"No. Not at all. We're bros, aren't we Arthur?" She leans down and scratches behind his ear. Mom was never big on pets. She claimed she was allergic, but Nicole always knew the real reason was their lifestyle. Their schedules were too busy to allow for anything that required that much attention or affection. "Were you looking for something?"

"No." Caroline settles into the chair across from the desk. "Just wanted to check in on you. Read anything interesting?"

Nicole supports her chin in her palm. "I think I'm starting to."

"Oh really?"

"Well, besides being written in reverse, most of this book has been pretty dry. Shipping manifests. Day to day events. Pretty run of the mill stuff. Interesting, but not all at the same time, you know? I mean; it gets my mind off of everything, but this entry is different." Nicole squints at the text. "Seems an anonymous employer wanted them to look into a missing ship. The Zuytdorp. It was carrying silver. A lot of silver. And it never reached its final destination. So these guys go looking for it, right? But they don't find a boat or mountains of silver. They find a castaway. A castaway who claims to be the sole survivor of the very ship they're looking for." Nicole pauses, feeling both completely comfortable being herself around this woman, and strangely rude for blabbing on at her about seemingly inconsequential findings.

When she looks up, Caroline encourages her. "Go on."

So this is what having someone interested in what you have to say feels like. She'd almost forgotten. "Um. The castaway tells them he can lead them to riches. More than just silver. Some lost treasure or something? Since the captain can't come back empty handed, he's totally into it. But the guy keeping this journal was skeptical."

Nicole straightens up, working out the stiffness in her back. "So, you know, hidden treasure and intrigue. It's starting to get good."

Caroline chuckles. "Has anyone ever told you how impressive you are?"

"Not really." Nicole blushes.

"Well, you are. To be able to do all that, *and* put up with your sister. You're down right remarkable." She flashes a supportive smile and combs her fingers through her dark hair. "Did you enjoy yourself this afternoon?"

"Sure." Nicole nods. "Zoe introduced me to your cousin. And then he promptly kicked her in the face."

"I sort of figured as much from the state of her." Gabriel's kick had left its mark on Zoe, splitting and swelling her lip. "I assume she started it?"

"Oh yeah." Nicole flips the page. "Has she always had trouble saying 'hello' like a normal person?"

Caroline shrugs. "It's her way."

"Gabriel seemed a little shocked we were staying with you." Nicole watches Caroline's expression out of the corner of her eye.

"I bet." The arch of her brow raises, amused. "He's not fond of Zoe."

"Why?" Nicole asks.

"I'm sure he has his own reasons, but things didn't exactly end well between your sister and me."

"I know it's none of my business," Nicole presses, curiosity getting the better of her, "but what happened?"

Caroline looks distant. She fusses with the hem of her skirt. "Your sister got restless. She missed working on the Trident. I wanted her to stay in Paris with me. We were both kind of selfish. I pushed too hard. She pulled away. In the end, we just tore apart. I didn't exactly handle the break-up well, and I leaned on Gabriel pretty hard. It's not like they were close to begin with, but seeing me hurt didn't help his opinion of her."

"Do you still love her?" She regrets asking even before she's finished saying the words.

There is a long silence.

"It's more complicated than that." A sad expression momentarily settles on Caroline's face. She forces her bravest grin and before Nicole can apologize, she is up and heading for the hall. "Don't work too late," she says. "You need your rest."

ELI DID NOT SEEM TO APPRECIATE her lack of cooperation this morning. When she refused to answer his questions, he stormed out, slamming the door hard enough to make the glass vibrate. At least he left her alone.

Lying bastard.

She hates herself for falling for it, her own fear and the weakness of maternal instincts rising up to bite her in the ass. Allison sits on her bunk, fingers combing through her hair, nails digging into her scalp.

The security camera light blinks off.

Allison watches the door as the locks throw back. Part of her can't help but hope to see the woman from the night before. No luck. Eli enters the room with two thuggish looking men.

She can feel herself begin to panic but buries the reaction, fighting to show no fear. She watches Eli as he walks towards her, slipping his hands into dark surgical gloves.

"I have nothing to say to—"

His interruption comes in the form of a hard backhanded slap across her face, latex sticking and stinging. The edges of her teeth cut the fragile skin of her lip, she can feel the blood pooling in her mouth.

Up until now, things have been intense but civil. Apparently, civility is over.

Eli motions to one of his men. "Get her in that chair."

Allison stands, objecting to the order like her opinion matters. "What? No."

Strong hands grab her arms and wrists, pulling her into the center of the room and forcing her into the bent-backed aluminum chair. She is not weak, and not beyond trying to futilely fight her way free. She kicks one of the men in the groin, but her struggling earns her a punch to the gut. She doubles forward, gasping desperately for air. Eli pulls her back, rubbery grip on her shoulders, pinning her down as her hands and feet are secured painfully to the chair with thick zip ties.

He leans in close, breath on her ear. "I do not appreciate being made a fool of."

Allison pulls away, rocking the chair. "Fuck you."

She spits at him, blood flecking his dark skin, spattering the collar of his white shirt. He chuckles, wiping his face with the back of his hand. Eli reaches into his coat, drawing his pistol. The heavy steel frame strikes her face. She can feel her skin split near her eye, hot blood running down her cheek. The pain is searing, sending tremors through her body, fingers tightening and twitching, wrists pinned to cold metal.

Eli grips her hair, pulling her head back sharply, shoving the muzzle of his gun into the soft tissue of her throat. Swallowing becomes a struggle. Blood drips slowly down her neck from the wound on her cheek. She prepares herself for the violence to come.

IF SHE FALLS ASLEEP IN HER contacts one more night, they may never come out again. Caroline closes her book and slips out of bed, wrapping herself in her robe and heading for the lavatory. Opening the door to a shirtless Zoe attentively inspecting her various injuries in the mirror is a complete shock. It's been so long since anyone has stayed with her, she forgot hers is not the only door into this room.

She takes a step back and averts her eyes, fighting the urge to blush if only to prove to herself she is capable of being an adult about this. "I'm sorry, I didn't realize you were in here."

"My fault. Forgot to lock the door." Zoe snatches a towel off the nearest bar and slings it over her shoulders. The thick fabric obscures her breasts, but not much else. She goes back to pouring rubbing alcohol over her scraped knuckles. "You need something?"

"Just my contact solution." She points to the white bottle on the glass shelf above the sink.

"Sure." Zoe grabs the bottle and hands it over, avoiding eye contact. "Here."

The split on her lip is more swollen than it was at dinner. Caroline winces out of sympathy. "That looks like it hurts."

"I've had worse."

"Even so, you should put some ice on it." As Zoe heads back to the sink, Caroline watches the shape of her: intersecting planes and angles converge, forming an athletic figure. Broad at the shoulders, narrow at the hips. She is as well muscled as ever, and substantially more tanned than Caroline recalled, but there is evidence she's not taking care of herself. Her ribs are visible, jutting towards the surface and pressing against deeply bruised skin. She's been in rough shape before, but Caroline wonders exactly how much she has gone through these past few weeks. "Nicole said you took her to the Gabriel's gym. You didn't go there to pick a fight, did you?"

"No." Zoe's response is surprisingly more chagrined than Caroline expected. She prods her wound and rinses her face, flashing a playful smile as she gingerly pats herself dry. "My face just kind of got in the way of his foot."

"You had to know he wouldn't be happy to see you." Caroline fiddles with the cap of her contact solution then sets it down on the vanity counter. "Of all the places in Paris you could take your sister, why there?"

"Don't know. We were out walking, and that's where we ended up. It just sort of happened. Think I was enjoying being in a familiar place for once, you know? Felt like coming home."

Something in the way she says 'home' sounds profoundly bittersweet. Caroline had often wondered if that was how Zoe viewed this place, but they never talked about it while she was living here. After she ran back to the Trident, Caroline couldn't help but wonder if she had been just another notch in Zoe Hudson's belt. Another conquest to talk about over beers with the guys. The confirmation to the contrary is as painful as it is pleasant.

Zoe frowns. "What's wrong? Did I say something?"

"No." Caroline shakes her head. "This is just—this is harder than I thought it would be."

"What?"

"Trying to be your friend." The marble floor is cool beneath her bare feet, but every fiber of her feels warmed from somewhere deep within. "I thought I was ready for it. I thought I had enough distance to be objective, but," she swallows the lump in her throat and continues, "this is confusing. I can't stop thinking about you. You make me feel so confused. It's like no matter how angry I am with you, no matter how frustrated I get, I just want to — I want things to be the way they were." Caroline stops inches away Zoe, her heart threatening to pound its way out of her chest. "I want to kiss you. Touch you."

Zoe's cheeks flush. "But you said—"

"I remember what I said." Caroline traces the curve of her split and swollen lip with the flat of her thumb. "But right now, in this moment, I want you to come home. To me."

"Caroline—"

She kisses Zoe deeply, drinking her in. Every feeling of anger and loneliness evaporates, and all that remains is desire. Fingertips search the topography of Zoe's body, rediscovering a once-familiar landscape. Strong hands slip beneath the fabric of Caroline's robe, gripping her skin with a fevered intensity.

They stumble blindly back into the bedroom, neither willing to break away from the other, and all at once removing her contacts doesn't seem very important.

FLETCHER ALERTED HER WHEN Eli left for the mainland. Wherever he is headed, he's in a hurry. Case wondered what was so urgent Kostich would abandon his prize in the east holding cells. When the door opens, Case gets her answer.

Seems Eli likes to break his toys.

The sight before her is messy and careless, the work of an amateur. Dr. Allison Hudson is in the center of her ten by ten cell, zip tied to a chair, left side of her face covered in blood. She appears to be breathing but unconscious. It's not the method that she disapproves of. She and Connor have used similar tactics to extract information from resistant sources. No. It's the fact Kostich could not accept he was beaten, bested at his own game by a superior opponent. Instead he took his rage out on the last person Hayden Thomas ever trusted.

She crouches next to Allison, checking her condition. Her wrists are badly chafed, rubbed red and raw from the plastic cuffs strapping her to the chair. There is a substantial gash near her left eye. Head wounds do produce an impressively gory display. Case pushes matted strands of blood-soaked hair from Allison's face.

The woman lurches forward at the contact, waking suddenly, panicked, her breathing erratic.

"He's gone. You're alright, Dr. Hudson," she says calmly. "I will not allow this to go on any longer."

"He's going after my girls."Allison groans, head down, chin pressed against the stained collar of her tank top.

Everything clicks into place. She underestimated his ambition. Instead of backing down, Eli is going after everything, just to spite her. Case curses him under her breath. "Bastard."

She pulls her cell phone from her jacket pocket and dials quickly. Fletcher's voice purrs into her ear. "Ms. Case?"

"I need a medical team to the east wing and a west corridor residence prepared. Immediately."

She can hear him typing. "Is there a problem?"

Case steps toward the open cell door. "Kostich made a mess."

"Ma'am." He does not ask questions. "The physician is on his way. I will send the room information to your mobile shortly." Fletcher ends the call.

Allison coughs behind her. It is a pained, gruesome sound. "What are you doing?"

Case leans against the jamb, watching the door at the end of the hall for the medical team. "I'm moving you to a private residence. You'll be more comfortable there."

"I don't want to be more comfortable." Allison growls through gritted teeth. "I want you to let me go."

"That is not an option."

"God damn it! You people can't keep me here forever!" Allison winces, drawing herself to her knees and glaring at Case. "Someone will realize I'm missing. They'll come looking for me."

"I doubt that, Dr. Hudson."

A buzzer sounds as the door down the hall swings open, expelling three men in monochromatic medical scrubs. She steps aside, allowing them access to the blood spattered concrete cell and their patient. "I doubt that very much."

- 7 -

WARM FINGERS TRACE THE LINE of her hip as soft lips kiss the nape of her neck. Zoe stirs, feet slowly rubbing together beneath the sheets as her brain reboots. When she rolls over, Caroline gives her a drowsy smile and kisses the steep angle of her nose. "Good morning, Ms. Hudson."

Her own grin spreads so broadly across her face that her cheeks begin to ache. She pulls Caroline close and kisses her. "Same to you, Ms. Royer."

Caroline strokes Zoe's chest, her warm palm finally resting on the curve of her breast. She lays her head on Zoe's shoulder. "I meant what I said yesterday. I think you should go to Zurich and meet with the man at Julian Baer. Ask him about your father's account. See if he has access to any contact information. A phone number. An address."

"Why would he give it to me?"

"I'm the signatory on all my parents' accounts. Maybe your father set up something similar. In case of an emergency." Coming from Caroline it all sounds so rational. "It wouldn't hurt to try. You've already come this far. Why stop now?"

The thought of being in a bank makes her skin crawl. Something about banks ranks right up there with taxes, law enforcement, and surprise phone calls from her mother. But Caroline seems so certain. Zoe nods, trying to ignore the knot growing in her stomach. "Are you trying to get rid of me?"

"Hardly." Caroline sits up, dark hair spilling over the smooth slope of her shoulder as her fingertips weave in between Zoe's. Her hands are so warm. "I'd rather you stay right here for as long as humanly possible, but this is your dad we're talking about. I'm not going to stand in the way of you finding him."

"Are you sure?"

"Positive." She kisses Zoe's cheek. "Now, get up and make me breakfast while I book you two train tickets."

"One ticket." Zoe corrects her. "Nik's staying with you."

"And what does Nicole think about that?"

Zoe shrugs.

Caroline arches an eyebrow, amused. "Don't you think you should ask your sister before you start making decisions on her behalf?"

"Nope."

"Don't be an ass." Caroline slaps Zoe's arm. "Ask her."

She slips out from under the covers and off the edge of the bed. Zoe watches her move across the sun-soaked bedroom towards her closet. "If she wants to stay with me, she's more than welcome. Arthur adores her."

Propped up on both elbows, Zoe watches the ebb and flow of Caroline's body. The muscles in her thighs and ass tense as she pulls the closet doors open wide. She leans against the jamb, sorting through hangers, perched on one foot while the other absently strokes her own calf. She is searching for something specific. The crisply starched button-down shirt she produces is far too large to be her own, and suddenly things click into place. Purchased years ago for some half-forgotten event, the shirt was something Caroline bought for Zoe to wear to occasions that required something more formal than her usual t-shirt and jeans.

She kept it after all this time.

"Since you're going to one of Switzerland's oldest and most prestigious private banks, you'll need to dress the part." She slips the dress shirt on. Its fabric hangs loose from her petite frame. Zoe's pulse quickens as Caroline makes her way back to the bed, crawling up the length of the soft mattress. When she settles, her thighs straddling Zoe's, the warmth of her radiates through the duvet. Her eyes are so bright. So very blue. So full of trust and love.

Caroline leans close, her long hair spilling forward, pooling against Zoe's bare breasts. She whispers softly, "We can't have you looking like you're going to rob the place, now can we?"

THE APARTMENT IS STILL. The only sounds are those of the kettle boiling and the click of Arthur's nails on the tile floor as he enters the kitchen to take his place in the sun spot by the french doors. She is not used to being the first one up.

The kettle whistles. Nicole steps over Arthur's outstretched legs, making her way around the island to prep her morning tea. Hushed voices drift down the long hall. Nicole drops a teabag into the steaming mug and leans around the corner to investigate.

Caroline is in a robe, her pale hands cupping Zoe's cheeks. She kisses her gently, then sets about rolling up the sleeves of her sister's dress shirt. Nicole has never seen Zoe in anything other than t-shirts and jeans. The crisp button-up is a stark departure from the norm. Zoe works to tuck in the tails as Caroline's hands roam across her broad shoulders, smoothing the fabric, then heading south. Feeling like a voyeur, Nicole lets out a cough. The women at the end of the hall both turn.

"Morning, ladies." Nicole tucks back into the kitchen. She hollers over her shoulder as she takes a seat at the counter. "Sleep well?"

Zoe comes around the corner, shameless smile on plastered on her face. "Morning, Nik."

Caroline follows, a blush creeping up her throat. She gives Nicole a fond squeeze on the shoulder before heading to the refrigerator for a bottle of juice. Caroline edges past Zoe, their bodies brushing. Zoe plucks a glass from the cupboard, handing it to Caroline over her shoulder as she passes. There is a fluidity to their movements, an ease. Nicole sips at her tea, enjoying the delicate domestic dance.

They look so happy.

Zoe takes a seat next to her at the counter. "How would you feel about taking the train to Zurich today?"

Nicole blinks. "Why?"

"That card Caroline found in the book has an account number on the back. Might be worth checking out." Zoe pauses, fidgeting with her fingers.

Nicole stares at her blankly.

Her sister's focus is on the counter as she continues to speak. "Caroline thinks they may know where my dad is, and I know that you don't approve, but I have to try to find him. So you can come with me if you want to." She gives Nicole a nervous look. "Or you can stay here with Caroline—"

"No." Nicole cannot hide her excitement. "I want to go."

"You're sure?" Zoe swallows hard, nodding.

"Yes." Nicole slips off her stool. "When do you want to leave?"

"In an hour, if you can get ready. Everything goes smoothly, we won't even need to stay in Switzerland. We can be back here in time for dinner." Zoe is all smiles as Caroline leans against the counter next to her and strokes her arm. "Sound good?"

"Sounds *great.*"

"Go get your stuff."

Nicole hurries off towards the office to gather her things. Only as she's collecting the book does she realize her excitement is not as directly related to what her sister said as to how she said it. Zoe asked her rather than just telling her.

She wishes that whatever happened last night had happened weeks ago.

THE DOCTORS DID A decent job of patching her up. It took thirteen stitches to close up the gash by her eye and another five to mend her split lip. They released her after a thorough exam, and she was escorted not back to a cell but to a fully-furnished apartment somewhere else in the complex. Its huge tinted windows look out over a strip of white sand beach and the ever rolling ocean. By the time she settles in, the sunrise is casting long shadows on the polished concrete floors.

Her surroundings may be more comfortable, but a new view and nice furniture does nothing to ease her pain. Every breath is a struggle, lungs expanding and pressing against fractured ribs. The doctor gave her a bottle of pain killers, but she is not terribly inclined to trust anything coming from these people.

There is a knock on the door. Allison glances over her shoulder, watching the entry and half expecting someone to barge in waving a gun. Instead there is another gentle knock, no more rapid than the first. Civil. Patient.

She crosses the spacious living area and opens the door.

A man stands before her. He looks elderly, but fit for his age. The rugged, hawkish features of his face are handsomely accented by a well-groomed mustache and closely trimmed white hair.

"Good morning, Doctor." His voice is low and even. Something in his tone is polite in the most off-putting of ways."Aren't you going to invite me in?"

She weighs her options, few though they are, and backs up, giving the old man room to enter.

"Such hospitality," he quips.

Before closing the door, she checks the hall. The same pair of guards who escorted her here so many hours before are still flanking the threshold. Allison turns her attention to her guest as the door swings shut. "Who are you?"

"Victor Sutton," he says cooly.

Knowing his name does not answer her question. She crosses her arms. "Why are you here? What do you want?"

"So many questions." He smiles, taking a seat on the couch. "Case did say you were rather inquisitive. I suppose it's in your nature, given your profession."

"Case?" Allison lowers herself gently into a chair.

"Tricia Case." Sutton adjusts his suit jacket, smoothing its fabric. "She is the one who vouched for you. She requested a change in your status."

"My status?"

He cocks his head. "She seems to believe you will be helpful."

"Helpful?" Allison scoffs, her anger boiling over. "You people abducted me at gun point. You've held me captive. Interrogated me. Beat me. I cannot help you. I don't know anything. No matter how many times you ask me, no matter how long you keep me here, that won't change."

Sutton flashes her a bitter smile. "Oh, I think it will."

"I haven't seen or spoken to Hayden Thomas in years." She lets out an irritated sigh. After all these years, Zoe's father is still managing to cause her problems. Allison scrubs at her neck. "I don't know anything about any book or anything he stole. All I want is for you to let me go and leave my family alone."

Sutton glares at her. "I will not do that."

She waits for him to expound on the thought. Silence settles. Sutton eyes are still trained on her. Scrutinizing her. She fights the chill running down her spine and a manages to stammer, "Why?"

"You're an intelligent woman, Dr. Hudson." He rises, buttoning his jacket and heading for the door. "I'm sure you will figure it out. Eventually."

THEY HAVE BEEN SITTING in an imposing office surrounded by opulence and dark woodwork for twenty minutes now. Zoe is starting to wonder if this was actually a good idea. She can feel herself sweating through the fabric of her shirt. Turns out the business card Caroline found tucked in the binding of the book was a little out of date. Fredrick Meier, Associate Investment Adviser is now Fredrick Meier, Director of Operations.

The door opens behind them and an elderly man with grey hair and a delicate mustache enters the office. Zoe stands, extending her hand. His handshake is firm and practiced.

"Please, sit, Ms. Hudson." Meier gestures towards her chair. His English is crisp and precise. "I trust you two have not been uncomfortable waiting in my office."

"No, sir." Zoe sits down, hands nervously smoothing the fabric of her pants with clammy palms. Nicole gives her a reassuring pat on the arm.

Meier takes a seat behind his baroque desk and begins to shuffle through a massive stack of papers, drawing a pair of glasses from his jacket pocket. "My secretary tells me you are here regarding your father's account."

Zoe nods stiffly.

"I'm glad you came to us when you did." He fnds the paperwork he was searching for and sorts through it, circling and marking different lines. "The assets were slated to be liquidated at the end of this year."

This wasn't how she was expecting the conversation to start. "Liquidated?"

Meier nods. "We had almost reached the statute of limitations."

"The what?"

"Statute of limitation." He fnishes shuffling the stack of documents. "It is customary to conduct an active search for the named apostle of any dormant account."

"Apostle?" Nicole asks.

Meier struggles to find the words. "A signatory? An authorized person."

"Back up a second." Zoe shakes her head. "What do you mean the account's been dormant?"

"The account number you supplied has been inactive for nearly ten years. Your father, Mr. Hayden Thomas, named you his apostle and requested, in the event of his death, that all assets and earnings be transferred to you." He clicks his pen and slides the stack towards Zoe. "I just need your signature on a few documents and we can complete the transaction."

She stares blankly at the papers.

"That is why you're here, is it not?" Meier's smile fades. "To collect the funds?"

She swallows hard, forcing her bile down and the question out. "He's—he's dead?"

The bank manager's expression falls slack. "Forgive me. I assumed you knew."

Her mouth is dry, tongue sticking to the back of her teeth. She shakes her head. Muted by shock.

Meier gives her a sympathetic look. "I—that is to say, I—Ms. Hudson, it happened nearly ten years ago. We've been trying to contact you ever since we received word. I assumed the coroner would have informed his next of kin."

"No one told me." She is weightless. Drifting. Meier's lips move, but she can no longer hear him. White noise fills her ears, crashing down on her like a wave during a storm.

All this time.

He was already gone.

Nicole takes hold of her hand. The physical contact snaps her back.

"I am terribly sorry for your loss, Ms. Hudson."

THE KETTLE WHISTLES. Caroline pulls it off the burner and pours the boiling water into the coffee press. As the grounds churn, the glass darkens. She slides the lid into place, leaving the coffee to brew while she retreats to her office. Personal day or no, she needs to do something more productive than wait by the phone hoping Zoe will call.

She takes a seat behind her desk, bare legs tucking underneath her as she boots up her laptop. She logs into the library's network and begins to cycle through the day's emails, hoping the monotony will offer some distraction, but her mind keeps wandering back to sweat-soaked sheets and the heat of Zoe Hudson's skin pressed against her own. It was like nothing had changed. Like no time had passed. They were together and everything made sense again. Caroline stretches the collar of Zoe's t-shirt over her nose and inhales deeply. Even after a day, the thin fabric still smells like her.

Caroline removes her glasses, setting them beside her laptop as she rubs the bridge of her nose. She pushes back from her desk and stares out the window at the Parisian sunrise.

A low growl drifts down the hall.

Her dog never growls.

"Come here, boy," she calls to him.

His growl turns to a deep bark. Caroline rises from her seat. Her pulse racing. "Arthur?"

There is a pop.

Followed by a pained whimper.

"Arthur?" She calls out his name again but the sound cracks in her throat. "Come here, boy."

The apartment is still.

He does not come.

As she creeps towards the door a tremor begin to course through her limbs. "Zoe? Nicole?"

There is no answer.

She enters the long hall, treading carefully towards the disturbance. Floorboards creak. At the end of the hall a dark shape rounds the corner. Caroline freezes. Her eyes struggle to bring the blurred man in her living room into focus.

"Who are you?" She steadies herself against the wall, edging back towards the office. "How did you get in here?"

As he draws closer she notices the polished silver pistol in his right hand. He flicks it at her, motioning for her to come forward as he closes the gap between them.

Her fingers find the jamb of the office door. She fumbles with the heavy door, trying to slam it closed, but the man moves too quickly. His grabs her wrist, pulling her back into the hall and tight to his chest. A massive forearm slips across her throat. He jerks her into the living room. Her body twists in his grip, legs stuttering beneath her, feet barely making contact with the floor.

He drags her past the kitchen. Caroline lashes out, her bare feet striking the cabinets hard. She pushes back with all her strength.

The man holding her may be huge, but his size doesn't mean much when he loses his balance. They topple to the ground, her head slamming against his chin with bone jarring force.

Metal skitters across the ground. Out of the corner of her eye, she sees his pistol collides with the leg of the coffee table. He shoves her off of him and scrambles into the living room, flipping the wooden table over to recover his weapon.

Her head is throbbing, vision swimming from the violent impact, but she scurries into the kitchen, grabbing hold of the counter top to pull herself upright. Panicked, she searches for a weapon. Anything to even the odds. Her fingers curl around the polished metal handle of her corkscrew lying next to the knife block.

Fingers latch into her hair. He is on her, flinging her around and slamming her painfully into the corner of the marble counter.

Through the blinding pain she catches a dark shape on the floor near the wide open front door. Arthur, limp in an expanding pool of dark blood.

This asshole shot her dog.

Caroline pinches her eyes closed, focusing her rage and fear into force. She brings the twisted piece of metal down hard, burying its tip into the thick flesh of the man's arm. Her strike is answered with one of his own. The muzzle of his pistol splits her forehead wide open and sends her sprawling to the floor.

Caroline scrambles past the island and into the far corner of the kitchen, her retreat is stopped only when her back hits the cabinets. She can hear his labored breath as he stalks towards her, corkscrew embedded in his bicep. There is no way out. She cannot get past him. No one can hear her. No one can help her. Her words are barely audible over her own panicked gasping. "Stay away from me. Don't you dare come any closer."

The man laughs, tucking his gun back into its holster. He rips the corkscrew from his arm. A ribbon of blood and tissue maps a gruesome trajectory as he flings the bottle opener over the island and into the living room. His thick fingers take hold of her hair, wrenching her upward.

She feels the edge of the counter against her shoulders.

Instinct takes over.

Her fingertips find the metal handle of the coffee press and she swings it with all the strength she has left, slamming the carafe into his scared face. Glass shatters, covering him with shards and scalding coffee. He releases her, hands flying up to scrape at the searing grounds sticking to his skin.

She grabs the skillet off the stove and strikes him across the face. The momentum of her blow sends him careening into the edge of the kitchen island. There is an audible crunch as his temple strikes the stone. His body drops to the floor with a thud.

After that, he does not move.

Everything is silent.

The skillet slips from her hand, striking tile floor with a clang that breaks the quiet. Caroline's knees give way. She slips down the cabinets until her body makes contact with the cool floor. Inches from her bare feet, a puddle of red seeps from under her attacker's head.

- 8 -

Sitting through that meeting was torture. Her stomach is still tossing and turning. If she had not just spent an entire month in Zoe's company, Nicole might have missed the cues, but she could feel the hurt radiating from her sister. She was different after their meeting with Mr. Meier. Broken.

And no matter how much she wanted to, there was nothing Nicole could do to help. She spent the rest of the meeting focusing on Meier as he explained the details of the transfer with succinct focus; initial here, sign there, please read this and sign. Within fifteen minutes, Zoe's father's accounts were turned over with robotic efficiency.

There would be no tearful reunion, no answers, only a bitter consolation prize: money. The unfettered access to her dead father's Swiss account will be helpful, but the entire transaction was cold, impersonal, and so deeply sad.

They've been walking for over an hour, Zoe quietly marching forward muttering softly to herself while Nicole hangs back, allowing her as much space and privacy as a public sidewalk can offer. The pub Zoe settles on is a quiet place reeking of smoke and alcohol. Nicole takes a seat in a shadowed booth and orders food from the stained menu. Zoe orders only a drink. Whiskey. Neat.

Nicole peers at her sister. "You should eat something."

"Not hungry."

When her food arrives, Nicole pokes at it, stirring the unremarkable bowl of stew with a comically oversized spoon. They sit in silence; Zoe restlessly twisting her glass between her fingers, Nicole staring at the gelatinous surface of her meal, trying to think of something to say, anything to start a conversation. But all she can come up with is *"I'm really sorry your Dad's dead. That really sucks."*

Before she can find words, Zoe is on her feet, bumping into the table as she drains the last of her drink. She sets the thick-walled glass on the sticky table and points at Nicole. "Stay put, alright? Be back in a minute."

Nicole nods, watching her stride off towards an antiquated public phone booth crammed next to the bathrooms. As Zoe tucks inside, pulling the bi-fold door closed behind her, a dim light turns on. Trapped behind wavy glass and bathed in warm light, her sister settles on the tiny bench and begins to dial. Her movements are sluggish and lingering. She is exhausted. Zoe pins the phone against her shoulder and rubs at her eyes, letting out a silent yawn. Yup. Definitely exhausted, but not oblivious. Her eyes lock with Nicole, but only for a moment. She turns away, kicking the door open just enough to shut off the lights, her frame receding into shadow.

Nicole switches back to poking at her food, pushing the ever solidifying mass aimlessly around the earthenware bowl until her skin begins to tingle and everything around her fuzzes out. The din of the pub settles over her.

Her stupor is broken when Zoe drops into the booth with a thud. Nicole does her best not to look startled. "Did she pick up?"

Zoe shakes her head and flicks at the empty glass.

Nicole tugs at the hem of her over-shirt, pinching a stray threads. "Did you leave a message?"

"No." Zoe motions to the bartender, wordlessly ordering another drink.

Nicole slumps forward, resting her chin on a hand. She stops stirring her stew and without guidance, the thick piece of bread swells and sinks below the surface. "You've got to let Caroline know what's going on."

"I know." Her sister scrubs at her face with both hands. After a deep groan of frustration she levels her gaze at Nicole. The bartender swings by their booth, depositing another pungent amber drink. Zoe sips from it slowly. "I kept trying to figure out a way, but I couldn't get it out. It didn't seem right to tell her about all... this... over voicemail."

Nicole understands that. And it's not like Zoe is an ace at communication to begin with. "So, what now?"

"Got us some tickets."

Nicole dips a hunk of stale bread into her stew. "Back to Paris?"

"Mumbai."

The statement is said so casually, Nicole almost missed it. Sort of like, *oh and by the way, I picked up your dry-cleaning on my way home*. She drops the bread and fixes Zoe with a confused stare. "Mumbai? Like Mumbai, India? Why are we flying to India?"

"Because the Trident's docked there. I need to go back and look into something."

"You're kidding, right?" Zoe's cringe is answer enough. Nicole pushes her bowl out of the way and leans across the table. "You're not kidding. Damn it, Zoe, I thought we were past all this you-make-big-decisions-that-directly-affect-both-of-us thing. I thought we were heading back to Paris. That we were going to stay with Caroline until we heard from Mom?"

She shoots Nicole a complicated look over the rim of her glass.

"I don't like that face. What's wrong?"

Zoe's eyes drop to the table. She drains her drink and stacks one empty glass into the other, then leans back against the wooden booth, hands digging deep into her jacket pockets. Her voice is hoarse. "Remember how you asked me if there was anything I wasn't telling you?"

"Yes."

"Well, when I talked to Mom, she sounded off. Scared. I haven't heard her like that since my dad left us." Zoe releases a measured breath. "I think she's in trouble."

"Why didn't you tell me before?"

"I'm telling you now."

No matter how hard she tries, Nicole cannot bring herself to be mad. Not right now. Not after everything that has happened. "What kind of trouble?"

"Don't know. I just need to find her." Zoe lets out a heavy sigh. As she draws her hands free from her jacket, Nicole catches a glimpse of something clutched between her fingers.

"What's that?" she asks.

Zoe opens her hand, exposing a weathered wooden figurine. "Meier gave it to me. It was with my Dad's stuff."

"Can I see?" Zoe hands the carving over. The wood feels smooth and warm in Nicole's palm. She inspects the ambiguously gendered effigy, turning it over and over in her fingers, taking note of the thick bands of red and white grain. The piece is no more than three inches tall, but the details are lovely—sloping forehead, broad, strong shoulders, deep set-eyes. One leg is extended as if the figure is about to kneel. It looks familiar somehow. Nicole tugs her bag open and digs inside the main pocket, pulling out the book. She flips through the entries, searching for an image.

The sketch she finds is accurate to the last detail. She turns the book towards Zoe. "This carving is in the journal."

Zoe pulls the book closer, squinting at drawing. She points to the text winding around the image. "What does that say?"

Nicole is so used to the flourished handwriting that translating the text comes easy, even across the table and upside-down. "'Blood and bone crafted from wood. A servant to the dead.'"

Her sister flashes her a skeptical look. "You're making that up."

"I wish." Nicole closes the book and sets the carving down on the table. The figure's hollowed eyes stare back at her. Her skin tingles. She picks up her spoon and attempts to fish the swollen hunk of bread out of her food. "When's our flight?"

"A few hours." Zoe responds. "How's the stew?"

Nicole takes a bite. It was probably better when it was hot. Or maybe it was better when the base ingredients were not mixed together. She swallows politely and pushes the bowl away. "It's pretty nasty, actually."

Kostich's Paris report was slipped into her morning briefings. It was a breezy read, full of half answers, self-glorification, and general cocky bullshit. Eli claimed to have a concrete lead on the Hudson sisters, and sighted the loss of a valued informant and a seasoned operator as acceptable collateral damage for the finding. The man's arrogance is impressive.

Case takes a deep drag off her cigarette.

She is waiting.

Eli, and the remaining members of his small team, landed on the mainland half and hour ago. He should be back by now. Case cleared her late morning schedule, allowing him time to realize Allison Hudson has been moved and his access to her restricted. Having Fletcher in her corner has been more useful than she could have imagined.

She can hear yelling just beyond her office door. Her secretary protests. "Mr. Kostich, you don't have an appointment. You can't just barge in—"

Case snubs out her cigarette and laces her fingers together, elbows propped on the armrests of her chair. She smiles to herself as Eli barrels through her door, red faced and furious, suit jacket balled up in his clenched fist.

"What the fuck are you playing at, Tricia?"

Past him, Case can see her secretary in the threshold. "I'm sorry, ma'am."

She stands, moving around the front of her desk, hand raised, calling her assistant off. "Hold all my calls, and please, close the door."

"Ma'am." The woman backs out of the office.

Eli's anger is radiating off of him. "You jacked my prisoner, you crazy bit—"

She cuts him off. "Shut your mouth. Sit down."

He glares at her.

"Sit down."

He flicks his jacket over the arm of the chair and drops into the seat, scooting the heavy chair back on the polished concrete floor.

Case picks up her tablet, pulling up his report. "You've been a busy little bee, haven't you? Your man in Paris made quite the mess."

He crosses his arms, an indignant scowl on his face. "I got closer to Hudson than you—"

"You tried to blindside me. You moved in on my objectives without permission. And you murdered an asset I spent years developing." Case slams the tablet down on her desk. "Muscling in on the mother wasn't enough; you had to go for everything. Come back to Victor looking like some conquering hero? Well, I won't let you take away everything I've worked for. Not now. Not ever."

The boredom on his face burns her deep inside. He does not seem to understand the gravity of the situation. Case pushes the police images Fletcher acquired to a larger display mounted on the wall. "You left two dead bodies in Paris! It is unacceptable! No matter how much you massage this report, you came back empty handed. You put everything we've worked for in jeopardy."

He glances at them, shaking his head. "Nothing connects the Russian to us. And your informant got greedy. He became a liability—"

"My informant was a reliable source of intel on a woman we cannot touch." She pushes a series of images to the screen, a mix of grainy telephoto surveillance and glossy publicity stills. "You sent an extractor after Caroline Royer? What were you thinking?"

A fine sheen of sweat appears at Eli's temple. "We tracked them to her apartment. Your bullshit asset held out on us. He tried to squeeze me for a bigger pay-off—"

"You don't get it, do you?" She presses off her desk, crossing the floor swiftly, finger stabbing the display. The crisp photo appears of Caroline, smiling politely for the cameras at a charity auction, flanked by her mother and father. "This isn't about the Frenchman. Going after this woman was never an option. We established that years ago. Zoe Hudson's girlfriend was too well connected, too high profile. That is why Durand was tapped. He drove a wedge, helped push them apart. It took years of constant pressure, and you ruined it!"

His smug expression crumbles, and for the first time, fear creeps in to his eyes. "I didn't ruin shit—"

"Shut your mouth." Case leans over him, sinewy muscles flexing as she grips the leather arm of the chair. Her voice drips with condescension. "You sent a hit man after Gerard Royer's only child. That man has defense contracts with every major intelligence organization. He could blow us wide open within a month if he could connect us to her."

His jaw clenches, cheeks hollowing out as his breath escapes through gritted teeth. "He won't connect us."

"You better pray he doesn't." Case glares, leaning back against her desk. "You're a fuck up, Kostich. Ever since you started here, you've been nothing but an ass-kissing leech. What Sutton saw in you, I will never know. But Victor will not live forever, and when he is gone, there will be no place for you in this organization that is not under me. Are we clear?"

He does not make a sound.

Case cocks her head and crosses her arms. "I said, are we clear?"

Eli chokes on his response. "Yes."

"Good." She sits down at her desk and starts reading the next packet. "Now get out of my office."

He stands, his movements more controlled than when he entered. He grabs his jacket and heads for the exit. The door closes quietly behind him.

Case smiles to herself, letting the sense of accomplishment wash over her. She dials her cell, holding the slim device up to her ear. "Fletcher? Get me on Sutton's schedule before the meeting." She stares at Eli's report. "I have promising news."

***

Captain Foster is going to be pissed.

She jumped ship, ditching her responsibilities with no notice. There was no time to explain. Mom sounded so frantic. She was so certain Nicole was in trouble. Though things between them have been strained for over a decade, Zoe knew blowing her mother off was not an option this time. As soon as the call was over, she raced back to her bunk, threw her things together and slipped off boat during the commotion of load out. An hour after docking, Zoe was sitting in the sun-drenched terminal of the Mumbai airport, waiting for a very expensive flight to New York City. And like that, she was gone. A thousand miles between her and the Trident before anyone noticed she was missing.

Yeah. Foster is definitely going to be pissed.

She leads Nicole up the gangplank and onto the deck of the Trident. Being back here makes her stomach swim. She pushes the feeling aside, weaving her way through the scattered cargo containers that litter the deck, heading for the navigation tower. Once inside, the cool, stale air calms her. No matter what has happened, this ship stabilizes her. She lets out a breath and nudges Nicole. "This way. Come on."

They walk quietly through the corridors and hang a left to go down a constricted stairwell. A few crewmen pass by. The men look familiar, but Zoe doesn't know them well. They each give her a stiff nod and continue down the hall past Foster's office. His door opens wide as always. She can hear him typing inside. The distinct sound of his index fingers seeking and stabbing keys.

This is going to be an unpleasant conversation at best. She raps on the metal door and motions for Nicole to follow. They tuck inside his office.

Foster looks up from the computer and grumbles, "Where in the ever-loving hell have you been?"

"Sir." Her eyes adjust to the dim light of his desk lamp. Zoe stands still and straight while Nicole fidgets behind her. She turns to her sister and gestures towards a battered leather sofa. "Why don't you sit down?"

Nicole sets her bag down and cautiously sits on the cracked cushion. Her expressive brown eyes are wide, searching her surroundings. Foster tugs off his wire-framed glasses and tosses them onto his desk. He points at Nicole. "Who the hell is that?"

"My sister." Zoe responds flatly.

"Didn't know you had one of those." Foster pushes away from his desk. His eyes narrow, cheeks turning a rutty shade of red above the peppered gray of his beard. "Why the hell is she on my boat?"

"I'm keeping an eye on her for a bit."

From the look on his face, Foster does not like that answer. He scrubs his chin. "So I take it you're not back to work then?"

"No." Her mouth is dry. She struggles to swallow.

"Why the hell are you here?"

No use pussyfooting around. "I need to take a look at the ship's communication record—"

"Like hell you do." Foster stands; the chair scrapes against the metal floor. His hands are braced against the edge of his desk. "You've really got a pair on you, you know that, Hudson? Sniffing around for favors after being gone for a whole fucking month. I try to give you the benefit of the doubt, but you left the entire team in a lurch during a peak salvage season—"

"The ship's still docked for repairs—" It comes out as a shout. Probably not the smartest move on her part.

"That's not the *point*, Zoe." He yells right back at her, crossing in front of the desk, drawing closer, accusatory finger pointed in her direction. "You ran off!"

"I know I probably should have talked to you first," she says shaking her head, "But there wasn't time—"

"Bullshit!" He grumbles. "This is your job, Hudson. You can't just ditch it whenever you feel like it. You have responsibilities. To the crew. To me." Foster shakes his head. "If you weren't so fucking valuable to this team, I would be seriously considering firing your scrawny ass right now."

It was never her intention to disappoint him. She has never felt like such a shit. "I'm sorry."

"Yeah, well, that's really nice, Hudson, but sorry ain't going to cut it this time." Foster crosses his thick arms. "I think you owe me some answers, kid."

He's right. She does. But answers are getting harder and harder to come by. Zoe exhales slowly. Avoiding his stare, she searches the details of his office, trying to piece together the most compelling argument she can manage. "The morning we pulled into port, I got a phone call from my mom. She told me I needed to get to my sister. Quick. I got a flight to the states and—"

"Your mom couldn't find a more convenient babysitter?"

"She's not babysitting me." Nicole's hoarse voice pipes up from the couch.

Foster squints. "Excuse me, young lady?"

"I'm seventeen. I don't need anyone to babysit me."

He arches an eyebrow, his jaw tensing with frustration. "Hudson, can you make her—"

"Nicole, please. Not now. Okay?" Her sister slumps back into the couch, arms crossed, bitter expression on her face. Zoe steps closer to his desk, speaking low, trying to keep her voice as calm as possible. "I know I screwed up. But I swear to you, it was something I had to do. And now it's been a month since I've heard anything from our mom, and really weird shit keeps happening to us. I don't know what's going on, but I think she might know. I just need some help finding her. That's all I'm asking for. Just a little help."

"So what happens after I give you the comm records?"

"I'll need Jake to trace the call."

"Shit, Zoe," he sighs, pinching the bridge of his nose. "Kohama's a little busy, what with rewiring half the comm relays in the bay. He doesn't have time for—"

"It'll take Jake an hour tops to do this."

He shakes his head, sitting on the edge of his desk. His hands bracing his bulk. The look he shoots her is slathered in sarcasm. "Since when are you so eager to help your mom?"

Zoe shrugs. "Things change."

"Like hell they do." Foster chuckles. "You've got no love for that woman, even I know that. Way you ran off, I figured this was about your dad."

"He's dead."

The captain looks shocked. His features grow pale. He looks how she feels inside, but she cannot let it show.

"It happened a long time ago." She pauses. "There was a fire. The coroner's report said it was the smoke—" Her throat closes. No more words come. A shiver rolls through her, and Zoe crosses her arms to stem the involuntary tremor.

"I'm sorry." Foster places a hand on her shoulder. "Are you going to be okay?"

Zoe nods. "I have to be, right?"

Her words come out light, but they drop like an anchor in her gut. Dragging up debris and worst of all, feelings; things she has kept hidden for years. The fear of being alone. No father. No mother. No one.

Except for Nicole. At least she would have her. A sister. They would have each other. But it would still feel empty.

Their mother is far from a perfect person, but at least she had tried to reach Zoe. She would track her down, usually at the worst possible times. And sometimes, the roles would be reversed. Zoe would get drunk and sentimental, missing the happy family folded up in her passport. She would call the good doctor, late at night, early in the morning. The conversation would be strained, awkward, ultimately painful, and always end in an argument. Emotions would churn, like sediment rising in clear water, clouding everything. Reminding her why she left in the first place. And then the loneliness would set in, crushing her chest like a weight.

There is a creak and she snaps back. Foster has taken his seat behind his desk; he forces a sympathetic smile. His attention turns back to whatever is on his computer screen. He puts his readers back on. "I'll let Kohama know."

"Thank you. Sir." And just like that, she gets her way. A part of her almost feels guilty. Zoe swallows the lump in her throat and changes the subject. "How are the repairs going?"

"Same as always." He shrugs. "We do the best we can with the budget we've got."

Even before she left, she could see money was getting tight. The Trident just wasn't running into the same kind of luck as previous years. Legitimate funding was drying up, and their contracted jobs were getting more and more legally gray. Jones started the exodus of quality employees years ago, but now other seasoned crewmen were turning in their notice, hoping to find more prosperous opportunities elsewhere. Foster tried to hide it, but the disappointment and mounting stress showed on his face and in the ever growing presence of gray in his once dark hair.

She owes him so much.

Zoe turns to her sister. Nicole is predictable, tucked up on Foster's couch, trying to keep herself out of the way, reading the tattered journal. Zoe crouches next to her, holding out a hand. "Can I have the journal?"

"Sure." Nicole marks her place and gives it over. "Why?"

Zoe stands, crossing back to the desk and setting the book on the scratched metal desktop. Foster looks confused. His broad hands pull the object closer, gingerly inspecting the brittle yellow pages.

"Wait a minute. What are you doing?" But Nicole's protests come too late.

"That belonged to my father," Zoe says. The words almost break her, but she continues. "I want you to have it. It's got to be worth something if you can find the right buyer."

"Zoe!" Nicole is up off the couch, tugging at her arm. Her sister sunburned cheeks flash even redder. "You can't do that. We need it."

"No, we don't, Nik. It's just a book." She understands why Nicole is upset, but the debt she owes this man is greater than her need to hold onto whatever scraps are left of her father. Zoe pulls free and looks back to Foster.

He is staring at the book. For a moment she thinks he might not accept it, that he might hand it right back to her. They are so alike. So unwilling to accept help. She hopes this time will be different.

His hands retreat from the pebbled cover. He leans back in his chair and scratches at his beard. "You two look tired as hell. Go bunk down. I'll page you when Kohama's finished tracing that call."

CASE SITS ACROSS FROM SUTTON, a smug smile of satisfaction on her face. She is still coasting on endorphins left over from her midmorning reaming of Kostich and the recovery of her op. Watching him sweat and squirm did wonders for her mood.

There was a wealth of valuable information in Eli's report. After a few necessary adjustments, Case felt confident she could present the findings to Sutton prior to the weekly meeting.

Though now chilled in a Paris morgue, her informant was able to confirm the Hudson sisters are in possession of the artifact. Her boss seems quite pleased with that bit of information.

Sutton places the tablet down on his desk. "This is excellent work, Tricia. I knew you would respond well to the introduction of competition."

Case gives him a modest nod. "Sir."

"When do you anticipate an acquisition?" Sutton checks his watch and begins to roll up his sleeve.

"Soon." She can just hear the swish of his office door.

Fletcher comes into her periphery, a small black bag in his hand. Sutton sits, draping his arm over his chair. He continues to talk, but her focus is elsewhere, distracted by the process being conducted before her. The meticulous way Fletcher opens the bag, withdrawing thick surgical gloves and a long syringe. The yellowish latex stretches over Fletcher's fingers, popping as he pulls the gloves into place.

A thick band of rubber tubing holds tension, forcing purple veins to the surface. Fletcher flicks at a syringe full of a milky liquid, watching air bubbles rise. Case watches as the needle penetrates the thin skin at the crook of Sutton's arm. Blood courses from his pale flesh, red mixing with the white solution in the syringe.

She has never been fond of needles. A shudder creeps through her.

"Is there a problem, Ms. Case?"

"No, sir." She fights for composure, still unable to take her focus off the process. Until Fletcher informed her, Case had never realized Sutton was ill. Now that she knows, she can't see anything but his weakness, his frailty. His skin is somehow thinner, more sallow, his cheeks more hollow, bones more pronounced. She watches Fletcher withdraw the needle, replacing it with the pressure of a small swatch of gauze. His motions are so practiced, so delicate.

Her cell phone vibrates in her jacket pocket, snapping her out of her daze. There are no scheduled field operative check-ins and her private line is not available to her lower-level subordinates. She checks the incoming number on the display. "Excuse me, sir. I need to take this."

Sutton rolls down his sleeve. He nods, giving her permission to connect the call.

Case stands, walking to the far side of the room as she presses the cell to her ear. "Yes?"

The connection is poor, but the gruff voice is familiar. "I've got them."

She can feel herself begin to relax. This is how things are supposed to go. Smooth. Clean. "Excellent."

"One more thing you might be interested in," he adds. "She had it with her."

Case's heart skips, lips curling into a wicked smile. "Do you have it?"

There is a pause. "It's on my desk."

"Good. Keep things quiet. I'll be in touch with a rendezvous point." She hangs up and turns to Sutton.

He cocks his head. "That was good news, I suspect?"

She pockets her cell, straightening her jacket as she exits his office. "Yes, sir."

***

Every corridor on this boat looks identical, all lined with the same brushed metal walls and gray paint, security cameras tacked up into corners. The place feels like a fortress, which, abstractly, should make her feel safe. But the oppressive color scheme and sideways glances they are getting from crewmen only make her feel more anxious. Zoe seems fine. Maybe she's not super talkative, but she's definitely comfortable with her surroundings. She leads down another narrow stairwell and comes to a stop outside a nondescript reinforced hatch. After entering a code on the keypad mounted next to the jamb, the locks disengage with a loud pop.

"This is me." Zoe pushes the door open. When it won't budge she gives it a stiff bump with her shoulder.

Once the lights are flicked on, Nicole begins to understand why the door needed coaxing. There are piles of clothes on the floor, a complicated mess of dive gear is flung on the cramped recessed bunk, and dirty dishes clutter the fold-out table. She's seen dorm rooms in better condition then this.

Nicole nudges a lone sock resting on a plate that maybe once held spaghetti. "You actually live in here?" Zoe rolls her eyes, and thought she may be annoyed, there is a twinge of shame present on her face that Nicole finds amusing. "This is impressive."

"It's not that bad." Zoe kicks at the hefty pile of laundry, scooting it into the corner of the room. "Just a little messy."

"A little messy? You're a filth wizard." Nicole closes the door and hangs her bag on a vacant hook. There are hooks, hooks where things could be hung and instead of being tossed all over the floor. There are even a few drawers built into the wall, but from the look of things, they don't get much use. "It looks like a tiny bomb went off it here."

"Ha. Ha. Funny." Zoe shakes her head. She carefully clears the gear off her bunk and begins to halfheartedly tidy the space. "Kind of had to leave in a hurry, you know?"

Nicole plops onto the now empty bunk. She never thought about how quickly Zoe had to act. When she showed up unannounced and started bossing Nicole out of the dean's office, the only feelings she could manage were confusion and frustration. There was no room for sympathy or gratitude. Her sister left her livelihood and flew to the other side of the world just in time to save her from men with guns. She has kept her safe. "Sorry."

"Don't be." Zoe flashes a lopsided grin as she shoves jeans into a drawer. "I am kind of a pig."

"No. That's not what I meant." Nicole fidgets with her sleeve. "I'm sorry you had to come get me. It really screwed things up for you."

"Nothing that wasn't already a little screwed up." She sits on the bunk. Her hands run the length of her thighs, smoothing the worn fabric of her jeans. "I don't regret coming to get you. It was the right thing to do and besides, you and Mom are all the family I've got left. Might as well start taking care of you two. Right?"

There is a pang of guilt. It's been days since Nicole has thought about their mother. Everything is happening so fast. She hasn't had time. Even as she thinks it, she realizes how poor an excuse that is. They were in Paris three days and she might have been exhausted and sick, but not once did she think to try and contact her mom. There were plenty of opportunities. She could have tried to call or asked to borrow Caroline's computer, logged into her email and sent a short note. *We're okay. Hope you are too. Love, Nicole.* Anything. Instead she obsessed over the journal; fussing over centuries old manifests and daily entries, as if translating them might help Zoe find her father.

Lot of good that did.

Nicole picks at a fresh hangnail on her thumb. "What if this doesn't work? What if he can't trace the call?"

"We'll find her, Nik," Zoe says softly, placing a hand on her knee. "I promise."

Nicole nods.

Zoe kicks her shoes off, launching the abused sneakers in opposite directions. "There's something I've been meaning to say—"

"What?" Nicole asks, worried. "Is something wrong?"

"No. Nothing's wrong," she sighs. "I just wanted to thank you."

"For what?"

"For going to Zurich with me. Having you there helped." Zoe scrubs her fingers through her hair. Her voice breaks a little, growing unsteady. "So, thank you."

It's the nicest thing Zoe's ever said to her. Nicole moves closer, looping her arm under her sister's. A yawn slips out between words as she speaks. "You're welcome."

Zoe pats the bunk's stiff mattress. "Now get some sleep."

"What about you?" Nicole asks.

"Not tired." Her sister rubs her neck. "Think I might actually go for a walk."

The dark circles under Zoe's eyes tell a different story. Paris may have offered a moment of rest, but she's been running on fumes for a while now, and Nicole sees it. She tightens her hold on Zoe's arm. "Can you just lay down with me for a minute? Until I fall asleep?"

"Yeah." Zoe gives her a weak smile and kisses the top of her head. "Sure."

Nicole scoots back, trying to make room. The bunk is small, barely enough space for one of them, let alone both. When Zoe lies down, her legs drape over the edge. The sight must look ridiculous. The two of them curled up like cats. Nicole rests her head on her sister's shoulder. The cotton fabric of her shirt is soft against her cheek. She focuses on the steady beat of her heart. How her breath grows softer. Deeper.

And within minutes, Zoe is asleep.

AFTER THE DOCTORS EXAMINED her and stitched up the gash in her forehead, they gave her a clean pair of hospital scrubs and turned her over to the police, who talked to her for what felt like hours. They walked her through the attack a hundred times, asking her the same questions over and over. The answers came out sounding mechanical and emotionless. No, she didn't know the man who broke into her apartment. He didn't tell her anything. He barely spoke at all. She had no idea what he was after. And no, she couldn't think of anything else, but if she did, she'll be sure to call. Certainly, Detective.

By the time her cousin is finally allowed to collect her, it is the middle of the night. She has already made up her mind.

Caroline slips into the passenger seat of Gabriel's car, slamming the door firmly shut. "Take me home."

He nods, indicating as he exits the parking garage. They drive in silence, her cousin fuming, hands gripping the steering wheel and shifter tight enough to turn his knuckles white. He is angry, or worried. She cannot tell.

They pass the turn for her flat. "Where are you going?" she asks.

"I'm taking you home to my place." He changes lanes, turning away from the river and towards his house, deeper in the city. Gabriel brings the car to a stop at a red light, and places a hand on Caroline's knee. "I want you to stay with me until things calm down."

She'll be damned if she'll let anyone coddle her right now. Caroline thumbs the door lock and slips out of the car, weaving in between the stopped traffic. Headlights cast long shadows on the pavement as she passes in front of the beams.

It's not that far. She can walk to her apartment from here. Horns honk behind her. Someone is shouting. She does not look back, focusing instead on the feeling of rough pavement under her bare feet.

"Caroline!" Gabriel yells. "Stop."

She quickens her pace, ignoring her cousin. He does not understand.

The snarled traffic behind her grows louder. People are yelling. A warm hand takes hold of her arm, stopping her. Gabriel turns her around, face red. "What the hell are you doing?!"

"I'm going home." She wrenches her arm free. "And if you're not going to help me get there, then leave me alone."

The light turns green. Angry motorists lay on their horns, protesting the obstruction caused by Gabriel's vacant vehicle. Exasperated, he sighs, "Fine. I'll take you home. Just please, get back in the car."

She leaves her keys in the lock and tears down the crime scene tape, crossing the threshold as her stomach flips inside her. Underneath the anger and the sense of violation, she can feel the twinge of fear. The rational part of her knows there is nothing to be afraid of. Gabriel is here, and the hulking man who broke into her apartment is lying on a slab in the Paris morgue.

There is no time for fear.

Caroline flicks on the light switch, bathing the apartment in soft, warm light, exposing the aftermath of the morning. The floor is dotted with outlines and evidence tags. Her kitchen is a sea of tiny markers, highlighting droplets of blood and broken glass.

For no particular reason, Gabriel's voice comes out as a whisper. "Are you sure this is a good idea?"

"I just need to grab a few things." She heads down the hall, trying to avoid looking at the blood spattered all over her kitchen cabinets. "It won't take long."

She pushes open the door to her bedroom. The sheets are still tossed about; Zoe's discarded clothes lay in the same place they fell two nights ago. She picks up the threadbare t-shirt, remembering how she poked fun at Zoe for not owning anything with buttons. She dressed her that morning after they showered. Delicate fingers taking great care to slip every button through its appropriate catch. Zoe looked so handsome. So beautiful. Her cheeks feel hot, tears threatening to slip free.

"This is her fault, isn't it?" Gabriel is leaning in the threshold, watching her.

She doesn't have to answer him. She rolls up Zoe's shirt and heads for her closet.

"God damn it, Caroline." His fist hits the jamb. "That woman is a hurricane."

She grabs a carry-on bag and begins to fill it. "She's in trouble and she needs my help."

"Your help?" he snort. "Caroline, listen to yourself. Someone broke into your flat and tried to kill you. You don't need to help her. You need to stay the hell away from her." He pauses, waiting for her rebuttal, but all she can manage is a stern look. "Whatever Zoe Hudson has gotten herself into, it's dangerous. You can't go throwing your life away for some woman who has done nothing but hurt you—"

She swallows the lump in her throat, shaking her head. "You don't understand."

"Make me, Caroline! Explain it to me. Tell me why you keep letting her do this to you?"

Her voice breaks. "I love her."

Gabriel sets his jaw, shaking his head in amazement. "She's not worth it, Caroline."

Everything stops. Her eyes close, hot tears roll down her cheeks. "Go home, Gabriel."

His expression softens. "I'm sorry. I shouldn't have said that—"

Caroline continues to pack. "Leave."

"Caroline, please—"

"*Get out!*" Her head pounds, stitches throbbing as blood pumps quickly through constricting veins.

"I'm sorry."

She can see the sincerity in his eyes, but it doesn't make what he said any less out of line. Gabriel leaves the bedroom as Caroline zips up her bag with shaking hands.

What she needs is someone who understands her. Someone who understands Zoe. A person who cares for them both.

She grabs her cell phone off the nightstand and thumbs through her contacts, stopping on the only man she knows who won't judge her right now.

The speaker pulses in her ear. "Please pick up, please."
The line connects.
"Matthew?"

IF FOSTER PAGED HER, she didn't hear it. Zoe checks the clock. It's been hours since she dozed off, plenty of time for Jake to trace the call, but she hasn't been able to bring herself to move, worried she will disturb Nicole. Her sister looks so peaceful, fast asleep, her freckled arm draped across Zoe's chest.

Nicole stirs, shifting her weight and murmuring softly. It's the best opportunity she's going to get. When Nicole begins to roll over, Zoe gently lifts her arm and slips out from under the warm weight of her sleeping sister. She mutters something unintelligible and presses her body tight to the cool metal wall. Zoe grabs a blanket from the foot of the bunk and tucks her in. Nothing wakes this kid. Zoe hits the lights on her way out, closing the door quietly behind her.

The hall is empty. That shouldn't feel odd at this hour; any time they pull into port for an extended period, the crew complement dwindles. It's a cost cutter. Keep the specialists and permanent employees. Let the seasonal sailors go. So many of the Trident's systems are automated, a skilled skeleton crew is all the old girl needs. Even still, it's unnerving. A part of her has always preferred the boat during peak seasons, when the corridors bustle with activity.

She walks slowly, hands dug deep into her pockets, headed for the crew lounge on the other side of the ship. She weaves her way through engineering, past the dimly lit medical bay and the massive airlock to the ship's launch bay. The steady hum of fluorescent lights fills her ears, calming her.

The feeling is short lived.

She enters the lounge and beelines for the coffee maker, searching the occupied tables for a friendly face—only to find Erik Bryce holding court over a handful of permanent crewmen. As she fills her mug, she can feel them watching her. Their eyes burrowing under her skin.

"Zoe?" A friendly voice drifts from behind her.

She turns, sipping the jet black mud from her mug. "Hey, Jake."

Jake Kohama is the youngest of the Trident's crew. Come to think of it, he can't be much older than Nicole. His dark, stick-straight hair flops obediently to the side, falling into his gentle eyes. He calls her over to his table in the far corner, where he is sitting alone. She can't fault the guy for wanting to keep to himself. Over the years, the two of them have always shared a certain black-sheep quality. Relieved to share his company, she takes him up on his offer.

Jake gives her a warm handshake and the broadest smile he can manage. "Foster said you came back."

"Yeah." She smiles. "Can't stay away forever. Who'll look after you?"

Jake lets out a sheepish chuckle.

Zoe sips her coffee. "You finished tracing that call?"

Kohama stares at her blankly. "What call?"

Zoe sets her mug down on the table and notices something that under any other circumstances would not worry her in the slightest: the ship's engines are operating at full power, churning deep in its belly, propelling the vessel forward at great speed. The diesel power plants thrum through all the surfaces of the ship. She didn't notice it before. She was too distracted, but she can feel it now against her hands as she rests them on the tabletop, and she can see it in the quivering surface of her coffee.

Jake's voice is timid. "Is something wrong?"

When she looks into the young man's eyes, she can see his discomfort. "When did we leave port, Jake? Where are we headed?"

"I—I don't—" He stammers his answer, refusing to meet her gaze. "I'm not supposed—"

She can feel bodies moving around her, other men in the lounge taking positions. Zoe stands, backing away from the table, away from Jake, and towards the open door that is now blocked by Bryce.

"Why don't you sit back down, Hudson?"

She doesn't have time for his bullshit. "Why don't you step the fuck out of my way?"

He laughs, shaking his head as he shoves her back. His tongue traces his chapped lips before he speaks. "Captain said to make sure you stayed put."

"What the hell is that supposed to mean?" She looks to the Jake. "What's he talking about? What did Foster say to you?" The boy is quiet. "God damn it. Answer me, Jake!"

Never one to pass up an opportunity to bully a younger crew member, Bryce barks, "Beat it, Ko-homo. The grown-ups need to have a little talk."

Jake avoids Zoe's stare and squeezes past the bulky man blocking the only way out of the lounge. She is left in the narrow room with a handful of former crew mates, most of them men she thought she could trust. Their hostility is like a current pulling her under.

"Get out of my way," she says it again, hoping for a different result.

He shakes his head. "Not a chance."

Zoe knows that look. If she is going to get past him, she will have to put him down first. Her fists clench, muscles twitching in anticipation. Finding the rage to deck Bryce will not be an issue. Getting away from the dozen or so other men in the room might be.

"You think you're so fucking special, don't you? Always Foster's little favorite. The biggest payouts. The best gear. Your own room. And a place at the top of the roster anytime you feel like gracing us with your presence." He surveys her with a sick glance. "That's not going to happen any more, Hudson. You stepped in some real shit this time, and instead of bailing your ass out like every time before, the captain finally made the right move." He sneers at her. "He's turning you in."

He is close. Within striking range. But her mind is misfiring, stuck on his words. "Turning me in? To who? Why?"

"You're done here, dyke." His face inches from her own, he stabs his finger at her chest, emphasizing each bitter word. "And you deserve everything that's coming to you."

Zoe grabs his collar. Cotton fabric stretches. Her head whips forward, hard bone of her forehead crushing Bryce's nose instantly. Blood gushes like a broken hydrant. She throws her knees up into his abdomen, repetitive strikes delivered as hard as she can manage as crewmen pull her off of Bryce.

He coughs. His distorted voice rings out over the din. "Fucking bitch! Broke my nose!"

She has to get to Nicole.

They have to get off this boat.

She writhes, fighting to break free of a dozen strong hands, fingers digging into her already bruised skin. She doesn't see his fist. Bryce's punch strikes her stomach, plunging deep, just below her ribs. Organs shift, muscles contract, and all the air rushes from her lungs. She is left coughing. He mouth gaping wide, breathlessly straining to recover. Her legs turn to liquid beneath her.

Bryce grips a fistful of her hair, wrenching her head back, stretching her neck at too steep an angle. Air sputters in ragged bursts from her nostrils. His mouth and chin are covered in blood, red is leeching into the stretched collar of his t-shirt.

"You're fucked." His lips pull into a caustic smile. As he speaks, cool spit and warm blood spatter Zoe's skin. He pulls a fist back and punches her. Hard.

Everything goes dark.

Nicole hears the door to the room quietly open. She pulls the blanket higher, pinching her eyes closed in an attempt to block out the bright light from the hall.

"Shut the door." Nicole mumbles her discomfort.

The door closes and the darkness returns. She scoots closer to the wall, making room for her sister on the bunk. "Finally got tired, huh?"

There is no response.

"Zoe?" Nicole rolls over, eyes squinting in the dark for her sister. "What's wrong?"

The size and shape of the person who entered the room does not match her sister. Nicole only realizes this when a strong hand reaches down, pressing a rag over her mouth and nose. The rag smells pungent and sickly sweet. She screams, taking in deep panicked breaths. Her hands slap limply at the shadow. Strong hands grab her wrists and press them firmly into the bunk's mattress. Her head swims, consciousness flees, her ears echo with the sounds of her own heart rate slowing. Every muscle shudders. She lets loose one final convulsion before her struggling stops.

- 9 -

SHE HASN'T SEEN MATTHEW JONES in a long time, not since his last visit some three years ago. At the time, he was all unruly long hair and bushy beard. So when a freshly shaved man in dark sunglasses and a buzz cut raps on her passenger door, it startles her. Caroline cautiously rolls down the window, worried she may be waiting in the wrong area. Once the tinted glass is down, she recognizes his easy smile.

Matthew leans against the door, plucking off his sunglasses to reveal a brutal black eye. "Going my way, sunshine?"

She grins and unlocks the door. "Get in."

He flings his duffel into the back and drops into the passenger seat. She can feel his stare as she merges back into traffic.

"I'd tell you you're looking good, but you kind of look like someone beat the shit out of you."

Caroline forces a weak smile, glancing at the battered man sitting next to her. "I could say the same for you."

"Yeah, well." Matthew adjusts his position in his seat, wincing. "Chicks dig scars."

She's never seen him in such rough shape. Two fingers on his right hand are taped together, and his knuckles are the sickly green of old bruises healing slowly.

It's the haircut and shave that she's really having trouble processing. Zoe often spoke of Jones's polarizing grooming habits, and how he had a shaved head and an intense handlebar mustache when she first met him. Caroline has a sinking suspicion his current look has less to do with whim and more to do with the abrasions, burns, and deep cuts that are still healing on his face.

"How many guys did they send after you?" He gestures at the stitches on her forehead.

She shakes her head, down shifting and slipping into a turn lane. "Just one."

"He grill you about Zo?" Jones asks.

"No," she says, "he didn't say much of anything."

"He get away?"

Her mind snaps back, recalling the crunch of bone against the edge of the counter. "No."

"Then you did better than me." Jones holds up his broken digits. The medical tape wrapping them together is dirty and frayed. "How'd you figure out he was after Zoe?"

Caroline focuses on the gridlock. "Trouble follows her."

"True enough." Matthew gives her a gentle bump with his elbow. "But I guess that's why we love her, right?"

Caroline changes the subject quickly. "You said you had a lead?"

He nods. "Got an ex-marine buddy who's CIA now. Guy owes me a favor, so he put me in touch with an FBI agent. A guy named Derrick Witten."

"FBI?" She cannot hide her disappointment. "But they only handle domestic issues. This is international. What good will that do us?"

"We won't know until we talk to him." Matthew pulls out his cellphone and checks the time. "We need a secure location for the meet up. You got one in mind?"

Caroline wrenches the steering wheel, guiding her vehicle past the snarled traffic, tires thumping against the lane reflectors as she accelerates down the on-ramp. "I know a place."

NICOLE FIGHTS TO OPEN her eyes and tries to focus on the dimly lit room she has awoken in. Her head is swimming. Her hands slip and sink into the distressed leather of a sofa. She pushes herself upright. Her equilibrium refuses to cooperate. The room warps around her. Every vein is being taxed beyond capacity, blood pumping through constricted pathways and making the space between her eyes and brain pulse. Her body feels sticky and slow.

She tries to get an idea of where she is, taking in the distorted information around her. She is no longer in Zoe's room, she knows that for sure. This room is different, larger. And there is the faint smell of smoke and dust. Her eyes still refuse to focus, but she can just make out the bulky shape of a man leaning towards her.

"Good. You're awake."

Nicole recognizes the voice. She squints, trying to get the shapes of Captain Foster's features to converge. Cool condensation touch her cheek. She flinches.

A water bottle pulls into focus. "Here. Drink this. It'll help."

Nicole slaps the plastic bottle out of his hand and presses herself as far into the corner of the couch as she can manage. She draws her knees up tight to her chest and presses her palms to her throbbing eyes. "What did you do to me?"

"It'll wear off in a little bit." He retrieves the bottle and sets it down on the floor near the edge of the couch.

"Wear off?" It takes her a moment to get his meaning. She drops her hands, dumbfounded, her voice cracking. "You drugged me?"

He doesn't answer, but his lack of response is just as good as an admission of guilt.

"Where's Zoe?"

Foster stays silent. He stands, retreating to his desk, taking a seat on its metal edge, his face falling into shadow. Now that her senses are clearing, "annoyed" really doesn't even begin to describe her feeling. "Furious" would be more accurate. She glares at the man, slowing her breathing to steady herself. "Where is she?"

Foster plucks the book from his desktop. "You were reading this."

"No." She shakes her head, and regrets it. Her stomach lurches. "No, I wasn't."

"Don't lie to me, kid. I saw you read it." There was warmth in his voice earlier when he talked to Zoe. It's gone now. "I need you to tell me what it says."

He expects her to help him. Nicole laughs bitterly. Her legs drop, bare feet stinging as they rest against the metal floor. She crosses her arms, jaw stiff, teeth clenched.

"Zoe's given me enough trouble as is." Foster rolls his eyes. "I don't need to deal with two Hudsons' worth of pain in my ass."

Bringing up Zoe is not going to help his case. And being uncooperative and stubborn is all she has left. "Fuck you."

Foster moves towards her. Nicole recoils. He gives her a half-hearted grin, sensing her apprehension, but under theses circumstances, it comes off looking far more sinister than he probably intended. "I won't hurt you." He offers her the journal. "Here, take it."

Nicole considers slapping the thing from his hand, but why take it out on the book?

He stoops in front of her and Nicole presses deeper into the couch.

"You had this page marked. Why?" He flips the book open to the drawing of a map and points at a series of numbers scrawled on the image. "These are nautical coordinates. Did you know that? What's at this location? Why did you mark this page? Just tell me and I promise I will leave you alone."

It was just a bookmark. A scrap of paper from an inflight magazine. She feels sick. "How could you do this to her? She trusted you."

Foster sighs heavy. He closes the book, righting himself and tossing the journal on the cushion next to Nicole. "This is just business."

"Business?" She cannot believe he is being so flip. Nicole is up, stepping into the captain's personal space. Her brain is running five steps behind her body and a hundred steps behind her mouth. "You bastard. This is the only place she felt safe and you do *this*. Why?" Nicole pushes him, palms slamming against his broad chest, rocking him back. Her own chest heaves, volume unchecked. "Tell me why!"

Foster does not retaliate, his face blank. At a full head shorter than him, she is not a threat. She is not Zoe. Nicole has no swagger. She's never hit anyone in her entire life. Violence does not come naturally to her, but now, in this moment, her fists ball, the tendons in her fingers strain, and her nails dig into her palms.

"I've got to pay the bills, kid."

The punch is instinctive. Her fist strikes his jaw. Her wrist collapses, painfully folding on itself, pinching nerves. A tremor runs through her, body reacting to an unfamiliar bone rattling impact. It hurt more than she would have ever expected, but she is determined not let him see her pain.

"You asshole," she growls.

Foster rubs his jaw. In the quiet she can just hear his fingers catching against his unshaved skin.

The phone on his desk rings. Eyeing her warily, he slap the flashing speaker button.

"What?"

The voice through the speaker sounds timid and young. "Captain, sir, their chopper is on approach."

"Okay, Kohama. I'll be right up." Foster disconnects the call. He smooths his mustache as he pushes away from his desk, moving past her

147

and pulling open the heavy hatch. Before he leaves, he turns back to Nicole, his face inscrutable. "Stay put."

The locks click into place after he slams the door.

DELICATE FINGERS TOUCH HER face, cupping her cheek. A thumb traces her lips. She opens her eyes to see Caroline hovering over her, long brown hair flowing over her shoulders, brushing the skin on Zoe's chest and neck. The sight of her is overwhelming. She shouldn't be here.

"Where—How are you—Why?"

She silences Zoe with a kiss, pulling away only to stroke her chapped lips. Warm fingertips move to Zoe's chin, then down her throat, slipping between the fabric of her shirt and her skin. Caroline draws closer. Her smile is so sweet, so calming. She whispers, her breath warm on Zoe's skin. Her voice is low and comforting, foreign words tumbling from lips just barely brushing the rim of Zoe's ear.

Caroline pulls away, withdrawing her hands as she sits up. "You need to wake up, my love."

"What?" Zoe tries to right herself only to feel an unbelievable amount of pain. Her muscles throb. Her hands are pinned behind her back, bound tight enough she can feel thick plastic digging into her wrists. Her shoulders ache.

Zoe knows this place. She remembers the steel supports, arching high like a cathedral. The ROV sways gently from its winch, and there is the familiar lapping sound of ocean water striking the metal grating of the launch pool.

Bryce tossed her in the damn launch bay. At least the coward had the good sense to put her somewhere secure so she can't finish beating the crap out of him. Getting out won't be impossible, but restraints and a lack of current security codes will make it take a while.

Zoe struggles to sit up, scanning for anything that she might be able to use to cut her bindings. If she could get her hands on a dive knife, she'd be in business, but they are all locked safely away in the gear cage.

Right now she'd settle for having her hands in front of her. At least then she could set to work on the door control, bound or not. Maybe she could short it out, somehow bypass the damn thing. Electronics and computers have never been her strong suit, but she is pretty sure she can break it if she can only touch it.

She squirms, folding herself in half, trying desperately to draw her arms forward and under herself, but the bindings are too tight. If she just had a few more inches of play, she could get her hands under her and down her legs. Just a few more inches.

Zoe spots something on the other side of the bay. The latch to the gear cage.

If she can dislocate her shoulder, she would be able to eke out the necessary distance. She lets out a sick laugh.

It happened before, years ago, at a bar in Hong Kong. Not that it was on purpose. Jones tried to warn her, but the vodka did most of the talking that night, earning her a busted lip, a serious concussion, and a dislocated right shoulder. It dangled there, limp and long, until the ship's medic reset it the next morning.

She rocks to her feet, stumbling across the metal grated floor to the gear cage. Once her bindings are hooked under the metal lever, Zoe lurches forward violently.

An audible pop echoes through her body.

The pain is blinding. She drops to her knees, disoriented, teetering forward until she crashes to the deck. Her cheek hits the metal floor hard. She can feel her stomach swimming, threatening to expel what little she has eaten in the last few days.

Zoe crumples into a tight ball, shaking as she begins to work her bound wrists under the curve of her ass. The thick plastic band cuts into her skin, but that pain is nothing in comparison to the fire in her shoulder. The extra length is barely enough. She tries to steady her breathing. Focus on breaking out of the bay, getting to Nicole. Anything to keep herself from passing out.

Her arms dangle before her, uneven. She staggers to the bulkhead near the hatch, adrenaline coursing, helping her concentrate, keeping her conscious. Her head rests against the cool metal. She lets out a manic laugh through clenched teeth, then counts to three before slamming her dislocated shoulder into the wall with every ounce of force she can muster. The impact drives the ball back into its socket, pinching nerves and sending electricity through her limbs. Her body spasms as convulsions take over.

She slips down the wall, crumpling on the floor.

THE MOST SECURE LOCATION she could think of is only a few hours outside of Paris. The Royer Aviation test site is off the map, a discretely guarded private installation most civilians mistake for a sleepy municipal airfield.

The man at the gate acknowledges her vehicle with a smile and a wave. He exits the guard shack, clipboard in hand. Caroline adjusts her hair, careful to hide the fresh sutures on her forehead. She rolls down her window, turning on the charm as she greets him in French. "Hello, Jean."

"Afternoon, miss. Going up today?"

"We're thinking about it." She nods towards Jones sitting in the passenger seat. Caroline gives the guard a sheepish shrug. "I actually have another friend on his way, but he had trouble keeping up with me."

He laughs. "Miss Royer, if you drive like you fly, I'll believe he did!"

For the first time all day, Caroline begins to relax. "When he gets here, do you mind pointing him to Hangar B?"

The guard grins, clicking his pen. "What's his name?"

"Witten. Derrick Witten."

The guard scribbles the name on the clipboard, then lifts the barrier, allowing them to pass. She lets out a sigh of relief as she watches the man drop the barrier and wave in her side mirror.

Jones smirks. "That was smooth."

Somehow Caroline thinks the rest of this won't go as smoothly.

They are not kept waiting long. The echo of unfamiliar footsteps on the concrete floor turns her attention towards the hangar door. Caroline ducks under the fuselage of the plane to get a better view of the man who has entered the hangar.

He removes his sunglasses, gesturing towards the jet. "Nice looking machine, miss."

"Agent Witten?" Caroline extends her hand.

"Stop right there." Jones exits the hangar office, pistol drawn and aimed at their guest. "Get away from him, Caroline."

"Matthew?" She pauses, startled and wondering where exactly Jones acquired a handgun. "What's wrong?"

The man holds up his hands. "Mr. Jones, if you will please lower your weapon, I can explain." He seems very collected given the fact he has a gun trained on him.

Jones steps between Caroline and the man, blocking her with his body. She tugs at the back of his t-shirt. "Matthew, what are you doing?"

"This guy's not a Fed."

"I assure you," says the man, "I am."

"Liar." Jones steps forward, brandishing his pistol aggressively. "You and that steroid freak-show left me for dead on my dock."

She has never seen Jones like this. Caroline backs away from him. "Somebody please tell me what the hell is going on? Now."

"He's not wrong about what happened in Brazil, Ms. Royer. He is, however, incorrect about my status with the bureau." Witten steps forward, lowering his hands slowly. "I am going to reach into my coat pocket to get my badge, Mr. Jones. Alright?"

She doesn't like the tension. The man withdraws a badge and tosses it to Jones, who catches it between his chest and the taped up fingers of his injured hand. He fumbles with the holder, careful to keep his gun on Witten. Not that she is the best judge of authenticity, but the document looks legitimate.

Jones seems to agree. He slips his gun back into the slim holster at the base of his spine and throws the badge back to the agent. "Start explaining."

"My name is Derrick Witten. I've been undercover with Victor Sutton's organization for nearly five years. My investigation was originally focused on his dealings in black market antiquities. Smuggling them into the States and selling to high profile collectors and museums. But it soon became very obvious that things went far deeper than that." He pauses, turning to Jones. "I am sorry for what I had to put you through, Mr. Jones. It was unfortunate, but necessary. I needed to maintain my cover. Your interrogation had to be—believable." Witten steps closer, slipping his badge back into his coat. "After our acquisition of Nicole Hudson was unsuccessful, I was skating on some pretty thin ice with my superiors."

Jones sneers, raising his taped fingers. "Yeah, sorry if I'm having a hard time giving a shit about your problems."

Caroline puts it together first. "You couldn't get to Nicole because Zoe interfered."

"Yes." Witten says. "She showed up right before I could talk to her sister. There was a chase. She took out my partner, which was no small feat. Then she took me down. Campus security found me unconscious in the parking lot."

Caroline can just make out the swollen lump on the agent's forehead, hidden by his dark complexion. Nice to know Zoe's worries about possibly assaulting a federal officer were actually grounded in reality. Caroline wonders what the legal ramifications might be for something like that.

"I tried to let Nicole know I was on her side. I could have gotten them both to a safe location if she had only trusted me. But she refused."

"Wonder why." Jones scoffs, his voice dripping with sarcasm. "Couldn't have anything to do with you chasing her down, could it?"

Witten presses on, letting the comment slide. "What I find shocking is that they chose to go after you, Ms. Royer."

"Why is that so shocking?" Caroline asks.

"You were on a black list. They labeled you too risky to use, coerce, or obtain. They had to settle for observing you. They've had surveillance on you ever since you and Ms. Hudson became involved."

Her stomach turns. "Surveillance?"

"You've been monitored by an informant for four years now." Witten pulls a photo from his pocket and hands it to her. "He turned up dead a few days ago."

If her gut was turning a moment ago, it drops to the floor after seeing the image. She covers her mouth with a hand, fighting back the bitter feeling rising in her throat. Jones takes the photograph as Caroline turns away from them both, nausea threatening to overcome her.

"What?"

"It's Max." Her voice trembles. Now is a strange time for Zoe to start being right about things. Caroline leans against the body of the plane, seeking whatever support it can provide. "He knew Zoe was in Paris. He knew she and her sister were with me. He—"

Witten draws closer, his look a mix of concern and interest. "What is it, Ms. Royer?"

Zoe never trusted Max. Caroline always thought it was classism paired with Max's puerile sense of humor. She never once thought he might be spying on them, but in retrospect it makes sense. His keen interest in their relationship. Always pressing for details. The way he treated Zoe. The little things he'd say to goad her. And then there were his is abrupt, extravagant expenditures. He was being paid to watch them. Caroline takes in a deep breath.

"Ms. Royer?" Witten presses.

Jones places two reassuring hands on her shoulders. "You okay?"

"Zoe had a book. Something her father left her."

Witten cocks his head. "Leather-bound? Very old?"

"Yes." She nods. "I didn't know what it was. She asked for my help, and I thought Max would be able to help. He appraised artifacts and antiquities for an auction house." Her voice breaks. "He knew about the book. He knew they had it, and I—"

Witten inhales deeply. "If Maxwell Durand knew they had the journal, the people paying him will definitely know."

The look of concern on Jones's face is impossible to mistake. "What does that mean for Zoe and Nicole?"

"It means you have less time to help them than I thought."

They have obtained both the book and the sisters simultaneously. If it hadn't been for Foster's data burst detailing some rather disappointing changes in the situation, this might have been a banner day. As the helicopter touches down on the deck of the Trident, Connor is the first one out the door. The wind whips at his clothes, pinning the fabric to his body. He turns, hand extended to help her from the carriage of the chopper.

Foster is headed towards them, mouth moving. He is trying to yell over the deafening sound of blades slicing through air. She cannot hear him. Case slams the door, rapping on the glass hard, signaling the pilot to leave. She watches the blinking red lights of the tail rotor ascend into the gathering darkness.

Case strides past Foster, heads for the nav tower. "Explain."

Foster grumbles, jogging to keep pace. "I already told you everything."

His report was not as thorough as she would have liked. The mention of the altercation and Zoe Hudson's subsequent restraint was mentioned as an afterthought, glossed over and buried. She expects more from her field operatives. Case tries to remind herself Foster is only a contract employee, and her expectations should be substantially lower.

Connor holds the door open for her. She slips past him and into the relative quiet of the ships interior. "Where is she?"

The captain scrubs his chin. "Which 'she'?"

"Don't get flip, Aaron." She has no time for his attitude.

"She's in the launch bay." Foster pauses, lowering his voice as a few crew members pass. "It was the safest place to put her after the fight broke out."

Case sighs, annoyed. "You should have kept a tighter leash on your men, captain. I swear, if your roughnecks damaged her in anyway, Mr. Sutton will not be pleased."

"Hudson's fine." The captain stares Case down. "And for your information, I don't have any problem keeping my crew in line—"

Case smiles mirthlessly. "Your men brutalized my target. If that's your version of control then I—"

"Don't bust my balls." He growls. "Zoe's not an idiot. She figured out where things were headed after we left dock. There was nothing I could do at that point."

A young man rounds the corner. He stops, sensing he has interrupting something private. The captain gives him a nod and waves him by. Case backs up, allowing the man to pass between them before she draws nearer to Foster. "You were told to be discrete. You failed. The corporation will not tolerate any further mistakes. Am I clear, Captain Foster?"

His nostrils flare. "Yes, ma'am."

"Good," Case looks down the corridor. "Where is the youngest?"

"She's in my office." Foster swallows hard and gestures down the long corridor.

"Take me to her."

She wasn't going to stay put for long. As soon as the locks bolt, Nicole is at the door, hoping there is a way to get it open from the inside. No luck with that. She scans the room, her head finally clearing from whatever Foster knocked her out with. There has to be another way out. But there are no windows. Everything is secured to the floor with large bolts, or built into the wall. Makes sense, considering how rough the waves can get. Can't have stuff slipping around. She's never been so annoyed at practical thinking.

The couch sits against the far wall, near the door and opposite a massive flatscreen television. She can see herself in the mirrored surface of the display. She is a complete wreck. Nicole rolls her eyes at her own reflection, tugging out the band holding her hair and combing her hands through her tangled curls. She pulls the entire mess back into something much more tidy, then moves around the captain's desk, pulling out the chair to gain access to the drawers. Pens, pencils, a stapler, and a half empty bottle of whiskey. Not exactly helpful. The rest of her searching is just about as uneventful until she rifles through his file drawer. There she finds a framed picture tucked under the hanging folders. It rests face down in the bottom of the metal drawer. Nicole removes the frame, turning it over to get a look at the image.

A younger Foster, sporting substantially less grey hair and a full beard, has his arm wrapped around a younger Zoe. Both of them are squinting into the sun. Her sister's skin is an even shade of golden brown, tanned as the day is long, her wetsuit pulled down to her waist exposing a bikini top and broad, well muscled shoulders. Foster is beaming, his big hand cupping Zoe's shoulder in a gesture of almost paternal pride. They are standing next to two massive cannon, their dark surfaces encrusted in barnacles and glistening in the bright sun. Seeing Foster smiling and holding her sister so fondly makes Nicole sick with anger. She tosses the frame on the desk and flops back into the chair.

She needs to get focused. There has to be some way out, some way to control the door from inside the room. She just has to figure it out.

Nicole snatches the phone off its base. It's a long shot, but maybe she could call out.

Hi. I'm on a boat. You know, in the ocean. We've been kidnapped. When you're not a kid can you still get kidnapped or are you just straight-up napped at that point? Whatever. Please send help.

She stabs out a number, but before she can complete it the receiver beeps harshly at her, refusing to connect. Someday, something will be that easy.

The locks snap back on the hatch. Nicole shoots up from behind the desk, expecting the captain. Instead, a tall woman in a crisply tailored suit enters the office.

"Hello, Nicole." Her voice is cold.

Nicole grips the edge of Foster's desk.

The woman's full lips pull into a sinister smile. She moves closer. "My name is Tricia Case. I represent a corporation that is very interested in a particular artifact you've been carrying."

Nicole sits, never taking her eyes off Case as she zeroes in on the discarded leather bound book sitting on the couch cushion. "What corporation? Who are you people? What do you want?"

"My, aren't you inquisitive." She purrs, picking up the book and carefully thumbing through its pages. "Just like your mother."

"Mom?" A tremor creeps into Nicole's voice. "H-how do you know my mother?"

"The man I work for is very influential. He was interested in meeting Dr. Hudson." She snaps the text closed and slinks towards the desk. Her heels click on the metal floor. "So I arranged an introduction."

Nicole sinks into Foster's chair as Case takes a seat on the edge of the desk. The closer this woman gets to her, the more it feels like all the air is being drawn out of the room.

"Now. Captain Foster tells me you can read this. That impresses me." Her voice is filled with mock disappointment. "But he also tells me you've refused to assist us in deciphering it."

She sets the book down in front of Nicole. Instinct takes over. Nicole reaches for the journal.

Case stops her, gripping her wrist with a dry, cool hand. She leans across the desk, whispering low, "I hope he's wrong about that. For your mother's sake."

Nicole freezes. And all at once she cannot breathe. Case's nails dig into her skin.

"Now why don't you be a good girl and tell me what it says."

- 10 -

ALLISON WAKES SLOWLY from the first decent sleep she has had in weeks. She is on her back, foot dangling off the edge of the bed, staring up at the ceiling, trying to memorize the texture of the concrete. It's not the most intellectual of exercises, but at this point any distraction will do.

They have left her alone for a few days now. Nothing to do. Nothing to read. She hates being alone with her thoughts. Stillness always brings back memories, and inevitably she circles back to the reason she is in this mess in the first place.

Zoe's father.

Hayden Thomas, with his bright green eyes and disarming smile. He made her feel like she was the only thing in the world that mattered. The only thing that was important. When she told him she was pregnant, he was elated. She let his excitement override her own fears. He assured her she would be an excellent mother and asked her to marry him that night. On the beach, under the stars, just past the dunes. It was so romantic. All too good to be true.

He was too good to be true. She should have known better.

A rapid knock sounds through the flat. Allison sits up, arms stretching wide as she rises to cross the darkened room. When she opens the door, a delicate young man is waiting outside.

"Good evening, Dr. Hudson," he says.

She has never seen him before. "Can I help you?"

He gestures towards the guard posted in the hall. "Edward informed me you asked to speak with Ms. Case."

Allison nods. She asked to see Tricia Case two days ago, but the stocky man guarding her door barely acknowledged her. She figured the request never got through.

"Unfortunately, Tricia is unavailable." In the sterile light of the hallway, the young man's pale skin is practically glowing. "But I am certain she will want to speak with you as soon as she returns."

Allison can sense something deeper in his meaning. "Where is she?"

"You'll know soon enough."

Allison's heart sinks. "It's my daughters, isn't it? She found them."

His smile is brilliant, a row of pearly teeth glistening between thin lips. He gives her a stiff nod and turns to leave. "Good evening, Doctor."

She watches him until he disappears around the corner. "Who was that?" she asks, feeling suddenly numb.

Edward shrugs, returning to his magazine. "That was Mr. Fletcher."

He says it like the name, in and of itself, holds enough meaning to be an answer. She waits for him to say something more. Anything. Instead, he peers over the top of his reading material and gestures for her to close the door.

She does so slowly, pressing her shoulder against the cool metal surface until she hears the latch catch. Her fears are overwhelmed by a surge of anger.

Allison shakes her head. All Zoe needed to do was keep Nicole safe, but apparently her wayward eldest daughter could not pull her shit together long enough to do that.

She is her father's daughter. Through and through.

NICOLE AGREED TO TRANSLATE the pages on one condition: she wanted to see her sister. Foster agreed to her terms. Case did not. But the captain managed to assure her Nicole's presence in the bay was in their best interests and would, in his words, "Keep Hudson from flipping out."

He's not wrong. Zoe is bound to be pissed.

Three men show up, and after the captain chews them out in the hall, Nicole is released into their custody. They guide her back down into the belly of the ship, only this time she's more aware of the cameras, their tiny lenses catching the light as they focus and follow. No wonder Foster had no problem letting her go; he can keep an eye on her no matter where she is. Nicole scowls at one of the cameras as they pass Zoe's room.

Always watching.

They reach a heavily secured hatch and everyone stops. The youngest of her escorts punches a code out on a keypad while the other crewmen flank her. There is a mechanical hum followed by a loud hiss as seals give way. An airlock? Really?

Red lights over the door turn green. The locks disengage. The young man fumbles with the lever, struggling to open the door. Of the Trident crew she's met so far, the poor guy opening the door looks to be the most anxious. His hands shake as he operates the airlock, and Nicole can see sweat soaking through his t-shirt.

He's not bruised up like the others. She has a feeling her sister is responsible for their injuries. Zoe does to love to head-butt people.

The muscle-bound pretty boy with the swollen eyes and seriously broken nose shoves Nicole towards the open hatch. "Move it."

She steps in. When the door closes behind her and the pressure begins to change, her ears pop with disapproval. They all wait there, listening to the low frequency hum as air is pumped out of the chamber. Once everything equalizes, the red lights go green and the thick-necked sailor covered in tattoos wrenches the hatch open. He grunts at her, insisting she exit first.

The surroundings are impressive. High-tech-looking machines sway from a complicated system of tracks suspended from arching bulkheads. And in the middle of it all, an eerily lit pool pierces the floor. That's why there was an airlock. They don't even have to go on deck to dive. They can do it from inside the boat. It's brilliant and strangely covert.

Her fascination comes to an abrupt halt. Zoe's limp body is sprawled on the floor just past the threshold. Nicole runs to her, dropping to her knees to carefully roll her over. Cupping her sister's face, she shakes her, urging her awake.

Zoe's eyes flutter open. She looks so confused.

"Hey, you." Nicole pushes strands of blonde hair out of her face. Her lip is split and swollen, bruises cover her face, and her hands are bound in front of her, wrists raw and bloody from the thick plastic band. She must have put up a fight, but they beat the crap out of her in the process.

"You're alright." Zoe's voice is unsteady. "No one hurt you, did they?"

"I'm fine. I promise." She tries to sound as reassuring as possible. "I'm not the one who got the crap kicked out of me."

There is a loud clattering and a sustained whir coming from behind them. The crew have gone straight to work prepping the bay. Zoe's attention is fixed on the men who accompanied Nicole. "Why are they prepping for a dive?"

She wants to tell Zoe about the section of the journal they made her decipher, but before she can get her thoughts organized, tanks and gear are dumped at her sister's feet. Zoe glares up at the man with the broken nose.

"Cap says you're diving."

"Foster can kiss my ass." She kicks one of the small tanks, sending it clattering across the floor. "You fucking do it."

"I'd love to, bitch. But the doc wouldn't clear me since you bashed my nose. So that means you're up." He crouches in next to the pile of gear. "Wonder how well you can swim with your hands all tied up like that?"

A timid voice calls out from the other side of the bay. "Leave her alone, Bryce."

"Shut your mouth, Ko-homo." Bryce yells, "Nobody's talking to you."

The young man turns away, lowering a huge yellow and white machine into the central pool.

"You never told me you had a sister." Bryce lets out a low whistle. "She's not so bad. And lucky for me ugly and titless doesn't run in your family."

Zoe is on her feet like a shot, pressing her way into his space. "Fuck off, Erik!"

"Bryce!" The tattooed sailor is half in a wetsuit at this point. He pulls gear from the lockers and yells across the bay. "Quit playing grab ass. Uncuff her already so we can get this shit over with."

"In a minute, Manny." Bryce moves in closer, his smile growing more sinister. "I'm just being friendly."

Nicole can see Zoe's body vibrating with rage. "You lay a finger on my sister and I'll finish what I started in the lounge."

Bryce smirks, smacking Zoe's bound hands. "Tough talk from the dyke in cuffs."

She lurches forward, raw hands clasped, ready to strike, but Nicole grabs Zoe's shoulders, pulling her back. The last thing they need right now is more blunt-force trauma. She holds her sister tight, pleading, "Please, stop. Don't do this."

"Listen to the girl, Hudson. You need to get your shit squared. This dive's a deep one. You'll be down for, what Reyes? An hour? Plenty of time." Bryce's lips curl into a sick smile. "And don't worry. I'll be gentle."

Case watches the surveillance feed from the bay on Foster's display. The captain is in his chair, nursing a bottle of whiskey. She could caution him about drinking in front of a corporate representative, but she doubts he would care. He is not in the most receptive of moods.

He sips his drink. "What if I send them down sixty meters and they don't find anything? What happens then?"

She rolls her eyes. "You should really try to be more positive, Aaron."

"Positive?" Foster lets out a stiff chuckle. "There's no telling if the artifact mentioned in that book will still be at this location. I hate to tell you, but the ocean doesn't stay put for anyone. Not even a man like Victor Sutton."

"We'll see about that, Captain."

He inhales deeply. The muscles in his jaw flex. They both turn their focus back to the video feed of the team entering the bay.

"What will you do with them when you're finished here?" Foster asks.

She can hear the fear creeping into his tone. His sentimental feelings are useless. Case keeps her eyes on the screen. "That is up to Mr. Sutton and absolutely none of your concern."

There is a flurry of movement on the screen. Two bodies collide, fists and knees connect with vicious force. Case can just make out Zoe, her hands bound at wrists and fighting with a ferocity Case rarely has the pleasure of witnessing.

"Shit." Foster exclaims as he scrambles out from behind his desk. The captain bolts out the door as more forms enter the fray on screen. Bystanders struggle to force the combatants apart.

Case crosses to his desk and plucks the half-empty glass of whiskey from the blotter. She moves closer to the display, downing the cheap alcohol and hissing as it burns down her throat.

***

She will pound Bryce through the floor if she has to. Zoe brings both fists down, striking the smug bastard across his already bruised face. He stumbles back, slamming into Reyes. The brawny man had dropped his gear and shot across the bay to separate them. Nicole is desperately trying to do the same. She has her hands clasped around Zoe's shoulders, nails digging in trying to restrain her. The kid is completely unaware how painful her hold is.

Nicole swings around Zoe, palms now firmly planted on chest. She shoves her. "Stop!"

Bryce struggles against Reyes, to little effect. Even awkwardly half dressed, and out of breath, Emmanuel Reyes is a formidable road block. He muscles Bryce away from Zoe and back towards the gear cage.

"Let me go, Manny!" Bryce kicks at Zoe, missing her and striking Nicole instead.

The kid's leg buckles. Her hold loosens. The opportunity does not go to waste. Zoe launches herself past her sister and directly at Bryce and Reyes. All she wants to do is hurt him. Her bad shoulder drives into his stomach, rocking the two men back and sending a shockwave of pain through her entire body. Bryce's knees slam upward, pistons striking her core. She can't block. She can't hit. Her bound arms are useless and tingling.

Salvation comes when two pairs of hands drag her backwards. Zoe gasps, sucking air into her battered lungs. Nicole and Jake support her weight. She scans the bay, searching for a weapon, an advantage.

Nicole twists her face towards her, forcing Zoe to make eye contact. "You have to stop! He's not worth it."

"You got fucked, Hudson!" Bryce calls out. "How's it feel, bitch?"

"Shut up, Erik." Reyes shakes Bryce by his shirt collar and shoves him back. Bryce is still twitching with anger but he turns away, pacing to catch his breath. Reyes points at Zoe. "Both of you."

Zoe nods. Jake and Nicole tentatively release her. She needs to cool down. Her wrists are bleeding from the cuffs, red soaking into the pale fabric of her button up.

Bryce licks at a fresh wound on his lips. "You're a fucking pathetic piece of shit, Hudson. You know that?"

He is baiting her. She knows it. It takes everything in her not to respond. Instead, it is Nicole who stalks forward and slaps Bryce full on the face, leaving a vivid red hand-print on his tan cheek.

"The only pathetic thing in this room is you," she exclaims.

Zoe stares in disbelief, so distracted by the protective display of affection that she doesn't see the knife Bryce has drawn until the blade is pressed to Nicole's throat.

Reyes steps closer. "Jesus Christ, Erik! What the hell are you doing?"

Bryce stumbles back, tightening his grip on Nicole and pressing the edge of his knife harder against the pale skin of her throat. She lets out a whimper. "I am sick of self-righteous bitches thinking they can fuck with me."

Zoe's brain is racing, trying to land on a solution to this situation that doesn't end in her kid sister's blood spilled all over the bay floor. "Please, Erik. Let her go."

"Fuck you." He draws the blade tighter. Nicole is shaking, her eyes snap closed. Fear takes hold.

There is a rattle and clank.

Bryce looks over his shoulder just in time to watch the oxygen tank crunch in to his face. The impact is intense, crushing his already broken nose. His grip on Nicole releases. She falls to the floor along with the knife. Bryce's unconscious body tilts backwards, crashing to the metal grating of the bay.

Foster sets the tank down and collects the knife.

"Reyes, get this shit-sack locked up." He pauses by Nicole placing a hand on her shoulder. "Are you all right, kid?"

Nicole nods, her body still trembling.

"Jake, I want you piloting that ROV. Get your ass in the online room. And you." Foster steps towards Zoe, hand fidgeting on the hilt of Bryce's knife. He cuts the zip tie pinning her wrists together. "Suit up."

There is shame written all over his face. A complete and utter self-loathing that is perfectly translated through his dead eyes. She doesn't have a choice in this. She understands that now. Without a word, Zoe turns to gather the gear she'll need.

Nicole steps between her and the row of lockers. "You can't do this. You're hurt."

"I'm fine, Nik." Zoe shrugs out of her sister's grip and fumbles with the pad lock on her locker.

"No you're not," Nicole says. "You need a doctor. You're just too stubborn to admit it."

Zoe stares at her, eyes losing focus. Mentally, she is no longer in the bay. She is already hundreds of feet beneath this place, her ears stifled by pressure, body heavy on the ocean floor. She is already gone and Nicole knows it. She looks furious, but her anger doesn't matter. Zoe pulls away from her and heads back to Foster. "I want her with you. She's on the comm channel the whole time I'm down, or I don't cooperate with whatever you've got going on. You got that?"

The captain nods.

"What! No. Zoe, don't do this. You can't—"

"God damn it, Nicole." Zoe slams her locker open. "Just shut your mouth and go with Foster."

Nicole protests fall quiet. She backs away, hurt.

Zoe returns to her preparations, pulling out one of her spare wetsuits. The hatch seals sound. When she glances back, Foster, Jake and Nicole are gone. The only people left in the bay are her, Reyes, and the unconscious dick-head locked in the gear cage. Zoe unbuttons her jeans, slipping them down her legs. She strips her shirt painfully off over her head and throws it into the wide open locker. Her skull is throbbing. She leans against the locker, hanging her head and breathing deeply through her nose.

Reyes's voice rumbles from over her shoulder. "I don't need you freaking out on me, Hudson. Pull your shit together."

He's right. She needs to get a grip. Focus.

Zoe pushes her discomfort aside and pulls her wetsuit on, tugging the neoprene over her bruised and mottled skin. This is her armor. Her protection. Something she understands. Something familiar.

The thick cable attached to the ROV continues to unravel from the winch, filling the bay with an eerie white noise. Her hands are shaking, raw wrists visible just past the sleeves of her wetsuit. She walks to the edge of the launch pool, fastening the straps of her buoyancy compensator. The heavy tanks clatter as she clips them into place. The shimmering skin of ocean is stretched tight across the mouth of the portal.

Reyes tilts his head, adjusting vertebrae in his neck with a few satisfying pops. He pulls on his mask, obsessively checking his gear one last time. Zoe's vision swims, and the room folds and buckles before her. She squints, tugging on her mask and checking the gate on her breather. The suction presses against every cut and bruise. She flicks on the comm link to hear static, then changes to the normal channel.

Reyes's steady breathing fills her ears, in stark contrast to her own erratic gasps. Her heart will not stop racing.

The tattooed man flashes her a bitter glare. "You ready for this?"

She takes another deep breath to settle her nerves and flips him off.

Reyes shakes his head. "Now that's more like it."

There is a buzz on the headset, followed by a burst of static and the muffled sounds of movement. Nicole's voice sounds distant, a worried murmur from a far-off place. "Zoe?"

She closes her eyes. Her thumb grazes the switch of her flashlight, igniting the bright LED beam as she steps into the ocean. The cold water presses against her wet suit. There is the familiar deafening sound of bubbles rushing past her ears. She begins to sink. Her weighted vest dragging her down, compensating for her natural buoyancy. The sensation hovers between weightlessness and drowning. Water moves around her and the light from her torch illuminates the turbulence created by Reyes as he breaks the surface.

Zoe grabs hold of the cable trailing behind the rover and slowly, hand over hand, follows the craft's decent.

- 11 -

николе sits in front of the complicated cluster of terminals and controls. She grabs a headset off the counter and pulls it on, dropping the mic into place. She is sitting between Foster and Jake. Both of them are flicking switches and turning dials. Systems are booting up. Screens blink to life. Nicole adjust the volume dial, but hears only silence. The boy to her right takes control of a sophisticated looking armature, and the static on the screens is replaced by live images of the dark water surrounding the Trident.

"Zoe?" She says softly into the mic. There is no response. Both men seem calm. This is routine for them. It is not routine for her. Nicole turns to the captain and asks, "Can she hear me?"

Foster pulls his headset's mic into place. "Hudson, you there?"

Scratchy audio hisses through her headset. She can just make out Zoe's garbled voice through the static. She sounds so far away, suspended in the dark, out of reach past locked doors, winding corridors, thick bulkheads, and thousands of gallons of water.

The ROV's lights kick on, illuminating the black. Nicole didn't even know it was night.

Through the popping, she hears her sister. "Switchin—channel —damn it—fix this—nel two."

The line goes dead. Foster adjusts a dial. The sounds are more crisp, but still faint. Zoe's raspy voice fills her ears. "Nik?"

"Hey." Nicole holds the headphones tighter, her own voice ghosting through the speakers. "I'm right here."

Foster leans back in his seat. "Kohama, what's up with the audio?"

The young man sound defensive. "I wasn't done with the rewiring when we left port."

"Great." The captain raps his fingers on the desk. "Hudson, Reyes. Stay on two."

Zoe grumbles, "You mind telling me what the hell I'm looking for?"

Nicole isn't the only one who picks up on her attitude. Foster looks to Nicole. "Tell her, kid."

She picks at the edge of the counter, not appreciating being put on the spot. "A wreck."

"That's vague," Reyes scoffs.

"I translated a section of the journal for them. It said diving bells were sent down to this location in the seventeenth century. The entry implied they found something, but the debris field was too deep. They had to abandon the expedition after four divers died."

Nicole watches the monitors, waiting for a response.

"That's fucking great." Zoe snorts.

"Just do your job, Hudson. You'll be fine." Foster rubs his eyes. "ROV should be down. Jake, light it up and give us the main camera."

The image on the center screen tilts, bringing the ocean floor into view. The beam of light thrown from the rover's powerful torches casts shadows on sea life moving in and out of coral structures. The sight is otherworldly and beautiful. Nicole's jaw drops. She scoots closer to the display, fixated on the flurried movement of creatures. The men with her continue with their tasks, oblivious to the fascinating scene on the screen.

Foster grumbles into the comm, "What's your ETA to the ROV? Reyes, Hudson. Do you copy?"

The static fizzes out the response, but Nicole doesn't notice. She cannot take her eyes off the ocean floor.

ZOE FLOATS ON A PLANE —her arms outstretched, her body oriented perpendicular to cable. It is a method Jones taught her, a way to decompress more evenly during a descent. Her legs churn slowly, the movement keeping her blood flowing as her fins displace the water around her.

Reyes joins her. He beats his legs hard, checking and rechecking his many gauges. He taps the dive computer on his wrist, showing her their depth. Zoe rolls her eyes. She found it hard to work with him before all this, but now it's completely nauseating. She can't trust him. It would be better if she was going down alone, but Foster would never allow it.

Zoe checks her own tank gauge and releases the cable, pointing herself down towards the sea floor. Leaving early will give her a few moments of solitude. The beam from her flashlight bounces as she pushes deeper, hands at her sides, legs together, fins pumping the water and forcing her deeper still.

The descent has always been her favorite part. The controlled movement, your body sinking through blue and into black. Something about it always felt natural to her.

She remembers the first time Jones took her out and how quickly she took to it. They dived the debris field of a downed Japanese fighter in the Pacific. The wreck was shallow enough to be safe for a first timer, but dicey enough to be exciting. They were only down for twenty minutes, but to Zoe it felt like hours. Time slowed.

That was it for her. Foster took her off the loading crew and had Jones train her. The Marine-style boot camp he put her through kicked her ass mentally and physically. She was hooked. Jones spent the next few years pushing her to go deeper and stay down longer. They quickly became Foster's go-to team for difficult or sensitive projects, Jones ever the prepared optimist, Zoe always the Houdini. With Jones at her side, it was easy to disregard the misogynist bullshit from the other dive teams.

Their luck was strong. Foster kept sending them down. Her bonus checks got bigger and bigger. And for a time it was fulfilling.

But it didn't last.

Her mask begins to press harder against her face, hard rubber pushing against her bruised cheeks. The suction is a familiar and painful sensation. Zoe depresses the regulator, adjusting the pressure inside her mask. Bubbles flutter in her periphery.

She can pick out the lights of the ROV in the blackness. Her pulse quickens. It's been a while since she has done a night dive. She rotates her body, checking around her. The water here is warm, a perfect climate for fast, deadly things. The extreme depth doesn't do much to improve the scenario, either. Best to get down, locate this wreck, and get the hell back to the Trident.

She makes it down to the rover, crossing in front of the main camera and waiting in the pool of light for Reyes to make his way to her.

He comes around the far side of the ROV, kicking up sediment and sand as he begins to run another round of checks on his gauges. Reyes always struck Zoe as a contradiction: calm and controlled topside, but a frantic mess underwater. He is a nervous nelly in a crew full of cowboys.

"What now?" she asks.

Jake's voice is garbled by static. "You're about a click off. I'll guide you in. Follow the rover."

The thrusters on the ROV kick up silt as they propel the machine forward. A single powerful LED torch cuts through the dark. Zoe swims alongside, her body undulating while every muscle screams for rest.

Ragged bursts of rock and coral jut up from the sea floor. Small schools reflect the rover's main beam, glimmering as they change course. The yellow and white submersible crests a ledge and disappears. Zoe floats over a drop-off, drifting upward to get a better look over the ridge. Her small flashlight is not powerful enough to cut through the darkness.

"How much deeper, Jake?" she asks.

His response crackles through the speakers in her mask. "Should only be a few more meters. Why?"

"Can we get some lights on down here?"

"What's up, Hudson?" Reyes joins her in the void, his face illuminated inside his mask. "You afraid of the dark?"

Zoe glares at him.

"I'll bring her overhead. Hold your position." The ROV moves smoothly, cresting the peak as the entire underbelly of the machine ignites. A six-foot tawny nurse shark flees the pool of light, heading for the obscured safety of darker water. Silt swirls with the creature's exit.

Zoe tilts down, her body drifting towards the scattered shards of coral-encrusted wreckage. Anything that was wood is now home to millions of tiny creatures, clinging firmly to the sunken vessel. She presses forward, her right shoulder aching with every stroke. There is an object projecting from the debris, a tapered metal pillar with a series of massive cast loops marching up its length.

"Foster, are you seeing this?" She swims towards the pillar, her hands reaching out to touch its craggy surface.

"I see it, Hudson." He covers his mic and dials the phone on the terminal, pinning the handset to his shoulder. He rubs his eyes. "We've got a positive ID on the wreckage, Ms. Case." Foster hangs up the phone and pulls his mic back down. "Cut that thing free and strap it. The rover will haul it in. You've got a torch in the gear box. Do you copy?"

***

NICOLE CANNOT HEAR ANYTHING in her headphones. She watches Foster adjust the dials on the terminal. "Reyes, Hudson? Do you read?"

Feedback blasts through the speakers, a brilliant, piercing sound that stabs at her eardrums. Nicole fumbles the headset off, tossing it onto the counter. Her ears are ringing. "What the hell was that?"

Jake cuts the comm system, stopping the piecing sound with a sheepish expression. "We lost audio."

"I told you to fix those relays, Jake!"

Jake winces at the volume of Foster's voice. "There wasn't enough time. We left port too fast. I didn't get to the forward cluster."

"God damn it." The captain rips his head set off and pushes back from the counter. Nicole imagines she can see his gears turning. Foster rakes his fingers through his thinning grey hair and shakes his head. "It's not a big deal. It happens all the time. They know what to do. They'll be fine."

She can't tell who he is trying to reassure.

THE HIGH-PITCHED NOISE that cracks through her mask's headset is debilitating. Zoe smacks at the exterior controls, cutting the connection. Reyes appears to be having the same issue. *Piece of shit comm system.* She swims back towards him, hoping to pantomime, since their link to each other is severed along with the link to the boat. Reyes is already scrawling something on his wrist display. Just one word: torch.

She nods and heads back to the hovering ROV. The gear box on the machine's flank houses a petrogen cutting torch and an ignitor. Reyes comes up next to her and removes two thick coiled bundles. He points to the pillar, drawing his fingers across his neck. She gets it. Cut the damn thing free. She's not an idiot.

Right about now, Zoe is missing diving in her own kit. This analog setup is getting on her nerves. All her gear is back in her room, uselessly sitting on the floor next to her bunk. She had stashed it there after talking to her mom, not wanting to repeat the experience she had when she got back from Paris. Her lock had been snipped. Thousands of dollars worth of military caliber re-breather gear Jones helped her pick out was simply gone. It took her weeks to track the shit down. Foster had not been happy with her method of investigation, but throwing punches got her seventy-five percent of her shit back and asking nicely got her squat. From then on, if she wasn't on the boat, her gear stayed in her room.

'In her room' isn't helping right now.

She checks the gauge on her primary tank. The reading is low. That doesn't seem right. She taps the glass. No change. The needle is hovering too close to empty. She'll have to cut over to her secondary supply soon.

Zoe swims backwards, gas line drawing out from the rover like an umbilical cord. She presses the tip of the cutter into the ignitor and feels the pop and push as the oxygenated gasoline touches off. All her focus turns to cutting the pillar free while Reyes works the heavy woven straps around the massive piece of metal. The lights of the ROV move around her, changing the directions of shadows. They have done this dance without communication before. Jake is a good pilot, fully capable of interpreting even the most erratic hand gestures.

She is halfway through the cut by the time the straps are attached to the reinforced undercarriage of the rover. She can taste the trimix turning stale and pauses her work to switch to her reserve tank. Zoe takes one last breath from her primary tank and checks the pressure on the new tank on a dangling analog gauge.

Her stomach sinks.

The needle is positioned firmly in the red.

Her reserve tank is empty.

She cuts the gas flow to the torch, letting the heavy bronze nozzle sink to the sea floor. Panic floods her body. She cannot stay here.

Her legs compress, pressing off the firm coral surface of the wreck. Her fins churn beneath her, driving her upward. Every muscle screams. She grabs hold of the ROV's tether and follows it up through the dark. Her head throbs. Her vision blurs.

She knows the ramifications of a rapid ascent. The bends. Tiny bubbles of inert gas permeating her tissue and joints. Irreversible damage. Pain. None of it will matter if the cerebral hypoxia hits her first. A total loss of consciousness underwater. Her body shutting down as she drowns in her gear.

Sixty-two meters down. It took twenty minutes to get that deep. She needs to make it back to the boat in under five without killing herself. If she can make it into the bay, Foster will see her. The observation team can call for the doctor. They'll take her to medical, to the hyperbaric chamber. She just has to make it to the bay.

Zoe fights to keep her breath steady, but it's a losing battle. Her chest tightens. As the lower edge of the launch pool comes into view, her lungs are burning. She focuses on the light in the bay, on the smooth metal lining punctuated by perfectly spaced rivets. Through the rippling surface of the water she can just make out the warped steel cathedral towering above the portal. Her heart slows, pounding hard against the neoprene collar of her wetsuit.

She releases the cable and makes one final push. Her hands stretch out above her. Reaching.

Her body breaks the surface of the water with tremendous force. Her gloved hands flail over the edge of the pool, searching desperately for purchase. Every joint is howling. Her lungs are turning inside out. She hauls herself half out of the water and collapses to the floor, her fingers clenching the bay's perforated grating.

Every limb is limp. Barely responsive. She manages to thrash at her mask, ripping it off her face. She gasps, craving oxygen.

A million tiny needles stab deep into every muscle, every joint. The pain is overwhelming. There is an erratic metallic pounding. A deep voice. Yelling. Zoe tries to find the origin of the sounds, but her vision is blown out, tunneling towards darkness.

Her head fills with the sounds of crashing waves.

Nicole drums her fingers on the counter. The cameras have been focused forward at the vacant ocean ever since Jake started to retract the ROV. She liked it better when she could at least sort of see Zoe. This silence is driving her crazy.

She feels a coldness in the pit of her stomach. Something is wrong. "Why is this taking so long?"

Foster quirks an eyebrow. "This isn't taking long at all. In fact, this is one of the fastest recoveries we've made in years. Good thing, too. I don't have the patience to deal with any patrols right now."

"What's that supposed to mean?" Nicole snaps.

"Considering where we are in the ocean, kid, what we're doing is not exactly legal." He forces a smile.

A channel opens from the bay, but the voice that comes through the speaker is not her sister's. "Get the doc to medical. Now."

She can hear the panic and anger in Reyes's voice.

Foster furrows his brow. "Reyes, what's wrong?"

"Just get the doctor." Reyes's breath is labored. "I'll meet him there."

There is a garbled sound in the background Nicole can't quite make out, the tinny noise of vibrating metal. Reyes's voice booms over the comm. "One more word out of you, Erik, and I swear to God I'll open that gate and beat you to death. Understand me?" The line goes dead.

That was not the most reassuring note to leave on. Nicole grabs Foster's arm after he hangs up on the infirmary. "What's going on?"

He pulls free, pushing back from the counter and heading for the hatch. "Not sure."

Nicole follows the captain. "Then I'm coming with you."

"No, you're not." Foster turns on the stairs, flashing her a look that stops her in her tracks. "Kohama. Keep her here."

The young man nods.

"And don't piss her off. " As Foster closes the hatch, he gives one last word of caution. "She hits like her sister."

The door closes and locks behind Foster.

Nicole turns to Jake. "What's happening?"

He stands, backing away from the armature. "I don't know any more than you do."

Maybe so. But he is the only person left in this room who can find anything out. The entire ship is wired with surveillance. There are cameras in every corner of ever corridor—she began to notice them while she was escorted to the bay. Jake isn't stupid. He either has access, or he can gain access. And he can definitely do it faster than she could.

He also looks worried. There is a sympathy in his expression that has been missing from the other crewmen on the Trident.

"You care about her," she says quietly. "Don't you?"

He nods.

"She trusted you people. That's why she came back here in the first place. She thought it would be safe." Nicole steps closer. "But it wasn't. These people betrayed her and now something's wrong. All I'm asking is for you to help me see if she's okay."

Jake glances at the display as it cycles through security cameras.

"Please, Jake." She can feel herself vibrating with fear and frustration. "Find her."

He hesitates only for a moment. "Okay." He nods, pointing to a vacant terminal. "I just need to—"

She moves out of his way, letting him take a seat at the computer. She watches over his shoulder as he cycles through the cameras in the bay. Bryce is pacing in the gear cage, soundlessly yelling and slapping the wire mesh.

She starts to chew on her thumbnail. "They're not in there."

"I know. Hold on." Jake types a command, and the video feeds begin to cycle.

She sees Foster running through one hall, arms pumping as he ducks around a corner, only to appear in another feed on the split screen.

Jake jabs his finger at the display. "There."

Reyes is carrying a limp form into a sterile room. The infirmary. When the tattooed man places the body on the exam table, Nicole can see Zoe's wet suit has been torn open. The doctor's mouth moves, barking orders. He pushes Reyes out of the way and sets to cutting off the rest the black material, peeling it away from her sister's pale skin.

- 12 -

THIS IS HER LIFE. This is her plane. And ultimately, it's her choice what she does with both. She put Nicole and Zoe in this situation when she involved Max.

She owes them.

Witten strolls back into the hangar office, dropping his cell phone into his pocket. His expression is not reassuring.

"What?" Caroline asks.

The agent takes a seat. "They're in custody."

Jones sounds about as angry as Caroline feels. "How the hell did that happen so fast?"

"Surveillance intercepted radio chatter between the compound and a ship in the Arabian." He gives them both a sympathetic shrug. "Looks like Zoe ducked into the wrong foxhole."

Caroline can't hide her confusion. "Why would she be on a ship?"

"Going back to familiar territory?" Witten rubs his neck.

Jones leans forward. "Familiar territory?"

"She went back to the Trident."

"What's the Trident got to do with any of this?" Matthew's tone sets her on edge.

"Aaron Foster has been in the corporation's pocket for years." Witten isn't exactly delicate with the information. "After he ran into trouble with the Italian government, the corporation stepped in. Bailed him out. Now they fund everything. Equipment, provisions, payroll. The entire operation."

"That's bullshit." Jones pushes out of his seat, slamming his fist on the desk. She's never seen him like this.

"I'm sorry, but it's the truth." Witten sighs. "That boat has been performing illegal salvage for years. It only got worse after you left. But the corporation never counted on Ms. Hudson leaving."

She desperately wants Witten to clarify. "Did she know she was working for these people?"

"I doubt it. She had to know her work wasn't on the up and up, but I can't imagine she would've headed back there with her sister and the book if she knew she was walking into a trap."

She wishes her voice sounded less panicked. "We have to do something."

"Ms. Royer, I understand and sympathize with your situation, but you cannot get involved."

"Excuse me?" She narrows her eyes at Witten.

Jones crosses his arms and smirks, happy to watch Witten step in it. "Careful there, pal. The lady doesn't like the sound of 'no.'"

Witten tries to backtrack. "I'm just saying, this is something you should leave up to law enforcement."

"You're law enforcement, correct?"

He nods.

Caroline cocks her head. "And how long have you been investigating them, agent?"

His answer is sheepish. "Five years."

"Zoe and Nicole don't have five years, do they?"

"Ms. Royer—" Witten sounds exasperated.

"No." Jones leans against a filing cabinet. "Caroline's got a good point. You Feds have so much red tape, you can't wipe your ass without getting a warrant. This isn't about building your case. It's about getting to our friends before they're dead."

Witten sits back in his seat. "Getting yourselves killed isn't the answer."

The boys do not appear to be getting along. Jones has his reasons for disliking Witten, but right now, he's not really helping their position by being aggressive.

"Then help us." Caroline pushes her chair back and comes around the front of the desk. "You know you have at least two kidnapped women. They're U.S. citizens. You're a federal agent. You know where they're being held." She rests her palms against the desktop behind her. "Arrest somebody."

The agent stares at her. "On what authority? There haven't been any demands. For all we know, Zoe went back to the Trident willingly. No one would consider her a hostage. She's an employee." He rubs his temple. "These people are smart, Ms. Royer. Even if I could get a naval cruiser to intercept the Trident and wrangle a warrant to board, Zoe and Nicole will be long gone."

A silence settles over the office.

"Where will they take them?" asks Jones.

"Back to the compound."

Caroline nods. "So we'll go there."

"It's not that easy." Witten scowls at her, pointing towards the private jet parked in the dark hangar. "If you approach that island in an aircraft registered in your name, you'll be blown out of the sky, no questions asked. They can chalk it up to terrorist activity, get a splinter cell to take credit. It's how they work."

Caroline looks out the window at her plane. The red Royer Aviation logo emblazoned on the tail might as well be a bulls-eye.

A solution hits her. She licks her chapped lips and draws them into a self-assured smile. "What would our chances look like if I had access to an unmarked, unregistered jet?"

Jones gives her a crooked smirk. "Share with the rest of the class, Caroline."

Witten shakes his head, rubbing his eyes. "I need to make it abundantly clear that I do not condone any vigilante actions—"

"And I need to make it abundantly clear that I'm not asking for permission, Agent. What if I had access to such a thing?" Caroline crosses her arms.

She recognizes the look of a man who has finally realized he is in an argument he cannot win. Witten lets out a heavy sigh. "There's an airfield the corporation uses on the mainland. Most movement to and from the complex happens through there. If they move Zoe and Nicole, they'll use that airfield. I can get you the satellite imagery, but it'll take some time—"

"Do it." Caroline says.

Witten rises, adjusting his jacket and tie. The agent pauses in the threshold. "Are you positive you want to go through with this?"

"Yes."

He gives her a nod and exits the office, heading back to his sedan parked outside the hangar.

Jones rocks his chair back on two legs. "Unmarked jet, huh? Should I call you Mr. Wayne, or just Bruce?"

Caroline barely manages a smile. "I'll use any asset I have, Matthew. I have to bring them home."

**

Bryce passed out. Again.

This will be the fourth time.

It is getting tedious.

Case shakes her head as she walks towards Connor. He is crouched by the launch portal rinsing his hands in the ocean water trapped in the pool. Her fingers trace the curve of his shoulder, gliding up his neck until they reach his chin. She plucks the lit cigarette from his lips. He smirks. She knows Connor is itching to be off this tin can. Boats have never been his thing. Too confined. They only have a few more hours to kill before they are in range for transport. She owes him this. An opportunity to blow off steam and inflict some brutality.

"Wake him up," Case hisses, breathing smoke deep into her lungs.

Connor slaps Bryce's cheeks, coaxing him back to consciousness. His eyes open, lids heavy and nearly swollen shut. He dangles from the ROV winch, twisting in the air as he jerks awake.

She would have almost considered him a handsome man before all this. Even with his nose mangled, she could understand his appeal. But now, his entire face is a pulp. Blood drips from his mouth and nose, mixing with drool and mucus. Case grips Bryce's chin and exhales smoke into his face. He coughs, sputtering up blood through cracked teeth.

"You were told not to hurt her," she coos.

The intimidation has always been her favorite part. There is something satisfying when a victim recognizes there is no way out.

Bryce stammers, "I-I-I didn't—I didn't know."

She shakes her head as she strokes his cheek. "Yes you did."

Connor strikes him from behind, cracking a length of pipe across his back and his bound arms. Bryce cringes, twisting wildly, his legs flailing beneath him. Case backs away, taking in the sight as Connor continues to batter the hanged man. She takes a deep drag of her cigarette and halts Connor's assault, taking a moment to inspect the bright red blood on the tips of her pale fingers.

"You knew. You knew the tanks you gave her were bad, Erik. That's why you did it. You knew what would happen."

"I just—I just wanted to—"

Case give him a bemused look. "Teach her a lesson?"

He nods, whimpering. Tears stream down his cheeks.

Pathetic.

Case grabs the straps that crisscross the front of the heavily weighted dive vest. She tugs Bryce closer, growling. "That wasn't your job."

She nods to Connor, who has picked up one of Hudson's empty oxygen tanks. He steps in front of Bryce and swings the cylinder into the man's gut. The force of the blow sends him spinning in circles. He vomits, blood and bile gurgle past his lips and down his chin. Connor drops the tank. It hits the metal grating with a hollow clang.

"It's so difficult to find competent help these days." She hands him back the cigarette, its ember still glowing a bright orange-red.

The big man takes a deep drag. Smoke rolls out his nostrils. He grabs hold of Bryce's head, stopping his rotation as he plucks the cigarette from his lips and buries it into the man's swollen eye.

The screaming is like white noise to her. She crosses to the winch control hanging from the ceiling. She can still hear his gasping and hollering over the whir of the motor.

"All you had to do was follow orders, Erik." Case yells as she wipes her hands on a rag. "Follow orders and do your job. But you gave your own personal bullshit priority, didn't you?"

The motor cuts, leaving Bryce suspended over the dark water of the launch pool.

His cries turn into manic laughter. He screams at her, "Fuck you, you crazy bitch. And fuck Zoe Hudson and her fucking bitch sister."

Too bad he is only showing this fire at the very end. It would have been more interesting if he had put up a fight from the start.

The bay smells of salt water, blood, and other bitter things. Case inhales deeply, letting the aroma permeate her senses. She never would have guessed this would have been the part of the job she missed the most.

She presses the clamp release on the control and the mechanism latched to Bryce's vest releases. He plummets into the water. His body thrashes as he begins to sink. She watches him fight against the weight of his buoyancy compensator. The pool begins to cloud. Bryce disappears beneath the cloud of bubbles created by his struggle.

Tendrils of red float in the blue.

HER EYELIDS ARE HEAVY. It feels like someone is standing on her chest. Every breath is a challenge. Her limbs are buried in sand. All her senses are failing her. Zoe twitches, trying to regain control of her own body, but every movement sends shockwaves up her arms and legs, directly into her brain. Pain is the punishment for action.

She squints, trying to focus.

She feels pressure and warmth against her hand. Someone leans over her, long dark hair falling against her skin. She tries to whisper, but her voice booms inside her own head. "Caroline?"

Another warm hand cups her cheek. Her eyes begin to align. Freckles and pale skin come into sharp focus. Not Caroline. Nicole. Zoe can't tell if her sister looks worried or relieved.

"Hey you." Nicole squeezes her hand.

The pressure of her sister's grip throbs through her nervous system, but the contact is too comforting to complain. Zoe tries to take in her surroundings, expecting the steel walls and thick glass of the Trident's infirmary and instead finding a windowless room of formed concrete and sterile polished surfaces. "Where are we?"

Nicole pushes sweat-soaked strands of hair from Zoe's face. "I don't know."

"We're not on the boat." There is no movement, no thrum of engines. She's disoriented, but once the statement leaves her lips, it sounds ridiculously obvious, even to her.

Nicole doesn't seem to care. "No. They helicoptered us— Somewhere else."

"Helicopter?" Zoe shakes her head. She doesn't remember anything except the panic underwater. Her body breaching the surface. Her fingers clawing at the deck. Her head throbbing as everything shut down.

An overwhelming sense of dread settles over her.

"We have to get out of here." Zoe tries to right herself, only to get painful resistance from the IV buried in crook of her elbow. The thick needle rocks in her vein, held firm by medical tape.

"Zoe. Don't." Nicole presses against her shoulders trying to force her back down. "You need to be calm."

"No." Zoe limply pushes her sister's hands away. "I need to get this shit off me."

"Stop, Zoe. Please." Nicole is practically begging.

There are so many tubes and wires and hoses hooking her up to different machines. She can feel her pulse begin to rise. The EKG beeps more rapidly in response.

The adhesive pads keeping track of her heart rate are the first to go. Zoe wraps the thin wires around her fingers and rips them from her skin. The steady pulse of the machine turns to a single long, loud tone. The frequency makes her head pound. "Turn it off."

Nicole searches for the switch, finally pulling the plug from the wall. The machine falls silent. Zoe drops her legs over the side of the bed, tugging the oxygen supply out of her nostrils. She feels the tubes scrape through her sinuses.

"We can't leave." Nicole moves in front of Zoe.

Her sister is searching for her eyes, but Zoe is not looking at Nicole. She is focused intently on her arm as her trembling fingertips extract the long IV needle from her vein. She hisses, flicking the tubing to the polished floor. Her skin feels suddenly cold. She looks down. Her feet and legs are bare, skin stippled with odd depressions. She begins to shiver. "Where are my fucking clothes?"

Nicole grabs a blanket off her chair and wraps it around Zoe. She grips her chin tight. "I know you're freaking out, but you have to listen to me. The people Foster turned us over to—" Nicole takes in a deep breath. "They have Mom."

"What?"

"He was working with them the whole time."

Zoe shakes her head. Nothing is making sense. Her head is swimming. She can feel warm liquid running down her arm and she pushes her sister away. "No."

A cold voice rings hollow in the sterile room. "Your sister is right, Ms. Hudson."

The sound of her name from an unfamiliar voice makes her turn. She does not recognize the woman in the doorway, but Nicole seems to. She is a wrecking ball in high heels, hips moving like the swing of a hammer. With an acidic smile plastered on her perfectly composed face, she steps closer, her focus bouncing from Nicole to Zoe.

"You should put something on." She places folded clothes on the end of the bed. "I'm sure your mother would appreciate it if you were clothed."

It's too late for company.

Allison rises from the couch and heads for the door. Her stomach is churning. Surprise visits here have not been positive. She has no way to prepare for the unpredictable. She opens the door, expecting Case.

Instead she finds Fletcher standing before her. He is wearing a different suit, but his face is the same—fresh, confident, and completely unnerving.

"Doctor." He gives her a stiff nod.

She doesn't have the patience to deal with him. "What do you want?"

Fletcher smiles and backs away, revealing her children.

Nicole sprints across the threshold, crashing into her mother. "Mom?"

Allison cannot maintain composure. Her eyes well up with tears. She embraces Nicole tightly, then holds her at arm's length, inspecting her. Her freckled cheeks are slightly sunburned, and she is much thinner than Allison remembered. Her right hand is badly bruised.

"Did they hurt you?" She inspects Nicole's injured hand. The anger in her voice is directed at Fletcher, still standing in the doorway.

"No." Nicole shakes her head. "I—I'm fine—"

If she kept speaking after that, Allison can't be sure. She is too distracted by the state of Zoe. Their eyes meet, but her eldest drops her gaze to the floor.

She releases Nicole, stepping carefully towards her oldest. "Oh my God. What happened to you?"

Zoe twitches. Her face is a mess of old and new wounds, bruises and cuts in various states of healing. Underneath the damage, Allison can recognize a familiar emotion: shame. She reaches out for her cheek only to have Zoe flinch and pull away.

"What did they do to you?"

"I'm fine." Zoe shrugs.

Allison has never understood her daughter's need to lie in the face of an obvious truth. A familiar flare of frustration runs up her spine. "Bullshit."

Fletcher bows slightly, smiling a knowing grin. "I'll leave you to catch up."

After the door is closed, the silence is deafening.

Nicole is the first to move, crossing the room to drop herself into the nearest chair. She melts into the cushions.

Allison hasn't been in a room with both her daughters for over twelve years. She hasn't seen Zoe in half a decade. And if their last face-to-face conversation was any indication, this will not go well. Maybe this time will be different.

"What happened?" She sighs, scrubbing her fingers through her hair. "How did they find you?"

Both girls are quiet.

"Tell me." She cannot take the edge off her voice. Neither daughter speaks. "You owe me an explanation. All you had to do was keep your sister safe. Why weren't you able to do it?"

Nicole comes to her sister's defense. "She did, mom. I'm safe. I'm fine."

Allison raises a hand to Nicole. "I didn't ask you, Nikky. I asked her."

Zoe fidgets with her fingers. She presses between each knuckle, contact briefly turning her skin white where it once was a sickly yellow-purple. Her green eyes are focused on the floor. Allison remembers this routine from when she was a teenager, always getting into trouble. "Look at me when I'm talking to you, Zoe."

Zoe glares at her. "I thought it would be safe back on the Trident."

"Well it wasn't," Allison snaps. "Was it?"

"I was trying to find you," she says softly.

Allison pinches the bridge of her nose, trying to stave off her growing headache. "I didn't need to be found, Zoe. I had everything under control. I'm a grown woman. I can take care of myself."

"Obviously." Zoe snorts.

Her daughter's single word response is so weighted in years of bitterness and sarcasm that Allison can no longer fight the urge to show her own anger. "Don't back talk me."

"Mom." Nicole tugs at her shirt from her seat on the chair. "Just calm down. Okay? We're all here. Together. We're all—kind of fine. We just need to—"

"Not. Now. Nikky." Allison snaps at her youngest. She turns back to Zoe, pointing an accusatory finger. "Why can't you ever just do what you're told?"

Zoe slaps her hand away, now yelling in earnest. "You didn't tell me anything! You never have. I didn't know what I was supposed to do!"

She turns away, resting her hands on her hips. "Come on, Zoe. Don't be stupid."

"Stupid?" Zoe's voice cracks ever so slightly. "I have never been good enough for you. Never. I have always been just one colossal disappointment after another to you. If this was so fucking important, you shouldn't have dropped it on me—"

Allison rubs the nape of her neck. "That's right. I'm sorry. I forgot. You can't be bothered to help your family."

Zoe grips her mother's arm, forcing her to turn around. "There were men with guns at her school, Mom. They were trying to take her. You didn't say shit about men with guns!" Zoe screams at her. "But that's just the way things work with you, isn't it? You keep everything important to yourself. Fuck! Hawthorne was the first person who was ever honest with me about my father, and he was a complete fucking stranger."

"Hawthorne?" Allison mumbles, confused.

"I should have learned that stuff about dad from you." Her daughter's expression is more hurt than mad. "But every time I asked, you lied to me."

"I cannot believe you." Allison jerks free of Zoe's grip. She feels a flush creeping up her neck. "I ask you for one simple, important thing: to take care of Nicole. And you go and make this about your father?"

"Mom." Nicole's expression is pained.

Allison ignores her. "He's the reason we're in this mess. Did you know that, Zoe? This is all his fault!"

Zoe is silent. Her bruised body trembles slightly.

There is no way she can hold back her rage at this point. "Hayden is the one who abandoned us. He's the one who lied over and over again. And he's the one who stole from incredibly dangerous people and, apparently, is more than willing to sit back and let us take the fall because he's too much of a fucking coward to step forward and deal with this."

Tears begin to collect at the edges of Zoe's swollen eyes.

"Mom," Nicole pleads. "Stop it."

Allison doesn't listen. She steps closer to her eldest daughter, her chest burning from years of resentment and frustration. Every feature on Zoe's face is a reminder of Hayden. It always has been. Her eyes. The steep slope of her nose. The shape of her lips. The tone of her skin. She looks so much like her father. A constant aching reminder of everything Allison lost. Everything that left her. Everything that hurt her.

A surge of emotion washes over her. Bitterness gives each word a sour taste. "Your father. The man you seem to idolize? Is a criminal, Zoe. Nothing more."

The room falls quiet.

Tears begin to flow. Zoe backs away, her palms feverishly wiping at bruised cheeks. She stumbles blindly, bumping the wall. With a quick jerk, she turns, ripping the door open and slamming it behind her. Just like her father, Zoe Hudson runs away.

Allison expected nothing less.

Beneath her skin, her heart is beating fast and erratic.

"Real nice, Mom." Nicole says flatly.

"I told her what she needed to hear."

"You don't get it, do you?" Nicole stifles a humorless laugh and shakes her head. "Her dad's been dead for over a decade. She only found out a couple days ago." Nicole rises from her seat on the couch, plunging her hands deep into her pockets. "So, salt in her wound. Great job."

"I didn't—" The floor drops out from under her feet. Her chest aches. She can feel herself floating in space, her heart rising into her throat. "Hayden's gone?"

Nicole isn't listening anymore. She isn't even in the same room anymore. By the time Allison tears her eyes away from the empty space Zoe left, the bedroom door has slammed closed, and she is alone. Again.

- 13 -

Connor's flat has always impressed her. This man actually has fewer possessions the longer he stays with the company. Case perches on his weight bench, centered in the vacant living area. She waits patiently, watching the tip of her cigarette glow brightly in the darkness. She didn't want to be alone with her thoughts, but instinct took over and carried her here.

She has been waiting for over an hour, ever since she transferred the Hudson girls into Fletcher's custody and turned over the artifacts to the research teams. It has been an uncomfortable and uncommonly quiet span of time.

The door swings open, flooding the room with light from the hall. Severe shadows are thrown against the bare concrete walls. She hears the sound of rustling of fabric, a pistol being drawn from its holster, the snap of the safety releasing.

Case stares listlessly out the plate-glass window, trying to focus on the crackle of tobacco burning as she draws the nicotine deep into her system.

The door closes.

She exhales slowly, smoke curling from her lips and nostrils. She can just barely make out Connor's hulking reflection in the dark glass. He steps closer, slipping his sidearm back into his holster.

"I did everything he asked. And more." Her words come out rough and uneven. "Why hasn't he called for me?"

"Who?" Connor's voice rumbles behind her.

"Sutton." She has been sitting in the dark of his living room, stripping gears in her mind, trying to figure out what she did wrong.

Connor lets out a low snort and takes a seat next to her on the bench. "Why do you care?"

"Because there's something I'm missing." His proximity is usually more of a distraction. She can feel his heat next to her, but Case cannot gather herself enough to fully appreciate it. "Something's not right."

"Doesn't matter." He plucks the cigarette from her fingers and takes a deep drag. "Old man's on his way out. I thought you cooked up a coup with Sutton's shadow."

Case smoothes the creases of her slacks. "I'm not sure I can trust Fletcher." She stands, moving closer to the window, welcoming the cold that radiates from the thick glass. "I don't know who I can trust anymore."

Embers at the tip of Connor's cigarette glow bright. She can hear the pop and hiss as the paper burns down. There is a bitter smell when the filter finally catches fire. Connor snubs the flame with sturdy finger tips. He flicks the butt to the ground and hovers behind her, his chest pressing against her back. Huge hands urge her to turn. Connor tilts her head up. The smoke flows from his lips as he speaks, curling around her. "What about me?"

Case's eyes narrow. "What about you?"

"You trust me."

Her hand drifts up the side of his body. Skilled fingers find the grip of his sidearm and withdraw it smoothly. Her thumb disengages the slide lock. Connor's weapon is always primed. A bullet is always chambered. Her finger slips over the trigger as she presses the muzzle to his stubbled jaw. "I'm not an idiot, Connor. If Sutton told you to take care of me, you would do it without hesitation. You're a company man. You'd make it quick, out of respect, but you'd do it all the same."

If she didn't know him better, she would think he looked hurt. His thick fingers drift up the length of her spine, pressing hard against the silk fabric of her blouse. Rough callouses catch and scrape their way past the base of her neck, tangling in her hair. He kisses her, sucking her lower lip between his teeth, then clamping down, biting hard enough to draw blood. Case can taste it pooling under her tongue.

Connor pulls back. "Never."

Her heart pounds in her chest. Her skin is on fire, burning as Connor traces a finger down her scarred breast. "He'd kill you."

He pulls her closer, whispering in her ear. "I'd like to see him try."

His tongue traces the length of her neck.

Her entire body begins to throb.

Case lowers the gun until the steel frame rests cold against her thigh. She focuses on his lips, on the pressure of his touch, the way his

187

blunted nails sink into her skin. The sensation is almost painful, but not quite.

She swallows hard, words hissing out in between gritted teeth. "You're an arrogant son of a bitch. You know that?"

"Yes, ma'am." His broad hands slip under the curve of her ass. He lifts her effortlessly and carries her into his bedroom.

THE WOODEN CARVING Zoe gave her in Zurich feels warm in her palm. She turns it over, paying close attention to its worn edges. Her freshly calloused thumbs trace the line of the figure's arms.

The door to the bedroom opens silently. A sliver of light pierces the dark. She sees her mother's shadow against the far wall. Nicole lets out a sigh, refusing to roll over. She closes her hand around the carving and crosses her arms. The bed's surface shifts.

Her mother's voice is strangely timid. "Are you okay?"

"I'm fine." Her mother has to know she's lying.

"I wanted to apologize."

"You should save it for Zoe." Nicole presses her head against the soft pillow.

"Nikky." Allison pulls out the pet name so easily, her tone becoming instantly dismissive.

"No, Mom." Nicole snaps at her. "You had no right to jump down her throat like that."

Allison stares down at the floor. "I didn't know Hayden was—"

"Because you wouldn't listen. To either of us! She could have told you what happened but you treated her like crap from the moment you set eyes on her. It's wasn't fair." Nicole can feel herself growing more and more frustrated. "Do you know what her first thought was after finding out her father was dead?"

Allison remains quiet.

"All she wanted to do was make sure you were safe. Because even through all the bullshit you pile on her, she still loves you." Nicole sits up. She takes a deep breath before she continues. "We went to the Trident because that was the last place she heard from you. She had no way of knowing those people would betray her, no way of knowing that this was all connected. She tried to do the right thing, and now her entire world is falling apart, and all you can do is chastise her."

Her mother shakes her head. "She put you in jeopardy."

"God damn it, Mom! Do you even listen to yourself?" Nicole's voice cracks. "Why do you hate her so much?"

Allison stares at her, shocked.

Nicole steadies herself, forcing herself to speak softly. "We are all the family she has left. Why can't we just be there for each other for once?" Her throat is raw from yelling. "Why do you have to keep pushing her away?"

The pained expression on her mother's face lets Nicole know the answer is not an easy one. After a long pause, Allison sets her jaw in a very familiar way. Her words are drenched in bitterness. "She's the one that always runs."

"Because you make it impossible for her to stay." Nicole knows that's harsh, but it's something her mom needs to hear. The rift cannot be blamed on one person alone. It took two shovels to dig this hole. Nicole fidgets with the frayed hem of her sleeve. "All she wanted to do was find her father. Is that really so wrong? To want that?"

She's not talking about Zoe now and Allison knows it. Her mother is quiet. All at once Nicole remembers the first time she searched for her father on the internet, ending up at a social networking site. She found out that he teaches high school history. He loves science fiction novels, spicy Thai food, and SEC football. Those things by themselves were all strange and foreign to her. They were abstract. What wasn't abstract was recognizing her own crooked smile on the lips of a complete stranger.

Anger surges from deep inside her. Nicole stares down at the carving resting in her palms.

"What are you trying to say, Nikky?" Her mother asks, eyes red. Her cheeks flush. There is the hint of shame in her expression.

Nicole hangs her head. No turning back now. "I have a father, too. Except he's alive. He even lives on the same coast as me. But before I was even born, you decided that we don't need him. You decided that I didn't need him."

"I did what I thought was best for everyone."

"No. You didn't. You did what was best for you." Her chest grows tight. "Just like always."

Nicole regrets everything seconds later.

Her mother's skin turns pale. She covers her face and begins to rock gently back and forth on the edge of the bed, her body shuddering. Nicole feels instantly ashamed at the way she's been talking to her. She tucks the carving in her shirt pocket and drops to the floor, trying desperately to comfort her mother. "Please don't cry. I shouldn't have said that. I'm sorry — "

A loud knock echoes through the flat.

They must have brought Zoe back.

Thank God.

Apologies will not change what she said. Nicole rocks to her feet and exits the bedroom. As she heads for the door she lets out a labored breath. There was a part of her that thought getting these things off her chest would make her feel better, but instead she feels worse. She went too far. How poetic to be saved from making an even bigger ass out of herself by none other than her sister. Zoe really does have some impeccable timing. Nicole tugs the door open.

Two armed guards are standing in the hall. Zoe is not with them.

Nicole balks. "Where's my sister?"

The men do not answer her. Their hands come to rest on the hilts of complicated looking sidearms. Stun guns? She doesn't want to find out.

"Nicole." Her mother's voice drifts over her shoulder. It is steady and calm. Her strong, protective hands rest on Nicole's shoulders. "Is everything okay?"

"You're needed in the lab, Dr. Hudson." The guard's voice is so even, so matter-of-fact. "Now."

SHE SHOULDN'T HAVE slammed the door.

The sound is still reverberating in her head, amplifying her dizziness.

Zoe rests against the wall, pressing her forehead to the cool concrete.

Fletcher is waiting behind her. His hands are clasped behind his back. He stands statue-still next to the stocky guard monitoring her mother's door. The way her stares at her, with clarity and intensity, makes her instantly uncomfortable.

He clears his throat and steps forward.

"I'm not going back in there," she says brusquely, her words catching in her throat. Tears well at the edges of her eyes. "You can't make me." Zoe pinches her lids shut, trying to quell the throbbing in her head. Everything hurts. Too much is happening. Nothing makes sense.

He is gesturing down the hall. "Please follow me."

There is something in his expression. Sympathy? No. More like amusement. He must have heard them all screaming at each other. Nicole did her best to play mediator, but it's not the kid's fault this is what happens when Zoe and Allison get in the same room.

Her mother hasn't changed. She still has no interest in listening, no interest in Zoe's side of things. All that matters is Zoe failed, and Dr. Allison Hudson is disappointed. Full stop.

Zoe lets out a sigh. After the month she's had, all she wants to do is get piss drunk and pass out for a good fifteen to twenty hours. Considering her current predicament, neither of those outcomes seem very likely.

She presses away from the wall. Her equilibrium instantly revolts. Everything tilts, careening uncontrollably. Bile rises in her throat. She throws out a hand to steady herself. Her callused palms strike smooth concrete with a sharp slap, but it isn't enough. She stumbles.

Fletcher catches her elbow before she goes down. His skin is cool and moist. The unwanted contact sends a shudder through her.

She jerks her arm free. "Don't touch me."

He backs away, his face neutral, waiting.

When the spinning subsides and Zoe rights herself, she breathes deeply through her nose and follows him.

They wind quietly through starkly lit corridors. Something about the color and cast of the light here reminds her of the Trident. Reminds her of the bay. The dive. Running out of air. Her lungs pulling themselves inside out.

She shivers at the memory, crossing her arms and tucking her hands into her armpits in an attempt to warm the icy tips of her fingers.

Fletcher leads her to an elevator. After pressing the button, he steps back for her to enter. The polished metal doors close before her.

The woman staring back at her in the mirrored surface is almost completely unrecognizable. Her face is blotched with deep, fiercely colored bruises and her skin still has a sickly dimpled texture to it. What was once tanned and smooth is now pale and pocked with dents, spiderwebbed with broken capillaries—her body's vain attempt to expel the toxic gases that built up in her tissue during the rapid ascent from the ocean floor. Her left eye is blown out, ruptured blood vessels coloring what was once white a bright red and putrid pink. The effect is unsettling.

Zoe's fingers begin to tingle. She glances down at her hands. Her knuckles are a patchwork of purple-green bruises, half-healed cuts and open wounds. No wonder her mother looked at her the way she did. She is grotesque. Horrifying. Shame swells inside her and she tugs the sleeves of her hooded sweatshirt down over her abused hands.

The elevator comes to a silent stop. When the doors slide open, Fletcher exits into a warmly lit hall. The polished, sterile concrete of the lower floors is replaced by rich oriental rugs and draped tapestries. He stops just shy of an intricately carved wooden door. This hall is vacant. No guards seem to be posted here.

Fletcher strides to the heavy door. When he pushes it open, the scent of ocean air hits Zoe hard. The sensation is instantly disorienting.

Against her better judgement, she takes a few steps forward. "What is this place?" she asks.

"Your room, Miss."

Tentatively, she crosses the threshold. The interior is spacious and open. Textured ceilings curve above her. Multifaceted star-shaped fixtures hangs low, their perforated spires casting amber light in all directions. As the wind blows, the fixtures sway, throwing shadowy patterns on sand-colored walls. Every window is flung open wide, sheer curtains billowing in the evening breeze. She can hear the sounds of crashing waves mix with the cry of seabirds. The ambience is soothing.

"Thank you, Joseph," says a deep voice.

Zoe turns to see an elderly man standing behind her. Was he there when she walked in? He had to be. She didn't notice him at all. How could she not have seen him?

He is dressed in black, which makes his tanned skin and close cropped white hair stand out all the more. The single color also succeeds in making his lanky frame seem imposing, and though he is thin, he is far from fragile. He looks at her with a squared gaze, unflinching and purposeful. As he moves cautiously closer, he motions to Fletcher. "Leave us."

"Sir." Fletcher gives a stiff bow and backs away, closing the door behind him.

There are so many reasons she should be frightened. She is in no physical position to defend herself. What's left of her family is in the custody of some shady criminal organization. She has so many questions and no hope of answers. She doesn't even know where she is geographically. And even if she did, there's no way to call for help. She is isolated. Alone in an unfamiliar room with a strange man.

Instead of fear, she grips hold of a stronger emotion. Anger. Rage. Zoe glowers at him.

He meets her gaze without hesitation. Minutes pass. He takes his time, silently considering her, before crossing the floor to a long dark wood bar stocked with bottles and shimmering crystal vessels. "Whiskey?" he asks cooly, pouring two glasses from a decanter.

Zoe can smell the alcohol from across the room, a rich, heady aroma that mingles with the salt air. Against her will, she begins to salivate. She nods.

He moves with graceful steps. Every motion is measured and precise. As he gives her the heavy glass, her hands begin to shake. The unconscious tremor sends a ripple through the amber liquid.

"There's no reason for you to be frightened." The old man smiles at her. "No one will hurt you here."

Addled, Zoe drinks deep, emptying her glass with panicked determination. The alcohol warms her throat but, unlike the medicinal lighter fluid she's used to drinking, it does not burn. Instead it travels through her body, permeating her blood and filling her belly with heat. His stare is harrowing, piercing her. She averts her eyes, focusing all her attention on the complicated pattern woven into the expensive looking rug.

"Who are you?" Zoe asks flatly.

His answer comes quickly. "Victor Sutton."

The name means nothing to her. Zoe keeps her eyes locked on the ground as Sutton passes by her, heading towards the windows. "You work for that blonde bitch?" she asks.

"Ms. Case? No." He chuckles, shaking his head as he lowers himself into an upholstered chair. "On the contrary, Ms. Case works for me."

This must be the man Hawthorne warned her about. This is her father's employer. The one who was looking for him. The wind kicks up, churning the air around her. The smell of salt and sea. She remembers the dunes. The scorched earth where her father's house should have been. Maybe she got it wrong. It had been so long and memory is a tricky thing. Nothing was familiar. She couldn't remember his address, just the feeling of home on a distant shore.

"And my father." Her knees grow weak. "He worked for you, too."

Sutton nods. "In a way."

"That book he left me." She swallows the lump in her throat. "It belonged to you, didn't it?"

"Yes."

"Then that's what this is all about? A book? You abducted my mother and chased me and my sister across the globe over some goddamn book?" Rage creeps into the edges of her voice. Her fingers strain painfully around her empty glass, threatening to crush it.

"That is an over-simplification."

"Bullshit!" Zoe flings the vessel at the wall. She is across the room and in his face as the thick glass shatters. Her sudden speed and aggression do not seem to affect Sutton. He sits still as a photograph. Studying her. Waiting. Zoe braces herself against the arms of his chair. "You got what you want. Let us go."

"I cannot do that." New emotion floods his weathered features. His body stiffens. "You must understand that the journal is not the end."

She does not understand. She wants to hit him. Her fist is already balled, but something in the way he looks at her is wrong. Her eyes dart around the room. Why are they are alone? He is vulnerable. Why would he do that? He has to know, has to see that she has the capacity for violence. She wears the evidence over every inch of exposed flesh.

There is a quiet confidence in his stare. He knows she will not hurt him.

Zoe's elbows and knees buckle. She shoves back, stumbling into the seat opposite Sutton, exhausted. Her muscles spasm as they relax, sending jerks and jolts of movement through her limbs. This is not just about her father. She is missing something. Her fingernails scrape at the thin fabric of her pants, picking stray threads as her head spins. "Whatever you want. I'll... I'll do it. Whatever it is. Just please leave Nik and my mom out of it." Her chest is heaving, lungs burning with every word. "Please."

Sutton cocks his head, looking out the window to watch black waves roll over the horizon. "That is a great deal of compassion for women who are essentially strangers to you."

"They're my family," she says plainly. The sentiment may be true, but somehow speaking the words out loud feels hollow. Zoe swallows hard, finishing her thought. "They're all I have left."

"My dear girl. How wrong you are." The sympathy in his voice is palpable. Sutton sets his glass down on the side table and leans close, placing a cool hand on her cheek. Her skin burns beneath his touch.

Warm light from amber sconces hits his face. His eyes are a deep, violent shade of green, flecked with hazel. Just like her father's. Just like her own.

All at once, Zoe cannot breathe.

- 14 -

THE LAB HAS AN INTENSE antiseptic smell to it. The fluorescent tubes on the low ceiling color everything a sickly blue. She can just make out their subtle flicker and low, steady hum. A polished metal table directly in front of her holds an all too familiar object. Nicole rolls her eyes. The book. Why are these people so fixated on this thing?

Her attention turns to the long lucite tank. It holds a thick pillar encrusted with sea life. This must be what Zoe found during the dive. Nicole had only seen the artifact briefly during its extraction from the debris field. The rover's visual feed did not do it justice. The sheer scale of the thing, the utter otherworldly appearance, is mesmerizing.

Nicole leans against the container, letting her fingers dip into the water.

"Where the hell did that come from?" her mother asks sternly.

Nicole pulls her hand away and turns. "Do you know what it is?"

Allison nods, lost in her thoughts.

"What is it?" Nicole presses.

"A masthead," her mother says softly.

"Seriously?" She looks back at the massive object suspended in the tank and cannot imagine anything that heavy staying upright on a boat.

"How did they find it?" Allison asks.

She swallows around the lump that has collected in her throat. Her words come out hoarse. "The location was in the book."

Her mother's eyes narrow into slits. "The book? What book?"

Nicole points to the leather bound journal resting on a long metal table near the tank. "That book. Zoe's dad left for her."

"So the artifact these assholes have been grilling me about. The one Hayden stole from them. Your sister has had it this entire time?"

Allison lets out a bitter bark of laughter. "Perfect. That's just fucking perfect."

"It's not like that, Mom." Nicole says. "She only found out about it a few weeks ago when we saw Professor Hawthorne. He gave it to her."

"Professor Hawthorne?" Her mother looks shocked. "William Hawthorne?"

"Yeah. He said he was a professor at the University of Cairo. He said he knew you. When you were younger. That you were his student." Allison will not look at her. "But you never said anything about going to school there. I mean, you would have told me if you did. Right? But you never mentioned anything about studying Egyptology." She tries to hide the hurt in her voice with middling success. "Seems like a big thing to not mention."

She will not look at Nicole. "Why were you in Cairo?"

"We weren't in Cairo." Nicole shakes her head, rubbing the intense knot she has been cultivating in her neck. She remembers the moldy smell of the apartment building. The dust motes drifting through the air like snowflakes. "He lives in Mombasa."

"Why would he live in Kenya? That doesn't make any... Wait a minute." Her words drift off. The realization takes a moment to sink in, but once it does, Allison's volume raises substantially. "Your sister took you to Mombasa? Jesus Christ, Nikky. Does she have any idea how dangerous that city is? She had no right to put—"

"Mom!" Nicole yells right back. "You've got to stop this. I understand you're pissed off at Zoe, but we've got way bigger problems. Like, for example, the gun-toting goons right outside the door. They brought us here for a reason." She presses off the tank and stalks to the table, picking up the book. The familiar texture of dimpled leather feels warm against her skin. She presses the journal to her mother's chest. "So, maybe we should focus and get to work."

Allison's jaw sets.

Her mother must have said those exact same words to her a thousand times while she was growing up. Focus and work. A tenacity for achievement was burned into Nicole at such a young age that she knew no other option. Life was work. She had her studies and her goals and she threw herself into them with obsessive dedication. A learned behavior, passed down from one workaholic to another.

After a moment, Allison takes the book from Nicole and drops onto a stool beside the long table. She begins to thumb through the pages. "Tell me what you know."

This is more like it. Straight to business. Nicole takes a seat next to her and peers over her shoulder. "From what I can tell it's a journal kept by a Dutch sailor from the 1700s."

Allison cocks a skeptical eyebrow. "You sound pretty certain of that."

Nicole shrugs. "Caroline had an appraiser look at it when Zoe and I were staying with her in Paris. He dated it. I just started translating what I could."

Allison looks confused. "Who's Caroline?"

She must not know. And why would she? It's not like Zoe would offer that sort of intensely personal information up for one of their incredibly uncomfortable biannual discussions/arguments.

Nicole presses on, ignoring the question. She points to the scrawled lines of words written in heavy black ink. "Writer was a lefty. That's why the text looks funny. It's mirrored. Right to left. I've been able to read most of what's written but there are some things, some words, that I'm pretty sure aren't Dutch." She pulls the book from her mother's hands and flips through the pages until she finds the passage she translated on the Trident. The one that led them to the mast. "Like here. Take a look at this." She slides the book back towards Allison. "This word is repeated multiple times, but I've never seen it before."

Allison traces the markings with her finger.

Nicole leans in closer. "What is it?"

"Where did you find it?" Her voice it distant. She drifts away from the table and stares at the Lucite container.

"I told you." She watches as her mom advances towards the lucite tank. "Hawthorne gave it to us when we saw him in Mombasa."

"Not the book, Nikky." Allison grips the edge of the acrylic, staring at the object suspended just beneath the water's surface. "Where did you find the mast?"

"In the Arabian. Why?" Nicole watches her mother work a path around the tank, inspecting the hunk of bronze intently. She plunges her hand into the water until she is touching the encrusted artifact. Her fingers search the surface with purpose, then stop abruptly. She withdraws her hand, flicking water to the floor and feverishly wiping her hand off on her pants before heading back to the table to flip through the pages. Nicole has seen her mother at work before. She's seen her get lost in dissertations and research documents,` but she has never seen her like this. "Mom?"

Allison's eyes are intense. "And there was nothing else? Nothing more?"

All at once Nicole remembers the carving. She digs into her pocket, withdrawing the wooden figure and setting it down on the pages of the open book. "There was this. But it didn't come with the book. Zoe got it in Zurich when we checked on her father's accounts. I have no idea what it is or if it's even related to—"

Allison exhales stiffly. "It's an ushabti."

"Excuse me?" Nicole squints. The word doesn't sound real, let alone familiar. "Yooba-what?"

"An ushabti." Allison flips back through the pages, landing on a crudely rendered series of symbols. Her voice instinctively slips into the steady, measured tone of a lifelong teacher. "An Egyptian burial tradition. The carving is placed with the dead. In lieu of a human sacrifice, the carved figure represented the soul of a servant meant to assist the deceased once they reach the afterlife."

"So you did study Egyptology?" Nicole cannot hide the hurt in her voice. All these years she never felt like her mother was keeping anything from her. She always felt like they connected, they were level with one another. That their relationship was different from the one Allison had with Zoe. "Why didn't you ever tell me?"

Her mother's focus does not break from the carving.

Nicole sighs and steers herself back on topic. "All the words that aren't Dutch, the ones that I couldn't figure out, they're—"

"Pidgin," Allison says.

Nicole's eyes go wide, she snaps her fingers. Dormant knowledge gleaned from two semesters of anthropological linguistics swiftly rises to the surface. When two cultures come into prolonged contact, sometimes concessions have to be made. Language may be about rules, but communication is all about compromise. "Those are words he phonetically simplified because he had no direct translation for them. He was probably using the sketches as reminders." Nicole pauses, scooting closer to her mother. She peers over her shoulder. "But that's a dead language, right? I mean, it was dead even in the 1700s. That's why the Rosetta Stone was so important. For a shipwrecked sailor to be translating ancient Egyptian, someone had to be speaking it to him, right?"

Allison is not listening. She is flipping through the yellowed pages, her finger frantically tracing the words Nicole could not translate. "Mom?"

She slams the book closed. "That son of a bitch."

THE TIMBRE OF CAROLINE'S VOICE is low and soothing. She speaks softly in French, murmuring words Zoe cannot understand "Ouvrez vos yeux, ma belle."

Her soft hands glide up Zoe's stomach, cresting the curve of her breasts. Her skin so warm. Caroline presses against Zoe. Her weight is intoxicating. Strands of her hair brush the bare skin of Zoe's cheek. She is so close. So tangible. Her breath hot against Zoe's ear. "Open your eyes."

Caroline is not there. There is no warm, intricate woodwork. No complicated coffered ceilings seamlessly uniting with delicate centuries old plasterwork. She is not in Paris.

She is alone, lying on a soft mattress as sunlight forces its way through blinds stretched across long windows. Her head is pounding. Her bleary eyes recoil from what little brightness punches through the gaps. Things are starting to come back to her. After Sutton left her, she drank. A lot. First, all the whiskey. Then other bottles. Something that might have been rum, maybe? It's not like the decanters were labeled, so she can't be positive, but it sure smelled like rum. She rolls away from the window and is confronted by a nightstand littered with empty bottles.

Zoe coughs, fighting the urge to throw up. Her stomach twists. Getting pissed and passing out was not the most adult way to deal with her avalanche of feelings, but she couldn't think of anything else to do.

Coping has never been one of her strong suits.

She pushes herself off the mattress and pads on bare feet to the bathroom where, thankfully, there are no windows. Every movement sends a pulse of pain through her body. Her joints are still swollen. The combination of being emotionally drained and physically weak infuriates her.

She leans over the sink and twists the tap, cupping her hands under the faucet's stream. The cold water makes her fingers ache. She splashes her face, once, twice, as many times as it takes to feel clean. The water drips off her chin, streaming down her neck and soaking into her tank top.

Elbows propped on the counter, Zoe stares at her reflection. The face looking back at her is barely recognizable. It's not the bruises, or the swollen lip, or even the blown out eye. The impostor is under her skin, a lie that courses through her veins, hiding somewhere deep inside her blood.

She combs through her hair, scraping her scalp too hard with too-long fingernails.

Everything has been fucked up since Zurich.

She should have stayed in bed with Caroline.

Zoe stops herself. Shaking her head in frustration. Caroline. Kind, beautiful Caroline Royer. She never got through to her. Everything fell apart so quickly on the Trident. There was not time to call. For all she knows, Zoe ran off yet again, abandoning the promise of their future. A storm churns in the pit of her stomach.

It's better this way. Caroline deserves more. More than Zoe can give her. She always did.

A loud knock echoes through the flat. She's not up for company. Zoe scrubs her face with a towel. She turns off the tap and waits, a silent hope that whoever it is will give up and leave her alone if she doesn't respond. That hope is dashed when the pounding continues, steady and insistent. Zoe slaps the counter, stalking out of the bathroom, through the bedroom, and into the main living area. She instantly regrets leaving the darkness. The morning light is intense, pouring through open windows, blowing out her vision and increasing the hammering behind her eyes. She stumbles to the door, flinging it open. "What?"

The man standing in the hall is sharply dressed but unkempt in the most calculating way possible. He smiles at her, his words coming out in a purr. "Good morning, miss."

"Who the fuck are you?" She swallows the bile rising in her throat.

The man extends his hand. "Eli Kostich."

Zoe rests against the jamb, squinting at her uninvited guest.

He lowers his hand slowly, slipping it into his pants pocket. "I work for Mr. Sutton."

She's already done with this conversation. "So?"

"So," Eli says, nervously checking the vacant hall before speaking. "I have some information about your father I'm sure you'll find interesting."

She already knows he's dead. Nothing this asshole can offer will change that. Zoe groans, rolling her eyes. The last thing in the world she wants to rehash right now is a past she had no control over. She pushes off the jamb. "Get fucked."

She closes the door as quickly as she can manage.

"The coroner's report was faked," he barks. Though he speaks quickly, his voice is confident. Smooth, sticky words seep through the gap. "It said he died in a fire, but it didn't say anything about the bullet in his brain, did it?"

Zoe stops. Her heart is drumming in her throat, threatening to choke her. Slowly, she pulls the door open again.

"Now. I can tell you who killed him," Eli says, a smirk on his full lips. His fingers loosely grip a slender computer tablet. He holds the device out to her. "Or you can find out for yourself. Choice is yours."

CONNOR HOLDS THE DOOR open for her. Though she is more than capable of taking care of herself—the behavior is a strange scrap of politeness and chivalry he has hung onto. Something he shows only to her. He has always treated her this way. Even before things between them grew complicated. And when her ambition took her away from field work and into a corner office, Connor stood by her, going so far as to refuse every internal transfer he was offered.

He is hers and hers alone. Steadfast and vicious.

Case slips past him, entering the waiting room just outside her office.

Her secretary looks up from her computer. "Good morning ma'am. You're morning appointment is waiting."

Case halts. She does not have a meeting on her book until well after noon. She glances toward her open office door. Broad shoulders and dirty blonde hair are an instant giveaway. Zoe Hudson is pacing the floor, disheveled and still wearing the clothes she was given yesterday in the infirmary.

"What's she doing here?" Connor tenses.

Case was just wondering the same thing. There should be a body man. Or two. Three, even, considering Zoe Hudson's record of violence. There is no way this woman would have been cleared to roam the complex unattended. A decision like that would be worse than sloppy. It would be stupid, and against every level of protocol.

Sloppy and stupid. Sounds like Eli. Victor must have put Zoe on his detail. Case snorts. This will be the final nail in Kostich's coffin.

Connor moves towards the door. She stops him, placing a hand on his chest. "No," she says, "I'll take care of it. Wait here."

She collects herself, then enters her office. The unmitigated anger seeping from Zoe is hard to miss. Case scans the room. "Ms. Hudson," she says cooly. "This is unexpected."

They are alone. Eli has really fucked up this time. It will be a pleasure to rub his nose in it. She smiles softly to herself and turns to face Zoe. "Is there something—"

The assault is quick. Zoe snatches up fistfuls of Case's blouse, driving her back, slamming her into the wall. Her head hits a framed mirror. Glass shatters. Case cannot process the event fast enough. Her physical response is sticky with confusion, every action is delayed. She tries to raise her hands as Zoe cocks a fist.

The hit is ferocious.

Case can see her attacker's mouth move. She is yelling, screaming. Spit flies from her lips, striking Case's cheek, but sound cannot penetrate the static pulse of her own blood coursing through her veins.

And just as quickly as it began, the attack is over. Pressure is released. The impact stops. Connor has wrenched Zoe off of Case. He drags her back, legs twisting and kicking. Case lifts a hand to her lips. Hot blood is pooling inside her mouth. She swallows it down as sound floods back into the room. Her jaw aches.

"Murdering bitch!" Zoe growls. She thrashes in Connor's arms. Fighting desperately to break his hold. He adjusts, gripping a handful of her hair and violently wrenching her head back. His thick forearm snakes across her neck. Her words sputter. He is choking her.

Case wipes her mouth, streaking red across the pale skin on the back of her hand. "Connor, stop."

He cannot hear her. Zoe is straining against his weight, fingernails digging into his arm. He draws her up higher until her toes hover inches off the ground. She flails, searching for traction but finding only air. Case has seen him like this a hundred times before. If he doesn't snap her neck, his hold will definitely force her to pass out, and an unconscious attacker cannot answer questions.

"Connor. *Let her go*," she yells. "Now."

His eyes clear, and silently he does as instructed. He releases Zoe, dropping her to the floor on shaky legs. Before Case can start her questions, Zoe lunges. Case should have expected that. In an instant, Connor's obedience is overwhelmed by a fierce instinct to protect. He lashes out, grabbing Zoe's raw wrist and twisting her bodily, wrenching her around. She swings at him wildly, striking with punishing force.

Case can hear a sharp crunch as Zoe's fist makes contact with Connor's cheek. It is all happening too fast. Where did this aggression come from? How did she get this opportunity? Who let her wander the complex alone? Case is so distracted trying to place why the attack is happening, she can't register what is going on right in front of her. Connor takes Zoe by the neck. His thick fingers crush her throat. As he raises her into the air, the cotton fabric of her tank top stretches tight across sinewy muscle. He'll kill her if she doesn't stop him.

"Connor. *Stand down.*"

He slams Zoe against the tempered glass of Case's desk over and over again. Her head whips back and forth, striking the surface violently. There is a choked gasping sound. A wet, sloppy attempt to intake oxygen. Zoe's struggling begins to subside. He is pounding the fight out of her. Only then does his grip on her throat loosen. Zoe is coughing, her head lolling listlessly. He pulls a fist back, preparing to strike.

"Connor!" Case snatches his wrist, her fingernails dig in deep enough to break through his frenzy. "That is enough."

The blind bloodlust in his eyes is replaced by indignation. He releases Zoe's limp body and takes a step back.

Case points to the door. "Leave. *Now.*"

She cannot allow him to handle this. Not this way. Not without orders. He glares at her, then stalks out, slamming the door behind him. Case winces at the sound, then turns just in time to watch Zoe slump off the desktop and crumple into a pile on the floor, her hands clasping her throat. After a coughing fit, she rights herself, propping an unsteady body against the desk.

"Now that we've all calmed down." Case inspects the blood on the back on her hand. "Do you mind tell me what this is all about?"

Zoe's voice is raw and filled with rage. "You murdered my father."

Case stares at her blankly. How could she know that? It happened so long ago. It was classified. Closed. Her wet work was immaculate, even considering that had been her first high-priority detail. The first time Sutton put her personally in charge of anything.

She had been so eager to please him. So tenacious. So calculated. She and Connor tracked their target for months until they finally cornered him in a tiny house on the Western Australian coast. It was surrounded by dunes and tall grass. The night was clear and moonless. The salty air stank of pungent gasoline. Smoke burned her lungs.

Fire was such an undignified way to go. No one deserved that. No matter what they had stolen.

"You put a fucking bullet in his head." Zoe is crumbling rapidly, tears begin to stream down her cheeks. Her words are nearly impossible to understand through her sobbing. "Why? Why did you do it?"

Case twitches, her skin growing cold and damp. She has never had to do this before; come face to face with the pain she has inflicted. Her response is unconscious. Mechanical. "I did what I was ordered."

"By who?!"

The force of her voice startling. Case grips the arm of the chair tighter, steadying her nerves. "Victor."

Zoe's face falls slack. Her green eyes dart around the room, losing focus. Damaged hands reach up, covering her mouth. She looks sick. Like she might vomit. A string of unintelligible words tumble from her lips. She rocks back, digging her heels in as her body tenses. All at once, she lets out a sharp, horrifying sound.

Case flinches and braces herself for another violent outburst. Instead, Zoe shoots past her, headed for the exit.

The door slams. The smoked glass partition separating her office from the waiting room vibrates with the force.

Seconds later, her secretary is standing in the doorway. "Is everything alright, ma'am?"

Case does not answer at first, distracted by the changed reflection staring blankly back at her, framed in the wide plate-glass window. Red spatters on a pristine white blouse. She applies pressure to her lip, feeling the split just inside her mouth with her tongue. The taste is coppery. Metallic. She glances over her shoulder at her secretary. "Everything is fine."

ALLISON SITS ALONE in Victor Sutton's office, stroking the dimpled spine of the journal with her thumb. Such a little thing. So delicate. At any point in history it could have been destroyed—the words could have faded, the pages could have fallen loose. But here it is, intact. The mast, the existence of the shipwreck in the Arabian, and the journal entries would have provided more than enough preliminary evidence to entice even the most skeptical of academic backers.

But there will be no academic backers. No organized research. Just priceless artifacts divvied up and sold to the highest bidder.

The thought makes her sick.

She releases a stiff sigh. How long she has been sitting here? Fifteen minutes? Twenty? There is no clock in this room. The walls are bare except for massive abstract paintings, their canvases heavy with reds and grays. She can only see a shadow through the obscured glass wall facing the lobby, but she can feel Fletcher's stare, piercing her from the other room. Sutton's assistant has not removed his eyes from her since he deposited her in the office.

Allison rubs the sweat off her palms, dragging open hands over the rough fabric of her pants. This has to be a tactic. They're trying to break her. Make her nervous. The guards came for her alone. Why wouldn't they bring Nicole? And what did these people do with Zoe? Panic begins to rise, clawing its way up from the pit of her stomach. Out of her periphery, a shadow moves beyond the glass. It strides quickly towards the door.

Sutton enters his own office with authority and purpose. "They tell me you already have results."

In this moment, all she wants is for this ordeal to be over. If she gives him what he wants, she has nothing left to bargain with. But if she withholds information there is a high likelihood conditions will worsen for her and her children.

Now is not the time to be proud or stubborn.

She clears her throat and begins. "The artifact in your lab is a masthead from an Egyptian longship. An ancient Egyptian longship. More specifically, from the 18th dynasty. The cartouche of the Pharaoh Hatshepsut is cast into the bronze." She pauses, looking down at her lap where white knuckled hands clutch the book. "This journal mentions an early attempt to investigate a shipwreck. The coordinates from that entry led your team to that mast which means the Egyptian wreck and the Dutch log book are connected."

"Go on." Sutton takes a seat across from her.

"But the entries never mention the Pharaoh. And they only mention Egypt in the very end. One thing does continue through all the entries, once the castaway shows up. One series of symbols. One cartouche. One name. Neferura." Allison pauses before she continues. "She was Hatshepsut's eldest daughter and was meant to inherit her mother's throne. A few years prior to the end of Hatshepsut's reign the girl simply vanished from the historical record. None of this information was known in the sixteenth century. Hatshepsut wasn't even confirmed as a Pharaoh until the early twentieth. If the dates I've been given are accurate, the man this crew picked up had incredibly advanced knowledge of Egyptian history."

"Is that all?"

"No." Allison stiffens, her anger growing. "How did you know about my undergraduate research?"

A smug smile spreads across Sutton's lips.

"I wrote my dissertation on Hatshepsut and her lineage. You had to have known that. That has to be why you brought me here. I just don't know how you knew," she says, trying and failing to mask the frustration in her voice. "My papers were never published. How did you find them?"

"William sent them to me," he says casually.

"William Hawthorne?"

Sutton nods.

"You're lying. That's not possible. Bill would never work with someone like you. Never." Allison shakes her head. Her eyes close. She doesn't want to believe it could be true. But Nicole mentioned him. Said Hawthorne gave them the book. And Hayden did know Hawthorne. He always said they went back a long way. She never made the connection until now. Allison pinches the bridge of her nose. "Even a passing connection to you would have jeopardized his entire career. He wouldn't do it."

Sutton chuckles at her and cocks his head. "Perhaps you didn't know the good professor as well as you like to think."

His condescension only incites her. She lurches forward in her seat and stabs an accusing finger at him. "He's a good and decent man."

"Even decent men need money, Doctor."

"So that's it?" The muscles in the back of her neck twitch. She straightens herself and glares at him. "You bought him?"

"William had expensive tastes." Sutton's demeanor shifts. There is a viciousness there, floating to the surface. "Strangely enough, your cooperation has been far more challenging to obtain."

"My cooperation?" She scoffs. "Is that what you call abducting me and threatening my family?"

"My initial attempt did not produce results."

"Your initial attempt?" Her mind races to complete the puzzle, haphazardly slamming the pieces together, forcing them into place.

"Hayden. You sent him to Australia. To the gala. You were using him to coerce me."

"Very good."

She remembers the night they met so clearly. It plays in her head every night, whether she wants it to or not. He looked so handsome. So confident. So charming. She trusted him instantly. It was the first of many mistakes. "So everything he said. Everything he did. It was all an act?"

"Unfortunately, I wouldn't know." Sutton's gaze is cold. "My son kept the details of his affair with you private."

Everything stops. A weight drops in her gut. "Your—"

"Son," he says. "Yes, you heard me. And now I think you understand."

Her mouth is dry. A dizzy, untethered sensation over takes her. "This isn't about the journal or the artifact. Is it?"

"There was a time when it was." Sutton sets his jaw and rises from his seat. Slowly, he walks to his desk. Allison can see his reflection in the wall of glass overlooking the ocean. A stern expression crosses his weathered features. "But now it's about family. My family."

Her words barely claw their way out of her throat. "Zoe is *not* your family."

"Neither is she yours, Allison." The bitterness in his voice hits her like a hammer. Sutton turns, his eyes narrowing. Every feature seems to grow sharper, more intense, seething with rage. And in this moment all she can see is her own daughter staring back at her, green eyes cloudy with disgust. "You pushed her away years ago. There is no sense in vainly holding on to her now. It's pathetic." Sutton presses a button on his computer terminal. Seconds later, the door behind her opens. "Joseph. Take the doctor back to her room. See that she stays there."

- 15 -

THE CONCRETE PATIO is bathed in sunlight. Salty sea air flutters across the lush leaves spilling from manicured planting beds.

Case checks her watch. "Who exactly are we waiting for, sir?"

Sutton's focus drifts over her shoulder; she follows his eyes as the patio door sweeps open. Fletcher exits the residence holding a computer tablet. He stalls the door for the woman following him.

"Thank you, Joseph." Sutton accepts the device from his assistant and gestures to the stiff modern deck chair next to his own. "Please have a seat, Zoe."

Zoe Hudson lowers herself into the chair. She stares vacantly out at the rolling waves beyond the greenery. Her skin is glowing red, visibly raw from vicious scrubbing. Her blonde hair is wet and pulled back into a tight bun. Beads of water trickle down her neck, leaving glistening paths over the bruises Connor inflicted the day before. The deep purple hues of his fingerprints are muddy against Zoe's honey-tanned skin. The collar of her dress shirt is spotted with darkness, water leeching into the starched grey fabric like blood from a wound.

She should not be here. She should be detained. Locked in a cell. Sedated and under surveillance. Not unbound, sitting at the right hand of Victor.

Why does he want her here?

"Trisha?" Sutton barks.

Case blinks. Her mind clearing. "Yes?"

"I asked you to bring Zoe up to speed." He is annoyed. His stormy green eyes are chiseled into narrow slits. "Is there some problem?"

His eyes.

Case catches her breath. She focuses on Zoe. The shape of her features. The hawkish sweep of her nose. The angle of her bone structure. Her sullen expression. Those same deep green eyes.

Case's lip begins to throb. She swallows.

Pull your shit together, Tricia.

"No, sir." Case taps her password onto the glassy surface of her tablet and begins her presentation. "The final entries of the journal mention a temple near the banks of Lake Nassar believed to hold the remains and burial treasure of the Pharaoh's daughter." An unsteady finger flicks her screen, selecting the next slide. "In the late 1950s, plans were drawn up for the construction of a hydroelectric facility that would aid the North African region in power production, as well as prevent catastrophic flooding of the lake. The Soviets assisted the Egyptian government in the project, while UNESCO stepped in to help with the relocation of monuments that were deemed too important to lose. I'm certain you will remember the reconstruction of Abu Simbel?"

Sutton nods. Next to him, Zoe slouches deeper into her seat. Case cannot help but watch her, trying to prepare for the unpredictable. For the briefest moment, their eyes meet, but Zoe turns away, muscles in her cheeks twitching and flexing as she clenches her jaw. Her bruised hand tightens around the arm of her chair, knuckles white with the strain.

"Dr. Hudson confirmed the location of the temple in question. It was not salvaged by UNESCO and, since it was directly in the flood plain, it has been submerged for over half a century." Case advances to the final schematic of the Aswan desert. The arial map twists at her touch, and the image warps into a modern rendering of the valley, complete with the reinforced perimeter of the dam.

Sutton studies the image. "Is there any chance the location has already been compromised?"

Case shakes her head. "No, sir. If anything had been academically excavated, the contents would have been meticulously cataloged. And if the location had been robbed, we would seen artifacts relating to Neferura on the black market. Neither have happened." She closes her presentation and turns off her tablet. "This is a solid lead. We have the location, the government connections, and the specialized personnel in place."

Sutton hands his device off to Fletcher. He plucks a water glass from the table between them and drinks deeply. Condensation drips onto his slacks. He places the glass back on the table. "How do you plan to gain access?"

This is what he pays her for. The planning. Even before he hired her, this is where she excelled. Her ability to cover all the angles kept her alive, kept her out of harms way.

Mostly.

Case clutches her computer and straightens her back. Her delivery has to be confident. Precise. "An extremist cell will call in a threat. The dam has been targeted numerous times before, and the UN takes each threat seriously. The facility in Aswan supplies power to all of North Africa and parts of the Middle East. Specifically Israel, Iran, and Jordan. The facility will shut down and the area will need to be secured. Under our current defense contract, the UN will rescind control of the site to our security firm for 48 hours while we conduct a preliminary assessment of the situation. Dive teams will survey the dam in search of biological explosives. While they provide a diversion, a lone diver will break off, breach the temple, and secure the artifacts."

Sutton looks away from Case to Zoe. "Will you do it?"

Zoe's brow furrows. Her lips are drawn into a tight line of frustration. The struggle inside her is obvious, but she nods stiffly in agreement.

"Excellent." Sutton says. He waves a hand dismissing Case. "Mobilize your teams, Tricia."

"Sir." She rises from her seat and follows Fletcher to the exit.

Before he can pull the door open, she see something. Reflected in the tinted glass surface, Sutton place a hand on Zoe's knee. The old man leans in close, his lips moving, saying words Case may not be able to hear, but she can feel their importance.

Everything is different now.

SHE IS DROWNING. Water fills her lungs. Her heart beats hard, slamming into bruised ribs. Darkness twists around her. Coating her skin. Chilling her body. She should give up. Right now. Let go. Allow herself to be taken under. Stop fighting.

A cool hand rests on her forearm. Her eyes snap open.

"Ms. Hudson," Fletcher whispers, "are you—"

Zoe flinches, withdrawing from his touch. "I'm fine."

She must have drifted off.

Her body tenses as she settles back into her seat and glances around the cabin of the luxury jet. Sutton is resting comfortably across from her, his head propped against the bolstered leather cushion.

Fletcher has turned his attention back to his tablet. On the opposite side of the cabin, near the reinforced cockpit door, Case sits alone, her pale skin glowing bright under an LED task lamp. As the woman adjusts in her seat, the black leather of her shoulder holster shows more clearly. Its thick straps are stark in contrast to the white of her shirt. She looks up, fixing Zoe with an emotionless stare.

Zoe's heart stutters.

She has to get away from here. Get space.

Her fingers fumble with her seatbelt until it unlatches and flops back against the metal arm of the seat. She shoves her aching body up and into the aisle, heading towards the cramped lavatory in the rear of the plane. With an unsteady hand she jerks the door open to throw herself inside. After the lock is flipped, fear overtakes her. She turns towards the polished metal mirror. Her knees bang against the brushed metal lip of the toilet. Her lungs refuse to pull in air. She pants. Quick, panicked gasps.

She has no plan.

Nicole and her mother were at the airfield. They were handcuffed and gagged. Nicole looked so frightened. Zoe watched, helplessly, from the tarmac as they were shoved onto a cargo plane, escorted up the ramp by the hulking brute who nearly strangled her in Case's office.

She had no way to help them.

No way to protect them.

Zoe runs the faucet, cupping her hands under the stream. She splashes her face. Once. Twice. The cool water runs down her cheeks, following the geography of her skin until it finally drips from her chin. In the mirror, a blank reflection stares back at her. She is still in her dream. Still drowning. Trapped on a plane with every person responsible for the death of her father. Killers. People she cannot trust. All the rage inside her wants to end this. Wants to walk out of the bathroom and tear Tricia Case and the man who calls himself her grandfather apart with her bare hands.

She would never land a single blow.

Case would put a bullet in her.

Just like her father.

Her knees buckle. She drops onto the toilet, elbows slamming into the narrow counter and the wall. Her entire body begins to shudder and the tears that come are uncontrollable. She covers her mouth with both hands, trying to muffle the sounds of her sobbing. Hopelessness pours from her, spilling out in waves.

There is a knock on the door.

Zoe jumps, startled. They must have heard her. She slams her eyes shut. *You have to be better than this. You have to be brave. Can you do that? Can you be brave?*

There is another knock. Harder this time.

"Just a minute," she stammers, standing right as turbulence hits the aircraft.

A red light glows above the door, telling her to return to her seat. Over the PA she can hear the pilot issuing the same warning. Zoe steadies herself against the edge of the counter and stares into the mirror. *No one else can save them.* She shoves a hand under the stream of water still flowing into the stainless steel basin. The cold makes her skin tingle. *It has to be you.*

"Ms. Hudson?"

Even hearing Case's voice muffled through the door sets her nerves on edge. Zoe rinses her face once more and cuts the faucet. She pads her skin dry with a few disposable towels and takes a deep breath. *You have to do this. For Nik.*

She unlocks the door and swings it open. Case is waiting outside, leaning against the bulkhead, her hands poised on her hips, so close to her sidearm. "We're on approach. Take your seat."

IT'S NOT THAT ROYER AVIATION doesn't make a respectable cargo plane—she has simply never taken the time to get the feel for one. Her interests have always leaned more towards the recreational and experimental. If she was going to fly for fun, the machine needed to break barriers and set records.

But this isn't fun. It's stupid. Reckless, even. She racks her brain, staring at the complicated instrument panels, trying to remember anything she picked up while clocking hours in the commercial jet simulators when she visited her father's training facility back in Quebec.

The scale must be what's throwing her off. The full-sized cockpit of the four turbine cargo jet is altogether monstrous and claustrophobic. Expansive blinking boards curve all around her. So many read-outs and switches, most marked in Russian, all of them unhelpful. Her confidence crumbles the longer she waits for Matthew to get back.

Sweat pours off her, soaking through her clothes at all points where the fabric makes contact with her skin. Caroline strips down to her tank top, throwing her over-shirt down on the co-pilot's chair. She glances at her watch. It's been over an hour. He is taking too long.

Something must be wrong.

The heavy metal hatch to the cockpit swings open. In the slanted glass above the main controls, a shape reflects that is most certainly not Matthew. A woman stands behind her, confused. Caroline's heart leaps into her throat. He told her to keep her head down, to stay in the cockpit and wait for him to get back. *Don't let them see you.*

Well, this is inconvenient.

"Who the hell are you?" The woman barks, her hand resting on the butt of her sidearm. "You're not supposed to be in here."

Caroline leans against the console. She stays quiet. The muscles in her arms twitch and pulse.

The guard draws her weapon. "Get your hands up. Turn around."

Caroline swallows hard, raising her hands but refusing to move. *Don't let them see you.*

"I said turn around!"

The woman won't fire in the cockpit and risk damaging the controls. She clings to this thought, trying desperately to steady her breathing.

"Do it now!"

You can't help them if you're dead. Caroline turns slowly, hands raised, blood pounding in her ears.

She keeps her voice low and level, covering her fear with gentle confidence as best she can manage. "I can explain. If you just let me—"

"Keep your hands in the air, bitch." The guard reaches for her radio. "Michaels, this is Welch. I've got unauthorized personnel on board the cargo transport. Do you copy?"

Static crackles from the small speaker, reverberating. There is no response.

She tries again. "Michaels? Do you copy? Michaels?" Her voice echoes back, tinny and hollow.

In the brief moment before Caroline realizes exactly what is going on, all she can do is smile. Her reflection on the windscreen is manic, muscles misfiring, contorting her features into some warped grin.

The guard slaps at her radio as a large gloved hand takes hold of her head, slamming it into the curved control board. Sparks jump from the display, electronics popping and hissing with the force of the impact. The woman's body drops to the floor with a thud.

Caroline exhales sharply, slumping back against the instrument panel. "Jesus Christ, Matthew!"

"What?" He tugs down a scarf covering his face. He is dressed the same as the guard at his feet. The name 'Michaels' is stitched across the tag on his vest. He tugs off his sunglasses. "She had a gun on you—what'd you expect me to do?"

"I don't care about her." She waves dismissively at the unconscious woman. "You've been gone for an hour."

He gives her a coy smile as he begins to strip the guard of her gear and uniform. "Were you worried about me, Mom?"

She rolls her eyes, wishing he would take what they are trying to do a little more seriously. The sharp sound of Velcro ripping open makes her flinch. He removes the woman's tactical vest, setting it carefully aside.

Caroline stammers, "W-wh-what are you doing?" The question comes out sounding more scared than she would have preferred. The guard twitches as Matthew removes her uniform top.

"We've got to blend." He balls up the dark shirt and tosses it to Caroline, quickly stripping the woman's boots and pants.

Caroline cannot watch. She turns, fumbling with the buttons of the stiffly starched shirt.

"You can fly this thing, right?" He doesn't wait for her answer, tossing the rest of the gear at her feet and hoisting the guard over his shoulder. He muscles the limp body out of the cockpit. His confidence in Caroline's abilities is complete. She wishes she shared his conviction.

She slips into the pilot's seat, twisting towards the controls. One hand rests on the four levers that make up the main throttle, the other loosely cups the wheel. She mumbles to herself, "I can fly it." Landing, however will be something entirely different. Matthew doesn't need to know that right now. She'll figure it out. It's just like riding a bike. A really big, ill-fitting bike where all the controls are labeled in Russian. Not a problem.

Matthew drops into the seat next to her. "Then let's get a move on, Ma."

She pulls her headset on with trembling hands.

"Royer?" He touches her arm, the synthetic material of his glove is strange, gripping her skin with little effort. He is serious now. "If you want to back out, I need to know. We still have time to get back to your plane and—"

"No." She drops the mic boom and flicks the radio on. "Tower, this is Charlie Alpha Vega Seven Six Niner. We have passed our maintenance inspection and are requesting immediate departure. Do you copy?"

The tower crew responds quickly. "Charlie Alpha Vega Seven Six Nine, you are cleared for take off."

"Roger that." Caroline cuts the radio, continuing preflight checks as best she can manage. She hears the click of Matthew's seatbelt fastening. Her right hand presses forward on the throttle sending a steady thrum of power through the aircraft's frame.

I lost her once. Caroline focuses down the dark, arid runway. *I won't lose her again.*

ALLISON STARES OUT the tinted window of the armored transport. Desert stretches out around them, seemingly infinite in all directions. A pale red horizon presses against the twilight, melding sand with sky.

She never intended to come back to Egypt.

The moment the plane touched down at the small airstrip near Aswan, she began to realize the true scope of Victor Sutton's influence. His armored convoy looked more like an army than an expedition. She tells herself a personnel movement of this size will not go unnoticed. There is no feasible way this many troops will be allowed anywhere near a protected historic site patrolled by UN forces.

She is getting used to being proven wrong.

Abu Simbel pulls into view through the dirty windshield, as does the simmering surface of the Aswan Dam. The convoy is waved through the gate and into a receiving area by heavily armed soldiers, none of whom bear the pale blue helmets or distinctive armbands of the UN. The site has already been secured. Vehicles fan out, screeching to a halt on the loose gravel. A cloud of dust and sand rises, but nothing can obscure the colossi guarding the entrance to the main temple. Crumbling effigies of Rameses II, their stony faces pointed south, staring down would-be invaders, challenging southern tribes to step foot in a kingdom at the height of its military might.

Seems ironic now.

An impossibly strong hand grips her arm, drawing her to her feet in the cramped confines of the transport. The mountain of a man who separated her from Nicole at the airfield forces Allison to the rear of the vehicle and out the wide hatch. Her knees buckle when her feet hit the sand. She stumbles, collapsing. Allison tries to convince herself her lack of coordination is related to poor blood circulation from too much sitting on her ass. She knows full well she is actually terrified of what might happen to them here in this secluded place.

The brute, who has been her handler since they departed the airfield, wrenches her to her feet and shoves her forward, deftly guiding her through the flurry of troop movement. Thick power cables snake up the carved stone stairs and into the temple's threshold. She's never seen anything like this. The speed at which these people are overtaking this site is remarkable. Men and women in fatigues unload crate after crate, generators, supplies, everything. This is an occupying force.

Allison's foot catches on a jumble of wires. Her escort stops her fall, steadying her with one massive hand gripped around her bound wrists. He pushes her into the main hall. She squints, raising her hands to block the unexpected light. The entire main chamber is awash in the bright light of halogen work lamps. Statues depicting Rameses II as Osiris march down the central isle. Their faces are lost in shadow, obscured by the blinding beams. They stare down, lifeless stone faces idly watching the technicians scurrying about their feet. In the dark beyond the columns, Allison can just make out the reliefs depicting the Pharaoh's countless military victories chiseled deep into the thick red granite walls.

"Connor," a woman barks. Allison recognizes the voice. Tricia Case waves them over. "Bring her over here."

Connor maneuvers Allison toward a cluster of widescreen monitors surrounding a square table covered in maps. In the center of the table sits the open journal. Case straightens, adjusting the line of her pale linen blouse as Connor shoves Allison towards her. She plucks a pair or pliers off a nearby hardshell case and works her way around the table and behind Allison. Allison holds her breath. Her heart skips.

There is a snap. Her wrists are free.

Case tosses the pliers onto the table and the clipped plastic ties into a nearby open crate. "Welcome to Abu Simbel, Dr. Hudson."

Allison rubs her raw wrists. "Where are my daughters?"

"They should be the least of your concerns." She pushes the journal towards Allison. "You have a lot of work to do."

"I'm not going to help you." Allison crosses her arms. "I refuse."

"Now is not the time to be stubborn, Doctor." Case's hand comes to rest on the butt of her sidearm.

"Where are they?" It takes everything in her to keep her voice from trembling.

Case narrows her eyes. Her tongue flicks behind her teeth. She leans against the table, arms spread wide. "I would assume Zoe is still with Victor. He does seem to love his new toy."

Allison recoils at the mention of the old man. Case has to see it.

"You don't like that, do you? Being betrayed." Her smile is acidic. "Children can be so ungrateful, can't they?"

"Where's Nicole?"

"She's in a secure location."

"I want her here. With me."

"No." Case shakes her head. "We have a limited timeline. You need to focus on the extraction."

"How limited?" Allison can barely believe she is asking.

"Two days."

"Two days?" she balks. "That's insane. An excavation like this can take years. Factoring in that the site is submerged—"

"You have two days, Doctor Hudson." Case grabs a pair of sunglasses off the edge of the table and moves to leave. "I suggest you prepare yourself. The divers will be in place shortly."

"Wait." She stops Case, grabbing her arm. Connor moves for his gun. Allison releases Case and takes a cautious step back. "Nikky... Nicole. She has more experience with the journal entries. She has a keener sense of the language... She'd be an invaluable asset to your operation. She would be helpful. To me."

Case pauses.

Don't beg. Don't show weakness. The words come anyway. "Please, Tricia."

The line of Case's jaw twitches. She looks to Connor. "Go get the girl."

Connor gives her a stiff nods. His heavy footfalls echo through the stone structure as he makes his way out of the hall.

"Thank you." Allison whispers under her breath.

"If you disappoint me," Case steps close. Her features tense. Sweat rolls down her cheek, following the rigid line of her jaw. She glares at Allison, hissing her words through gritted teeth. "I will make certain you regret it. Am I clear?"

Allison dips her head.

Case exits the main chamber, leaving the doctor under the watchful eyes of armed guards.

SHE WOULD GIVE ANYTHING NOT to be alone. Nicole can barely remember how to cope with her own mind as it races about, drawing oblique connections, making impossible plans, and finally drifting off to dark, scary places. She'd give anything for someone to talk to.

She'd give everything to talk to her sister.

No one will tell her what's going on. Her mother wasn't in any mood to share what she and Sutton spoke about after their impromptu meeting. Hours later they were cuffed with plastic zip ties and escorted to the roof where they were shoved onto helicopters. Nicole probably protested too much because the neanderthal escorting them gagged her. When they touched down, they were at an airfield. A big one. It seemed to roll on for miles. Hangars and different types of airplanes dotted the landscape. She saw Zoe briefly as they were being manhandled onto a cargo plane. She was dressed in dark clothes, her hair pulled back and pinned up. She looked different. Angry, severe, and distracted. She didn't even look in their direction, which, given the argument she had with their mother, Nicole could understand. Allison Hudson wasn't winning any parenting awards at the moment.

But what Nicole could not understand was why her sister wasn't handcuffed or under guard. These people were treating her differently.

Like she was one of them.

There has to be a reason for it. It has to be part of her plan. But all Nicole can come up with sounds less like logic and more like Star Wars-y dark side bullshit. Zoe has to have a reason for switching sides. She has to know what she's doing. Nicole just hasn't figured it out yet.

She scrubs the sweat off her face with her hands. Her focus shifts to the steel plates welded over the room's lone window. Bright light punches through the gaps. With no clock, the passage of time is difficult to read, but if the light and growing heat are any indication, it's coming on afternoon. Afternoon in a desert. That much she could tell from the drive in from the airfield. All she saw was sand and dust. Somehow, she can't imagine that being stuck in a sealed metal box baking in the noonday sun will be good for her. She tugs the band out of her hair and rearranges her mess of curls into something tighter and higher, further from the sweat cascading down her neck.

Nicole unscrews the cap on the huge bottle of water she was left and takes a deep drink of its lukewarm contents. In the stillness, she can just hear voices outside the door. She stands, turning towards the sound, straining to make out what they are saying. A fan kicks on, filling her ears with a low mechanical hum, obscuring all other noises until the bolt is thrown back on the lock and the door swings open, bathing the small portable in harsh light. The shape lingering in the threshold is familiar.

"Zoe?" she murmurs softly.

Her sister takes a tentative step as the door slams shut. Nicole's eyes fight to adjust, vision filling with white bursts, floating in space and clouding her sight. The dark, slender shape of her sister comes back into focus. She looks exhausted.

Zoe inspects her with bloodshot eyes. "Nobody's hurt you, have they?"

"No," Nicole answers.

Her sister begins to sway. She nervously wrings her bruised hands. "Good."

"What's going on? Why did they move us? Where are we?"

Her barrage of questions gets a lone answer. "Egypt."

"Egypt?" Nicole repeats the word like it will somehow make more sense coming from her lips. Her sister's restless movement turns into pacing. She makes a deliberate circuit of the container. Nicole follows her. "Why are we in Egypt? Does it have to do with the book? With the artifact? With Mom? She won't talk to me, Zoe. Tell me—"

Zoe turns around and takes hold of Nicole shoulders. She fixes her with a desperate stare. "I need you to promise me something."

"What?" Nicole asks, confused. "Why?"

"No matter what, I need you to be brave. Okay?" The intensity of her gaze increases. Zoe tightens her grip. "Promise me."

"Zoe, I don't—"

"Promise me, Nicole!" She growls.

"I promise." She barely manages the response. Nicole blinks, swallowing the bile rising in her throat. "What's going on? Why are you acting like this?"

Zoe's eyes dart around the metal container. "They murdered my father."

Nicole's stomach twists.

"They shot him. Burned down his house. Paid off the police. Covered it all up. Made it an accident." Zoe's breath hitches. She pauses for a moment, licking her parched lips. "You and Mom aren't safe."

She shrugs out of Zoe's grip. "What do you mean? Are they going to try and kill us?"

Her sister may be looking right at her, but Zoe doesn't see Nicole. She's deep in her own mind. Fighting with her thoughts. Rage flows off her in waves. Nicole cautiously reaches out to touch her sister's cheek, but she recoils from the contact. The world begins to shift beneath her feet. "Zoe. Please talk to me."

Tears well in her sister's eyes. Sweat beads on her skin, rolling down her face and neck, leeching into the dark fabric of her shirt. There is a silent determination in Zoe's eyes that Nicole can feel more than see. Her heart races. She knows that look. Zoe gave it to her on the boat as the pirates approached. She flashed it in the bay before she dove. And all at once Nicole knows what her sister is planning. She knows why she is here. She knows what this visit means. This is no rescue. No convoluted escape plan.

This is goodbye.

The realization hits her like a punch in the gut. Her breath is gone. She draws in deep, ragged breaths, forcing oxygen into her blood, trying not to pass out. Hot tears give way, rolling down her cheeks as she stammers like a child. "Please don't. Don't do this. Please, Zoe. Please."

She snatches Nicole's sweat-soaked flannel over-shirt and pulls her in close, hugging her tight. Held there against Zoe's chest, time slows. She is surrounded in the strength of her sister's arms. It is the safest place Nicole has ever known. This woman has been her protector. Her friend. Her family. And if she goes through with whatever she's planning, she will be gone forever.

She sobs into Zoe's chest. "Please don't leave me again. Please."

Zoe kisses the top of her head and whispers softly into her tangled hair. "Take care of Mom."

Nicole wraps her arms around Zoe's waist in a vain attempt to stop herself from coming undone. Everything inside Nicole wants to hold onto her. To keep her here in this stuffy, windowless portable shelter until she changes her mind. But that is not how this will work. She cannot change Zoe's mind. There may be a million rational protests racing through her brain, but they all crumble in her throat. Their wreckage blocks even the simplest sounds from exiting her mouth.

"I love you, Nik." Zoe says, gently kissing her damp forehead. "I always have."

She breaks free of Nicole's grasp and exits the dark trailer into the blinding desert light.

- 16 -

Case steps out of the shadowed temple and into the unyielding heat of the desert. Sweat instantly evaporates from her skin, soaking through her linen blouse only to dissipate in the still air. She slips her sunglasses on and scans their make-shift base of operations. Things seem to be going smoothly. Boats are already circling the dam.

Amidst all the movement, Fletcher catches her eye, coming around the rear of an armored transport parked at the base of the steps. His three-piece suit is out of place in the desert heat. Its dark fabric appears pristine, except for a smattering of red dust over his dress shoes and the up-turned hem of his pants. He sees her and begins to stride up the steps. His movements are casual, but she can see an uneasiness in his expression.

He should be uneasy.

He should be fucking terrified.

She marches down the steps to meet him.

Fletcher gives her a weak smile. "The recovery plane has touched down. The crew radioed in. They are awaiting further—"

"You slimy little prick." She cuts him off. "You never told me Hayden was his son."

He responds flatly, obviously amused by her anger. "You never asked."

"This isn't a joke, Fletcher." She could slap him, but there are too many witnesses. She doesn't have time for games. "Why didn't you warn me?"

Fletcher seems offended. "It isn't relevant."

"She's his fucking granddaughter." Case barks. She checks over her shoulder again to see if anyone paid attention to her outburst. The troops seem to be going about their tasks, unaware.

Sutton's assistant takes her by the arm and pulls her away from the center of the steps and closer to the rubble of the felled statues. She wrenches free of his grip as he begins to speak. "Zoe Hudson is nothing more than a distraction to him."

"She's family."

Fletcher shrugs. "She may be related to Victor, but that doesn't make her your competition."

"I murdered his only son." She feels more panicked than she would like, but given the circumstances, she cannot imagine feeling any other way. Why is he being so nonchalant?

He steps closer, pressing into her space with unearned familiarity. Case wants to back up, but forces herself to stand steady. When he speaks, his words are soft but firm. There is the slightest hint of frustration in his voice. "You did what Victor ordered."

Case scowls at his response. "And what if Victor stops seeing it that way?"

"Zoe will only become a complication if *you* make her one." Fletcher moves closer still. She can smell his sweat mixed with something bitter. Astringent. It makes her head swim. He whispers in her ear. "You have to trust me on this, Tricia."

The space between her eyes begins to pulse. She watches the boats crisscross the glassy surface of the dam. An acrid scent smoke and gasoline burns her nostrils. A wall of heat bears down on her. She did exactly what he ordered. She did what he told her to do. Case's knees buckle. She steadies herself against the toppled statue.

Fletcher checks over his shoulder before he speaks. His words come out low and rapid. "Now, Sutton is fatigued and under enormous amounts of stress. If we combine those factors with the extreme heat and a minor alteration in his medication, I can manufacture a seizure. It will look completely natural."

She cannot believe he is suggesting this. Here. Out in the open. "Fletcher, I don't—"

"He is old and feeble, Tricia. This organization needs a stronger leader." His attention is directed only at her. The intensity makes her skin crawl. "Your succession is guaranteed. No one will contest Victor's will. All the board members will ratify his choice. They will support—"

"Stop." Case grabs hold of his jacket and shakes him. She cannot do this. Not now. Not like this. "Just stop, Fletcher. Stop."

Time halts.

Fletcher peels her hands off his lapels. He straightens himself and his rumpled clothing. With a curt nod he turns on his heel and stalks away, heading up the broad stone steps to the main command post inside the temple.

Case watches him until he disappears through the shadowed portal. Shutting him down like that was probably not one of her smarter moves. She checks her watch. The second team of divers should be in the water any minute now. Zoe will be among them. The breach will begin soon.

She needs to be ready.

AS THE ZIPPER SLIDES CLOSED, she can feel the familiar tightness of the fabric. The neoprene cups her form perfectly, as it should. This is her gear from the Trident. Her wetsuit. Her rebreather. The only pieces of kit that are new to her are a complicated looking dive mask and some sort of fancy wrist computer. Zoe focuses all her attention on running equipment checks, tracing the lines, checking the hoses, inspecting the gaskets. She shouldn't even be doing this, not so soon after her bout of the bends, but when Sutton asked her, she didn't feel like she had the luxury of saying no.

A crewman dressed all in white tosses a weighted guide line into the water. It sinks fast, rope unraveling from the deck and plunging deep into the dark water of the dam. The same man saunters up and crouches next to her, slapping her thigh. A plastic grin spreads across his face. The unearned familiarity is off-putting. Zoe can't see his eyes through his mirrored sunglasses, but the rest of his mannerisms seem to communicate 'asshole' easily enough. He hands her a bandolier of reinforced ripstop fabric loaded with a dozen thin bullet-like objects.

"You're gonna like these," he says.

She takes the strap and pushes one of the bullets free to inspect it more closely.

No, it's not a bullet.

"What are—?" She begins to ask.

The crewman plucks the device from her fingers and stabs it, tip first, into the bench right next to her thigh. She flinches at the ear-shattering pop. He releases the cylinder. The end begins to glow a brilliant blue and six inches of polished aluminum stands perfectly perpendicular to the moulded bench. Zoe tilts forward to check under the seat. The spiked tip passed directly through the thick steel support and splayed out, locking the beacon in place and showering the deck with splintered fiberglass and flakes of metal.

"They're navigation beacons. Loaded charge. Just stab 'em in and move on. Better than stringing line. Nothin' to get tied up on." He gives her a hearty slap on her back. "You start spacing these suckers out every twenty meters or so once you get in and they send out a pulse. Map your route. Readout will show up on the HUD, along with all your communication controls and your rebreather info. Pretty self explanatory."

Zoe secures the beacons to her thigh.

The crewman heads off towards the cockpit. "She's all yours, sir."

Sutton emerges from the cabin. He is wearing light-colored practical clothes, perfect for the desert heat. He squints in the unforgiving sun, the wrinkles around his eyes fanning out, growing deeper. No matter how much she doesn't want to see it, she can recognize the similarities between this man and her father. Sutton takes a seat next to her. "I hoped you wouldn't mind, but I took the liberty of retrieving your gear from your previous assignment. I thought you might find it comforting."

His proximity forces a shudder to roll through her body.

"Are you ready?" He smiles at her. Almost sweetly. He barely waits for a response before paternally cupping her shoulder. His touch feels like lead, weighing her down. "Of course you are. You're a natural. You were born to do this."

It takes all her strength not to shove him away. She stares down at his hand, the tanned skin stretched over broad knuckles and prominent veins. They are the hands of a man who used to be strong. Hands so much like her father's.

"Are you alright?" he asks.

"I won't let you hurt them." After she says it, he stares back at her, confused, but he knows who she is referring to. Zoe pushes forward with the only strategy she has been able to come up with. The only way she can think to protect the people she loves. "You have to let them go."

His face changes, displeasure filtering through the cracks. "And if I refuse?"

"You don't want to find out."

He focuses on the horizon. "Are you giving me an ultimatum, girl?"

Zoe stares down at her equipment, her jaw set so tight the strain makes her head pound.

"Why do you even care what happens to them? All your life that woman has done nothing but bring you down. She doesn't care for you.

She never has. Why show her an ounce of your compassion?" Sutton stops himself, visibly attempting to reign in his anger. His expression softens, but the effect is more threatening than comforting. He takes a deep breath before speaking. "If I agree to release them both, I will need something from you in return."

"I know." Her stomach twists inside her as she forces herself to throw down the only thing she has left to bargain with.

"Will you stay?" Sutton asks. There is an edge to his tone that is impossible to gauge.

This is it. It is all she has to offer him. The only thing she's willing to part with. It has to be enough. She prays he cannot hear the fear swirling inside her. "Yes."

He quietly considers her response. Does he doubt her sincerity? Does he question her motive? Why won't he say something? All she can hear is his shallow breath, the lapping of water against the hull of the boat, and the far-off hum of motorboats circling the dam. Zoe fidgets with the rubber strap of her dive mask.

"Once the objective is complete," Sutton says, rising from his seat, "I will let them go."

Relief swells inside her.

Zoe watches her grandfather walk away, leaving the sun-soaked deck for the shade of the boat's cabin.

Her heart races. She pulls her mask on, feeling the comforting suction press against her face. The dual hoses snake over her shoulders. She adjusts the straps. Her kit is compact and comfortable—definitely more so than the bulky half-empty tanks Bryce set her up with on her last dive. She checks the rebreather's capacity a third time. Everything is green. She keeps reminding herself this is her gear. She can trust it. The internal computers are calculating and configuring the gas mixes. They will scrub and recycle any unused oxygen. She will be fine.

Zoe taps the device strapped to her wrist, and it blinks on, instantly connecting to a heads-up display in her mask. It reminds her of all the video games she's played with Jones. At least that'll be easy to get used to.

This is it. She scoots to the edge of the boat, gripping her mask tight to her face. Her body tilts back, slipping from the edge and tumbling into the water below.

The sound is intoxicating.

A muffled rush of liquid envelops her as bubbles burst and flee towards the surface in a concussive staccato.

And then the stillness.

She begins her descent, her muscles surging, just a streamlined neoprene form pushing through the calm water. The actions, feet together, fins churning, forcing her deeper, are ingrained. There is still a dull ache in every joint, a residual side effect of the bends. It has lessened over the past few days, but the pain brings uncomfortable memories to the surface.

She pushes them aside. She needs to focus.

Her wrist computer begins to blink. A soft tone chimes through her headset. Zoe opens the communication channel, trying to stifle her disappointment. She had been looking forward to some well earned solitude.

"This doesn't have to be anything showy or complicated. Just get in and get the artifacts secured. Dr. Hudson will be assisting you with prioritizing targets." Case's voice rings through the speaker, crystal clear. "We're marking the telemetry for you now. Do you acknowledge the beacon?"

"I see it." Vibrant blue numbers appear in the corner of her vision, counting down her forward progress and guiding her direction. Zoe makes the adjustment, her body twisting and torquing in the cool water of the dam.

Case continues, "I will be monitoring your progress from the surface."

"Great."

"Oh, and one more thing, Ms. Hudson." Her voice lowers to a whisper. "Don't fuck this up."

"Wouldn't dream of it." Zoe grumbles into the mic and closes the channel. "Bitch."

FOR SOME REASON, she had not expected to have a direct visual and communication link to her daughter during the dive. In hindsight, it makes complete sense. She just wasn't prepared. Watching the crisp video feed and hearing Zoe's raspy voice boom over the speakers sends a chill straight through Allison. She has always known what her daughter did for a living, but she's never had to watch her do it.

She knew Zoe was a salvage diver. A highly trained treasure hunter. It's an extremely questionable occupation for the child of an anthropologist. The boat Zoe worked on was known in academic circles as an opportunistic outfit that often took advantage of legal loopholes to make their finds. They weren't interested in science or history so much as money. Allison made her displeasure clear from the start, and further discussion of her daughter's career path only ever led to arguments.

So she kept her mouth shut. The few times a year she managed to get Zoe on the phone, she prayed the interactions would be pleasant. They rarely were. Zoe didn't want to talk about her personal life. Allison didn't want to talk about the work she was doing. Neither of them broached the past. Their conversations were short, impersonal, and intensely uncomfortable.

It was like making small talk with a stranger.

Sutton was right. She has lost her daughter.

The realization stings.

"Mom!"

Allison turns. PMCs move aside as Connor drags her youngest girl through the threshold of the temple. The armed soldiers snap back into position as he releases Nicole with an unceremonious shove. She runs for her mother, launching herself into a bone-rattling embrace. Allison rocks back from the force, but she holds Nicole tight, stroking her dark, tangled hair. After a few moments, she pushes her back gently. Nicole's cheeks are stained with tears.

"Did he hurt you?" she asks.

"No," Nicole says, scrubbing at her face with the tattered sleeve of her oversized flannel shirt. She forces an expression of confidence. "I'm fine."

But something is not right. Nicole seems hyper-vigilant, completely aware of her surroundings in a way that Allison is not. Her eyes dart around the room, taking in everything. The shadowed statues. The high-tech gear. The soldiers. Nicole watches Connor carefully, tracking his movements until he takes his place next to Case. She takes her mother's hand, squeezing it hard. Her voice is low, barely more than a whisper. "I have to tell you something."

A sinking feeling settles in the pit of Allison's stomach. She looks towards the array of computer terminals clustered in the center of the room, their huge flat screen displays monitored by militant technicians. "Now is not a good time, Nikky."

"It's important."

Allison keeps her eyes firmly trained on the group collected around the central hub. Connor is watching her in return. She wraps an arm around her daughter's shoulders and kisses her forehead, hoping to mask their conversation. "What?"

"It's about Zoe," Nicole whispers. Allison lets out an irritated sigh, but Nicole continues, her speech growing softer and more rapid. "These people murdered her father."

The world grows fuzzy around the edges. Boots scuff against the stone floor. Out of the corner of her eye, Allison sees the armed guards part again, allowing Victor Sutton space to enter. His assistant Fletcher meets him halfway and hands over a computer tablet. Sutton studies the screen as he proceeds to the hub.

Nicole has to be wrong. Hayden was Sutton's only son. How could he murder his only child? "Who told you that?"

"Zoe did when she came to see me." Nicole checks over her shoulder at the men and women monitoring equipment. When she turns back, she hisses through gritted teeth. "Mom, I think she might do something stupid."

Allison glances back to the readout screen. Zoe is currently pushing a depth of sixty meters. She's getting closer to the monument. She'll be breaching soon. They don't have much time. Allison whispers in Nicole's ear. "Did she tell you what she was planning? Did she say anything? Give you any clue?"

Before Nicole can answer her, Sutton turns towards Allison. "A moment of your time, Doctor?" He waves her over to the tactical table in front of the cluster of monitors. "We should be nearing the temple any moment now. I'm sure we will require your expertise."

His expression is disquieting. Vicious. He flashes her a pale row of perfectly shaped teeth, white and tidy behind thin lips.

If he killed his own son, nothing will stop him from killing them.

Allison clutches Nicole's hand and walks towards the displays.

SHE IS NEARING THE BOTTOM. Her flashlight begins to illuminate the deep lake's uneven floor. Every surface is coated in thick, grainy sediment.

"What is your position?"

No matter her depth, the audio connection is crisp and clear. It's easy to pick up the irritation in Case's voice. Zoe pauses her descent, her body hanging in space, weight offset by her equipment.

"I'm closing on the marker."

Diving this deep alone is a surreal experience. There are few sounds to distract her from the quiet hiss and suction of the rebreather. Her own breath. Air flowing in and out of her lungs.

Don't think about it. Focus on something else. Zoe flips and heads down, pointing her light in the direction of the digital marker blinking in the corner of her vision.

The floor drops steeply, then levels. Ghostly figures come into view. Zoe swims past eroding stone sculptures of winged women, carefully perched on simple granite pediments.

She twists, floating on her back to slow herself and get a clear look at the blurry silhouettes. Their stoic faces are fading, deteriorating in the harsh waters. She's seen them before. The journal had sketches of these in the back. Nicole showed her when they were on the plane to India.

As she draws closer, her movement churns sediment, filling her vision with billowing clouds of earth. She went too fast. She needs to calm down. She has plenty of time. Plenty of air.

Knowing that doesn't stop her heart from thrumming against the tight collar of her wetsuit.

A blue light blinks rapidly on her HUD right as a crumbled structure comes into view. It's obviously man-made. Chisel marks are still visible on the surfaces of the large support stones around the opening. Zoe presses closer to the toppled pediment blocking the entrance.

There are two triangular crevices between the massive pieces of stone. Only one is a viable entry point. She shines her light into the fissure. The beam barely penetrates the blackness. Whatever this place is, it goes deep into the granite.

The gap is tight but she manages to squeeze between the massive stones.

The tunnel behind the fallen pediment is remarkably narrow. She extends her arms, gripping the walls with her fingertips, pulling herself deeper. Her flashlight dangles from her wrist, slamming into the rock, its beam swinging wildly in the darkness. Turning around isn't an option. If this starts going south, or if the way is blocked up ahead, she'll have to back out, blindly inching her way to freedom in reverse.

It's happened before.

It wasn't comfortable.

If she had been thinking more clearly, she would have planted her first beacon before squeezing into the crevice. Zoe groans, contorting her body to reach the devices strapped to her thigh. Her shoulders scream as the awkward movement pinches out-of-place nerves. The sound of her gear scraping against the surrounding stone makes her cringe. Her fingers grope down the length of her thigh until they come to rest on the slender cylinders nestled in the bandolier. Gripping one of the beacons tight, she struggles to draw her arm back up. Every muscle seems intent on disobeying even the simplest instruction.

Zoe adjusts her position, searching for an out of the way spot to slam the beacon. The task is difficult in such a confined space. She settles on a seam a few feet up and to the right. With a jerk she stabs the device into a thin crack. A flurry of bubbles ejects from the tip. The loud pneumatic pop she heard on the boat is diminished by the surrounding water. When she lets go, the beacon stays in place, its end slowly blinking a bright blue. She presses on.

After a few meters the entry tunnel plunges down at a sharp angle, then after a few more meters it abruptly begins to head steeply upward. Thankfully, it also begins to widen out. Her terminology is probably wrong, but she has a feeling she is no longer in a "tunnel", but more of a corridor. The passage is void of any ornamentation. It almost seems unfinished. The ancient chisel blows are still visible on the walls and uneven stairs carved into the floor below her.

Zoe places a second beacon and rolls slowly, shining her light on the rough surfaces surrounding her. The structure appears to have been carved directly into the granite. There are few visible seams. This would probably be impressive to her mother, but all it means for Zoe is this place is sturdy. It's a reassuring thought, as any kind of structure collapse would not end well for her.

The corridor continues upward. Eventually the carved stairs disappear and give way to a smooth floor. Broad cylinders begin to take shape in the murky water. The walls fall away, flaring into a chamber, its ceiling supported by marches of thick, tapered columns.

"You getting this?" Zoe murmurs softly into her headset. "What the hell was this place?"

"It's a monument." Her mother's voice crackles through the speakers, blunt and matter of fact. "Get closer to the walls. See if there's anything carved on them."

Zoe wasn't prepared to hear her voice.

"Sure." She stammers, threading her body through the march of columns, swimming closer to the wall, her beam pointed straight ahead.

Floating particles catch the light, every movement she makes stirs up long settled sediment. There are carvings on the wall, but as she draws closer, a strange sensation travels up her leg. She is caught on something. Zoe turns her focus, aiming her light down toward her feet.

The black neoprene of her wetsuit registers first. It takes a moment to recognize tattered fabric and leather, then bones brown with age. Human remains. Her heart lurches. She jerks back and the body tumbles apart, collapsing into the silt. The crumbled corpse is not alone. As the flurries settle she can see another body, decomposed, its forehead slumped against the wall. When she shines her light on the corpse, a jagged hole becomes visible near the base of the mottled skull.

Zoe slaps at her radio controls. "There are fucking bodies down here."

Case responds, her irritation swelling. "Disregard them. They are not your objective."

"They've been shot—"

Case cuts her off. "Continue the inspection, Ms. Hudson."

Zoe struggles to regain her composure but she cannot take her eyes off the pair of corpses pressed against the wall. They are old, but not ancient. Not Egyptian. The clothing is too modern; high leather boots and heavy canvas pants hold their pale bones in place. Nicole said the book was written by a sailor. These men look like sailors. What were they doing so far from the sea?

"Get back to work." Case growls through her speaker.

She tries to shake the thought and presses away from the wall, swimming more carefully this time. Being underwater is one thing. Being in a confined space is another. But being two hundred feet beneath the earth and trapped with corpses is bullshit. This place is a grave. A tomb.

The walls begin to press in on her.

Her heart races.

She cannot calm down. Her hands translate the tremor rolling though her body, shaking the beam of her flashlight as she continues her circuit of the room. When she edges around the last column and points her light towards the far wall, a carved figure comes into view. A woman in profile sits on a throne, her arms outstretched, long, sharp wings extended as a symbolic sun beats down upon her.

Zoe twists, rolling onto her back and shining her flashlight at the ceiling above the carving. The beam strikes stone, then plunges deep into darkness. There's a shaft. A way out. Her heart races. The gap is smaller than the one she had to squeeze through to get into this place, but at this moment she cannot imagine backtracking and would give anything to be out of this chamber. Away from those bodies. Even if that means trading her tomb for a coffin.

"There's an opening. In the ceiling. I'm going up." Zoe doesn't wait for permission, she slips into the gap, her gloved hands extended. When the walls bear down on her, she grips at the stone, pulling herself up as her legs churn tight circles in the confined space. She's dived plenty of caves with Jones over the years, from the Bahamas to Australia. She's searched the interiors of sunken submarines and the jagged remains of downed aircraft in the Pacific, but there is something entirely different about this, something that is slicing through her years of experience and training and turning her into a panicked mess. Sweat beads up on her skin, salty and cool. An abrupt sense of terror consumes her as her gear scrapes against the stone walls. Everything is pressing inward, narrowing. She stops. Pinching her eyelids shut, her heart hammers in her chest. She cannot breathe.

Case's voice echoes in her mask, the sound is distorted by the blood pounding in her ears. "What are you doing? Why did you stop?"

Why did I stop? I can't stop. She needs out. Zoe presses off the rock, her body vibrating with anxiety as her gloved fingers claw at the stone entombing her. Each stroke of her legs propels her upward. Her knees strike the stone hard, sending shockwaves of pain through her body. Everything aches.

The shaft has to end. It has to open up.

Please, God, open up.

She surges upward.

All at once, her body breaches the surface. She must have hit level with the lake outside, but she is still far below ground. Confused, she claws at her mask, ripping it off her face and flinging it back against the stone wall. She gasps, drawing in deep swells of musty air. Air that hasn't been inhaled for thousands of years. Murky water floods her open mouth as she bobs in the darkness, trying to regain control. Zoe tilts her head back, shutting her eyes tight. Dirty liquid dribbles out of her gaping mouth while her aching legs pump beneath her, desperately straining to keep her body afloat.

"Zoe?"

At first the sound of her own name doesn't register. There are far too many other thoughts racing through her addled brain. She opens her eyes. Daylight punches through debris further up the shaft, illuminating dust and particles floating in the stale air.

Light.

Sunlight.

She's close to the surface.

"Zoe! Answer me!" Her mother's frantic voice fills the narrow passage. "Are you all right?"

She ignores the call and aims her light up the shaft, slowly turning her body to better inspect the walls. The bright beam reveals an offshoot further up the main shaft, a break in the sheer wall about a body-length or so above the water line. It's not that far up. She can get to it. Then she can rest. Regain her strength. Calm down. Think.

The distance to the ledge may be short, but it's nothing she can span unaided. She reaches down, her fingertips tracing the line of her gear until they rest on the cylinders strapped to her thigh. With all her concentration fixed on the plan haphazardly forming in her mind, her legs briefly stop churning, sending her head below the water line. Foul tasting liquid floods her mouth.

Exhaustion is already setting in.

She will only get one shot.

Her heels rub together, forcing the straps of her fins off her feet. They slip free and rise up, bobbing at the surface. In each hand she clutches a beacon. Zoe orients herself so she is facing the wall below the ledge. She spits and sputters dirty water from her mouth.

"What is happening? Talk to m—"

She doesn't have time to explain.

Zoe punches the dive computer on her wrist, cutting the communication link entirely. The shaft falls silent except for the sloshing of water and her own spastic breathing.

She stabs the beacon into the granite wall as high as her left arm will allow. After a concussive pop, the device remains sturdily lodged into the rock, glowing in the dim light. If it can bear her weight plus her gear, she'll be in business.

Zoe goes limp, dangling from the cylinder

The device seems to be strong enough to support her. *God bless technology.*

She draws herself out of the water, lurching upward, pinning another device into the wall with her right hand. As she hangs in space, her left hand fumbling for another beacon, the nerves in her right shoulder shift, pinching between bone and socket. The pain is excruciating, a reminder of an all too recent dislocation.

Her cry echoes through the shaft.

She halts her ascent, pressing her face to the cool stone. *Keep going. Don't stop.* Her left arm swings up, then her right, slamming the tips of the sturdy pneumatic beacons into the rock face. The higher she pulls herself from the water, the more strain she can feel on her arms. On her shoulders. Her own weight and the bulk of her equipment threaten to pull her back into the darkness. Zoe's feet press against the stone, seeking support. She scrambles, compressing her body until she finds toeholds formed by the blinking locators.

As the beacons activate, the narrow passage begins to glow, pulsing blue light.

She can see the ledge. She is so close.

Every muscle in her body is quaking with exhaustion. Just the idea of being able to stop and rest, even for a moment, in the adjacent shaft is exhilarating. Zoe takes hold of another beacon and with a desperate lurch, propels herself up, hooking her torso just over the ledge. The stone is smooth. She begins to slip. Her feet kick the wall, groping for another toehold as she begins to fall backwards. Flailing, she slams the beacon into the granite. It pops loudly. Her momentum stalls, elbows torqued at an painful angle. She grunts, hauling herself into the pitch black tunnel.

The feelings of accomplishment and relief she feels are short-lived.

Her body pitches forward, balance offset by the weight of her rebreather. She slips, tumbling head first down the steep shaft. Her hands claw at the walls, desperately trying to slow her fall. Her flashlight bounces and slams off the stone, casting long, strange shadows in every direction. She is yelling. Not screaming, just yelling, more out of frustration than fear. This was a bad idea. It was a bad idea from the beginning, and she knew it, but her desperation forced her here.

Her velocity increases with the angle. Plastic and metal begin to snap off her gear. The expensive equipment shatters, flying apart and gaining speed, tumbling with her down into the darkness below.

A loud all-body crack resonates through her body. She hears it before her brain can process the strike. Whatever she hit was brittle. The cloud of dust that fills her mouth tastes like dry earth. Her body plummets, arms and legs flailing. The free fall comes to an abrupt end when she strikes water. The impact is a slap to the face. Her head plunges deep into brackish liquid before hitting the solid surface beneath. Her teeth rattle in her skull, threatening to snap free. Water forces itself into her gaping mouth, burning its way into her nostrils, down her throat. She whips back, disoriented and coughing violently.

It is pitch black.

She needs to see where she is.

She fumbles for her flashlight. It is gone. It must have ripped off her wrist during the fall.

She gropes at her dive computer on her wrist. Shards of glass stab through her glove, catching in the fabric and piercing her fingertips. She pulls her hand back, wincing as she tears off her glove and sucks on her punctured fingers. Something hot and wet is dripping down her face, flowing into her eyes. As she wipes it away, she can feel the wide, sopping gash on her forehead.

She begins to count the ways she's totally fucked:

One. No light.

Two. No communication to the surface.

Three. She has no idea where she is.

Four. She's bleeding, probably concussed.

It is all too much.

Her consciousness begins to slip away.

She tilts forward, dipping back into the foul water.

She flails, crawling and spitting, seeking shallower water. Her hands find what feel like steps. She slumps against the hard stone, her body shaking. She gropes down her thigh, searching for metal cylinders. Only two beacons are left after her fall. She clutches one in a trembling hand and stabs its sharp point into the rock. The device releases, popping loudly, echoing in the darkness. The light on the end of the beacon comes to life. Zoe leans back, resting against her broken gear. The blue light pulses. Hot blood pours down her face. Her breathing begins to slow to shallow gasps.

She is so cold.

- 17 -

THE AREA JUST OUTSIDE the command center is in complete chaos. Personnel are scrambling to reload equipment onto the armored vehicles before they abandon Abu Simbel. It's been like this ever since they lost communication with Zoe. Case heads down the stairs at the entrance of the temple, slipping her sunglasses on to block the late afternoon light.

She had ordered the vehicles moved half an hour ago.

None have left yet.

She catches sight of a PMC milling about and stalks towards him. "Why aren't these trucks headed to the beacon site?"

He snaps to attention. His words come out in a jumble. "Ma'am. We weren't anticipating a location shift. We're still loading—"

"Move these trucks." Case stabs her finger at the man's chest, then at the stalled convoy. "Now."

"Ma'am. Yes, ma'am." The soldier nods stiffly and turns on his heel. He begins barking orders at other troops.

Case squints into the low-hanging sun, the combination of heat and light amplifying her seemingly ever-present migraine. The pain has become sharper, burrowing deep behind her eyes and pulsing in a constant and tedious fashion. She pinches the bridge of her nose, letting her fingers linger until the pressure becomes pain. Out of the corner of her eye, she catches a hulking shape. Connor exits the temple and casually saunters down its steps, heading towards her, an unlit cigarette dangling from his lips.

"Sutton's pretty pissed." He pulls out his lighter. The silver shape reflects sunlight into Case's eyes.

"He's the one who suggested her as the infiltrator." Case rubs her temple. "It isn't my fault his granddaughter's incompetent."

"He was saying you should have sent a whole team down." He cocks his head, regarding her with a malicious sort of amusement. "You know he's gonna pin this on you if it goes to shit?"

"It's not going to go to shit, Connor," Case grumbles. She pushes stray strands of hair behind her ear and rubs her neck, working the tight muscles that have wound themselves into unforgiving knots. "The beacon signal is close to the surface. It's ghosting a network of caverns and tunnels. I need you to punch us in with some Semtex charges."

Connor nods, chewing at the filter of his cigarette, his attention briefly drawn towards the entrance of the sanctuary. Case follows his eyes. Sutton exits from between the seated colossi, followed by a team of armed guards escorting Nicole and Allison Hudson. They board one of the armored cars and merge seamlessly into the line, exiting onto the access road in a cloud of dust, tires struggling to gain traction on the loose earth.

She can feel her heart beating in her throat. "This will all be over soon enough."

Connor grunts and flicks his cigarette to the ground and grinds the smoldering butt into the gravel with the toe of his boot. He stalks towards one of the jeeps, his thick frame casting a long shadow on the red sand.

The primary transports are moving in a slow but orderly fashion, kicking up clouds of earth in their wake. All but one. Case glares at the stationary vehicle parked at the edge of the entry, engine off, driver at the wheel. She lets out a frustrated sigh and stalks towards the truck.

Fascinating how some people cannot manage to follow one simple order. "Get this truck in the convoy."

The woman does not respond.

Case grabs the mirror and pulls herself onto the running board, getting on level with the obstinate PMC sitting in the driver's seat. "I told you to move this fucking truck." She whips her sunglasses off and leans further into the truck, inspecting the soldier's name tape. "Did you hear me, Ms. Welch?"

The soldier stares blankly forward out the windshield, refusing to make eye contact. Sweat drips down her face and neck. She gives a quick nod and starts the loud diesel engine.

"Good. Then do it." Case releases the mirror and drops to the ground, backing away. She catches what looks like a nervous sideways glance from the PMC as the woman slips into gear and turns a controlled circle around Case before speeding away to join the line of armored vehicles heading for the beta site.

She watches the vehicle blend with the horizon.

The second Zoe cut communication was the moment this situation began to slip away from her. Case inhales deeply, pinching her eyes shut tight. A wall of heat presses against her back. She can hear the pop and crackle of flames behind her. Smoke rises, removing oxygen and burning her lungs.

"Hey. Tricia."

Her name mixed with the sound of screeching tires on loose gravel snaps her back into reality. Connor's jeep is idling next to her. Waiting. Case takes one last look at the support convoy and climbs into the cab, threading her way under the roll cage to take a seat in the back.

Connor turns towards her as the driver accelerates. His brutish glare effectively hides his emotions from everyone. Everyone but her.

"What wrong with you?" He barks, but she can hear the concern in his voice.

"Nothing," she says, looking past him. "Everything is under control."

"I NEED YOU TO BE BRAVE, OKAY?"

He sounds panicked.

"Can you do that for me? Can you be brave?"

She is standing in a desolate parking lot dotted with cars while the rain pours down. Fat droplets soak through her clothes. Her body shivers uncontrollably. Her father is crouched behind a parked car. His hands are cupping the cheeks of a frightened girl. She can feel the heat of his skin against her own.

"Dad?" She stammers.

He can't hear her.

Why can't you hear me?

She is everywhere at once.

Simultaneously experiencing and observing.

"I need you to run away from here. Okay? Run home." He kisses the top of the girl's head and urges her to move. She clings to his wet jacket with pale, shivering hands. He peels small, desperate fingers from his clothes and grips the girl's shoulders delicately. "You have to do this, sweetheart."

Heavy footsteps echo in the wide open space. Something ominous looms behind her. A dark figure just outside her vision. She cannot bring herself to turn around. Her breathing stops. Blood pounds through her body. The rain slows, each droplet slamming with the force of a bullet, rippling the network of interconnected puddles covering the black asphalt.

Her father's mouth moves silently.

Zoe can hear each word loud inside her head. "Run, Zoe. Now."

She remembers.

She ran.

Through the parking lot and over the grassy embankment.

The crunch of brittle branches beneath her feet was so loud.

She fell down. Slipping on mud and dead leaves. Tumbling. Her skin catching and tearing. The fall scraped her knees and palms raw. Made her bleed. But her father told her to be brave.

He told her to run. And that was exactly what she did.

She was seven years old.

"What the hell were you thinking, Hayden? She's only a child!"

Her parents are fighting.

Her father is packing.

Zoe stands in the darkened stairwell, a passive observer to her own forgotten history. She hides in the shadows, listening to an argument she is too young and frightened to understand.

"Just tell me what happened." There is concern in her mother's voice, but it is lost under a swell of rage.

Her father's lip is split. Blood dribbles down his chin. The left side of his face is a mangled mess. His eye is nearly swollen shut. His jacket is missing. His shirt is torn and soaking wet.

Her mother told her to go to her room. She didn't listen.

"Don't you walk away from me," her mother screams.

A hand grips her shoulder, spinning her around. There is no one behind her.

The lights are on in the dining room. People are arguing. She takes tentative steps down the stairs. The transition from shadow to brightness is disorienting.

Standing next to the table is a scrawny seventeen-year-old version of herself. She is angry, and bitter, and yelling hurtful things at her mother. "This is all your fault. If you hadn't been such a bitch, he never would have left. I'd still have my dad."

Allison looks so very tired. "Your father made a choice. He left both of us, Zoe. There was nothing I could have done to stop him and you know that."

"You're a fucking liar." Even the memory of saying those words twists her stomach.

Her mother's face changes. She sinks into the wooden chair at the head of the long table.

"And you're an ungrateful child." Her mother lets out a bitter sigh and rubs her temples, her voice trembling with rage. "You have no idea what I've had to sacrifice for you. Every time you get in trouble, every time you act out, I'm the one who cleans up your mess. I'm the one who has to fix all your mistakes. I am getting so tired of it. Just once, just once, Zoe, I wish you could understand how hard you've made everything for me, for yourself and for this family."

The teenager storms out of the room, evaporating into the darkness and leaving Zoe alone with a memory of her mother. The lights begin to flicker as she steps closer to her.

"I'm so sorry," she says.

Allison cannot hear her.

Why can't you hear me?

She crouches and places a hand on her mother's knee. "I'm trying to make it right. I'm trying to—"

Lightbulbs burst. Her muscles spasm. Her head pounds. Her cheeks feel warm. Zoe pinches her eyes closed as the darkness swallows her.

A rough hand cups her cheeks.

"Wake up. Please wake up, Zoe. Please."

Her brain tries to process the blurred shape looming over her. The air is musty and cold. Every breath is painful. Zoe coughs and a million tiny needles twist inside her chest, stabbing into her lungs.

"Stay still, sweetheart. Everything will be okay."

She recognizes the voice. It's the tone that confuses her. Zoe croaks, choking on the blood and bile resting in the back of her throat. "Mom?"

Allison leans down and kisses her forehead, whispering softly as she strokes Zoe's hair. "Try not to move too much."

Heavy boots crunch through gravel and stone. Zoe rolls her head, trying to get a better look at her surroundings. She moves to sit up and immediately regrets the decision. She winces sharply. "How are you here?"

"They followed your signal." Her mother points at the beacon protruding from the stone step, its blue tip still pulsing bright. Allison places a steady hand on Zoe's back, helping her upright. "Careful."

Her mother's concern is an entirely alien thing. It's too uncomfortable. Zoe can't bring herself to make eye contact. She stares over Allison's shoulder at a worried-looking Nicole sitting on the steps. Her freckled cheeks flush as she forces a crooked smile. "Hey you."

"Nik." Zoe tries to smile back. She becomes painfully aware of the gash on her forehead. A cautious hand reaches up to inspect the damage only to find tacky medical adhesive has sealed the wound. The same is true for the numerous cuts on her fingertips. A medic must have gone over her. How long has she been unconscious?

A strange hum fills the chamber, like a bass line changing in pitch but not in tone. Large work lamps switch on, flooding the room with brilliant light and throwing distorted shadows against the thick columns lining the central pool. Soldiers move purposefully about, depositing large reinforced crates and heavy bags of tools near a stone altar on the far side of the pool. Her grandfather is across the room, deep in conversation with the leggy bitch and her attack dog. Case must feel her stare because she gives Zoe a knowing sideways glance, her lips pulling into a malicious grin.

Zoe pulls free of her mother's grasp and clambers to her feet, clutching her aching ribs.

"I really don't think you should be getting up quite yet," Allison cautions.

Connor extracts a wrecking bar from one of the canvas equipment bags near the altar. He grips the heavy metal rod with both hands, testing its weight by swinging it like a bat. The bar cuts through the stale air with a high-pitched hiss that makes Zoe flinch.

Nicole places a hand on Zoe's arm as she whispers into her ear. "What is he doing?"

CASE CUPS HER HANDS TO HER MOUTH, amplifying her voice through the chamber. "All nonessential personnel are to clear the area immediately. Take your assigned positions and await further instruction."

The crew that hauled down the gear begins to evacuate. Heavy boots disturb the soil, crunching the rock and raising a fine cloud of bitter dust. Men and women file through the chamber's lone entrance in an orderly exodus. In the end, a lone PMC is left positioned by the door, his assault rifle trained on the Hudson women. This is not how she would have preferred to do things. There were far too many eyes in this room. Too many mouths to have to keep quiet. Her past operations have been more precise. Smaller. Every variable carefully analyzed and exploited for maximum efficiency. But this op has been a disaster from the beginning.

It is a game that refuses to conform to her rules.

Her body is drained. Her head is still pulsing with a migraine. Sweat pours off her and even though the room is cool, the heat from the work lights sets her skin on fire. Case rolls up the sleeves of her blouse past her elbows. She gives Connor a nod and gestures towards the slab behind the altar. "Bring it down."

He stoops and draws a six-foot pry bar from one of the canvas equipment bags. The muscles in his arms and back ripple as he swipes the tool through the air. He is a perfect wrecking ball. He takes his place. Stepping in front of the slab and over and over, he slams the pry bar's tip into the stone. The sound of the impact rings like a bell through the chamber. His precision is mechanical. He makes quick work of the obstruction, weakening the surrounding area until a seam begins to splinter and widen. Sweat soaks through his shirt, clinging tight to the shapes on his back. A lit cigarette dangles from his lips, cinders shaking loose with each blow, smoke curling from his nostrils. Case watches his body twitch and contract with every strike. The ferocity is mesmerizing.

The dull ache pulsing in the center of her mind explodes in a brilliant burst of pain. Case leans forward, closing her eyes and pressing her palms hard against her lids.

There is blood on the floor, slippery and congealed. Her nostrils burn with the smell of gasoline. Heat from the flames set in the surrounding rooms presses down on her. Wood begins to pop. Paint sizzles. The entire structure groans with the strain.

She asks him again. "Where did you hide the book, Mr. Thomas?"

His face is coated in blood. He convulses. The spasms run down the length of his arms, past the restraints cutting into his wrists and terminate at the tips of his scorched fingertips.

She crouches next to him, whispering in his ear. "Tell me and I will end this."

His silence is his answer.

Fire is such an uncivilized way to die.

She pulls her sidearm and levels it, closing her eyes as her finger contracts around the trigger.

There is a loud pop.

Her eyes snap open.

She hurtles out of the memory just in time to see Connor plant a boot on what is left of the slab. He presses hard, sending it crashing backwards into the darkened antechamber. His pry bar clatters to the ground and he takes a step back.

"Excellent work, Mr. Shaw." Sutton give Connor's back a congratulatory slap, then gestures to Case. "Shall we, Tricia?"

She nods, grabbing a flashlight from an open gear crate. As she passes Connor she whispers to him, throwing her head in the direction of the three women and their armed guard. "Watch them."

He rests a broad hand on the butt of his pistol. The chance is remote, as Zoe is in no physical position to start a fight, but that hasn't seemed to stop her before. For some reason, leaving him alone with them while she and Sutton investigate the antechamber sets her on edge.

She reminds herself: *Everything is under control.*

Case flicks on the bright LED lamp as she crosses into the darkness. Her feet slide beneath her, searching for traction on the mound of rubble that litters a gradual set of carved steps. Cautiously, she makes her way down, steadying herself with a hand outstretched to trace the wall. Another beam shines behind her as Sutton follows her through. His dress shoes slide on the crumbled debris.

She reaches the base of the steps and sweeps the room.

The intricately carved walls stretch out twenty feet in any given direction, but other than the art adorning the granite, the chamber is completely empty.

This cannot be happening.

Her heart begins race. Her head pounds.

Sutton moves past her, his light grazing the dusty web covered walls.

There is nothing here.

Nothing.

She begins to panic.

He will blame her for this. She will wear this failure for the rest of her career.

If Sutton even allows her to have one.

Her vision blurs.

There is no way Fletcher's plan will work now. This will ruin them both.

One way or another, she's dead.

Her breathing becomes rapid. The musty air of the chamber burns her lungs.

She has to think. Why can't she think?

Sutton's hand closes around her arm. "Tricia—"

Synapses fire. Electricity travels through conduits and terminates in action. She strikes him hard, the rigid metal barrel of her flashlight hitting his face with explosive force. His body twists, sprawling to the floor. His head hits the stone steps with a thud.

Her chest is heaving, brain struggling to catch up to her outburst.

She shines her light on his body. He isn't moving.

She steps closer.

A pool of blood has formed under his head, growing steadily, staining the dust that covers the ground. His chest is still rising. He is still breathing. As she comes closer, the old man feebly shuffles in the dirt, trying to press himself up. He coughs and rolls over, flecking his shirt with specks of red.

Without a word, Case drops to her knees, straddling his frail frame. One hand slips over his mouth, pressing hard, her palm mashing his lips into his teeth. Her thumb and index finger pinch his nose closed. Her other hand grips his throat, fingers sinking into his skin.

She can feel his pulse and the sick contraction of his neck every time he tries to swallow.

Her arms begin to tremble. Sutton claws at her, desperately searching for anything that might force her to release him. His fingernails dig into her skin, tearing as they slip down her face. Warm blood runs down her cheek, dripping dark droplets onto the old man below her. As his struggling grows weaker, Case presses down, forcing all her weight onto his fragile neck until she hears a crack. His eyes bulge, veins pulsing beneath sallow skin.

She closes her eyes as his body convulses beneath her.

"Shhh."

CONNOR HAS NOT TAKEN his eyes off them since Case and Sutton disappeared beyond the threshold of the antechamber. He leans quietly against the altar, his hand resting on his gun. Nicole chances a look over her shoulder at the PMC hovering behind them. His imposing shape is still blocking their only exit.

This is not really how she envisioned her summer, trapped in an ancient subterranean Egyptian monument flanked by burly men with guns. But things could be worse.

Couldn't they?

Zoe is pacing. Knowing everything she's been through, Nicole is amazed Zoe is still alive, let alone standing. When they lost radio contact it was like being back in the online room of the Trident, watching her sister's limp body over the closed-circuit camera. Her skin begins to tingle. Sound fizzles out, muting everything, until all Nicole can hear is indecipherable murmurs and Zoe's bare feet sweeping over the rough stone floor.

"Nikky?" Her mother's voice cuts through the static. "I asked you a question."

"What?" She sits straight up. She didn't even notice her mother had sat down next to her.

"The journal. You said the sailor they picked up. The castaway. He was Dutch, right?"

Nicole nods stiffly. "Why?"

"Did they ever mention where they found him?"

"Umm." Nicole becomes keenly aware of movement behind her. The PMC adjusts his position. Metal and plastic realign on his webbed harness. She whispers, "I don't think so."

Allison waits until the guard settles. "Did they mention the name of his ship?"

Her mother looks so serious, so worried. Nicole turns inward, trying to recall any memory of the requested information. "I can't—"

"Try." Her mother is holding the carved wooden figure. Her thumb absently strokes the deep red and white hued wood.

Her mind races. The ship, it held silver. A private investor wanted the cargo recovered. She read it aloud to Caroline the night before they left Paris. It was there. Right in front of her, but everything is so jumbled in her memory, she can't see it. So many things have happened since then. So many things have changed. Nicole lets out a hiss of frustration. She can remember everything from her freshman semester of Latin with crystal detail, but she cannot for the life of her remember the name of the ship. She closes her eyes, trying to call up the placement of the letters. The shape of the sound. "It was weird. Eight letters. It started with a Z."

"Zuytdorp." The name falls from her mother's lips with ease, like she has said it a million times before.

"How did you—?"

Allison closes her hand around the figure. "We're in the wrong desert."

Flashlight beams bounce around the void beyond the crumbled stone slab. Nicole can just make out the sounds of scuffle emanating from the darkened threshold of the antechamber. Her heart begins to beat in her throat. Allison stands, cautiously advancing towards Zoe, slipping the carving back into the pocket of her jeans.

"Mom?" No matter how hard she tries, Nicole can't get her voice louder than a whisper. Allison turns, motioning for her to stay quiet.

Connor pushes off the stone altar, his hand still resting on his pistol.

Something is wrong.

Nicole scrambles to her feet, flashing a nervous look over her shoulder at the PMC still standing next to the exit.

When she looks back, Case is exiting the antechamber. She steps into the flood of halogen work lights. Her well-manicured facade is completely shattered. Clothes disheveled, a fine layer of dirt coats her pale linen blouse and vibrant red blood is soaking through the white handkerchief she is clutching to her face.

Nicole stares in shock, her brain working to quickly connect the information. Sutton's absence and the frantic way Case is searching the chamber speaks volumes. Her wide eyes finally rest on Connor. Her features twitch, searching for composure. She lowers the handkerchief, exposing four jagged gashes down the left side of her face.

"We're leaving." Case gestures towards the Hudson women as she moves past Connor, clutching the cloth to her face. "Keep it quick. Shoot them."

Everything went from bad to worse in a second. Nicole grabs hold of her mother's hand. Zoe is to her right, practically vibrating, her fists clenched at her sides, knuckles turning pale with the strain. The room is so quiet Nicole can hear the gears stripping in her sister's brain. It's not long before anger overcomes her own fear. This is probably not the most convenient time for her to find her voice but she yells anyway, her words echoing through the main chamber. "You can't do this."

Case stops in her tracks, her head twitching as she digests the words. She turns, giving Nicole a look of vivid contempt, fresh blood pulsing from the wounds on her cheek. "Meet me topside when you're finished."

The big man nods stiffly, drawing his sidearm. In one smooth, controlled motion, he levels his gun in their direction. Nicole flinches, closing her eyes.

There is a loud crack and a concussive wave she can feel deep inside her chest.

She waits for the bullet to tear through her. Seconds go by. It feels like minutes. There is no pain, only a sudden heavy weight that knocks her off her feet and sends her crashing to the stone floor. Her head hits the ground. The impact is brilliant and crippling. Her brain surges forward, soft matter ricocheting inside her skull.

Stillness settles over her, dampening all sounds in the chamber. Everything is muted, fuzzing out like the static of a dead television channel. Her eyes flutter, failing to focus. There are sounds of splashing water, frantic yelling and panicked gasps.

The world tilts on its axis, dissolving into shadow.

- 18 -

HER LEG IS ON FIRE. She is on her back.

Zoe charged Connor as soon as he pointed his gun at Nicole. There was a flash of light. Her equilibrium faltered and she tumbled back, crashing into Nicole.

He shot her. The bullet tore through her thigh. Blood is leeching into the sturdy fabric of her pants.

Allison twists, gripping her thigh with both hands as she scrambles to check on Nicole. Her daughter is still breathing, but she isn't moving. In her periphery she can see Zoe fighting a futile battle with a man twice her size.

She made a mistake.

A tremor builds inside her. The wound on her leg begins to pulse. She can't stop shaking.

The room begins to swim.

Strong hands slip under her arms and draw her back, dragging her out of the chamber and away from her children. When she tries to break free, the arms hold her tighter. They cross from the well lit chamber into the shadows of the outer corridor. Allison twists, pivoting in the grip of her captor and sending them both off balance. She falls, crying out in pain as her leg hits the uneven ground hard.

The man is big. In the dim light of the corridor she can make out his dark uniform, the embroidered name tape on his bulky bullet proof vest reading 'Michaels'. The PMC guarding them in the chamber. He advances towards her, reaching out a gloved hand, silently asking for her to take it. Allison scrambles away, clutching her wounded limb. Her pants are dark with blood.

"It's okay, Doc. I'm a good guy." He tugs off the balaclava, revealing a battered face with kind eyes.

She presses herself against the stone wall. "Wh-who are you?"

The man crouches next to her. "I'm a friend of your daughter's. I can help you, but I don't have a lot of time. So you have to trust me. Okay?"

Her vision is blurring around the edges, compressing into a tunnel. Muffled sounds of fighting fill her head. She can hear water splashing and fists pounding flesh. This is the wrong place. It's all her fault. She was angry and arrogant and she didn't take her time. She didn't look hard enough.

"Help Nikky. She hit her head. And Zoe. Help her..." Allison's words trail off. Her whole body begins to quake. Her teeth chatter painfully, their vibrations transmitting through every bone. She is so cold.

He lifts her, cradling her against his body as he carries her out of the dimly lit catacombs. "I'll come back for them. I promise."

She wants to believe him.

SHE WASN'T QUICK ENOUGH.

He got a shot off.

Zoe pushes Connor's gun hand down at a steep angle, forcing the weapon towards the ground as she punches him square in the face, knuckles bashing hard against his nose, the cartilage giving way. His grip loosens. The gun clatters to the stone floor. She kicks it into the water. Only after the gun is out of play does she chance looking back at her mother and sister. They are both sprawled on the ground. Neither is moving.

Rational thought evaporates. All that's left is rage.

She tucks in close, searching for gaps in Connor's defense. Her punches are followed by elbows and knees, thrown into his core with punishing force. He takes the beating, barely registering the abuse. Her body is the one that screams. Every breath, every hit that connects, a knife plunges deeper into her lungs. Zoe can feel her strikes growing weak and careless.

Connor snatches hold of her wetsuit and hoists her effortlessly into the air. He flings her into a nearby column like a rag doll. Her back and hip strike stone. She drops to floor, stunned and gasping for air. Connor has every advantage; his size, his stamina, his enormous strength. But the odds have never stopped her before.

She staggers to her feet.

Connor sloshes out into the pool, sweeping huge hands through the filthy water in search of his gun. Zoe charges towards him, her bare feet slipping on the stone. She launches off the edge of the steps surrounding the sunken basin, wrapping him up in a solid tackle. They both plunge beneath the surface of the pool.

Dark water surrounds them. Time slows. As she sinks to the bottom, her mind latches onto a distant memory: scorched earth on a barren shoreline. She stood in the burned-out remains of her father's house, certain she must have remembered it wrong. She was positive he was still alive.

She was wrong.

Case and Connor tracked her father to that tiny house by the sea looking for the journal. They tortured him, beat him nearly to death. And when he didn't give them the information they wanted, when he refused to give in, this man set fire to the house and left her father there to burn.

Zoe translates her anger into momentum. She twists, squirming around the bigger man, churning the murky water. She wraps her legs around his torso, pinning his hands to his sides. As he sinks beneath her, she takes hold of his t-shirt, feeling the wet fabric stretch in her grip. She pulls his head just above the surface and strikes him in the face with all the force she can summon. The impact splits her already raw knuckles, spattering his face with her own blood. She can feel him press against her, struggling, his core flexing, feet searching for traction on the slick stone.

She hits him again, and again, crushing his nose flat to his face and splitting his lips. There is so much blood. It leaches out into the pool, turning the water around them red.

As his eyes lose focus, a perverse satisfaction swells inside her. Zoe presses him under, her hands slipping around his thick neck, fingernails digging into his skin. She holds him there, below the surface, pressing against his throat as bubbles explode to the surface.

Zoe glances back at her family.

Nicole is still there, but her mother is gone.

Her confusion is interrupted by the sensation of strong, square fingers working their way around her right hand, clutching her thumb.

Under the murky water, Connor's eyes are wide open. His lips curl into a grimace as sporadic bubbles float up from the corners of his mouth. He begins to rotate her thumb, his strength easily overwhelming her own.

As he rights himself, he twists her arm further, folding it back upon itself. Zoe tries to stand, to move with him. Anything to keep her arm from breaking, but her feet slip on the slick bottom of the pool.

Ligaments in her thumb are the first things to tear, the joint separates, distending. Her wrist shatters next, tiny bones reaching their apex then cracking with horrific volume. Connor continues to torque her arm around until her forearm gives way. Her elbow and shoulder grind, bones mashing together, pinching nerves until they finally dislocate. When he's done, she is twisted around, her back pressed against his chest. Connor releases her shattered limb and plants a boot on her back. He kicks her, sending her crashing face first into the filthy water.

Zoe chokes. Liquid fills her gaping mouth as she tries to breathe. She sloshes through the water, trying to crawl away, her useless limb dragging against the slimy bottom of the pool. A part of her knows she is screaming, but the only thing she can hear is the sound of waves breaking on a distant shore.

PAIN PULSES THROUGH HER BODY, forcing her awake.

The room is off kilter, tilted too far. She can barely think. Nicole struggles to her feet, stumbling blindly. Bile rushes up her throat. Her chest heaves, body spasming as she chokes on the bitter fluid. She drops to her knees, spattering the dusty stone floor with spit and stomach acid.

She looks up.

The man guarding the entrance is gone.

So is her mother.

How long has she been unconscious?

Her ears are ringing. She hit her head. Hard. Everything is distorted, emptiness mixes with static and pulse. A wounded cry cuts through the vacuum. Something is splashing in the center of the chamber, flapping around in the pool like a bird fallen from its nest. Connor towers over the disturbance, a sick smile on his flattened, bloody face. It takes Nicole a moment before she realizes the broken thing in the water is her sister.

Zoe is trying to get away. She sloshes through the water, flopping like a dying fish. Connor snatches her ankle and drags her back. Her face plunges below the surface, open mouth taking in filthy water until she gags. He flips her over and with one hand tangled in her hair wrenches her out of the water. He cocks his fist.

Nicole tries to scream, anything to distract him. Anything to make him stop. But she can't. She's frozen, her body unwilling to cooperate. Connor's fist crushes into her sister's face like a piston, over and over again. Each strike increasing in force and fury. His laughter rings out, filling the room as he shoves Zoe beneath the murky water. Bubbles surge upward, escaping from Zoe's open mouth and exploding once they cut the skin of the pool. A single mangled hand slaps at the big man, while the other claws at his massive arms. Her strength begins to evaporate.

He's going to kill her.
Right here.
Right now.
In front of her.
She has to make him stop.
Nicole searches the chamber for anything that might even her odds.

Left on the steps with the rest of Zoe's discarded diving gear is one of the menacing looking navigation beacons. Its polished metal tip gleams in the light from the halogen work lamps. It will have to do. Nicole plucks the device from the webbed strap and wades into the dirty water. The fabric of her jeans grow heavy. Her steps become sluggish and unsteady, feet slipping on the slimy bottom of the pool. She stops behind him. He cannot hear her. He does not fear her. Nicole's brain shuts down, leaving her body to be piloted by everything that is raw inside her.

Her eyes close.
She is lying on the deck of the 303 staring up at the stars.
She is in a soft bed in Paris, waking to warm sunlight streaming through tall windows.
She is sitting next to Zoe on the train ride to Zurich.
Her hands have never been more steady.
Be brave.
She brings the beacon down with every ounce of strength she has.
Nothing could have prepared her for the sound.
After a pneumatic pop, the point of the device plunges through Connor's thick neck. A long spike surges forward, expanding and locking into place. There is a wet crunch and the sickening sound of suction. His arms spasm. He slaps at his neck, groping at the three inches of cold metal now protruding from his throat.

He looks so confused.

His body goes limp, slumping into the dark water, pinning Zoe below the surface. Nicole shoves at the body, trying to roll the beast off her sister. Second lasts for eternity. She grabs hold of Zoe's wetsuit and pulls her, drawing her lifeless form out from under Connor.

Her hands come away red. She can't tell where or who the blood is coming from.

Her sister's skin is pale and cold.

She drags Zoe towards the edge of the pool, struggling to lift her out of the foul water. Her feet slip. She tumbles forward, slamming her hip into the stone steps. Zoe begins to sink. Nicole frantically clutches at her wetsuit, fingernails digging into the thick neoprene, fighting to draw her sister's head above the surface. No matter how hard she tries, she cannot draw Zoe's heavy body from the pool. Nicole collapses, exhausted, sinking to the submerged steps, her arms still wrapped around her sister's chest.

"No. No. Please. No." She strokes Zoe's face, leaving streaks of red on her skin. Her voice comes out as a whisper between panicked gasps. "Please don't leave me. I don't want to be alone, Zoe. Please. You have to wake up. I can't do this. You have to wake up. Please wake up. Please. Please. God. Please."

She closes her eyes. Hot tears stream down her cheeks. Blood pulses loud in her ears, pounding out a steady rhythm like footsteps on stone.

"Nicole!"

"I've got her." A warm hand cups her cheek. "You can let her go, Nicole."

She opens her eyes.

THE ANTISEPTIC STINGS.

Case flinches, pulling away from Fletcher as he attempts to sterilize the deep gouges on her face. She has never seen him look so angry. He reapplies the iodine and continues. The pressure of his touch grows harder. He forces the soft gauze too deep into her wounds. She grips the bench, knuckles turning white as she holds back her discomfort.

He masks his rage with practiced professionalism. "Obviously, these will scar."

She slips off the bench and begins to pace, cutting tight circles in the claustrophobic confines of the medical transport.

"How could you let that happen?"

"I have everything under control." She is saying it more for herself than him.

"You killed Victor Sutton."

"I had no choice." Case rubs her temples, trying to forget the way the old man had looked at her. The shock. The fear.

She had never seen him so feeble.

Fletcher stares at her, a look of frustration on his delicate face. "You ruined everything."

Case chuckles bitterly, turning away. "It's not like you didn't want him dead."

"You're right." He peels off his latex gloves and throws them in the biohazard bin. "But my way would have been discrete. It would have looked natural. You—You murdered him. I can't cover this up. It will look exactly like what it is: a coup. The board will want answers. There will be an outside investigation. What do you expect me to tell them?"

"Tell them she did it." Her skin stretches painfully as she smiles. "His granddaughter. She had a motive. She had a history of violence. She found out Victor ordered the death of her father, and she attacked him. I tried to stop her, but—"

Fletcher cuts her off. "What about the mother and the girl?"

Her smiles broadens as the idea finishes taking shape. It is too perfect. A simple solution to a complicated problem that eliminates all their problems at once. "They were caught in the crossfire. It's quite tragic, in a way."

Fletcher chews on the idea. "I can work with that. Where's Connor?"

She looks at herself in a small polished metal mirror. Red seeps from beneath the iodine. "He's taking care of things."

"Do you need me to schedule a wet team?"

"No. Focus on the withdrawal. Move the convoy back to the airstrip. I'll pick a small team to stay behind." This is her mess. She can clean up after herself. "I have this under control, Joseph."

She pushes the door to the medical transport open wide and descends the vehicles grated metal stairs. The cool night air makes the gouges on her cheek sting. She speaks softly, repeating the words she needs to hear. "I have everything under control."

Sounds around her meld, blurring into an unwavering wall of noise. The thrum is unbearable, setting her on edge even before she hears the first explosion.

The network of work lights fade. Generators fall quiet, plunging the makeshift camp into darkness. Tires squeal, fighting for traction on loose sand. Case turns around just in time to see one of the transport trucks explode, bright orange flames expanding, shattering every window and littering the desert with glass and twisted metal. The smell of burning fuel fills her nostrils.

The sensation takes her far away, to a different place, on the other side of the world: A tiny house by the sea, creaking and moaning, consumed by fire.

So much heat. So much smoke.

Another vehicle explodes. Closer this time. The concussive force knocks her off her feet. Her ears are ringing.

Fletcher takes hold of her hands and yanks her to her feet. He turns away, coughing as sour fumes billow from the nearby wreckage. When he turns back, he is screaming at her. She sees his mouth moving. Spit strikes her skin after every word, but she cannot hear him. Nothing can cut through the high pitched whine pervading her senses.

Soldiers scramble to put out the flames. The remaining vehicles begin to explode, one after another. Their flames burn bright, producing thick clouds of black smoke that blot out the night sky.

"—you listening to me?" Fletcher shakes her hard. "We have to contain this. Now."

Another blast detonates close by. The generators powering the work lamps in the chamber explode in a bright shower of sparks and light.

"Tricia!" Fletcher screams.

Panic overwhelms her. Choking her. Stealing all her air and replacing it with fear and smoke.

All she can think about is the man she left below ground.

Fletcher tries to hold, tries to keep her with him, but Case shoves her co conspirator aside and sprints for the portal the demolitions team blew in the bedrock. She needs to get to back to the chamber. Back to Connor.

Her boots slip down the steep metal ramp. Darkness swallows her. She fumbles through the corridor, feeling her way along the path, her fingers tracing the chiseled walls. Her feet catch on the thick electrical cables snaking towards the room where she left Connor to deal with the Hudson women.

He's fine. He's always fine. All these years, all the assignments, he's been hurt plenty of times, each wound adding to the ever growing patchwork of scars that crisscross his body, but he has always healed. He has always been fine.

She never would have left him alone if she didn't think he could handle himself.

It was just three women. Not even. Two women and a child.

Nothing Connor can't handle.

Case rounds the corner. A faint glow emanates from the chamber. She moves towards the threshold, tentatively stepping through and into the eerie blue light. A navigation beacon is floating in the center of the pool, bobbing slightly, its LED tip illuminating a large form drifting alone in the center of the murky water.

Her knees grow weak.

She knows the shape. The slope of his back. The way the wet fabric clings to his muscles. Connor is face down in the water, six inches of metal protruding from the back of his thick neck.

The light pulses gently in the darkness.

Epilogue

THE DEADBOLT HAS ALWAYS STUCK. Having to open the thing with her left hand isn't helping. Zoe jostles the key in the cylinder, fidgeting and pressing until the tumblers finally give way.

With her good shoulder she pushes the door open, sweeping a path through a mound of unopened mail. Letters scatter across the battered wood floor. She hasn't been here in over a year. This place is not home. It's just an address, a required field on her taxes, and a place to crash when she finds herself in Boston.

She steps into the cramped studio apartment and kicks the door closed behind her, tossing her keys down the empty hall. They skitter across the floor, stopping once they finally reach the baseboard. There is no furniture to speak of. The bare walls are ghosted with the decorations of former tenants, evidence that the apartment used to be occupied by people with more than a passing connection to it.

Zoe stoops, snatching up a random selection of mail with her left hand. The awkward movement sends a throbbing ache through her right side. Her arm pulses inside its cast. She makes her way to the main room, where warm autumn light drifts through the window. Something about the quality of the sunlight makes the dust floating in the air more evident than usual, but it's also possible this place is always dusty and she is usually too drunk or too tired to give a shit. She drops the envelopes on the mattress near the wall and heads straight for the refrigerator.

The pills the doctor prescribed make her puke. She hasn't taken them since she signed herself out against doctor's orders and caught a Greyhound from D.C. to Boston. She was tired of the surgeries, all vain attempts to get her arm back into some sort of working order. Eleven in total. Breaking and resetting her bones. Rods and pins inserted to keep everything stable. Reattaching tendons and ligaments. Trying to mend the extensive nerve damage to her right shoulder. She's a mess. She accepts that, but she was tired of all the coddling, the doctors and nurses telling her what to do and how to do it. After everything she had been through, she just wanted to be left alone.

A part of her almost wishes they had just amputated the damn arm at the military hospital in Saudi Arabia. Waking up to find out she was a freak would have been better than finding out she was a cripple. There would have been a finality to it, instead of this nagging hope that things could be mended.

It would have all been over.

No doctors. No medication. No pain management. No impending physical therapy. No hefty hospital bills.

When she pulls the fridge open, everything is where she left it over a year ago. Zoe selects a beer and bumps the refrigerator door shut with her hip, then tilts the bottle against an opener mounted to the counter. The cap pops off, flipping through the air and dropping to the brittle linoleum floor.

She takes a deep drink and turns to stare out the apartment's lone window. Through the dirty glass she watches the cars on the street below, obeying the traffic light as it changes color. Slow down, stop, go. Rinse. Repeat.

Zoe sinks to the windowsill, wincing as the sling holding her casted arm in traction disagrees with her motion. She pushes through the stack of mail with the her foot, kicking credit card offers and junk mail off the end of the bed until one envelope catches her eye: foreign stamps and delicate script addressed to Ms. Z. Hudson from a Mr. F. Meier.

She takes a deep drink and sets her beer down on the uneven floor, leaning down to pick up the envelope with still wet fingers. Her left hand struggles to open the document, tearing a jagged, excessive flap in the thick yellow paper. There is a letter from Meier, a very business-like update on her father's account. No. On her account. Pages and pages of numbers, graphs and charts tracking the activity of the various investments and assets. It's all gibberish to her, but wrapped inside those papers is another envelope with a small note taped to its face that reads: *"You forgot this. FM."*

Zoe pulls the note free. The writing underneath is crisp and blocky.

"To my daughter."

She presses herself upright and heads back to the kitchen, pulling drawers out until she finds a knife. With her cast pinning the envelope to the counter, she slips the point of the blade under the flap, pulling it along, careful not to rip the note inside. It's written in the same blocky handwriting, on a piece of the bank's heavy stationary.

"Zoe - I wish things had been different. I wish I could have seen you grow up and been the father you deserved. But I had to protect you and your mother from my past. I'm sorry if you didn't understand and if it hurt you when I left. I didn't have any other choice. I've done a lot of things I regret. Made a lot of mistakes, but I need you to know that you were never one of them. I love you. Be strong. Be brave. And know that I will always be proud of you. Forever yours, Dad."

She sets the letter down on the stained counter. Her throat closes up. She steadies herself, pressing her hips against the metal edging. She can feel the tears welling up, and opens the cupboard searching for something stronger than beer. Her hand closes around the neck of a heavy, dusty bottle.

She wants to drown.

A knock on the door wakes her.

She managed to fall asleep sitting up, back pressed against the cold wall, sticky hand gripping an empty glass. Her neck is stiff from passing out in such an awkward position.

There is another knock.

Zoe struggles to her feet, stumbling over bottles that didn't quite make it in the bin. There is barely any light. It's early. *Who the hell is knocking on her door before the sun is up?*

She tugs the door open.

"Hey." Nicole stands in the dimly lit hallway, a sturdy jacket draped over her arms and a bright scarf hanging loosely around her neck. She gives Zoe a cautious smile. "Are you going to invite me in?"

Zoe steps aside, letting her sister enter. The kid looks good. Healthy. Her dark hair is pulled back in a tidy braid. Zoe can only imagine how shitty she must look in comparison. She hasn't bathed in days, unwilling to take the necessary steps to keep her cast dry. At this point, even she can smell the alcohol seeping through her skin.

Nicole glances down the narrow hall, eyebrow cocked. "Wow. I love what you haven't done with the place."

Zoe closes the door and pushes past Nicole. "You're supposed to be back in school."

"I'm taking some time off."

"Me too." She grabs a half-empty bottle of beer off the windowsill and drains it. The shock on her sister's face gives her pause. "What?"

"Are you stupid?" She gestures at the empty bottles on the floor. "You can't drink."

"I'm a grown up, Nik. I can have a beer."

"Not when you're on pain medication." Nicole tugs the bottle from Zoe's hand. "Unless you're trying to melt your liver."

"I'm not taking the damn pills, Nik." She sits on the sill and pinches the bridge of her nose. "Why are you here?"

"You ran off. You didn't tell anyone where you went. I've been looking for you for almost a month. I had to call Mom at her research site to get this address." Nicole's voice stiffens, her freckled nose crinkling. "And by the way, if you hadn't noticed, this neighborhood is a hell hole, and this apartment looks like a crack den. You can afford some place nicer. Hell, if you wanted to, you could have come to live with me."

Zoe stares down at her bare feet, watching her toes flex against the wood floor. She's not in the mood to be berated, but she doesn't have the energy to fight right now. "Yeah. I'm sure you would've loved that."

"I would have, actually." Her sister crouches in front of her, placing warm hands on Zoe's knees. "I miss you."

"Really?"

Nicole nods, flashing a crooked smile.

Zoe forgot how much she missed that ridiculous smirk.

"Get up." Nicole stands and holds out a hand, tilting her head towards the hall.

"Why?"

"Because I'm getting you out of here."

"Where are we going?"

"Does it matter?" Nicole asks.

Zoe glances around at her empty apartment.

It doesn't.

THE WAITING IS ALMOST UNBEARABLE.

Caroline sits alone in a far corner booth nursing a scalding mug of something people in North Carolina think is coffee. She watches the two lane road outside the plate glass window, and waits.

It's been raining all morning. Nothing serious, just a constant mist that covers everything with minute droplets.

Caroline sips at her coffee. Her stomach is getting good at backflips. She hasn't seen Zoe in months, not since the Army hospital in Saudi Arabia. Witten came through after all, calling in a career killing series of favors to secure them an military evac from the Aswan airstrip. Good thing, too, because without his help, both Zoe and her mother probably would have died from blood loss. He even pulled strings at the hospital to make sure Caroline could stay at Zoe's bedside.

She sat there for days, steadfastly holding onto Zoe's lifeless hand until Gerard Royer showed up and dragged her back to Montreal. Apparently, Gabriel had done a decent job of lying to her father. He gave Caroline more time than she had expected. Needless to say, Gerard figured out something was amiss he was informed that his experimental aircraft was sitting on a less than reputable airstrip in Dubai. He was not happy.

Caroline tried to explain the circumstances, but the only person who seemed to understand was her mother. As far as her father was concerned, Caroline stole his plane and put herself in an enormous amount of jeopardy for a troublesome ex-girlfriend he had never liked to begin with. He wasn't particularly receptive to her reasoning.

The waitress stops at Caroline's table to top off her mug. "You still okay with just coffee, hon?"

The woman's drawl is pleasant and friendly. Caroline smiles and nods, then turns her attention back to the window, watching the quiet highway and the calm ocean just beyond. "I'm good. Thank you."

The waitress rests a hand on her hip and gives Caroline a knowing look. "None of my business, I'm sure. But whoever he is, he's a fool for keeping a girl like you waiting."

Caroline smiles and turns her attention to the rain-spattered window.

A silver sedan pulls into the lot, windshield wipers flicking water in all directions. Nicole is at the wheel. Caroline can feel her heart quicken as Zoe slips out of the passenger side door. Her right arm is still in a thick cast and secured to her body by a complicated system of black straps.

A weight she did not realize she was carrying lifts from her body. When she left the hospital, the doctors weren't certain they'd be able to save Zoe's arm. There had been so much damage. She was so broken.

The bell above the diner's door rings. Zoe walks up to the counter and leans carefully against the edge.

"Yeah. Hey," she says brusquely, "can I get an order to go?"

The waitress hands her a menu. She begins to flip through it as Nicole's car abruptly backs out of the parking lot and turns onto the highway, heading south.

Zoe looks over her shoulder with a familiar expression, confusion mixed with annoyance. She watches her sister's car speed away and mutters something under her breath. She turns on her stool and scans the room. Her eyes fall on the diner's only other patron. Zoe shakes her head, pressing away from the counter and walking down the aisle towards her.

Caroline sets her mug down and waits for what feels like an eternity.

Zoe lowers herself slowly, sitting on the edge of the booth's bench, unable to slide in further due to her bulky sling and cast. She chuckles softly. "You and Nik. You two worked this out?"

"You're a hard woman to find, Ms. Hudson." Caroline grins, leaning across the table and whispering softly. "I needed help."

The Army hospital wouldn't tell her where Zoe had been transferred. She tried to get something out of Matthew Jones, but he left Saudi Arabia after being discharged and thoroughly grilled by Witten about where the hell he had obtained enough explosive to destroy every car in a three mile radius. It was actually Matthew who suggested she get in touch with Nicole, though it turned out finding a seventeen-year-old student was almost as difficult as dealing with a military hospital. Columbia University was guarded about Nicole Hudson's whereabouts, but that may have had more to do with her abduction from their campus earlier in the year than her status as a minor. Regardless, they were not helpful.

It was Nicole who found Caroline. She showed up at her parent's home in Montreal with Zoe's Boston address and a plan. The girl was a professional. All Caroline had to do was get to North Carolina and wait in the roadside diner.

She twists her mug on the tabletop, uncomfortable with the deepening silence. "How are you?"

"Been better."

Terse, but at least it's a response. Caroline presses on. "You look good."

Zoe scoffs, flashing her a skeptical sideways glance before focusing on her mangled right hand. "No, I don't."

In Caroline's eyes, she looks amazing. She is conscious and no longer attached to life-support. Her face is no longer swollen with cuts and bruises. It is a miraculous improvement.

"Look." Zoe fidgets with the frayed straps of her sling. "Jones told me what you guys did. You shouldn't have. You shouldn't have done anything. You just should have kept clear. If anything had happened to you—"

Caroline stops her. "Matthew did most of the heavy lifting, I was just his wheelman—"

"Heavy lifting? Wheelman?" Zoe flinches. "Listen to yourself. You helped my ex-special forces best friend infiltrate a crooked multinational, Caroline. I expect that kind of crazy shit from Jones. Not you. You could have gotten yourself killed."

"I didn't." *And if I hadn't come after you, your whole family would be rotting in the desert right now.* She feels justified. Zoe sounds just like Caroline's father, unable to comprehend the basic reasons behind her actions. She had no other choice. Caroline gives her the most sympathetic look she can manage. "I wasn't going to let you go."

"Maybe you should've." Zoe murmurs and stares down at the floor.

"Never." Caroline reaches across the table and places her hand on Zoe's. "I hate to break it to you, Hudson, but you're sort of stuck with me."

She tries to read Zoe's reaction. Hoping, praying she won't withdraw like so many times before.

Her eyes dart around the diner, finally focusing on the edge of the formica table. She looks so lost, so scared. Caroline keeps waiting for her to pull her hand away, but she doesn't. Instead, her features soften and her thumb gently brushes Caroline's fingertips.

The rain has let up. Sunlight breaks through the heavy grey clouds. Caroline tucks a five under her mug and slips out from behind the table, keeping hold of Zoe's good hand. "Come on."

"Why?"

"Because I want to show you something."

Zoe flashes her a skeptical look.

Caroline gives her hand a tug. "Oh, just get up, Zoe."

They leave the diner and cross the gravel parking lot then the quiet two-lane highway. Caroline leads her down the wooden steps to a small moorage. Boats gently sway in their slips, pressing against the thick ropes and wood supports. The creaking and lapping of water is strangely soothing. She can feel her heart beating in her throat, making it hard to breathe. It's hard to tell if it's the anticipation or her proximity to Zoe. Probably both.

She stops, turning to face the confounded woman following her. She cups the cool skin of Zoe's cheeks.

"Caroline, wha—"

She stops her with a kiss, fingers sliding up her neck, working their way into long blonde hair. When Caroline finally draws back, Zoe's eyes are closed, her pulse visibly pounding. Caroline slips her arms around her waist and relaxes, melting into her sturdy body as she rests her head carefully against Zoe's good shoulder.

They stand in a comfortable silence, reacquainting themselves with the other's presence.

Zoe kisses the top Caroline's head and clears her throat. Her voice is uneven and raspy. "What'd you want to show me?"

Caroline points to a streamlined yacht at the end of the pier. She bites her lip, waiting for Zoe's response. The shock on her face is priceless. She wraps her arms carefully around Zoe's waist and kisses her cheek. "I was hoping you'd run away with me. You know. If you weren't up to anything important."

Zoe pulls her closer and Caroline takes comfort in the strong arm latched around her shoulders. Low, dark clouds roll in, their heavy shapes blurred by rain falling over the open ocean. The faint autumn sun is obscured as the sky grows darker. The wind picks up, forcing the waves into white tipped peaks. A storm is closing in. Rain pelts the wooden dock, pounding out a steady rhythm. Huge drops soak through her clothing. She takes hold of Zoe's hand, letting their fingers entwine and she draws her forward, pulling her towards the shelter of their yacht.

She has never felt more safe.

HIS NAME IS KEVIN RAMER. He's a high school history teacher at a public school in North Carolina. He is thirty-nine years old. He is her father.

Those are only things Nicole knows for sure.

Whether or not he wants a now eighteen-year-old daughter in his life is an entirely different question.

She was glad Caroline had been so adamant about helping her do this. Zoe needed to be coaxed out of her isolationist bullshit, and Nicole needed a reason not to lose her nerve. She needs to do this. Or at least, she thinks she needs to do this. The remainder of the drive from the coast to her father's modest home has been filled with hypothetical outcomes. She has been sitting in her car, parked across the street from his house for ten minutes now. Courage is a finite thing, and she is gathering all she has left.

The sky is grey. Fat raindrops spatter her windshield, turning the street into a blurry impressionist landscape. There is a car parked in his driveway. The lights are on in the front room windows, casting a warm glow through the curtains. The house looks so inviting.

She could go for some comfort right about now.

The past few months have been hell. Ever since they left Egypt, her world has tilted on its end. Her arm wasn't shattered like Zoe's. She didn't get shot like her mother. But something inside her broke when she killed Connor.

She is different. Strange, and empty. But no one around her seems to notice.

It scares her how well she hides it.

Agent Witten assured her it was a natural response to a very traumatic event. She did what she had to do. She still hasn't told Zoe. How could she? It's just one more thing that her sister would blame herself for, and she doesn't need that right now.

Witten has been remarkably understanding, considering the fact that her sister did knock him unconscious and nearly cost him the case of his career. He has stayed in contact with Nicole. He even gave her contact information for a bureau psychiatrist near her apartment in Brooklyn. An impartial person who she could see if she needed someone to talk to. It was a kind and sympathetic gesture from the most unlikely of places.

She hasn't gone yet, but she keeps the card in her wallet just in case.

She wants to remember what normal feels like.

A few weeks ago, punch-drunk from lack of sleep, she convinced herself this was the way to accomplish that. But now that she's parked on this quiet residential street, she's not so sure it was actually a good idea.

Don't wuss out, Hudson.

Nicole takes one last deep breath and pushes herself out of her car. The air is crisp and smells of burning firewood and wet leaves. She digs her hands into her pockets, drawing her coat tight around her as rain pelts her head, working its way through her thick hair until it hits her scalp and rolls down her neck. The sensation makes her shiver. She checks for traffic out of habit, then crosses.

The chain-link gate pushes open with a creak. She lets it sweep shut behind her. There is a hollow metallic clank when the latch strikes the post. Apprehension seizes her.

Her desire to turn around and head back up the highway, back to the diner, back to the boat, back to Caroline and her sister, intensifies. But it's just her fear talking, and now is not the time to be scared. She has already come so far.

Nicole swallows the lump in her throat and heads up the well-worn porch stairs. The screen door hinges groan as she opens it to rap on the heavy wooden front door. She lets the screen door slam shut and backs away.

Rain pelts the porch roof through the canopy of trees, channeling down the gutters, the sounds mixes with the gentle hum of traffic from the main road. Her brain grinds, processing a million excuses, coming up with all the reasons to just turn around and leave.

He's probably not home.

Lots of people leave their lights on.

Maybe that's not his car, or his driveway.

"Can I help you?"

She didn't even hear the door open. His voice is deep and kind, with the slightest hint of a drawl. The porch light flicks on and she can see him clearly through the screen. He looks younger than she had expected, but kind; with gentle brown eyes, a full beard, and dark, close cropped hair about her color. Most striking of all is his easy, albeit confused, smile.

Nicole pushes out the only word she can manage. "Hi."

Her father leans against the door jamb. "Can I help you, miss?"

There is no look of recognition, not even a hint of familiarity. She feels stupid. What did she expect? Why would he have any idea who she is? Her throat tightens and the words don't come, stalling inside her. This was a stupid idea.

Nicole freezes, choking.

His smile falters. "Are you okay?"

"No." She murmurs softly and turns, feeling tears welling up in her eyes. She has to get back to her car. He can't see her cry. "I'm sorry. This is the wrong house."

She heads down the steps towards the gate.

The screen door slams behind her.

"Nicole?"

Her feet stop, body shutting down as her brain expends all available energy processing what she just heard.

"Is it you?"

When she turns around, her father is directly behind her, barefoot on the wet concrete. Rain falls on his broad shoulders, soaking through his sweater. His face twitches, muscles too shocked to move but trying to pull into a smile. Nicole knows how he feels.

She forces herself to nod. The motion comes out spastic and involuntarily exaggerated.

He moves closer, shoving his hands into his pockets and looking sheepish but happy. He gives her a crooked smile. Her crooked smile. "Hey."

Her fears evaporate. She still doesn't know what to say to him, but he knows who she is, and that feels like a start.

SHE IS BACK WHERE SHE BELONGS.

Sweating in the intense heat of the western ranges.

Allison squints into the afternoon sun. In the distance, an SUV approaches the bustling excavation site. She hands her tools to an intern and gives the girl a reassuring pat on the back. "Go slow. You'll do fine."

Navigating the outcrop of twisted rocks that lead back to the cluster of portable research buildings and storage units is a slow process. She's not as agile as she used to be. Being shot in the leg will do that to a person. The cast over her thigh is a daily reminder of the titanium rod replacing her femur. The Army surgeon let her know in no uncertain terms how lucky she was she hadn't bled out when the bullet shattered the bone. The fragments missed the femoral artery and a tourniquet had been applied at just the right time. She had Zoe's friend Jones to thank for that. But timely medical treatment did not stop her from being crippled. Mere months earlier she had been climbing through windows and racing through crowded streets in Baghdad. Now she needs a cane just to get out of bed in the morning, and navigating her own dig site is exhausting. The irrepressible pessimist in her hardly feels "lucky."

The white SUV is coated in a fine red powder. It rolls to a stop just outside the main research trailer, cutting its engine. The passenger side door swings open, exposing a familiar face from her past. The man spreads his arms wide, an infectious smile on his rugged face. "Ally!"

She stalls in place as his arms wrap around her. She gives him a gentle pat on his broad back as she whispers in his ear. "Always the professional, aren't you, Craig?"

He pulls back, cupping her tanned shoulders. "What? You want me to call you Dr. Hudson? I think you get enough bowing and scraping from your grad students. Somebody has to keep you intellectual types grounded."

Funny coming from the person whose article made both their careers so many years ago. She watches as two other men exit the vehicle and begin to remove camera equipment. "So you're working for CNN these days?"

"My agent tells me I'm too pretty for print. I left the Geographic after my Pulitzer." Craig gestures at her cane with a look Allison can only interpret as amused concern. "Dapper. What the hell happened to you?"

"I had an accident in Baghdad. It's not a big deal."

"An accident, huh? That's funny, because I heard you got shot." Craig raises an eyebrow and waits for her response.

She stops, her lips pulling into an involuntary nervous grin. "Really?"

"Yeah," Craig says cooly. "In Egypt."

Allison shakes her head and pats his back. She continues to head towards the main excavation site just up the outcrop of oddly formed rocks. "You might want to check your facts, Mr. Talbot."

"My source is reliable, and it puts you doing recoup in an American military hospital in Saudi Arabia less than four months ago. And now you're privately funded and back in the field after two decades, limping around aboriginal burial grounds in hundred degree heat. Level with me, Ally. What's going on?"

A group of dusty interns pass by carrying clear plastic bins and murmuring excitedly to each other. Allison waits for them to pass, then continues towards the main excavation location: A natural cave worn into the red rock outcrop. Maybe chastising him will get their conversation on track. "CNN didn't fly you all the way out here to talk about my limp."

"True." He shrugs. "They said you found mummified remains."

Allison gives him a coy smile, raising her eyebrows.

"Last time we talked, you told me your team was investigating the Zuytdorp shipwreck. Now, I'm no anthropologist, but I'm pretty sure shipwrecks happen on the coast." He gestures around at the low horizon. The vast expanse of empty, low desert, reaching out and touching the pale blue sky. "And I sure as hell know 17th-century Dutch sailors didn't mummify their dead."

"They didn't." She pauses leaning against her cane to relieve pressure on her leg. "But Egyptians did."

"Egyptians?" Craig's eyes narrow. "You're telling me your team found an Egyptian mummy in the middle of the Australian outback?"

"Yes."

"How?"

She chuckles. "Wouldn't you like to know."

"If you're giving me an exclusive, hell yeah, I'd like to know. These things need provenance. How did you find it?"

"Not it," she corrects him. "Her." She pauses to summon the vaguest answer possible that is both true and not. "Luck."

"I'm not buying that, Ally." Craig rolls his eyes and crosses his tanned arms. "This all sounds too convenient and way too mysterious."

Allison give him a weak shrug. "I thought men liked women with a little mystery."

"I'm not a man, Ally. I'm a reporter. I like facts. Facts are sexy."

She leans against the red rock outside the cave, resting her aching leg and squinting at him as sweat beads up on her tanned skin. "Sexy, huh?"

"What can I say?" His playful grin is back, though less disarming than before. He rubs at the back of his neck. "You're not going to tell me how you found this place, are you?"

"Maybe later." Allison smirks at him, slipping her hand into the pocket of her pants, searching for her flashlight. Her fingertips brush against the ancient hardwood carving. Red-white grain smoothed by the passing centuries. Only one place in the world it could have come from. "Over a drink."

"Fair enough." Craig pulls out a small digital recorder and turns it on. The light glows red. "Why don't you tell me why I'm here, Dr. Hudson."

She fishes the LED flashlight out of her pocket and aims it into the cave. "It'll be more fun if I show you."

***

The transition has not been smooth.

Though Sutton's death in the desert was easily pinned on Zoe, and Fletcher's alterations to his will were flawless, her control of the corporation has been shaky at best.

Aswan was a bloodbath that attracted far too much attention. Their private security contracts were nullified, and investors were getting jittery. Confidence was not on her side. The past few months have been a delicate dance of dodging one bullet just to step in front of another.

All eyes are on her now. Scrutinizing her. Watching her every move.

She wasn't prepared for it.

Fletcher has seen to it that the legal department takes care of things quickly. He told her not to worry, to instead focus on her responsibilities and ingratiate herself to the standing board members, assuring her a show of strength will calm even the most timid of shareholders.

But her mind will not rest.

She cannot sleep.

Her head throbs, eyes aching and listless but unwilling to close. The lights are dimmed, their amber filaments glowing steady behind opal glass, ribbons of heat struggling to illuminate Case's residence. Unlike every other flat on the island, hers is personally furnished, possessions slowly accumulated over years of service. The hyper-modern leather furnishings have been replaced by heavy fabrics with hardwoods. She sits in her living area, surrounded by her own things. Personal mementos line a pair of exquisitely carved antique bookshelves that flank a handful of intricately framed classical paintings. Sutton may have built the sprawling concrete complex, but Case has seen to it this room is a place of her own design. A conscious decision to break the old man's mold.

She is seated on the couch, legs drawn up, lean frame sheathed in a smooth silk robe that holds tight to her skin. The large television hanging on the far wall is on, muted and cycling through news networks. She has been watching for hours.

She leans forward and plucks a cigarette from the crinkled pack on the coffee table. Connor's lighter sits next to the foil wrapper, the engraved silver metal catching the dim light. She flips it open and strikes the flint. Her nostrils fill with the scent of fuel. Even after the cigarette is lit she stares into the flame of the lighter, watching it undulate in the air. His ghost fills her lungs and clouds her judgement.

She can't stop seeing him.

Face down in the dark water.

Dead.

I never should have left him.

Case snaps his lighter shut and inhales deeply, watching the tip of her cigarette glow a brilliant red. The smoke crawls through her, seeking an exit, rolling out of her mouth and nose.

There is a knock on her door.

Her rise from the couch is fluid and controlled. She had almost forgotten her meeting with Fletcher. When she opens the metal door, he is waiting in the hall, pale grey three-piece suit perfectly pressed. Case allows him to enter, closing the door behind him. She can already see his brain churning as he absorbs and catalogs every item in her residence. She doesn't normally allow visitors. Agreeing to meet him here was a choice, one she is trying not to regret. He pauses in front of a large pastoral painting on the wall opposite the television. Its warm soothing autumnal colors and heavy lines are a stark contrast to the motion and violence on the muted news channel.

"Flemish. Interesting. I would have thought you'd be into the early Impressionists. Something more ambiguous. Don't get me wrong. I can appreciate the literal." Something in his inflection and tone is off-putting. "I, myself, prefer photography. Preferably black and white."

Case stands behind him, resenting the voyeuristic way he inspects her possessions. Fletcher's body doesn't move, but his attention diverts to the screen, then to her, a bemused expression slipping across his face as he watches the delicate woman anchoring the muted news station. "We can talk about art some other time, I suppose. Our South American contacts need immediate attention. The Peruvian cartels who have been instrumental in exporting ancient textiles are claiming we have unpaid debts. It's completely unfounded. They've gotten greedy due to the transition in power. We may need to look into a rigged election to get our muscle in the right places before we deal with them." He pauses, clasping his hands behind his back as he turns to face her. "On a different, but related front, the FBI has seized the Trident. Our litigators say they have enough evidence to support the charges of illegal salvage and antiquities trafficking. Most of the violations happened within national waters. The lawyers insist this is not a battle we can win.

Considering the crew's recent performance, my recommendation would be to let them twist. Foster and his men are due a lesson."

Case moves around Fletcher and takes a seat, her robe falling away from her thigh as she crosses her legs. Her cigarette is balanced between her fingertips. Ash drifts from its tip to settle on the linen couch. She's not listening to him. Her eyes are glued to the screen. Watching. Waiting. Her hand closes around Connor's lighter, thumb flicking the top open and closed. The metal makes a hollow pop with each motion.

It's obvious the sound annoys Fletcher, but she can't bring herself to care.

He lets out a labored sigh. "Tricia? Are you even listening to me?"

She clicks her tongue. "What about the Hudsons?"

"What about them?"

"Where are they?" She stares past his shoulder, losing herself in the deep brushstrokes of the pastoral scene, the dark hues of brown and red set against a pale autumn sky. So many deep shadows and brilliant highlights. She absently strokes at the deep gouges around her eye.

"Their whereabouts do not matter. We've wasted enough time and energy on those women. You have more important things to focus on. You have responsibilities." He must sense her distance. His jaw clenches, muscles tense and release. "This is a business, Tricia. You have to start running it."

Case drifts further, her mind tumbling deeper into distraction.

She pulled him out of the water. His blood was all over her. The tip of the beacon protruded from his mangled throat. His eyes were wide open.

I never should have left him alone.

Fletcher clears his throat and her focus snaps back. She shifts her position and drapes an arm along the back of the couch, eyes returning to the screen, dismissing him both figuratively and literally. "Is that all?"

His smile is reptilian, his eyes pull into thin crescents. He shakes his head in disapproval. "You can't stay locked in here forever."

"That will be all, Mr. Fletcher." Her words are growled more than spoken.

He lingers.

"Get out." She sinks deeper into the couch, lifting her fingers to her lips and inhaling deeply from her cigarette. The tobacco burns, paper crackling, edging ever closer to the filter. She can feel his stare, but her focus remains on the television, ignoring him until she hears the door latch click shut. Case presses her palms into her aching eyes. The jagged scars running down her face are always a surprise, always a reminder. She can feel the heat from her cigarette radiate against the sensitive skin.

All the years of sacrifice, all the things she has ever done, they have all been for this. Power. Control. She achieved everything she strived for.

But the victory is hollow

She has no one to share it with. No one she can trust.

And no one to blame but herself.

The female anchor taps her stack of papers on the counter's reflective surface and looks directly at the camera, lips moving as the ticker tape below cycles through headlines. Case raises the volume on the television. "—still reeling over a shocking discovery. A team of anthropologists have uncovered the mummified remains of an Egyptian princess. Neferura, The Beauty of Ra, was found in a remote corner of the Western Australian outback. DNA testing and carbon dating confirm the remains are directly related to ancient Egypt's only female pharaoh, Hatshepsut, and solve a centuries old mystery of what happened to the young woman after she disappeared from the historic record during the end of her mother's reign. For more on this exclusive story, we take you live to the excavation site with senior correspondent Craig Talbot and anthropologist Dr. Allison Hudson."

A handsome man comes into focus against a backdrop of red-orange rock and brilliant blue sky. "Thanks, Kerri." The reporter smiles at Allison as she limps into the frame, supporting her weight on a metal cane.

"This is the find of the century, Doctor."

Case hurls Connor's lighter at the television screen. The glass fractures, spiderweb-cracks extend from the point of impact, distorting Allison Hudson's smiling face. Case's pulse pounds in her ears like waves crashing against the shore.

She is adrift.

She has nothing.

Made in the USA
Lexington, KY
06 November 2017